TORN HART

THE HARTY BOYS, BOOK 3

WHITLEY COX

For Jodie Esch
A fellow author, a friend and a beautiful soul gone too soon.
I will forever treasure our VIRA picnics on your patio,
your kind words, constant support and encouragement.
The world is certainly a lot less bright without you in it.

CHAPTER 1

Fuck, sweet and sour pork was goddamn delicious. Particularly when he didn't have to share his six-person combo meal with anyone.

Rex's stomach grumbled, demanding to be filled.

Every last bite was for him, and he was more than okay with that.

Was there anything better than the smell of Chinese food wafting up from the back of your vehicle?

He sure as fuck didn't think so.

Well, maybe the smell of Chinese food wafting up from the back of your vehicle while a woman's head bobbed in your lap in the front seat.

But he only had one of those things currently, and his angry belly was winning out over his full balls and lonely dick.

Especially after a long fucking day at work—he'd been up since four and on the job by five—followed by an hour at the gym hitting the punching bag. He'd earned every damn carb that he intended to consume tonight and then some.

He'd have to make do with his fist tonight. He was too tired to send out messages to women he knew would be interested in a little no-strings fun.

Maybe tomorrow night.

With enough Chinese food to feed a family of six, and a six-pack of beer from a local microbrew in the back seat of his truck, he was gearing up for a satisfying evening alone.

It was late Wednesday afternoon, but considering he started work before the sun was up, he'd put in a full day and then some. He was going to head up to his apartment, grab his dog, Diesel, and take him for a quick piss outside. After Diesel did his thing, they'd head back inside, he'd feed his dog, strip down, have a shower and nut one out. Then, finally, at long last, he'd sit in his incredibly expensive recliner, put his feet up and eat a fuck-ton of chow mein and sweet and sour pork, drink his beer and watch a riveting documentary on the Discovery Channel while his dog snored and farted at his feet.

Was there a better plan out there?

There sure as fuck wasn't.

Unless of course, while he did all of that, a beautiful woman's head bobbed in his lap.

Again, tonight he'd settle for the chow mein and beer, followed by his fist.

With his belly continuing to grumble like an angry bear woken up mid-hibernation, Rex pulled his big, black Chevy into his parking spot behind his apartment building and turned off the engine.

Thank fuck the weather was starting to get better.

Spring had arrived and with it, longer days, warmer weather and the heady and sweet scent of blossoms on the air.

Always on the alert, even when he wasn't on the job, he scanned the parking lot as he climbed out of his truck, slammed the door, then opened the back cab to grab his beer and dinner.

He'd been in his apartment for nearly two years, and so far, nothing weird or nefarious stood out to him. It was a decent neighborhood, not too far from the University of Victoria, and the building was only about five years old. The majority of his neighbors were students, but nobody was rude, loud or obnoxious. And the odd party he heard didn't affect his sleep at all.

He'd been to hell and back during his time with Joint Task Force 2 and the special operative team he and his brothers joined after their stint in the Canadian Navy. He could sleep on a concrete floor next to a mosquito-infested swamp while ten other men farted and snored around him.

If he was tired, he could sleep.

He tossed his coat over his arm, grabbed his gym duffle bag, and heaved the Chinese food and beer out of the back seat of his truck, his keys in his teeth as he struggled and juggled all his shit before finally getting to the lobby door. He'd done this over a hundred times, this exact same scenario. You'd think he'd have figured out a more productive and effective way to carry all his shit.

He was just checking his mail when the sound of sobs and sniffling drifted down the hall, followed by the sweetest smell of wild strawberries and summer sunshine.

He'd always had the nose of a bloodhound.

As a kid, he could usually guess what his mother was making for dinner simply by how she smelled when she picked up him and his brothers from school.

He glanced up from where he was scrutinizing a misaddressed letter only to come face-to-face with a beautiful woman with tear-stained cheeks and red-rimmed eyes.

She was stunning, tall and lithe, with feminine curves, long auburn hair that coiled down just past her shoulders and wide, deep-set hazel eyes. Eyes that were filled with sadness as tears continued to fall. She looked up at him, her nose red, while her cheeks held a rosy glow.

Rex had never met this woman, but he'd seen her around the

building—only from a distance, however. She liked to run on the weekends, and he liked to watch her leave. She pulled off Lulu Lemons like no woman he'd ever met.

He instantly felt the need to protect and find out what or *who* made her cry and make them pay.

He wasn't sure how he could fix her, but he really wanted to try. Those weren't just tears from a sad movie or seeing a three-legged dog on the side of the road. Those were tears of pain. Heart-break. Devastation.

Protect those who are unable to protect themselves.

And although that often meant "protect the weak" he didn't see this woman as weak; he just saw her as sad. Hurt.

Either way, he wanted to help.

It was just how he and his brothers had been raised.

If someone was in trouble or needed help, you helped them. Simple as that.

And right now this woman looked like she needed help.

"Are you okay?" he asked.

She shook her head, her breath catching as she struggled for words. "N-no."

"Is ... is there something I can do to help? Do you need me to beat up an ex-boyfriend or something?"

She snorted a small laugh and wiped the tears from her cheeks and beneath her eyes. "Unless you're willing to kick the shit out of a twenty-six-year-old, hundred-and-thirty-pound chick, I don't think your muscles are needed."

"Uh ..." He scratched the back of his neck. "Ex-girlfriend?"

"No." She sniffed loudly. "I was fired!" And then before he knew it, she flung herself at him, collapsing against his chest and wailing.

He'd dropped everything in his hands to check his mail, so he was able to comfort her now. His hand gently fell to her back, her small body feeling like a child's in his giant palms. Then he found himself petting her back and shushing her like he did his nieces and nephews when they fell and hurt themselves. "It's okay," he hummed. "It'll be okay."

He shifted her under his arm and with his free hand grabbed his dinner, coat, gym bag and lastly—and most importantly—his beer, and he ushered her toward the elevator.

"Which floor are you on?" he asked softly. She didn't say anything but hit the number three. They rode in silence, and then when the door opened, he figured she'd take off, leaving him to his Chinese and microbrew, but he suddenly found himself inside this stranger's apartment, watching her take off her shoes and then slump onto her couch, clutching tissues to her nose.

"You know I've *never* met a nice girl named Odette?" She sneered. "Not that I've met a ton or anything, but the few I've come across have been the biggest bitches ever. The one I went to grade school with was a mean girl—even two years younger than me, she was still just a little witch—and this cow was no different. I worked there for one month. Did EVERYTHING right, went in early, stayed late, bought my own supplies, took work home with me. I spent three hours of my own time at home sewing up the holes in the canvas parachute and the big stuffed alligator that sits in the reading corner. I never asked for money for doing it. Never even told them I did it. I just *did* it. I was an exemplary employee, and she waltzes in as the new manager, is there for less than a week and she fires me because she thinks I'm after her job."

Rex watched her reach into her purse and pull out a brown paper bag, the neck of a booze bottle sticking out. She took a swig, then made a face, only to take another sip before offering it up to him.

"No, thanks." He grimaced. "I have beer."

She shrugged. "More for me." She tipped the bottle up and took another drink. "Have you ever met a nice Odette?" She caught a rather dainty burp with the back of her hand before offering him a crooked, slightly embarrassed smile.

He snorted. "Can't say I've ever met one. But I did date an Odessa briefly. She dumped me."

"Why?" Another cute little burp, followed by a hiccup.

"Ah, you know, same old story ... she complained that my penis was too big." He grinned wide, hoping his joke made her smile.

Her sweet little rosebud mouth hung open for the briefest of seconds before she shot him a skeptical look, hiccuped again and then burst out laughing.

Good. His joke did the trick.

He widened his smile. She had a really adorable laugh, and at least for the moment, he'd managed to take her mind off her problems. Little did she know that it was actually a true story. Odessa *had* dumped him because she said his cock was too big. If he remembered correctly, she'd called him Godzilla dick, said he nearly split her in half and then tossed him out of her apartment in nothing but his boxers and his work boots.

Good thing she hadn't tried to sleep with his brother Heath. He might be the baby of the family, but he was also the *biggest*. She'd probably chase him down the hallway—at a cowboy waddle—claiming he was part horse.

He snorted hard at that thought.

He lifted his shoulder. "So ... uh, can't you just get another job? What did you do?"

She mimicked his shrug before taking another sip from her brown paper bag of secrecy. "I was working full-time at this day care and loving it. I got the job midyear because another teacher went on maternity leave. It was perfect. Monday to Friday, eight until five. Then they hired a new program manager. She's younger than me and doesn't have near the experience with kids that I do. I've been babysitting since I was thirteen, then I nannied and babysat all through college. I got my preschool teacher certification as soon as I finished my teaching degree because I knew that I wanted to teach little kids. I'm also certified to teach Montessori and special-needs kids.

"But preschools aren't open as long as day cares and the money isn't as good—unless you're at a full-day Montessori or a Waldorf or some fancy private preschool. And I applied to those, but they had no available positions—or they said I was overqualified and they couldn't afford me. So I found this job. It's the best of both worlds. A preschool in the morning, then day care for the rest of the day. I still get to teach—sorry, I still *got* to teach, past tense and all since I was canned." She sighed. "Canned from the perfect job by the biggest bitch on the west coast."

"Did you try telling them this?"

"*Pfft*," she scoffed. "I was still within my three-month probation period. They could fire me for having a hangnail if they wanted to."

He looked around her apartment, unsure what to say next. Her place wasn't quite the carbon copy of his, but it was close. Small but open concept. A big bedroom, small but homey living room and kitchen, new stainless appliances and cramped bathroom.

Or maybe everything just felt cramped and small to Rex, but to an average-size person, it was all completely normal. She'd decorated her place in a very feminine way, with soft oranges and light blues. A white overstuffed leather couch faced the television with a slew of throw pillows on it, while paintings of seashells and flowers in black plastic frames hung behind the couch. He saw very few photo frames or pictures of people, except for a small black and white photo of what he could only assume was her as a little girl, maybe six or eight, at the beach with a man and woman who he would guess were her parents.

"So what's your name?" she slurred, appearing to be bored or perhaps just too upset to want to continue talking about her job or lack thereof. "I've seen you around the building a bit. You have the big black truck and the pit bull puppy, right?"

He nodded. "My name is Rex. What's your name?"

"Lydia." She yawned. "Rex, eh? Like *T. rex*."

He rolled his eyes. "I suppose."

"Is it short for anything? Like Rexworth, Rexwell or Rexington ... Rexthalomew?"

"Rexthalomew?"

She shrugged again. "Rexly?"

He simply snorted and smiled, ignoring the grumble of his belly. Man, she was drunk. "It's not short for anything."

She shrugged again. "Do you have any siblings?"

"Three brothers."

"And do they all have weird names too?"

"I personally don't think Rex is weird, but no, they don't. We all have one-syllable names, though. Brock, Chase, and Heath. And our dad was Zane, and our mother is Joy."

She made an interested pout. "And what's your middle name?"

"You looking to steal my identity? Want my social insurance number next?"

She stuck her tongue out at him.

He grinned. "My middle name is Barry."

That had her nose wrinkling like a cute little bunny. "Why Barry?"

"What's wrong with Barry?"

She shrugged, and her eyes lost focus for a moment, reminding him of her inebriation. "Nothing. But why? Is it like a family name or something?"

He exhaled through his nose. "My parents—in their infinite wisdom—thought it would be fun to give my brothers and I the middle name corresponding to the artist they were listening to while we were conceived."

"Gross."

"Indeed."

"So you're Rex Barry after ... Manilow?"

"White. You know, 'Let's Get It On ...'" He made sure to drop his voice to baritone level when he sang that little bit.

She nodded in understanding. "And your brothers?"

"Brock Lionel, Chase Marvin and Heath Leppard."

"Leppard?"

"'Pour Some—'"

"'Sugar On Me'!" she finished with a wide smile. "That's hilarious."

"At least it's our middle names and not our first names."

"True enough. What's your last name?"

"Hart."

She rolled his name around on her little pink tongue like foreplay. "Rex Hart ... Rex *Barry* Hart," she murmured, cocking her head to the side and giving him a once-over. "I like it." He continued to watch her, wondering when the bottle of whatever spirit she'd chosen to numb the pain was going to hit her like the freight train it inevitably was and send her rushing to the bathroom to go and vomit.

"What's your full name?" he asked. "Fair is fair, right?"

"Lydia Andréa Sullivan." She tipped back her booze bottle, then frowned when she realized it was empty. She set it down on her coffee table, and her eyes darted to his case of beer. "So ... *sexy* Rexy, how are you going to make me forget about my jobless woes?"

He searched her face for a moment.

His belly grumbled again.

He needed to go let Diesel out.

He needed to shower.

He needed to fucking eat.

His bald head was covered by a black knit cap, but he pulled it off and ran his hand over his bare scalp. "I'm not in the habit of taking advantage of drunk women," he said slowly, choosing his words carefully. "So I can offer you some dinner—got enough

Chinese food here to feed a family of six—but as far as *sexy* Rexy goes, I'm afraid I'm going to have to say no."

Her face fell. "How old are you?"

Well, that was a random and abrupt subject change. Though, he was grateful for it none-the-less.

"Thirty-six. How old are you?'"

"Twenty-eight." She pursed her lips. "So you reject me but then you offer me food. What the fuck?" Her anger was building, and without thinking, his gaze flitted to the door. She saw him, and he watched heat and embarrassment creep up her neck and into her cheeks.

Rex took a deep breath. Despite his hunger and how drunk this woman was, he could already tell she was a good person. Anyone who wanted to work with kids usually was. He'd already come up with a few ways that he might be able to help her. "What kind of qualifications do you have?"

"I told you. I have a degree in education and preschool teacher certification and a Montessori teaching certification. I've also taken courses to work with children with special needs and kids who are on the autism spectrum. I have my first aid certificate, a clear criminal record and a clean driving record. Why? Do you have kids that need watching?" She took a hard swallow before standing up and heading to her kitchen, where she ran the tap in the sink and filled a small tumbler of water.

"I don't have kids. But I know a lot of people who do, and they are looking for childcare. It might not be completely full-time, but it will probably be close. Unless this is just you licking your wounds and allowing your ego to heal and you could go out and get another similar job tomorrow. Seems to me you're crazy-qualified and people would be champing at the bit to hire you."

Her eyes formed thin slits as she stood in her kitchen, her hip cocked against the counter as she sipped her water. "It's hard to get hired in March for anything school-related. I lucked out with covering that maternity leave. And I was looking everywhere before I got that job. It's slim pickings. And I don't want to teach older kids." She huffed. "Even if I did, the on-call teacher list is a mile long, and the school districts have put a moratorium on hiring new substitute teachers."

Well, that was shitty.

His gaze drifted to the fur ball that had wandered into the living room from the bedroom. A calico cat with bright yellow eyes sauntered toward him and rubbed its back up against his leg. His mind immediately flew to Diesel upstairs, and he knew that he had to get to him and take him out for a walk. Poor guy was probably pacing the living room with a full bladder.

He made to stand up, but the intense look in her eyes had him pausing where he sat.

"I can't figure you out, Rex *Barry* Hart. You turn me down for sex, then you offer me food, and now you might have a job for me? What's your deal, dude?" Her words were only slightly slurred for someone who should be struggling to remain vertical if she'd consumed that entire mickey like he figured she had.

Relaxing his shoulders, he stood up, reached for his duffle bag, beer, coat and dinner. "I'm in unit four-eleven if you want to come up and have some dinner. I need to get my dog out first. But I'm more than happy to share my food with you."

She stumbled back into the living room and squinted at him. She was either on the verge of passing out or puking. And even though he normally found drunk chicks to be nearly as intolerable as two cats mating at midnight, Lydia was a cute drunk. "What's your angle ... *Rexly?*"

Rexly? Oh lord.

His head shook. "No angle. Just a nice guy. Give me twenty minutes. I need to get Diesel out and then have a shower. I was just at the gym."

Her eyes struggled to roam his body in a new way—a way of appreciation—but she finally smiled. "Maybe."

He was not one for head games. If she didn't come up, then so be it. More food for him. But if she was going to come up for dinner, she needed to get there before he ate it all.

His stomach made another noise of impatience and desperation. If he didn't get something in it soon, it was going to start consuming him from the inside out.

"Am I not pretty enough?"

Oh, good lord.

This was one of the things he hated most about drunk chicks. The self-deprecation and melodrama.

However, Lydia was an unusual case. She wasn't drunk simply to party. She was nursing a wound. She'd been fired out of the blue from a job she loved. She deserved to wallow for a night with whatever spirit was her vice, and he needed to cut her some slack.

"Lydia, you're fucking gorgeous, and you know it. Let's not play that game. But you're also drunk as fuck, and I don't fuck drunk chicks." He paused for a moment. "Unless we're already together and it's a consensual thing, but you know what I mean. But I'm turning you down for sex because we just met, you're drunk off your cute little ass, and you're sad. The only kind of man who would tap you in that state is not a man worth knowing. If we have sex, I want you sober and knowing what you're agreeing to. If I fuck you, it'll be until you're damn near cross-eyed, and forgive a guy for wanting the chick awake and aware for something like that." He headed to her door and rested his hand on the knob. "I'm upstairs in four-eleven if you're hungry for Chinese food and want to know more about the job."

He went to open the door, but her voice had him pausing again. "I know what I want," she slurred.

He highly doubted that.

She tossed her feet up onto the couch and slid down into a horizontal position, her eyes closing like a vintage doll when her head hit the orangey-pink checkered throw pillow. His mother would probably call that color *coral*.

Turning the knob, he opened the door but glanced back into her apartment. "Well, if you still want it tomorrow when you're sober, you know where to find me."

But she didn't reply. A low and very unladylike snore rumbled up from the sad little drunk woman on the couch, while her cat hopped up and snuggled up next to her leg.

Rex took a deep breath, closed the door again and stepped back into Lydia's apartment. The glass she'd been drinking water from was empty on her counter, so he filled it again. Then he opened up a couple of kitchen cupboards until he found a bottle of Advil. He shook out two tablets and carried them and the water over to her coffee table.

Reaching for the baby-blue knitted blanket off the back of her couch, he draped it over her, making sure not to disturb the cat. "I hardly know you, but I don't like how sad you are. I'd like to help," he whispered.

CHAPTER 2

As MUCH AS she loved Pia, the cat seemed to have the most impeccably bad timing for waking up Lydia. And today was no different.

A meow, a purr and then some very aggressive, very painful claw retractions on Lydia's hip caused the dirty dreams she was having about a bald beast of a man, with deep dimples and a killer smile, to evaporate into the ether before she even had a chance to remove the sexy bra she was wearing in her dream.

Her eyes opened to a dark living room. A quick glance at the window showed that it was dark outside.

What time was it?

She found her phone on the coffee table—next to a glass of water and two tablets of Advil.

Huh?

Her phone said it was nine thirty—at night.

Had she slept for over twenty-hour hours?

No. Pia wouldn't let her get away with that. The cat was on her like dirt on a toddler to get her meals ready, and if Lydia was even ten minutes late, Pia was clawing at the furniture and knocking valuables off high places.

She glanced outside. It was late March in Victoria. The dark sky made sense. But what didn't make sense was why she was passed out on her couch at this time of day with a blanket over her.

She spied the paper bag on the table and grabbed it. An empty mickey of cheap rum fell out onto her lap.

Oh yeah. *That's* why she was asleep on her couch at this time of day on a Wednesday.

Because she'd been fired from a job she loved by a bitch with an ax to grind, then she got drunk and had a very interesting and possibly somewhat embarrassing conversation with a man too sexy to be real.

That's the part where her dream and reality got a little hazy.

Was Rex real?

Or had she dreamt him up completely?

Her damp panties and the flashes of her dream a moment ago said he had to be real, because never in her life had she conjured a man that sexy into her thoughts without having seen something in real life for inspiration.

And she'd definitely noticed him around the building. The man had dimples for days and calf muscles she'd love to sink her teeth into.

She squeezed her eyes shut for a moment, lay back down on her pillow and pressed the heel of her palm to her forehead.

Stupid. Stupid. Stupid.

She'd propositioned him, hadn't she?

She thought harder but couldn't bring herself to open her eyes.

Yes, she had.

Fuck.

Groaning, she rolled off the couch, causing Pia to leap off onto the floor, obviously perturbed. She popped the Advil into her mouth and drained the full water glass before crawling on all fours, like the cat who'd been digging its claws into her flesh a moment ago, the twelve or so feet to her bathroom. She didn't feel like she needed to puke, but she did want to see what kind of a train wreck she was dealing with visually.

Using the counter to pull herself up, she flicked on the light for the bathroom. At the sight of the woman who stared at her in the mirror, she gasped like she'd just been stabbed in the back with a dagger.

Her makeup was smudged around her eyes so bad she looked like she'd been punched, her auburn hair was all over the place and tangled, and she had salty tearstains on her cheeks, which were also sporting some pretty deep pillow creases.

Had she been drooling in her sleep too?

That would round out things in the devastation department quite nicely.

She needed a shower.

Peeling out of her clothes, she made a point of not glancing at herself in the mirror any more than was necessary. Then when the water was hot enough, she leapt in and stood beneath the spray until she started to feel human again.

She was just rinsing the conditioner from her hair when the gentle knock at her front door had her jerking where she stood and flailing her elbow out, which only knocked the shampoo bottle into her bodywash, sending them both to the floor in a mighty crash.

"Fuck." Mumbling more curse words, she bent down to pick up the bottles.

Knock. Knock.

"Lydia? I'm checking to make sure you're still alive."

She gasped. But that only caused her to suck in air—and water —from the shower and start coughing.

Fuck.

With the bright lights of death and the afterlife blinding her, she managed to catch her breath, put the bottles back up on the ledge and turn off the faucet. Now if she could only exit the tub without tripping and cracking her head on the edge of the granite counter.

Wouldn't that be a sight for the firefighters to find.

Her, naked and dead on her bathroom floor, with a cracked skull and a starving Pia eating her eyeballs to survive.

"Lydia? You okay? I heard a crash. The door's unlocked, but I don't want to come in if you don't want me too."

Double fuck.

"Just a second!" she called through the open bathroom door.

She did a mediocre towel-dry of her body, found her fluffy hot pink robe and flung it on before twisting her hair up into another towel on the top of her head. Then, making sure she'd gotten all the makeup off her face and she didn't have big black tracks down her cheeks, she took a deep breath and headed to open the door.

Dear God, had she ever been drunk earlier. Never in a million, trillion and the made-up word *bajillion* years would a sober Lydia have had the cojones to proposition, let alone flirt with and talk to, a hunk of burning love like Rex Hart.

How damn deep did those dimples go? How blue were those eyes? And they weren't like your typical sky-blue either. No. They were like midnight with a thousand stars. With white flecks around the pupil and an intensity that made her lady parts tingle.

She'd never been big into bald men—well, except for The Rock, Vin Diesel, Jason Statham—okay, maybe she did have a thing for bald guys or at the very least the actors of the Fast and Furious franchise. But none of those A-listers could hold a candle to the man standing in her doorway with a plate of food and a sexy smile.

"I figured you might be hungry," he said, offering her up a plate covered in aluminum foil. "I also wanted to check to make sure you were still alive. How are you feeling?"

Without a word—because her tongue had quadrupled in size and was having difficulty navigating its way around her mouth—she took the plate from him and stepped inside. He followed.

"Cat got your tongue?" he asked with a grin that brought the dimples out into full-on attack mode. Like seriously, those things should not be legal. He should need a permit for those babies or a license to carry or something. At the very least, he should be required to issue a warning to all females in a certain proximity before he busted them out. They were about as lethal to her resolve and the existence of dry panties as the sun was to a Popsicle.

Pia wandered into the living room and wove her way around Rex's ankles.

And another thing, he was wearing goddamn gray sweatpants and a fucking white T-shirt that showed off EVERYTHING he had to offer. Including the nipples that appeared to be tight and pointing directly at her.

Dear God, it'd been way too long since she'd been with a man. Way. Too. Long.

She'd also done a damn good job of scrubbing any memories of that last guy from her brain. So her spank bank was so empty, the echo of a pin dropping there would sound more like thunder.

His smile faltered, and his eyes turned cautious. "Are you okay? You *do* know who I am, right?"

Speak, you idiot woman! Speak!

She nodded. "Yes, I know who you are." She lifted up the plate of dinner. It was warm. Her belly rumbled. "Thank you."

That seemed to mollify him a bit. "How are you feeling?"

"Not great," she said, pulling out the stool for the bar slash island in her kitchen and taking a seat while removing the foil from the plate. Dinner looked incredible. Sweet and sour pork, chow mein, lemon chicken, chop suey, fried rice, and he'd even left a spring roll for her. She dove in.

Rex entered the kitchen and pulled out the other barstool, making her more than aware of not only his size but his heat and scent as well. Fresh from the shower with just a hint of ... was that almond? It wasn't overly sweet, but it definitely smelled like almonds.

Interesting. She'd never met a man who used almond-scented bodywash.

But the man could probably wash himself in bubblegum body-wash and it wouldn't detract from his raw, animal magnetism for a second. It'd probably add to it and make him all the more mouth watering.

"I reheated it," he said. "I wasn't sure if you had a microwave or not."

She thanked him again, her mouth full of food.

She did have a microwave, but the fact that he was thoughtful enough to reheat it for her on the off chance she didn't have a microwave was very touching.

"So do you remember our conversation before you passed out?" he asked with a hint of a smirk.

She didn't remember much.

Not that she really wanted to. She knew she'd propositioned him for sex—*that* she remembered but would sooner forget. Maybe her brain was doing her a solid and blocking out the even more embarrassing stuff from her memory.

She kind of hoped it wasn't and that she hadn't made an even bigger fool of herself.

"I'm going to take your silence as a no." He stood up, went to her cupboard and pulled down two water glasses. Then he filled them both from the tap and brought them over, setting one in front of her and taking a sip of the other. "I told you I might have a job opportunity for you."

Right!

The nanny job. Not that she was keen on being a nanny, given all her education, but she could do it even just for a few months, to get her through the summer.

She sipped her water. "Yes, I remember that."

"Good. Anyway, I called my brothers, and both their women are interested. My buddy James, his wife, Emma, would like some help as well. She's trying to head back to work part-time, and my one sister-in-law Krista is a cop and doesn't like relying on my mother so much for childcare. She's a nana, not a babysitter, and they don't want to abuse the grandmother generosity, if you know what I mean?"

She did. Not that she had a family life like that, since it'd only ever been Lydia and her mom for the most part, but she understood what he was saying.

"I mean, obviously, they'll want to meet you and see how you mesh with the kids, and want some references—you don't have to include Odette on that list—but at least it's a start, right?"

Right. At least it was a start.

She had enough money in her savings to pay rent for two months without a job, but after that, she'd be searching for coins in the couch cushions of the doctor's office if she didn't find a way to make some money.

"So how sober are you right now?" he asked, finishing his water and setting the empty glass on the island. A bead of moisture clung to his upper lip, and Lydia found herself mesmerized by it. Like a diamond glinting in the sun, it seemed to almost shimmer on his lip in the glow of her kitchen track lighting. His forehead wrinkled, and he cocked his head to the side. "You okay?" His tongue darted out—oh mama—and swept across his lips, taking the droplet with it.

Lydia shook her head and the dirty, desperate thoughts from it, then took a much-too-big bite of the spring roll. "Mhmm. Just fine," she replied like an uncouth cavewoman. Fitting, since the thoughts she was having about the man in front of her were primal, carnal and involved less clothes than a loincloth. If T-Rex knocked her over the head with a mastodon bone and dragged her back to his cave, she wouldn't complain one bit. Hell, she'd probably race him back to the cave and gather all the animal furs, leap on top and say, "Take me, big boy!"

"You sure you're sober?" The look Rex was giving her was like she was crazy. Like he was calculating the steps and maneuvers he would need to get to the door unscathed and unmounted.

Triple fuck.

She swallowed the spring roll, took a sip of her water to wash it all down and smiled, praying that there wasn't any food in her teeth. "I'm pretty sober now. I mean, I *feel* like I just drank almost an entire mickey of cheap rum, given my pounding head and overall feeling of *blech*, but cognitively I'm sober ... *ish.*"

The mickey hadn't been completely full when she started—thankfully. Because if it had been and she drank the whole thing—which she would have—she'd probably be getting her stomach pumped at the hospital instead of sitting in her kitchen with her dimpled and delicious neighbor.

She took another bite of the spring roll. "I don't think I should drive anywhere, though. Not that I have anywhere to be. No boyfriend, no job. No friends, since I only just moved here a couple of months ago. My mom doesn't live here. Where do I have to go? Nowhere."

"I can be your friend."

With benefits?

She told her libido to go stand in the corner and be quiet.

"Why? You hardly know me."

Rex's enormous shoulder lifted, which only caused those thick muscles that connected his shoulders to his back to bunch. If she remembered her biology class right, those were the trapezius muscles or "traps," as the gym-bros called them. Not that she hung around with a lot of gym-bros.

Whatever they were, Rex had them, and the ones he had were big, sexy and well-defined. She kind of wanted to lick them.

Down, girl. Back to the corner. Sit down. Be quiet.

"I like to help people," he said. "And I'm also a friendly guy." Color bloomed in his cheeks. "Or at least that's what I've been told. Why can't we be friends?"

Because you're gorgeous and I don't think I could just be your friend. Do friends always want to jump their other friends' bones?

Quadruple fuck.

Her libido was not listening. She needed to drag that needy little brat into her bedroom, tie her to the bed and lock the door—which her libido would probably like, given her proclivities.

Quintuple fuck.

"I ... I'm embarrassed about what I said earlier." Well, that was true, though she was kind of wishing now that she hadn't said anything. He was kind enough to act like it hadn't happened. Why wasn't she taking her cues from him?

"About propositioning me for sex?"

Lydia nodded, her cheeks growing hot—in fact, her whole body was an inferno. She reached for the belt loop of her housecoat and was in the process of throwing it off her body when Rex's eyes went wide.

Sextuple fuck.

Oh, why did that word have to have *sex* in it?

"Shit! Sorry." She tightened the housecoat around her body, leaped off the stool and ran to her room, nearly lopping off Pia's tail with how quickly she slammed the door.

"No need to apologize," Rex called through the door from the kitchen, an obvious chuckle to his tone. "I'll never tell a woman *not* to take off her clothes in front of me. Though I was kind of hoping I'd get to take you on a date first."

A date?

She located her fuzzy flannel pajama pants, the pink ones with the avocado halves turned into cats on them. *Avo-cat-o.* Get it? Then she found a black tank top with a built-in bra and tugged that over her torso. A quick pick-comb through her wavy auburn locks and she was opening the door and braiding her hair as she entered the kitchen.

"That's cute, too," Rex said, all dimples and devastatingly sexy smiles.

Her cheeks were now hot enough to probably fry an egg. She secured the end of her braid with a hair elastic from around her wrist and let it fall over her shoulder. "Sorry. I forgot I wasn't wearing anything under the robe. You knocked as I was just getting out of the shower."

There you go, girlie. Nice, articulate adult conversation. See, you are capable of having a normal conversation.

He held up a hand and shook his head in protest. "No need to apologize. Like I said, I'll never discourage a woman from taking off her clothes in front of me. Won't complain either. And for the record, that little bit of top breast that I saw ... very nice." He made the OK sign with his thumb and forefinger pressed together.

Lydia's head dropped, and she stared at her lap. "Are you trying to mortify me even more?"

"On the contrary." He actually sounded a little hurt. "I'm trying to make you smile, even laugh if you're up for it. You had a shitty day. It can only go up from here, right?"

She lifted her gaze but kept her head down. He was back to smiling.

It was alarming how disarming his smile was. How much those dimples made her want to smile just as wide as he was. She smiled too. It was downright impossible not to when such a gorgeous specimen of a man was grinning that hard at you.

"There we go," Rex said. "Is that so bad?"

Still smiling, though now it was more like a smirk, she twirled some chow mein around on her fork like it was spaghetti and shoveled it into her mouth. "No."

"Good. Because you have a very pretty smile." His own grin faltered. "Not that I'm one of those douchebags that tries to tell women to smile or that they'd be prettier if they smiled. I'm a woke man—or at least I'd like to think I am. My brothers and I were raised by a single mother who is a feminist and a sex and relationship therapist. If any of us boys told a woman to smile more or that she'd be prettier if she smiled, and our mother found out about it, she'd throw her slipper at us, then make us write an essay on women's rights and the feminist movement."

Now Lydia's smile came as naturally as breathing. "Your mother sounds amazing."

Rex's smile was big again, his eyes wistful. "She is. You'd like her. And I think she'd like you."

The thought of meeting Rex's mum, of being introduced to her as … someone Rex was seeing, or even just as a friend, made tingles form in her belly.

"So, if you're sober … *ish*," Rex started, standing up and heading to the sink with his glass. He filled it up again from the tap, then leaned back against the counter and crossed his ankles. She had to keep her tongue in her mouth, otherwise it would fall out and she'd drool all over. "How about we go on a date?"

A date?

Her libido broke free from its shackles, picked the lock on the bedroom door and was now running around naked like a streaker at the Super Bowl, waving her arms in the air and cheering.

"A date?" she asked, needing more water. She drained her glass. He leaned forward, took it from her hands, their fingers brushing just enough to send all kinds of sparks and zaps to her cobweb-cluttered lady parts, and he filled the glass back up in the sink, then passed it to her.

"Yeah, a date. You just said you don't have a boyfriend, and you *did* proposition me for sex earlier, so unless only drunk Lydia is attracted to me, I figured it was probably a safe bet to ask you out. What do you say?" He sipped his water and studied her over the glass, a brow bobbing as he said, "Wanna go out with me, Lydia?"

CHAPTER 3

Damn, she was cute. And not puppy or kitten cute—he'd been reprimanded by his mother enough times over the years to not call women *cute*. But Lydia really was cute. She was adorable, in fact. Honest and bright-eyed. Expressive and quirky. A refreshing change from some of the women he'd dated recently—all from a hookup app. Great body, no substance. They rarely got past the second date.

"Ever thought maybe you're only meeting a certain *caliber* of women because of the app you're using?" his mother had chided on more than one occasion. "Why not try an app not actually called *Huukup?* It's in the name, for goodness' sakes, you buffoon."

"You want to go on a date with me?" Lydia practically squeaked, pressing her hand to her chest like she'd just won an Oscar and was surprised they'd picked her over Meryl Streep and Kate Winslet.

Rex nodded. "Yeah, is there something weird about that?"

"Well ..." Her hazel eyes raked his body from loafers to bald head and back, growing wider as she casually slid her gaze over the

V of his sweat pants, his stomach, chest and arms. Color filled her cheeks, and her pink tongue darted out and slid across her lips.

See? Cute. She was fucking cute.

Hot too, of course.

Smoking hot, actually. Like set your sheets on fire hot. But she was also fucking cute. Though he could tell she had a little wicked side too. The day-drinking out of a paper bag like some train-track hobo, propositioning a stranger for sex—those weren't the actions of a virtuous girl next door.

Plus, the more time he spent in her apartment and glanced around the room, the more he noticed. Before he left earlier, he'd spied a photo of her dressed up for a burlesque show on the bookcase in the corner of the living room. It was a small frame, but he was trained in surveillance and observing his surroundings and all the threats that lurked nearby. Not that Lydia in a black bustier was a threat—well, maybe to the front of his sweatpants remaining flat. But she looked comfortable in the outfit, and something told him this woman had a wild side that only the closest people to her got to see.

"Let's grab breakfast tomorrow," he said, letting his gaze wander back to the woman sitting in front of him. He'd allowed his eyes to take in her burlesque attire one more time, committing that image to memory for later. The way her eyes had clung to his body and she questioned him so surprised-like made him wonder if she thought he was out of her league.

Au contraire, Miss Lydia, it is you who is way out of my league.

"Breakfast?" she asked, like she had never heard the word before and was trying it out for the first time on her tongue.

He pressed his lips together to stifle his amusement. "Yeah, you know, the first meal of the day? Usually consists of a big cup of coffee, maybe some eggs and bacon, or granola or cereal. And if you're my little brother—all of the above, plus more. You *do* eat breakfast, right?"

She nodded. "I do, yeah."

"Then let's go grab some together. My treat. I don't have any jobs tomorrow, and you, well ..." He twisted his lips.

"Don't *have* a job," she finished, her shoulders slumping and face falling.

"I didn't want to say it out loud." He felt bad for her. He didn't know much about her, but what he did know, he liked. And to be fired from a job you loved—well, that just sucked no matter who you were.

"You didn't have to," she said with a deep sigh. "It's the truth whether we verbalize it or not. I'm jobless. It's the first time I've ever been fired from anything. I've been employee of the month at other jobs, received nothing but glowing references and recommendations. I was named teacher of the year at the first preschool I ever worked at. I'm not somebody who gets fired. I'm just not."

"We'll find you another job. Trust me."

"I don't even know you."

That was true, but she'd invited him into her home twice, propositioned him for sex, and he couldn't forget her flinging herself into his arms down in the lobby and crying against his chest. As much as he hated to hear her cry and know that she was hurting, it did feel good to be that place of comfort for someone, to be needed. He always liked being needed.

He flashed her a grin that he knew made his dimples dig deep into his cheeks. "Then let's change that. What do you want to know?"

She eyed him suspiciously for a moment but then seemed to relax and speared a piece of sweet and sour pork onto a fork and popped it into her mouth. "What do you do for work?"

"A few things. I'm a plumber when I'm not doing my other job."

"Which is ...?"

This was always where it got a bit tricky. Some women were

either super attracted to a man with his "talents" or they were super turned off and ran for the hills. But he was all about transparency, and he'd dated women from every facet of life and the career world with no judgment, so he expected the same. If they didn't like what he did, then they weren't for him.

He wasn't going to change who he was or the jobs he loved to make someone else feel comfortable. If a woman was going to love him, she was going to love all of him, just like he would love all of her.

Lydia lifted a brow and tilted her head in waiting.

Rex took a deep breath. "I was in the Navy for a while. Then my brothers and I were all recruited by Joint Task Force 2, which is basically like the Navy SEALs in the States, but in Canada. We were then recruited by a covert special ops team—off the record, ghosts in the night, doing the tough shit that nobody else wanted to do—and I did that for a while."

Her hazel eyes went wide. Her chewing stopped too.

But as much as he was good at reading a situation and his surroundings, he still wasn't the best at reading women. And Lydia was no different.

Was she turned on? Turned off? Intrigued? Terrified?

He swallowed. "After we all retired from that, we did work for a surveillance and security company—my brothers and I—for a few years based out of Victoria. But we were sent all over the place. Wherever the job was needed. But then Brock—my oldest brother —bought the company and now he runs it. Chase is our tech specialist, and Heath and I are kind of the grunts, though we all do a bit of everything. Heath is also our language specialist. He speaks six languages, including American Sign Language. I'm kind of the explosives specialist, too, you could say. I've done a lot of bomb-tech training."

"And you're a plumber?" she asked slowly, her eyes once again traveling the length of his body at the speed of a sloth on Valium.

She spent a considerable amount of time studying the front of his sweatpants. A *very* considerable amount of time.

Rex lifted a shoulder. "Need something to fall back on. Won't always be able to do this, won't always *want* to do the hard, dangerous stuff. So when I wasn't on a job, I was apprenticing with a plumber. Did the schooling when I could. Got my ticket when I was thirty-two, and I work on-call when I'm available for a guy here in town."

"So you're like"—she swallowed and licked her lips—"a real badass then?"

That made him snort, smile and turn away. The look she was giving him was one he'd seen before. She was turned on—big-time.

"We—*I*—get the job done," he said, intentionally adding that innuendo, which caused her to suck in a sharp breath. "Got all the right tools."

Eyes squinted at him, and lips curled into a sassy smile. "I bet you do."

That had him grinning. She had a wicked side to her, he just knew it. "So breakfast?"

"Still don't know enough about you, *Rexington*." She stabbed a piece of broccoli with her fork and pulled it off provocatively with her teeth. "Favorite color?"

"Blue."

"Favorite food?"

"You're eating it."

"Favorite animal?"

"Pit bull. Rescued one late last year. He's upstairs. Fucking adorable."

"Favorite—"

"Let me help you out here, hmm? Blue, Chinese food, pit bull— or dogs, I guess you could say—chocolate chip mint, July ninth, Barbados, nothing, cinnamon gum."

"Cinnamon gum?"

"Can't stand it. Makes my tongue go numb and feel weird."

"And nothing?"

"I'm not allergic to anything." He pointed at her. "Your turn."

"Barbados?"

"Favorite vacation spot."

She smiled and pushed her plate away, making a face like she was full.

"I hope you'll eat that later," he said. "Letting Chinese food that good go to waste is sacrilege."

Lydia nodded and yawned. "I will. And thank you. It was perfect."

He stepped away from the counter, grabbed the foil from the island and wrapped it back over the Chinese food before opening her fridge and stashing it inside. "Grab your water, go sit on the couch, and let's learn all we can about each other."

———

WHO WAS this bald man with thick thighs and dimples for days?

A man fresh out of her fantasies, that's who.

Normally, Lydia wasn't a big fan of being told what to do by a man, but the way Rex did it, so casually and almost gently, she found herself obeying without even a second thought.

He took up purchase in the chair opposite her couch, cocked one ankle on his knee and studied her.

She squirmed under his scrutiny. Did she have sauce on her cheek?

A booger on her upper lip?

"So, what's Lydia's story?" Rex asked, leaning back in the chair and causing it to creak.

Damn, he was big.

And not fat big.

Hellllll no.

The man was pure muscle. And those arms and the way they were squeezing out of his T-shirt like sausage from a casing—she had a vague feeling she'd felt those arms around her at some point but wasn't sure how that could be.

"Hmm?" he probed, giving her another smile that had her saying goodbye to her dry panties.

Oh, where to begin ... there were parts of her life—a lot of them, actually—that she would rather forget, so to dredge those up now, particularly with a person she just met, wouldn't be wise for either of them.

Keep it simple, stupid.

"Favorite color: aqua-blue. Favorite food: Thai. Favorite ice cream: butterscotch ripple. Favorite animal: turtle. Favorite vacation spot ... I haven't really been too many places, so I guess Mexico? My mum took me when I graduated high school for a girls' trip. I have no allergies, and I do not like yams." She did a quick checklist in her head. "Oh, yeah, and May tenth."

He nodded, still smiling. "Coming up then."

"Not too far away. But I'm not big into birthdays." Not anymore, anyway. Not since the last one.

His eyes fell back on the picture in her corner-style bookcase. She'd noticed him looking at it earlier but hadn't said anything. "Looks like you have a *hobby*." He bobbed his brows. "Do you do that here?"

Her smile spread slowly, pulling the corners of her lips upward. "You mean the burlesque dancing?"

He nodded eagerly.

"Not *here* in Victoria. But I know they have a burlesque club. But what I do is more *burlesque aerobics*. It's a workout. I've also done pole dancing as a workout too. When I lived in Vancouver, I did it like four or five nights a week." It had not only been an incredible workout, but she'd never felt sexier or more in tune and confident in her body. She missed the workout and the friends she made a great deal.

But she needed to get away from that life. *He* was in Vancouver, and even though she knew he wasn't himself and didn't want to hurt her, he was still there, and if he knew where she lived or saw her across the street, there was no telling what he might do.

Victoria seemed like a safe bet. Still close enough to her mom, who lived in Hope, but far enough away from Dierks that he might not think to look on the island.

The twinkle of interest in Rex's dark blue eyes set her body to tropical temperatures. "Pole dancing, eh?"

She nodded. "Yep. It's a *great* workout."

If she ever owned her own home, she planned on installing a pole of her very own. Ah, life goals.

"Should we consider this our first date?" he asked, all sexy smiles and salacious, penetrating glances.

"First date?" She reared her head back in surprise. "What makes you think this is a *date?*"

There went those manly shoulders again. Bobbing and drawing her attention to his muscles and the cords in his neck and those lick-worthy traps. "I bought you dinner. We're getting to know each other. Why can't this be a first date?"

She was enjoying herself as much, if not more than her last several first dates—not that she'd had many—but she also wanted to tease him a bit. "I dunno ... seems like a bit of a lazy first date, if you ask me. I mean, you brought me your leftovers and we're just sitting in my living room. I'm in my pajamas."

"Are you wanting to be wined and dined? Because I don't think you need any more booze, but the night is young, so if you'd like to continue this date, why don't we throw on some jackets and shoes. I can run upstairs and grab Diesel, and we can go for a nice walk. It's not raining outside, and I'm sure your drunk little butt could use the fresh air."

What was it about Rex that made her feel so at ease? Like she'd known him way longer than the few hours since she'd wandered into the apartment lobby drunk and crying. For a man who could probably snap a redwood in half over his knee, he had a very gentle way about him. A genuineness to him that she struggled to see in people these days. It was refreshing, and if she was being honest with herself, she was trying to figure out a way to spend more time with him tonight. She didn't want to be alone. She hated being alone.

"Hmm? Fresh air? Walk? You can meet Diesel."

"I'm in my pajamas," she said, glancing down at her avocat-o PJs.

He shrugged. "So? Either go for a walk in them and not give a shit, or change into another pair of pants. Both choices seem pretty damn simple to me. Nothing like the choice poor Sophie had to make." He grinned, and she nearly fainted from the effect of his dimples. Then she found herself mesmerized by his bunching muscles as he pried himself out of her chair and slapped the side of her knee playfully. "Get some jeans on and meet me in the lobby in five. I'm going to go grab D." Then before she could argue or say *no* —not that she had any intention of saying *no*—he headed to her door and was gone.

And she was smiling more than she had in God only knows how long.

She was on a date, and it felt great.

CHAPTER 4

AFTER TOSSING on a pair of skinny dark wash jeans, some socks and a red hoodie, Lydia locked her door and headed down to the lobby to meet Rex. She didn't bother with the elevator since the stairs were just as fast and she wasn't sure her slightly queasy stomach could handle the motion of the elevator.

He was waiting for her just inside the lobby, with a tail-wagging, tongue-lolling, bright-eyed brindle pit bull whimpering next to him. The dog tried to lunge for Lydia, but Rex held tight onto his leash. "Hey, Diesel, knock it off."

The dog only whimpered louder, his whole back end now moving with his frantically wagging tail.

Grinning, because she loved dogs—all animals, really—Lydia approached slowly and offered Diesel the back of her hand to sniff. He did so eagerly, but his determination to give her all his attention and love was still present and persistent.

"Let's get outside before he starts whining for attention." Rex hit the button so the door opened on its own.

She followed him, admiring the breadth of his back and the

way his muscles moved beneath the tight-fitting royal blue zip-up hoodie. He was still in those sweatpants. Yum.

"He's adorable," she noted, falling in line beside him on the sidewalk. "You say you rescued him?"

Rex nodded and glanced down at her. "Yeah, he was from a puppy mill that got raided. They were breeding and raising dogs for fighting. His poor mother was one of those females that gets strapped down for breeding. It was horrible. I was actually part of the crew that raided it, and when I saw Diesel, I knew he was mine. Those eyes, man, how can you not fall in love with someone who looks at you with eyes like that?"

As if on cue, the happy-go-lucky pup turned around with a big smile on his face, giving them a good look at his whiskey-colored eyes.

He was definitely a looker.

"I brought him home and adopted him, and it was the best decision I ever made."

"Who watches him when you're away for work?" She became keenly aware when their hands accidentally brushed and heat and electricity shot through her as if she'd just touched an electric fence meant to keep the cows from wandering into the vegetable garden.

But there were no cows around, just her raging hormones and libido with a mind of its own. Both needed to be caged though.

"My mom or one of my brothers if they're not on the job with me. But he's pretty good. I know he seems hyper right now, but he calms down quick. He's a great apartment dog. Not that I want to live in an apartment forever, but for now it works for us." He stopped so Diesel could lift his leg, exposing his white belly, and pee on a bush. "If you ever want to take him for a walk or a run or something, you're more than welcome. He's great company. I feel way less alone or lonely now that I have him."

A sadness flitted across his face that hit Lydia hard in the solar plexus.

He'd been such an upbeat guy until now, the idea of him being lonely seemed almost absurd. Particularly since he had so much family here in town. She had nobody. Nobody besides Pia, and Pia only offered up her affections when she felt like it, which was when Mercury was in retrograde or there was a harvest moon—at least that's what it felt like.

"But you know what I'm talking about, right? You have your cat. Pets are great, aren't they?" They went single file, with Rex in front of her, and they walked through a turnstile gate into a field that was labeled as off-leash. It was empty, but you could tell by the way the grass was all kicked and trampled that a lot of dogs had burned off some steam there earlier.

"Pia's great," she agreed, "but she's a typical cat. Her moods shift almost with the tides."

Rex made Diesel sit. The dog looked up at his master with hopeful eyes, and his tail swished quickly on the ground. "You come when you're called, you got it? If I have to chase you, there will be no off-leash fun for a while. Got it?"

She could have sworn she saw the dog nod.

Rex made him sit there for a moment longer, Diesel's eyes seeming to get wider and his tail wagging faster. But otherwise, he didn't move or make a sound.

After a few more heartbeats, Rex unclipped the leash from the harness, said, "Okay, go!" and Diesel took off like the field was full of rabbits and he had to catch every single one.

Lydia's smile hurt her cheeks as she watched the pup sprint around the wide-open space in joy. It was dark out now, but there were loads of orange street lights around, and Diesel's harness had a flashing blue light on it, so he was easy enough to see.

Rex reached for her hand, startling her and causing her to pull it away.

Shit.

"Sorry," she said, the instant nausea from her nerves making her swallow down some bile. "I didn't mean to jerk my hand away."

He shook his head in dismissal. "I wasn't trying to hold your hand, truly. You just look cold, and I wanted to see if your hands were cold." He reached into the pocket of his hoodie and pulled out a pair of black one-size-fits-most gloves. "Here."

Now she felt like an even bigger idiot.

It was a clear night, and even though it was late March and finally spring, her hands were cold. "Thank you." She pulled the gloves on and felt instant relief.

He nodded, smiled and pulled a ball out of his other pocket. Diesel seemed to spot the ball from all the way across the field and came bounding back, his long, pink tongue hanging out of his mouth like one of those clams whose body sticks out of its shell. She was pretty sure they were called geoduck, and she was also pretty sure they were delicious.

Rex pressed a button on the ball, and it lit up. Diesel leapt up and barked, his whole body wiggling now, not just his long, muscular tail.

"You don't want this, do you, bud?" Rex teased, doing a couple of fake throws and making Diesel start to run but then turn back around with a confused look on his face. Finally, Rex actually threw it, and Diesel took off like a bolt of lightning. "My brother Brock has two kids—Zoe and Zane. Zo-zo is just over three, and Zane just turned one. My brother Chase has two kids as well. Connor is four, and Thea is not quite a year. Then my buddy James and his wife have twin girls who are just over a year, I think." He turned to face her. "I doubt you'd have to watch more than two kids at a time. I know Connor and Zo-zo are in preschool too. But between the three families, I'm sure we could get you pretty close to full-time. Even if it's just for the summer to make you some scratch. I know you're too old to be 'babysitting,' but these are also people with connections. James knows nearly half the city as a project developer and business investor, my sister-in-law Krista is a cop, my other sister-in-law Stacey is a nurse, and Emma is an ESL teacher. These are people to know. They're also just great people—if you're looking for friends."

She was.

It sounded so sad and pathetic to say, but she was looking for friends. Desperately, actually. She was a fairly social person, had a small but tight group of friends back in Vancouver, but since she moved to the island a couple of months ago to get away from Dierks, nobody had reached out. She'd even reached out, but her texts and calls went unanswered.

She knew her friends disapproved of her leaving Dierks, but she just couldn't stay with him. He needed more help than she was capable of giving him, and she didn't deserve the abuse while he struggled with the realization that he wasn't the man he used to be.

Even after his outburst at the restaurant for her birthday last year, where he screamed, caused a scene and made their server cry because she brought him a coke and not a diet coke, wasn't enough for her friends to think Lydia was right in leaving him. That had ruined birthdays for her entirely and now she'd rather just treat it like any other day.

No, none of it was his fault, and she knew the man that he once was—kind, caring and gentle—but he wasn't that man any longer, and the man he was now needed serious psychological help.

"I'd like to meet with these people," she finally said, having gotten briefly lost in her own thoughts about Dierks, her friends and life before the accident. "I'd like the nanny job. Even if it's just for the summer. They all sound like nice people, and I need more nice people—I need more *people* in my life. Since moving here, I've been really lonely."

Diesel brought the ball back, panting. He dropped it at Rex's feet, and Rex picked it up. She could see the thick coat of slobber glowing from the LED light inside the ball. But Rex didn't seem the least bit fazed and chucked it to the other end of the field once more. He glanced down at her. "Why did you move here?"

That was a loaded question if ever there was one.

She also wasn't in the right frame of mind to get into the details, and as nice as Rex was, as easy as he was to talk to, she also didn't know him *that* well.

So she'd give him the canned response she gave anyone else who asked. "A relationship went south, and I needed a fresh start. Too many memories, too many mutual old haunts and mutual friends. I just needed a clean break."

And all of that was true. It just went a little deeper. She tried leaving Dierks and staying in Vancouver, but it was (a) too expensive to live on her own, even with her decent-paying job at the elite Montessori Preschool in West Van, and (b) he wouldn't leave her alone. He found her, called her, showed up on her doorstep. And even though he wasn't violent when he begged her to take him back, she now knew what he was capable of, and she didn't want to be anywhere near it.

That response seemed to satisfy Rex, and he nodded, offering her a grim smile of understanding. "Yeah, breakups are tough."

Understatement of the century right there, but she wasn't going to say that.

She only nodded.

Diesel came bouncing back to them, his chest heaving with spent efforts. He dropped the ball at Rex's feet again, then flopped onto his back and wiggled his whole body, his tongue still hanging out of his mouth.

"He's done," Rex said, reaching down and grabbing the ball, turning it off and stowing it back in his pocket. "I took him for a long walk earlier while you were sleeping off the rum spins, so he didn't really need this extra exercise, not that he'd ever complain." Diesel flipped over to his belly and gazed up at both of them, smiling. "Would you, buddy? You don't complain about much. As long as you get food, ear scratches and walks, you are a happy camper, hmm?"

Once again, it looked like Diesel was actually nodding in agreement, but maybe that was the leftover rum in Lydia's system.

Rex re-clipped the leash to Diesel's harness, and they turned to head back to the turnstile gate. Rex allowed her to go through the gate first, and when he joined her on the other side, she reached for his free hand and laced her fingers through his.

His grin down at her wasn't surprised but simply pure joy—and incredibly disarming. Damn, those dimples were lethal.

"We doing this?" he asked her, giving her fingers a gentle squeeze.

"I'd like to try," she said, enjoying the feel of her hand in his more than she was ready to admit. "This has been a great first date, and I am very much looking forward to the next one."

He released her hand, tugged her close and wrapped his arm around her tight. "Me too. My gut tells me this is right."

"Well, then, let's listen to your gut." She bit her lip to contain her excitement.

She had a boyfriend, and he was gorgeous, nice and smart. Maybe things for her were finally starting to turn around.

Maybe this was her life starting its upswing.

Maybe Rex was the one.

How UTTERLY UNCONVENTIONAL but no less wonderful. She started yesterday off with a job and no boyfriend. Now she was waking up today to no job, a new job prospect and possibly a boyfriend.

Oh, the universe and its kooky plans.

Grinning and stretching in bed, Lydia gripped the wrought-iron bars of her headboard and pointed her toes beneath her plush duvet. She'd had a very dirty dream about one handsome bald man with more muscles than the sky had stars, and she knew her panties were damp.

A quick glance at her phone on her nightstand said it was only seven thirty, and Rex was going to knock on her door at nine so they could go grab breakfast.

Plenty of time for a little morning one-on-one time.

She had an impressive collection of battery-operated boyfriends, but her default was the one she'd nicknamed Marley.

Battery-operated boyfriend. B.O.B. Bob Marley. Get it?

She thought it was clever at the time.

With a lazy sigh and placid smile, she reached over into her nightstand for Marley and pulled him out. He greeted her with the same look he always did—blank and indifferent.

Conjuring up an image of Rex in his sweatpants, she slid Marley down beneath the covers and under the waistband of her pajamas, pressing the button on the end a couple of times until she got the right speed.

Marley knew what to do. He slid inside her pussy and got to work.

With Marley firmly inside her buzzing away, Lydia rubbed two fingers over her clit, feeling shockwaves of pleasure sprint through her right down to her toes and up to her peaked nipples. With her other hand, she began working Marley back and forth inside her, hitting her erogenous zones and trembling across her slick entrance.

Thoughts of Rex's arms wrapped around her, his muscles rippling and damn near ripping his T-shirt, and his big hand engulfing hers had her close in no time.

What would it be like to make love to a man so big and powerful? To feel his weight on her?

Dierks hadn't been a small guy, but he was a Yorkshire terrier compared with the Great Dane or St. Bernard that was Rex. Damn, even his name ... *Rex*. Like a *T. rex*. King of the dinosaurs. Strong and mighty.

Her fingers picked up speed on her clit, and it swelled as she got closer to her climax.

Was Rex her boyfriend now?

They'd spent time together last night, getting to know each other, and then they held hands on the walk home, but he'd been the perfect gentleman walking her to her door and saying good-night. A big part of her wanted him to lean in and kiss her, but he didn't, and it spoke more of his character that he didn't. Another part of her—the part between her legs—had wanted him to do more than just lean in and kiss her, but again, it spoke a lot about his character that he didn't expect more from her. He was what her mother would call *a keeper*.

She pressed the button on the base of Marley, and he increased his vibration speed, taking her body from not-quite-there to so-close-she-could-taste-it.

Rex.

He wasn't like any man she'd ever dated before, and maybe that was a good thing.

She tended to play it safe with the men she dated. Men who were soft-spoken, calm and collected, not much bigger or taller than her, and with safe, boring jobs.

Yeah, and Dierks was that kind of guy and look what happened. He was a mild-mannered carpenter before the accident.

That was true.

But even so, Rex didn't have a safe or boring job. Even as a plumber, his job probably wasn't boring. But he wasn't just a plumber. He was ... a protector.

And boy oh boy, did that turn her on.

Her fingers picked up fervor on her clit, and she worked Marley in and out of her pussy quicker until heat and tingles formed in her lower belly. What would it feel like to have Rex *protecting* her? To be the person he looked out for, guarded with his body, and kept free from danger?

A girl could only be so lucky.

Rex.

Rex Hart.

He had a good name.

Strong. Powerful.

Just like him.

Her fingers brushed her clit. She pushed the tip of Marley up against her G-spot, squeezed her eyes shut, and her body went off like a keg of dynamite doused in lighter fluid. Her back bowed on the bed at the same time her toes curled.

"Rex," she breathed out as her orgasm reached its crescendo. "Oh God, Rex."

And at that moment, Pia deemed it a good time to leap up onto the bed and crawl across her body, settling on her chest.

Her orgasm simmered away, and she removed her hands and Marley from beneath her pajamas, turning off the buzzing B.O.B. "You've always had *impeccable* timing, Pia," she said, kissing the cat's head when Pia sat on Lydia's chest, bent her head and nuzzled her face. "You avoid me like I'm the plague all night, and then when I take a couple of minutes to indulge in a fantasy and do a bit of stress release, you're right up in my business."

Pia began to purr.

Rolling her eyes, Lydia kissed her cat once more before sliding out from beneath the covers, much to the meowing protestations of her feline. She padded barefoot to her bathroom, where she washed Marley and used the toilet.

She really should be going for a run before breakfast, but a big part of her just wasn't up for it. What she'd rather do was spend the next hour back in bed with Marley and more thoughts of Rex.

She hadn't had too many partners in her twenty-eight years—a few long-term boyfriends and one or two shorter-term flings—but over the few relationships that she'd had, Lydia had learned a lot about what she liked and what she didn't like in the bedroom.

She liked to be dominated, for one thing. And not in a Dom/sub kind of way. More in an organic, he takes control and makes assertive but respectful demands and she acquiesces and has all the orgasms her body can handle.

It worked better with some partners more than others. Dierks hadn't been super authoritative in the bedroom, but he tried. He did, however, like to use the restraints—so did she, and she had those restraints attached and tucked behind her bed now, just in case the next man she brought into her room was into tying her up and taking control.

And something told her Rex just might be.

Pia had found a new spot to occupy on the other pillow, and for a brief moment, Lydia contemplated jumping back into bed with Marley for another round of hide the salami, but the idea of masturbating next to her cat just didn't sit right. She stowed Marley back in her nightstand, grabbed her phone and headed to the kitchen to make some coffee.

She was just dumping the beans into the grinder when her phone buzzed.

It was Rex.

On his insistence, and zero balking from her, they'd exchanged numbers before saying goodnight.

Want to go for a run. Work up an appetite for breakfast.

She could think of other ways they could work up an appetite, but seeing Rex run and get all sweaty next to her was an alluring close second.

He would probably run laps around her, though, with those long legs and thick thighs. She wasn't exactly fast. Slow and steady won the race, right? She ran to accommodate her penchant for wine and bread, not because she enjoyed the burning sensation in her lungs like some masochist.

But her fingers did the talking—along with her unsated lady parts—and she found herself texting *Sure* before the kettle had even boiled.

Awesome! I'll be by in ten to grab you, he texted back, following it up with a winky-face emoji.

She smiled like an idiot and shot him a winky face back, loving how easy all of this felt and that for the first time in a long time, she'd met a nice guy *not* on a dating app and he wasn't expecting to jump into bed with her on the first date.

Maybe nice, respectful guys still did exist out there and Rex was one of them.

Was her luck finally changing?

She sure as heck hoped so.

CHAPTER 5

HE CONSIDERED himself a man of immense willpower.

Hell, he'd been tortured and never gave up the information.

And yet, Lydia running next to him, with her tight ass tucked into those running pants and her chest bouncing in her bra, was enough to make him give up every last bit of intel to the enemy just for a glimpse of creamy, soft flesh.

He'd never been a man for head games, so as they sat there at breakfast and the server rattled off the specials, including the three-dollar mimosas and four-dollar breakfast Caesar cocktails—the Canadian version of Bloody Mary, but with Clamato juice instead of tomato—he knew he had to come clean with Lydia.

Her reaction, however, had surprised him.

"I'm a gentleman," he started. "I respect women, their consent and boundaries. No means no."

Her brows narrowed, and she sipped her water. "Good to know."

"But if you have a mimosa or a Caesar, I won't be taking off your clothes today. Like I said yesterday, I want you sober when we ..."

Her throat bobbed heavily, and her nostrils flared. "When we ..."

"Do you want a mimosa?" he asked, glancing at the menu briefly before lifting his gaze back to Lydia. Damn, she was fucking hot. Even in the baby-blue T-shirt and soft black jersey leggings, she was a knockout. Her auburn hair was in a ponytail that swished down behind her in gentle waves, and her hazel eyes widened behind thick lashes.

"Not as much as I want other things," she whispered, looking up at him seductively from beneath those heavy eyelashes.

Well, fuck if his dick didn't jerk like it'd just been zapped with a Taser. He cleared his throat and grinned. "So, two orange juices then? Hold the champagne?"

She nodded. "Hold the champagne."

He'd like to say that they took their time having breakfast and getting to know each other even more, but they didn't. They ate like they were in a rush to catch a flight. He tossed way too many bills onto the table, probably leaving a fifty-percent tip, then they raced out the door and to his truck.

Her grin as they drove through town had his cock surging to life in his jeans and pressing uncomfortably against his zipper.

He wanted to do this right with Lydia, get to know her and be the gentleman his mother had raised. But she was making it really fucking hard when she looked at him like she wanted to sink her teeth into his neck and rake her nails down his back.

Laughing, they ran through their apartment parking lot to the door, both of them smiling like fools who knew very well what the plan was but were both playing coy to keep the game and fun alive.

Once inside, she headed for the stairs, but he snagged her hand and pulled her toward the elevator. She didn't resist, and they stumbled through the parting door, laughing once again.

When the doors shut and the lift engaged, he tugged her against him, reached behind her and pulled out her ponytail, pushing his fingers into her hair and cupping her cheek in his palm. She allowed him to tilt her face up, her gaze hooded, pupils dilating.

They hadn't even kissed yet.

It was kind of bizarre but also wonderful.

He'd never held such giddy anticipation about a first kiss with a woman before. Normally, he went in, the clothes came off, and they did the naked horizontal mambo like adults were known to do. He rarely knew as much about a woman as he did Lydia before he got her into bed, and yet here they were, on their second date in less than twenty-four hours, and he'd like to think he knew a fair bit about her.

He'd like to know more.

But he was off to a good start as far as relationships went.

"Are you going to kiss me?" she asked, batting long lashes at him.

One side of his mouth lifted up into a lopsided smile, and he nodded. "I will."

The elevator dinged, and the doors opened. Reluctantly, he removed his hand from her face and his fingers from her hair and took her hand, pulling her along until they came to her front door.

Impatiently, he waited for her to dig her keys out of her purse and open the door.

His dick throbbed in his pants, and his balls ached, they were so full.

She put the key in the lock, turned it, but it didn't engage or click open.

She tried it again. But that only made her lock it and then unlock it.

"Did I not lock it before I left?" she asked, more to herself than to him.

"No, I'm pretty sure I remember watching you lock it," he said, sifting back through his memories from just over an hour ago.

They'd gone for a run, then parted ways to shower, then he came back to her place, knocked on the door, then they left. He remembered standing behind her, checking out her ass as she locked the door, her phone in her other hand, purse over her right shoulder.

She gave him a concerned look.

The hair on the back of his neck stood straight up, and he gently nudged her aside. He didn't want to scare her, but something wasn't right. If they both remembered her locking the door, why was it open now? Why was it unlocked?

"Get behind me," he ordered, turning the handle slowly.

"Pia," Lydia whispered. "I hope she's okay. What if someone broke in and took her?"

A possibility, but he was more concerned that whoever broke in was either still there or had taken more than just Lydia's cat.

The door opened silently, and he pushed Lydia behind him more, entering the dim entryway. All the lights in her place were off. He couldn't hear anything, and he had exceptional hearing.

They paused just inside the apartment, and he held his breath.

Nothing.

Releasing his breath, he stepped a bit more into the unit, and he gave the air a couple of long, deep, lung-filling sniffs. Nothing but the scent of Lydia's bodywash and just the slightest hint of litter box coming from the direction of the bathroom. But as far as litter box smells went, this one wasn't bad. He'd been to some houses where the smell was overwhelming and made your eyes tear.

They stepped into her living room, and Lydia let out a sigh of relief behind him, stepping out and making a *psst psst* noise to a curious, hesitantly walking Pia. The cat approached Lydia and allowed her owner to scoop her up into her arms.

"Oh, I'm so glad you're okay," Lydia said, nuzzling the cat and kissing her head.

Rex left them in the living room and continued on through the rest of the apartment, checking for signs of disturbance.

Nothing.

"Maybe I didn't lock it," Lydia said when he returned to her in the living room.

No, he remembered her locking it.

He had a good memory, a keen sense of smell and almost bionic hearing. Out of all the brothers, Rex was the one most in tune with his senses. They each had their strengths. Brock was the leader, Chase the tech savant, Heath the language aficionado and Rex— along with being the guy best trained in blowing shit up—was the one who understood and could really engage with the world around him. He could hear things others couldn't, could smell different underlying odors and scents when others smelled nothing but the bleach used to cover up the mess. He was also really good at detecting the slight physiological changes in people close by. Beads of nervous sweat on an upper lip, a quickened pulse, dilated pupils, nervous ticks, darting eyes, increased temperature or heart rate.

When he was in Joint Task Force 2, they used to call him The Lie Detector. He could often tell when someone was lying just by getting into a room with them. He rarely had to touch them, and if he did, it was no more than two fingers to the inside of their wrist.

"But maybe I didn't," she said again, the concern for her own sanity clear in her tone.

Nothing nefarious stood out to him. Nothing seemed out of place, but then again, he hadn't spent much time in Lydia's apartment to know if a knickknack was moved or a closet door was ajar.

"Take a look around," he said, rejoining her in the living room after scoping out the whole place. "See if anything is missing or amiss."

She didn't let go of the cat but slowly wandered through her apartment. He could tell she was scared, the way she hugged Pia close and stepped softly and slowly through each room like the floor was covered in glass.

She went into her room and not three seconds later gasped.

Rex was in there and beside her in a flash. "What is it? What?"

Lydia shook her head. "I'm pretty sure I shut that drawer. I never leave them open like that. And why are there like four pairs of my underwear on the floor? I wouldn't leave them out. They belong in the drawer or the laundry hamper."

He glanced down at the carpeted floor where she was pointing, and sure enough, four pairs of brightly colored cotton briefs were in a heap. The middle drawer of her five-drawer dresser was also half open, and the neatly folded clothes appeared to have been trifled with.

"Is anything *missing?*" he asked. What would be someone's motive for breaking into her apartment but not taking anything? Why wouldn't they put everything back where they found it and lock the door?

Lydia glanced around her room. "I don't think so. I mean, maybe a pair of my underwear, but ..." Her head shook. "I don't think so." She shivered and clutched Pia tighter. "I've got the serious willies right now. Someone was in my apartment. Why?"

"I don't know," he said, more to himself than her as he continued to look around her room. "Did you have anything of great value in here?"

"No. My computer, my TV, maybe a hundred bucks in cash that I keep in a jar in my freezer. But ..." She pointed to her computer, which was still plugged in and sitting on her desk seemingly untouched. And her television was still mounted on the wall in the living room.

"Go check the freezer," he ordered. Maybe he should call Chase and have him bring a print kit by so they could see if whoever broke in was dumb enough to leave behind some damning information about themselves.

She did as he instructed. "Money is still here."

Even weirder. "Come on," he said, joining her in the kitchen. "Grab Pia and let's go to my place. We'll call Evelyn, the landlord, and let her know. We definitely need to change the locks and report this. Even though nothing was taken, clearly someone was in here, right?"

Her head nodded slowly. "Yeah ... I mean, I think so. Unless ..."

"Grab the cat. Grab what you need, and we'll go to my place until we can get shit figured out." He headed for the door and checked to see if it had been pried open, but there was no sign of forced entry. Had she locked the door?

Shuffling sounds deeper inside the apartment drew his attention back to Lydia. She was visibly shaken and rightfully so. She probably felt violated. Someone had been in her home, in her underwear drawer of all places.

With Pia still in her arms, Lydia gathered up what looked like a travel-style litter box, a small bag of cat litter and a travel cat crate.

At first, he wondered why she was bringing all that stuff, but then he remembered his own pet upstairs and realized Diesel had never been around a cat before—at least not indoors or in his own home. They needed a safe place of refuge for Pia just in case Diesel tried to maul her with love or drown her with drool.

"Got what you need?" he asked, taking everything but the cat from her.

She nodded.

"It was the drawer, the underwear and the unlocked door," he asked, just needing to clarify what was touched.

She nodded again. "Yeah, I think so. I mean—" She pressed her fingers to her forehead and squeezed her eyes shut for a moment. "I mean, maybe it was me? I had a long shower after our run, and by the time I finished drying my hair, I was scrambling to get ready. Maybe I just forgot to close the drawer? Maybe I left the underwear drawer open and Pia got into it? Maybe I didn't lock the front door?" She looked at him with hopeless confusion and mounting self-doubt. "Maybe it *was* all me and I'm just going crazy."

What she said made sense.

He'd been so busy staring at her ass while she locked up, maybe she hadn't turned the key all the way. Or maybe she didn't lock it on purpose?

No. That didn't make any sense. He didn't get the crazy vibe from her, and he was usually a pretty good judge of character.

Usually.

He got the lonely, lost and sad vibe from Lydia, but not the crazy vibe.

Particularly not the "does this shit for attention" kind of crazy. He'd dated one of those before. She flooded her apartment, claimed her ex came by and beat her up, then ran out onto her front lawn naked and started howling, all just to get Rex's attention—or so she claimed—after he ended things with her.

Yeah, Lydia wasn't like that—he hoped.

He stepped back into the apartment, went into her room and took a few pictures with his phone of what she said was "askew" before rejoining her by the door. "Better safe than sorry," he said. "We'll call Evelyn from my place."

She seemed smaller than usual. Like she'd retreated into herself and was hiding.

He got that.

When shit hit the fan, no matter how much of a splatter it caused, human instinct was to fight or flee. Most people fled. Not him, of course.

"Don't touch the handle," he said, just as she was about to open the door with her hand. "I'm sure it's a long shot, since we've both touched it, and door handles are riddled with prints, but I'll call my brother to come by with a print kit and we'll see if we can lift anything." He tucked his hand beneath his shirt and turned the handle gently so as to not smudge any prints or leave any new ones.

Once they were out in the hallway, he took her keys from her trembling hands and locked the door, videotaping himself doing it with his phone just for good measure.

He shoved her keys into the pocket of his jeans, lifted the cat carrier and box in one hand and placed his other hand at the small of her back, urging Lydia to head toward the elevators.

"What if it's nothing?" she asked, when they stepped back through the opened doors. "What if it's all in my head?"

He shrugged. "Then it's all in your head. But better to be safe than sorry, right?"

All she did was nod and adjust Pia in her arms.

"Hey." He wrapped his arm around her waist and tugged her into his embrace, the soft curve of her hip beneath his palm. She was warm against him and fit just right beneath his arm. "We'll figure it out, okay?"

She nodded again. "Yeah, I'm just worried that if it isn't me losing my mind, then it might be Dierks. And if it is him, I need to move. I need to leave Victoria. I honestly don't know which one I'd prefer."

Ice filled his veins. His hand dropped from her hip, and he glanced down at her. "Who's Dierks?"

CHAPTER 6

LYDIA TOOK A DEEP BREATH, pressed her lips to the top of Pia's head and swallowed. "My ex-boyfriend. We were together for about two years. He worked construction and was big into skateboarding. He had a really bad skateboarding accident and was in a coma for nearly three months. When he finally woke up"—she glanced up at him—"he wasn't the same person I fell in love with."

"Did he hit you?"

The elevator dinged, and the doors slid open. Rex's hand fell back to the small of her back, his touch reassuring, comforting and oh so welcome. She stepped off first, cradling Pia against her chest and taking comfort from the warmth of the cat's body.

"Lydia?" Rex's hand slid to her hip bone, and he squeezed, making her stop in her tracks and face him. "Did Dierks hit you?"

They were in the hallway again, identical in appearance to the one below, where her apartment was. The only difference was that the apartment numbers all started with four instead of three.

She shook her head. "No. But he became an angry man. He punched holes in the walls, broke dishes, took a knife to a piece of canvas art, smashed a few windows. He never laid a hand on me, but his anger was out of control, and I worried that one day it might get so out of control that ..." She could still remember the sound of her favorite coffee mug hitting the wall of their apartment and shattering. And all because she'd forgotten to buy more cereal at the grocery store for Dierks's breakfast. "The smallest things set him off," she went on. "If his phone battery died or he burnt his tongue on hot coffee, the bus was a couple of minutes late." She shuddered. "That poor bus driver. It was only his first week of work, and the way Dierks tore a strip off him, the man quit on the spot."

"He can't drive, then?"

"No. He hasn't been deemed fit to drive since the accident. Not that we really drove anywhere in Vancouver anyway. The SkyTrain, SeaBus and public transit are really good. A vehicle, insurance, gas and parking are unnecessary expenses when you live in the city. We used a car-share program for a while, but then when I ended things with him and moved in with some roommates, I bought a car."

"Did he go back to work?"

"He tried to, but his anger was out of control, so they fired him. He's on disability now. Problem is, he doesn't think he needs help. He refuses to see a counselor or a doctor or get medicated. He knows he's angry, but he thinks it will just heal over time." But even if that was the case, which Lydia didn't believe it was, she didn't want to risk her own health and safety by waiting around for that time to come. What if it never did? She wanted children and a family, and as lovely a person as Dierks had been before the accident, she didn't want to risk having children with him if he never returned to being that person.

Mutual friends of hers and Dierks called her heartless for leaving him. They all thought she should have stuck by him and helped him work through his issues. But you can't help a person when they're unwilling to accept it or admit they need it, and

Dierks still didn't believe he needed it. And she wasn't about to put herself or her cat in harm's way.

Maybe she was heartless, but if she didn't look out for herself, who would?

Her explanation seemed to satisfy Rex enough, and he released his death grip on her hip and encouraged her to head toward his unit again.

"And you think he might be the one who broke into your apartment?" He set the cat carrier and litter box down on the floor and dug into his jacket pocket for his keys.

She shrugged. "Maybe. I mean, when I broke up with him, I didn't immediately move to the island. I sublet a room in a house with four other people for a few months, as I had a great job at a Montessori preschool I didn't want to leave. But Dierks found out where I was living and would wait for me on the sidewalk. He followed me on walks, showed up at my work. He was never *aggressive*, but it was still harassment. He said he wants me back and is willing to work on himself if I take him back, but I don't do ultimatums. He needs to get better *first* and for himself."

He unlocked the door. "Hold on tight to the cat, eh. I don't think Diesel will hurt her, but he will be curious." He opened the door, and nails on the wood clickety-clacked like crazy as Diesel scrambled to gain his footing and greet them. "Hey, buddy. Did you miss us?"

Diesel didn't quite ignore Rex, but he didn't give him much attention either. He was too caught up in the fur ball that was digging its nails into Lydia's arm.

"You think he'll be okay with her?" Lydia asked, murmuring shushing noises into Pia's ear at the same time Diesel shoved his big nose into Pia's stomach and did the muffled snuffle sniff. His tail was wagging like crazy too.

"We'll have to see," Rex said, toeing off his shoes and stowing them on a two-tiered shoe shelf in the entryway. He set the carrier and litter box down just inside the living room, then took Pia from her arms and wandered deeper into the manly, immaculate but somewhat sparse living room.

A dark brown leather sofa with what appeared to be two recliners on either end sat across from the enormous mounted television, and a big snake plant nearly as tall as her sat in a black pot near the corner, next to the sliding glass door to the balcony. There was only one piece of decor in the place, and that was a big, blown up photograph on the wall over the couch. It was grayscale and seemed to be treetops in the mist taken from a mountain or hill summit.

Diesel followed Rex, who gently held on to Pia as he sat down on the edge of the couch. "She's not food, dude. She's a new friend, and I expect you to be nice to her. No roughhousing, no play biting. Just respect and cuddles. Got it?"

Either Lydia was losing her mind or Rex's dog really knew what he was saying all the time and nodded in acknowledgement.

Pia looked scared out of her fur as she sat on Rex's lap and Diesel went nose to nose with her, whimpering and sniffing up a storm. His tongue poked out of his mouth and touched her face, and she reared back and swatted at him with her paw.

But that didn't seem to deter Diesel at all. He leapt back, kicking his hind legs for a moment before bouncing forward again and pressing his nose back to hers.

Then Pia did something Lydia wasn't expecting at all. She leapt down gracefully from Rex's thighs and silently sauntered over to Diesel's big bed in front of the gas fireplace and beneath the television. She pawed at it, circled a couple of times, then nestled down smack-dab in the middle of it. Diesel watched the whole thing, cocked his head side to side, did a few more weird puppy leaps, then trotted over to the bed too, climbed on behind her and lay down until they were spooning. In less than thirty seconds, both of them had their eyes closed and were snoring.

"Well, I'll be," Rex said, standing back up and joining Lydia where she stood gobsmacked in the middle of his living room, staring down at the two new best friends. "Didn't think it would happen like that or that fast, but I think it's a good sign our pets get along so well." His hand found her hip, and he drew her near to him. "I still haven't even kissed you, but my dog has licked your pussy." His joke worked, and she tossed her head back to laugh.

"Oh, you are a slick one, Mr. Hart."

There went those dimples.

There went her dry panties.

"Just trying to take your mind off the scary stuff," he said, allowing his thumb to brush across her hip bone in a way that made her insides turn warm and gooey. "We don't have to do anything, but I want you to know that I'm here if you need me. I won't let anything bad happen to you. We'll figure out who if anybody was in your apartment and, more importantly, why?"

A shiver careened through her when his thumb pushed up the fabric of her shirt so he was now touching flesh.

"Let's do something fun," he said, taking her hand and pulling her toward his bedroom. "Go crazy."

Go crazy?

Another tremble took her by surprise, but her feet followed him anyway.

Just like the rest of his house, his room was sparse, manly and tidy. A dark brown duvet cover lay flat across a made bed, and dark blue curtains hung on either side of the big window, letting in what little daylight there was. Just as they were climbing back into Rex's truck after breakfast, thick, fat, gray clouds had rolled in and the sky had opened up.

Spring showers bring May flowers or however the saying went, but why couldn't it rain at night while they slept?

He glanced out the window. "It's really coming down out there now, eh?"

She swallowed hard and fought the urge to shut her eyes from how good his thumb on her hip felt.

"I don't know about you, but this is the perfect weather for some extracurricular activities. What do you think?" He guided her to the bed and helped her sit down. "Close your eyes."

She did as she was told, her entire body now trembling as if she were sitting on a block of ice. Even though she'd only just met this man, they seemed to have this connection, and he put her at such ease. Made her feel safe and desired, cared for. He wanted her, which just blew her away, since a man like Rex was far out of her league. Not only appearance-wise but also in life experiences, education, strength, probably financially too. What did *she* have to offer him?

"Put your hands out," he ordered.

Shit!

A flash of memory from their conversation yesterday while she was very drunk came back to her like a splash of cold water to the face. Had he actually said a former girlfriend broke up with him because he was too *big*?

Was that why he told her to put out two hands?

Oh God!

"I don't know if I'm ready for this," she said, trying to mentally prepare herself to have a German sausage laid across her palms like a baton in a relay race. But it wouldn't be like a baton. It would be more like a javelin. She opened her eyes, expecting to find him with his pants down, python out, but he wasn't. He was still dressed, and he had a box in his hand and a hilarious expression on his face.

Damn, those dimples.

"What did you think I was going to put in your hand?" he asked slowly, teasingly.

"I ... uh ..." She stood up to look at the box. It was a beautiful one-thousand-piece puzzle of a coral reef.

"I got this for Christmas from one of my brothers. I love jigsaw puzzles. I figured we could crack this baby open. I could make us some hot chocolate and we could spend the day getting to know each other and building a puzzle. What do you think?"

I think you're my dream man.

"I noticed you had a bunch of puzzles on your bookcase, so I figured you'd be into it, but"—he lifted a brow—"now I'm not sure, based on your current expression and the weird look you're giving me."

Her butt plopped back down onto the bed. She stared straight ahead and blinked.

Was she disappointed?

She'd been nervous, no, terrified to have him lay his anaconda across her palms a second ago, and now she was disappointed that he didn't and instead wanted to do a puzzle with her?

What was wrong with her?

Where do you want to start? Childhood and work your way forward, or present day and work your way backward? You're jobless. We have time.

Rex set the puzzle box down on the bed before sitting beside her and taking her hand. His lips fell to the back of her knuckles. "I know when we got in the elevator, hell, when we got in my truck, we were planning to come back here, rip each other's clothes off and make the beast with two backs for the rest of the day ..."

Well, if that didn't conjure images in her head.

"But after what just happened in your apartment, I don't want to push you. We have all the time in the world to get naked and nasty." *Naked and nasty.* More images. "But I want it to happen when you're in the right headspace. When you want me because you want me and not because you're drunk or feeling scared and just need to feel safe or distracted. You'll always be safe with me, but I just don't think sex is what you need right now." His mouth twisted ruefully. "Unless I'm way off base here and sex is exactly what you need, then I can be naked in under two seconds and hard in like five."

Gah! The dimples.

To be honest, a jigsaw puzzle and hot chocolate sounded perfect.

"I also need to text my brother and get him to bring a print kit over, and I'd rather not have our first time in bed together be interrupted by somebody who used to sit on my head and fart until he shat himself."

She snorted a laugh, which turned into a smile.

Rex cupped her cheek with the other hand. God, his hands were big. Maybe he really did have the Loch Ness Monster in his pants. She was unable to stop herself, and her eyes drifted down to the V of his pants.

"Later," he said, drawing her gaze back up to his face and the penetrating blue of his irises. "But first, before we puzzle, I think I should at least kiss you."

She wasn't going to argue with him there. She'd been dreaming about what his lips would feel like against hers. About what kind of a kisser he was.

She fluttered her lashes. "I think you should at least kiss me, too."

He smiled again, disarming her completely until she melted into him, closed her eyes and waited.

It was soft at first, gentle and almost a whisper of a touch. His lips were like velvet against hers. Warm and inviting. His hand on her cheek and jaw tightened its grip, and he encouraged her to tilt her head a little more, giving him better access to dive in. She did. And he did.

Rex's tongue swept inside her mouth, soft, wet and warm.

He was a really good kisser. Like *really* good.

He knew when to nibble, when to suck, when to twirl his tongue and how much pressure to apply. It would be a safe bet to say she'd never had anyone kiss her the way Rex was kissing her. So thoroughly, so expertly. She was mesmerized by the way his lips moved against hers, the way his tongue tangled with hers.

She made to recline onto the bed and welcome him on top of her, to hell with the jigsaw puzzle. He'd advertised *naked and nasty*. She wanted *naked and nasty*. But he resisted the pressure she applied to his back, and she was forced to stay sitting up.

"Nuh-uh," he said, his lips creating a gentle but electrifying buzz against her mouth as he spoke but also kept kissing her. "Puzzle and hot chocolate, no sexy time."

Lydia whimpered, released his back and let her hand slid down to the apex of his thick thighs.

Holy fuck!

It was like a goddamn redwood in his jeans. She pulled her hand away as if his pants had caught fire.

Rex broke the kiss and gauged her warily. "Are you scared?"

She shook her head.

No.

Scared was not the right word.

Nervous?

Yeah.

Intrigued?

Oh yeah.

But she also had this feeling that because Rex was so ... well-endowed, he also knew how to be gentle. She was seeing him gentle right now, and it was wonderful.

He wouldn't split her open like an ax in a cedar stump; he would take care of her. Make sure she was good and relaxed, thoroughly turned on, wet and open for him before he released the cobra from its denim basket.

She shook her head and slowly put her hand back on his erection. "No, I'm not scared. I trust you, and I know you won't hurt me."

"I won't," he said, staring down at her. "But I'm also not going to fuck you right now."

She whimpered again, which only caused him to smile, beautiful and bright, and stand up abruptly from the bed. The kielbasa in his jeans was unmistakable, particularly because she was now at eye level with it. She licked her lips.

Rex smacked her thigh playfully. "Later. But right now, I'm going to make us some gourmet hot chocolate with my mom's homemade marshmallows, and you're going to set up the puzzle pieces and box on my kitchen table." He adjusted his erection in his pants and glanced at her. "Put the pout away before a bird poops on that bottom lip."

Like an idiot, she glanced up at the ceiling looking for birds.

That only caused him to start laughing as he made his way out of his bedroom and into the living room and kitchen. "Did you honestly just look to see if there were birds up on my ceiling?"

Heat infused her cheeks, which was actually rather welcome, since that meant the volcanic temperatures in her belly and between her legs were forced to cool off a bit.

Grumbling, she grabbed the jigsaw puzzle box off the bed, but as with a fruit fly or toddler, her attention was diverted to something else.

Black straps with red stripes were fastened to the corner posts of Rex's bed. The ones on the headboard and the ones at the foot.

Double-checking that he wasn't standing in the doorway staring at her, she pulled up the duvet cover at the foot of the bed to confirm her suspicions.

Yep. Just as she thought.

Restraints.

Now her lady parts were back on fire.

"Whatcha doing?"

Jesus!

Lydia jumped nearly a foot in the air from where she sat on the corner of the bed, and she released the duvet like he'd just told her it was coated in hobo cum.

If her cheeks did not have flames dancing across them, she would be very surprised.

"I, um ..."

He entered the room, crouched down next to the corner post of the footboard and pulled back the duvet she'd just had in her hand. "Do you know what these are?"

She nodded. "Yes."

His brows lifted slightly. "And what do you think of me having them?"

Lydia's throat was dryer than Pia's freshly changed litter box. "I, um ... I have them in blue?"

CHAPTER 7

Well, that sure as hell wasn't the answer he'd been expecting from the rosy-cheeked, bright-eyed, deer in the headlights Lydia.

But he had to say, he liked this answer a hell of a lot better than the one he was expecting.

"You have them in blue, do you?" he asked, having to stand back up because the way he was crouching was making his still semi-hard dick get increasingly uncomfortable against his zipper.

She nodded. "Yeah."

"On your bed right now?"

She nodded again. "Yeah."

"Have you used them with anyone since you moved here?"

She shook her head. "No. But I put them there just to save time for when I *do* finally use them again."

That was the same reason he always kept his attached to the bed. Saved time. He usually did a better job of tucking them away so as to not scare women he brought home as soon as they walked into his room, but on the off-chance he and Lydia did wind up in his bed today, he'd changed his sheets that morning and must not have tucked the restraints away well enough.

But the fact that Lydia neither minded nor was turned off by them, and the fact that she had her own in blue in her own apartment, just made his already white-hot burn for her even hotter.

Now his resolve to be the gentleman and take care of her with a jigsaw puzzle and hot chocolate was crumbling. He hadn't done any kind of play in a while, and to know that she was into it and he wouldn't have to carefully approach the subject had his cock twitching in his jeans big-time. If he wasn't careful, he might lose his load in his pants just from thinking too hard about Lydia naked and spread-eagle on his bed.

"Do you like to be tied up or the one doing the tying up?" They needed to settle that plaguing question quickly. He knew some people were able to switch, but not him. He'd been tied up before with a woman, and it'd only triggered shit from his past that he didn't feel like revisiting. Not that he had any serious hang-ups— not like his brothers—but he'd been bound and tortured before and not in a sexual way, so to have anybody restrain him just felt fucked up and was a total boner-killer.

It was also the reason why he did so many puzzles. It distracted him from his thoughts—from his memories. Made him concentrate on something else so intensely, that the other thoughts were pushed out, or at the very least blurred and made less significant. He'd tried everything: yoga, meditation, reading, self-help books on tape, but the only things that seemed to work, seemed to distract him from the memories that popped up for no fucking reason sometimes, were working out, sex and puzzles.

All four of them, his brothers and him, had been kidnapped and held against their will at some point. They didn't really talk about it though. It just came with the territory of the job in a lot of ways. And even though Rex hadn't even been held for more than forty-eight hours before Brock and Chase got him out, the intensity of the torture still stuck with him. Bound to a pole, naked, while he was whipped with a switch. He still bore the white criss-cross scars across his back, though they were faint now after so many years.

But he never gave up the intel. Never told those fuckers where their wives and children were hiding. And Rex would take a thousand more whippings if it meant not one child had to go through what those women and children went through for way too fucking long.

She drew her bottom lip into her mouth and scraped it with her top teeth, drawing him out of his wandering, distracting thoughts with the subtle, but erotic move. "I like to be tied up."

Phew.

Another win for the both of them.

"Do you like to be tied up?" she asked.

He shook his head. "No." For now, he'd leave it at that. Maybe in time, when he felt more sure of things and could trust Lydia completely, he'd tell her why he preferred not to be the one restrained. "Do you just play or ..." How far did her penchant for kink go?

"I haven't done anything else besides be tied up. I like the feeling of being totally exposed and my entire body open for exploration." A small, almost embarrassed smile tilted her lips, and she huffed a laugh through her nose. "I don't know if you could consider it *playing*. I just like to be restrained ... and not all the time, just ..."

"When the mood strikes you?"

"Yeah." Her throat bobbed on a swallow. "When the mood strikes *us*."

Hot damn.

"What about you?" she asked, pulling the duvet back, taking the ankle restraint from it and erotically running it through her fingers. "How hard do you play?"

Well, that was a loaded question.

But he believed in honesty and transparency, and if what he was about to tell her next had her running for the hills, then so be it.

"I don't play hard," he said. "Pretty much just restraints, too. But I used to swing."

Lydia's hazel eyes went wide. "Like orgies?"

That was always the first thing people asked him when he said he belonged to a swinger's club.

"Kind of. There's a big group of swingers up on Bear Mountain, and about once a month, someone hosts a party. It alternates between houses and hosts. But it's a bit of a free-for-all. Anything goes as long as it's consensual and protection is used." He hadn't been to a party in a while, but when he did go, they were always fun. Men freely allowing and watching their wives get fucked by other men, sometimes more than one man at a time. It was wild. It was also a great distraction from his thoughts. He'd been introduced to the lifestyle and the club by an ex. She was *big* into the lifestyle but almost more than Rex could handle or keep up with. She wanted nearly every sexual encounter they had to involve another person. Rarely did just the two of them have sex.

Sure, the threesomes with Cynthia and another chick had been hot as hell, but sometimes he just wanted to pleasure one woman, then curl up around her soft, warm body and fall asleep with his nose in her hair.

But Cynthia wasn't into that. She had a high sex drive and wanted it a lot with a lot of different people. In the end, they realized they just weren't compatible, and they went their separate ways. She also ended up moving to Toronto for work, where he was sure she was having all of her sexual fantasies and demands fulfilled. Bigger pond, more kinky fish.

But Rex was welcomed back into the swingers' club with no problem, and he still received the monthly email invites even though he hadn't gone since before Christmas.

"I ..." Lydia's nostrils flared. "I don't think I can do that. I ... it sounds super hot, but I think I'd lose my shit if I saw you doing anything to another woman."

Fuck, he liked her—a lot.

"That's like the best fucking answer ever, babe. I'm not a jealous guy and didn't have a problem watching another dude rail my ex when she and I went, but something tells me that I wouldn't be able to handle watching you get stuffed by anybody but me."

Even though he was no longer in a crouch position, his dick was still angry about being locked away in his jeans. But he ignored his dick's onslaught of grievances and reached down and cupped her face like he had earlier.

The pad of his thumb swept across her bottom lip, and he pulled on it slightly. "Nothing more I want to do right now than tie you up to this bed and slip inside you, but I also want to do this right, and I think we should spend a little more time *out* of bed getting to know each other, don't you?"

Her mouth dipped into a frown. "If I disagree, that make me a slut?"

Rex tossed his head back and laughed. "Not at all. You are *not* a slut. And my feminist mother raised feminist sons, and I don't like that term to begin with. If men were treated the same way women were treated for having a plethora of partners, the world would be a very different place. You're just as entitled to play the field and sow wild oats as I am."

She blinked slowly, and her bottom lip relaxed, which made her mouth open into a very sexy little O. "You just know *all* the right things to say, don't you, Rexthalomew?"

He smiled and snorted at her playful tease on his name. "I try. Though I've stuck my foot in my mouth a few times over the years. I'd like to think I've learned from it though. We can't grow if we don't learn from our mistakes, and as *painful* as it might be right now"—he reached down and adjusted his cock again—"I want to do this right with you. But I'll make you a deal."

She lifted a brow in interest.

"Let's go out into the living room, have some hot chocolate, work on the puzzle for a bit, and then after my brother Heath comes and we get some prints from your apartment, then we'll come back here and we can spend the rest of the day in bed getting to know each other on a more *intimate* level. Hmm?"

"Naked and nasty?" she asked with a smile that had his revolving door of a heart suddenly throwing on the brakes and slamming shut.

"Super naked and nasty," he confirmed.

She nodded. "I can get on board with that."

"Good."

"But first—" She reached for his belt and tugged him off balance and on top of her. "More kissing. You're really good at it."

Rex smiled as his lips fell against Lydia's. "Not going to argue with you there."

The knock at the door made Lydia jump. She'd been focused on a terribly difficult section of the puzzle for quite a while, and when that happened, the world around her tended to disappear.

"That must be Heath," Rex said, standing up from his spot at the table across from her.

Leave it to Rex, a man she barely knew but was pretty smitten with, to know exactly what she needed. For a small while there, she'd actually forgotten about the weirdness in her apartment and that his brother was coming.

Until the knock at the door, that is.

Rex opened the door, and even though she didn't think it was possible, a man even bigger than Rex stepped into the entryway, all smiles and shoulder-length blond hair. "Geeking out today I see, big brother." His midnight-blue gaze—the same as Rex's—landed on Lydia, and his smile turned from playful to charming. "Hello, I'm Heath."

She greeted him with a big smile. "Heath Leppard, nice to meet you. I'm Lydia."

That earned her a gorgeous toothy grin in return from the big blond man. "I like her."

"She's off limits," Rex said, his deep and serious bass catching her off guard and making her nipples peak beneath her bra.

"No need to go pissing on things to mark your territory," Heath said, slapping Rex on the back. "I'm just being friendly."

"Your version of friendly and my version differ greatly," Rex said, still giving his brother the stink-eye.

"I didn't think they did. I'd consider us both *friendly* guys, wouldn't you?"

Rex merely grunted.

Heath lifted up a small black duffle bag. "Lead the way. Chase is busy with Stacey and the kids, so he sent me. But I'll take him the prints so he can run them. Need to print you too, Lydia, so we can rule you out."

Lydia nodded and stood up from the table. Her hot chocolate was long gone, and even though Rex had offered to make her something for lunch, she wasn't hungry. A pit the size of a grapefruit was in her belly at the thought of someone being in her apartment and rifling through her stuff.

Pia and Diesel were snuggled up on Diesel's bed, both of them content and snoring. If that wasn't a sign that she and Rex were supposed to be together, she didn't know what was. Pia rarely liked anyone, let alone another animal, but she'd taken to Diesel right away and the two were spooning like besties.

She grabbed her keys from her purse, and the three of them headed to her unit. "So you still don't think we should call the police?" she asked, glancing up at the brothers as they stepped into the elevator. Jesus, they were tall. And big.

Heath shook his head. "Not much they're going to do. Not much they can do. If nothing was taken or damaged ... plus, who's to say that it wasn't all just you and you just forgot to lock the door and close the drawer? Cops don't have time for this kind of thing. Not until a real threat is present."

Rex grunted and nodded in agreement, but he also wrapped a protective arm around Lydia and tugged her into his body. "He's right, I'm afraid. Though I believe you when you say it wasn't you. And I want you to feel safe going back into your apartment. But just because the cops wouldn't do anything doesn't mean we can't. First step is ruling out our prints and then changing the lock on the door." He glanced at Heath. "You bring the stuff to change the locks?"

Heath's head bobbed, causing his blond tresses to swish majestically. "If she's got a smart lock, it'll be easy peasy, but either way, yeah, we can do that."

"But what if whoever broke into my apartment wore gloves? Or their prints aren't in the database or whatever you're going to use to cross-reference them? Aren't the only people with prints in the system criminals and government employees?" Lydia asked, not feeling nearly as reassured about any of this as she hoped she would. Even if they found prints that didn't belong to her and Rex, that didn't mean it still couldn't wind up being a dead end.

"Your ex, does he have a criminal record?" Rex asked at the same time the elevator dinged and the door slid open. He and Lydia stepped out first, and Heath followed.

"Dierks? No, at least I don't think so. I mean, we were together for a few years, and I would like to think he would have told me if he was on probation or had a history with the law. But I don't think so. He worked in construction, but he always wanted to be a cop. He just had a heart condition that kept him from passing the physical. I can't see him doing something to break the law, not when his dream had been to uphold it."

They reached her apartment door, and she slid the key into the lock.

"Yeah, but you said so yourself—he changed after his accident, right?" Rex said, drawing a latex glove out of his pocket and tugging it over his giant right hand. He gently nudged her out of the way and turned the handle to open the door.

"Yeah, I guess."

Maybe Dierks was capable of more than she thought. He'd been such a kind man until the accident. Then he became downright terrifying. Maybe he no longer cared about what happened to him and he just wanted to get even with her for leaving him, the law and his dreams of being a cop be damned.

Rex opened the door, and they stepped inside.

Even though this was her home, it felt weird entering it. It felt cold and lifeless, foreign and unfamiliar. A chill wracked her body from top to toe, and she clutched her arms around herself tight to keep the shivers at bay.

Rex watched her and was instantly by her side, grabbing the baby-blue blanket off her couch and wrapping it around her shoulders. "You don't have to be here if you don't feel comfortable. You can go back to my place and we can meet you there when we're done."

She shook her head. "No. This is my home. I also want to double-check that nothing else has been touched or tampered with."

Rex nodded, then jerked his head at his brother toward Lydia's bedroom. "This way."

Heath nodded, then tied his hair behind him at the nape of his neck with a black hair elastic he pulled off his wrist. She'd never been attracted to men with long hair, but Heath pulled it off like nobody's business. The man was made to have hair like that, and it worked for him. He could be a model for Pantene or the next Fabio for sexy romance book covers. Her mother had always loved Fabio. She had nearly every book he'd ever been on the cover of, and as Lydia grew older and started to notice boys and the changes in her body, she'd snuck a few of those books off the shelf and read them in her room with the door locked.

Wrapping the blanket tighter around herself, she wandered through her apartment as if it wasn't her own. She scanned the bookcase, reading each title and studying each face in the picture frames like she'd never seen them before. She did the same in the kitchen, opening the cabinets with a napkin. She perused each shelf, the contents of every drawer.

Nothing seemed amiss.

Nothing was out of place or missing.

She opened the fridge. Everything was there.

Maybe she was overthinking all of this and she just hadn't closed her underwear drawer or locked her front door. Maybe this was all just a big misunderstanding and a memory lapse. Not that she'd ever had any like this before, but it was possible, right?

She was in a state of depression since getting fired. Maybe her brain was misfiring and she was forgetting to do everyday things that she thought had become habit.

She heard Rex and Heath murmuring in her bedroom. Was she wasting their time getting them to do this?

Was Rex only indulging her worries to be kind? Did he actually believe her?

Continuing on her exploration, she entered the bathroom. Her shower curtain was open.

She never left it open.

Never. It was habit for her to close it as soon as she hopped out of the shower. Not that she had a lot of guests, but she hated the idea of anybody snooping around in her stuff, and that included her bathtub.

"Rex?" she called from the bathroom, her breathing shaky, fingers trembling as she gripped the corners of the blanket.

"Hmm?" he answered, coming around the corner. "What's up?"

"Did you pull open the shower curtain earlier when we were here?"

He shook his head and scrunched his brows. "No. Why?"

"Because it's open."

His expression remained confused but not alarmed. Meanwhile alarm bells were blaring inside Lydia's head. "And that wasn't from you?"

She shook her head, her throat raw as she forced the words out. "No. I *always* close it. *Always.*"

His eyes widened. Now he was starting to take it as seriously as she was, probably because she looked like she was going to puke. "Was it closed when we were here earlier?"

She couldn't remember. Maybe it had been. Or maybe it hadn't and she'd just overlooked that because she was so shaken up about the unlocked door and underwear drawer.

Now she really did feel like she was losing her mind.

"I ... I don't remember. I mean, I always close it, so I think so. But maybe it wasn't. Maybe it was open and we just didn't notice because we were so caught up with the unlocked door." Her eyes darted around the bathroom. Nothing else seemed out of place or missing.

Was she making all of this up? Was it all just her being forgetful?

Heath came out of the bedroom. "Okay, now let's do the door, unless there's something else you need me to take prints from?"

The look Rex was giving Lydia just confused her more. Like he *wanted* to believe her, but as things progressed, he was having a more difficult time thinking this was more than just her being absentminded and distracted.

"The door," Rex said to Heath. "Lift prints and change the lock."

"It's a smart lock, so that'll be easy," Heath replied. "I have loads of spares and duplicates."

Lydia pulled the shower curtain closed, then closed the bathroom door before joining the men in the foyer. "I'm really sorry you had to come and do this," she said, taking in the wide expanse of Heath's back as he crouched down and used what resembled a blush brush in black powder on the door handle.

"No worries," he said. "Between jobs, so it's all good."

Rex had said that Heath worked with him doing security and surveillance, but did he have another job as a backup like Rex did as a plumber?

"Out of curiosity, how easy is it to pick a lock?" The itch at the nape of her neck was not from the blanket. She'd never been so forgetful in her life. This couldn't have all been her.

"You can buy a pick kit online, and YouTube has videos for everything, so not that hard," Heath said, lifting the prints off the handle with something that looked like transparent Scotch tape.

"Well, that's not the least bit reassuring," she murmured, glancing down the hallway and nodding at a neighbor entering her own unit, wearing a curious expression.

Rex's big arm wrapped around her. "Yeah, but you can buy all the materials at a hardware store and watch a how-to video online to make a pipe bomb and not everyone does it. People who do this kind of shit do it for one of two reasons."

She glanced up at him and lifted a brow.

"To help people, like what Heath's doing, or to hurt people."

"Not reassuring," she said again.

Who would want to hurt her?

She wracked her brain as they stood there watching Heath

change the keys, trying to figure out who would want to hurt her. Who had she made such an enemy of that they'd break into her apartment, not steal anything but just ... mess with her?

"There you go," Heath said, standing up with a slight groan. He handed her three identical keys. "Legally, you'll need to give one to the landlord or property manager or whatever or at least let them know that you changed the locks."

Lydia nodded and thanked him, taking the keys from his catcher's mitt of a hand and clutching them in her fist.

"Try it out," Heath encouraged, stepping back and stowing everything into his bag.

She did as he instructed and slipped the key into the deadbolt. It went in smoothly. She locked it, unlocked it, then relocked it.

"Not ready to go home just yet?" Rex asked.

She shook her head. "Not yet."

"We'll go let Evelyn know what's going on, then we'll go back to my place," he said, his voice gentle and calm but verging on the edge of patronizing—or was she only thinking it was because of how much self-doubt she was struggling with? Rex had done nothing but show her complete patience and understanding. Not once had he expressed any doubt or misgivings with her claims.

Heath held out a digital fingerprint scanner. "Just need your prints, Lydia, to cross-reference and rule you out when I take these prints over to Chase's."

She complied with his request, but the uneasy feeling in her gut remained like a big wad of gum. She knew it was a myth that gum didn't digest and remained in your stomach for seven years, but right now, it felt like she would feel like this forever. At this point, seven years would be a welcome sentence.

Heath checked each print on the screen, and when he was satisfied with how they came out, he turned off the machine and stowed it in his bag. "I'll run this to Chase now. Stacey had an appointment, so he's with the kids, which is why he couldn't come himself."

Rex nodded. "Appreciate it."

Heath's gaze roamed Lydia for a moment, but like a gentleman, he didn't blatantly allow it to travel down her body. He kept it on her face, his expression grim and sympathetic. "Hopefully, it's just forgetfulness. But either way, we'll get to the bottom of it."

She'd never wished so hard in her life that she was losing her mind. Because the alternative was that someone had been in her apartment and tampered with her stuff.

They made their way to the elevator.

"You coming to dinner on Saturday?" Heath asked, his eyes flicking between Lydia and Rex. "Both of you?"

Rex cleared his throat, shot his brother a look that Lydia could decipher like a riddle designed for preschoolers, then she glanced away to hide her discomfort.

"Yeah, we'll both be there," Rex finally said, tightening the hold he had on Lydia's waist. "I think Mom will love her."

Wide-eyed, she glanced back at Rex.

Heath's expression was one of amusement: a crooked smirk, crinkled corners of his eyes just adding to his appeal. "Maybe next time you should *ask* your date before you commit her to something like a Hart family dinner."

She swallowed. "The whole family?"

The elevator dinged, the doors opened, and three college-age students stepped into the hallway. Rex, Heath and Lydia stepped inside.

"Not a big deal. We're all cool. Just my brother Brock, his wife, their two kids, who you need to meet anyway if you're going to start nannying for them; Chase and his woman, Stacey, their kids; me, you and Heath." Rex shrugged, reached out and pressed the button for the lobby.

"And Mom," Heath added. "She's my date, seeing as I'm the only single one left."

"Single by choice," Rex added. "Your bed is rarely empty though."

Heath was all grins as he pulled the elastic from his hair and let the shag fly free. "Haven't had a different woman in my bed in a while."

"Used to," Rex retorted. "All those lonely soccer moms."

"Lonely soccer moms?" Lydia asked. Though now she wasn't sure she *wanted* to know.

"Heath coaches a kids' soccer team, and all the single moms fawn over him. They show up at his house with a casserole or some other dish. He earned himself the nickname *The Big Eater*."

"Wasn't because of my appetite for food though," Heath said slyly, flashing Lydia a big, toothy smile. "If they bring me a lasagna and then take off their clothes, who am I to turn down a meal? Or dinner?"

Oh Jesus. Yeah, she shouldn't have asked.

"But Pasha and I have something casual going on. Don't feel like dipping my dick into anybody but her." Heath shrugged. The elevator dinged, and the doors slid open. "We're not serious, but we're not sleeping around either. Only way I can get away with not needing a wrap."

"The doctor down in Seattle?" Rex asked, a genuine look of surprise on his face. "Since when?"

"Since Chase's little incident. We got friendly and have remained *friendly*." Heath dug his keys out of his pocket. "She was here last weekend. I'll head down there next weekend. Not as frequent as I would like but ..." A wistful yet raunchy look took over his face. "She's worth it." He lifted his chin. "I'll have Chase call you when he gets the results." His gaze drifted to Lydia. "It was nice to meet you, Lydia, and I'm sure we'll get to know each other better on Saturday." His keys jangled as he waved goodbye, then headed toward the front door.

Rex's fingers flexed on her hip. "Let's go talk to Evelyn, then we'll head upstairs and finish what we started."

Confused and with her head brimming full of thoughts, Lydia nodded. "You mean the puzzle?"

His brows bobbed, and he kissed the side of her head. "Or other things."

CHAPTER 8

"I'm really sorry," Lydia said for probably the tenth time in an hour.

Rex shook his head and took a bite of his pizza. "Nothing to apologize for. When I get you naked, I want your head completely in the game, and right now it's just not."

"I know, but—"

"Lydia, seriously, it's okay. We've known each other a little over twenty-four hours. The fact that we haven't had sex yet is *not* a big deal. I'm not a jerk, and I don't *need* to get my rocks off immediately after I meet a woman." He nudged her shoulder playfully and grinned at her with a closed mouth full of pizza.

She nudged him back and picked up another slice from the platter on the coffee table. They'd finished the puzzle around seven thirty, both of them with grumbling bellies, so Rex pulled a pizza out of the freezer and popped it into the oven. In twenty minutes, they were sitting side by side on his couch watching the first Daniel Craig James Bond movie and filling their faces with pizza.

Pia and Diesel had only briefly moved from their spots on Diesel's bed to eat dinner. Rex took Diesel out to do his business, and Lydia gave Pia some much-appreciated ear scratches. Then they were back on the bed, cuddled up tighter than ever. You'd think neither of them had had a decent sleep until they met the other, the way they spent the entire day deep in REM.

"You're welcome to eat all the pizza you want," Rex said, reaching for another slice, "but I'm going to be hungry after this. I usually eat one of these myself, plus more."

"I still have leftover Chinese food in my fridge," she said, loathing the idea of even going back into her apartment until they found out if someone else had been in there. Though the more she thought about it all, the more she figured it was just her forgetting to close the drawer, the curtain and lock the door. If the results came back with just her and Rex's prints, then she'd lay it all to rest and move on.

Nobody would be sophisticated enough to wear a glove to pick a lock and then *not* take anything once inside, right? That was just epic levels of stalkerness, and she couldn't think of anybody who would do something like that. Not even Dierks. Not even now. It just wasn't in his wheelhouse. Follow her? Yes. Show up on her doorstep? Yes. But break into her place and rifle through her underwear drawer and open up her shower curtain? Nope. That just wasn't him and it never would be.

"Ooh, that's right," Rex said, his eyes going wide. "I have some chow mein left in my fridge too. Do you mind if I run to your place and grab the leftovers?"

She shook her head. "Not at all."

He was off the couch and out the door lickety-split.

While he was gone, she took another opportunity to check out his apartment but not in a snoopy way. She did so simply with her eyes from the comfort of her spot on the couch, with her baby-blue blanket draped over her lap. His place was bigger than hers, not by much, but by enough. The appliances were the same, but the living room had a wider layout, whereas hers was narrow and long, not very conducive to rearranging furniture. There was really only one place for her couch to go, and that was opposite the wall that housed the television and gas fireplace. Rex's bedroom was also a little bigger. So was his closet, or at least it appeared bigger—the entire length of one wall, actually, with sliding doors. She just had your run-of-the-mill bifold door closet.

And he lived quite minimally.

It wouldn't take much for her to move her stuff in here or chunk out and use mostly his stuff.

Holy shit, you're getting awfully ahead of yourself there, crazy lady. Like he said, you've known each other for all of twenty-four hours, and suddenly you're making plans to move in? Back the psycho truck up a bit and just focus on figuring out who the fuck was in your apartment before you go trying to figure out a way to move into this one. Yeesh.

She mentally slapped herself and then, for good and extra measure, smacked her palm to her forehead too.

The door opened, and Rex stepped back inside, carrying the plate he'd kindly brought her last night. "Gonna pop it into the microwave. You want some?"

She nodded. They'd skipped lunch, and now that she'd had a bit of time to relax doing a puzzle and spending some time with Rex, she finally had an appetite again.

Too bad it wasn't an appetite to get naked and nasty with Rex.

Not that she didn't want to, because God almighty, did she ever. She just knew she wasn't in the right headspace for sexy times, particularly first-time sexy times with the Vin Diesel of her dreams.

The microwave beeped, and seconds later, Rex was back on the couch with the plate of leftover Chinese food balanced on his palm. He handed her a fork, and she speared a piece of almond chicken.

"Feeling better?" he asked, taking the fork back from her and shoveling some fried rice into his mouth.

She nodded. "A lot better. Thank you. I honestly don't know what I would have done or how I would have handled things if you hadn't been there. I probably would have just called the cops or started living in my car if they told me there was nothing they could do."

He snorted a laugh. "Glad I was there to help then."

She glanced at him out of the corner of her eye before focusing back on the television. But as hard as she tried, her gaze kept wandering back to him sitting there placidly eating and watching the movie. He was such an easy guy to like. Such an easy guy to be around. There were zero false pretenses when it came to Rex. What you saw was what you got. The man was transparent, calm and patient. She didn't feel like he was harboring a storage locker full of deep, dark secrets—unlike her.

Not that any of her secrets were harmful to other people. They were just her past—slightly tormented and full of near misses—but nothing illegal or dangerous.

Either way, though, she felt like she could be herself with Rex and when the time felt right for her to tell him about more of her past, he wouldn't run away or end things between them because he took life in stride.

Or at least that was the impression he gave her after spending a little over twenty-four hours together.

"What's on your mind, Sunshine?" he asked, flashing her those dimples and making her lady parts quiver.

Dammit, she was staring at him.

With a dismissive headshake, she focused back on the television. "You're a really easy guy to like, that's all."

"And you're a really easy gal to like." He set the empty plate of Chinese food on the coffee table, grabbed her around the waist, which caused her to squeak, and hauled her into his lap.

"Is it really this easy?" she asked, snuggling into his big, warm, safe body.

"Is what?" He rested his cheek against the top of her head.

"Just *being* together? I've never done anything like this before. I mean, we've known each other for all of a day and yet ..."

"It feels a lot longer."

"Yeah."

"I think when things are supposed to work, they just do. Don't you?" He pulled his cheek away and looked down at her, those beautiful dark blue eyes deep enough, she could so easily drown in them. "My gut tells me this works. What does your gut tell you?"

Lydia blinked earnestly at him. Was her world finally looking up? After the debacle that was Dierks and getting fired from her job, was this dreamboat with the dimples a sign that her life was finally starting to turn around?

She sure as hell hoped so.

"Hmm?" he probed.

Crap. She realized she hadn't answered him. She'd been too busy staring into those eyes, getting willingly lost in his gaze and the way it made her warm and tingly all over.

Slowly, she nodded. "I think so, too. This just ... works. And although I don't listen to my gut nearly as often as I should, and it's probably not as right as often as yours is, it's telling me this is a good thing and to go for it. And this time, I'm definitely going to listen."

His smile made her buoyant, and she wrapped her arms around his neck and pulled him in for a kiss.

With a growl, he adjusted them on the couch until she was beneath him, the blanket draped over their bodies as the movie played in the background and their lips meshed in the foreground.

He really was an excellent kisser.

———

LIGHT STREAMING in from behind the blinds had Lydia groaning and tossing her arm over her eyes. She tried to roll over but quickly realized she wasn't in her bed. She was on a couch, and rolling over wasn't nearly as easy.

She blinked a few times.

This was the second time in two days that she'd woken up on a couch.

But this time, she remembered why.

She was in Rex's apartment.

They'd made out a bunch, watched more television, eaten ice cream, and she'd fallen asleep sometime around eleven thirty.

Pia was curled up with Diesel on the dog bed—had they even moved? And she assumed Rex was in his bed.

Despite the unease surrounding her circumstances for staying the night at his place, she'd had a wonderful evening with the man. A wonderful day, in fact. He was easy to talk to, easy to like and easy to be around. She'd never been so able to be herself this early on in a relationship. Normally, she felt like she had to be "the best version of herself" or some variation of, because if the guy found out who she really was—a slightly neurotic homebody who talked to her cat—he'd run for the hills before they reached the third date.

And yet Rex didn't seem to mind.

He talked to Diesel nearly as much as she talked to Pia. He liked puzzles, staying in and watching movies and cuddling just as much as she did.

Sure, he had a super dangerous job, but that just added to his well-rounded appeal.

Speaking of appeal, the dirty dream she'd just been having made her want to *peel* Rex's clothes off him.

With a stretch and a yawn, she pried herself off the couch, found her purse on the chair by the kitchen table and pulled out the package of moist towelettes.

After a thorough visit to the bathroom, where she tidied herself up downstairs, splashed some water on her face and did a finger brush with some of Rex's toothpaste, she tiptoed into his room.

Oh, mama.

Fast asleep with the sheets bunched up around his waist, he was on display for her like a Greek god. His abs had abs, his pecs had pecs, and, oh fuck, was he naked? Was that the V? Was that the penis line or whatever you wanted to call it? Two diagonal lines running from his hip bones down beneath the linens, like road maps of where she simply must travel.

The longer she stared, the more she saw. And the more she saw, the more she liked.

A small dusting of dark blond hair peeked out from beneath the sheet, and there was a similar dusting on his chest.

She licked her lips and felt her temperature rise. She was too hot for clothes. Much, *much* too hot. Without a second thought, she shimmied out of her leggings, tugged off her socks and pulled her sweater off. Then, in nothing more than her black panties and baby-pink bra, she climbed into bed on the empty side.

"'Bout time," he murmured, not bothering to open his eyes but reaching down beneath the sheets and leaving nothing to the imagination about what his hand was grabbing or tugging.

She swallowed and pushed her hand beneath the sheets too, finding his hand and nudging it away. "I'm in a better headspace now. Had a good sleep with some *good* dreams."

He popped one eye open at the same time she gripped his length and began working it from root to crown. "Good dreams how?"

A small smile slid across her mouth when she reached the tip of his cock and slid her thumb across the head, swirling the damp precum. "Naked and nasty good dreams."

He groaned, then growled. "Sit on my face."

Lydia's eyes flared, and her hand stopped working his cock.

Rex opened both eyes. "What's wrong?"

"Um ..."

His lazy, sexy smile dropped, and he propped himself up on his elbows. "Please don't tell me you've never had a man go down on you before."

Her head shook quickly. "No, no, it's not that. I have. It's just ... I mean, I washed myself, but I haven't *tidied* things up down there in a while. I don't go bare as a peach, but I like to keep the hedge, well, *groomed,* if you know what I mean."

He rolled his eyes and flopped back down into his pillow before reaching for her hand from where it was still wrapped around his cock. "Don't care about that. Like fruit, like topiaries, like the wild, untamed wilderness. Now climb up onto my face, woman. I'm hungry."

Warmth and lust infused her.

"Lydia ..." he urged, hauling her over him with all his rippling muscles. "Listen to your gut and climb up on my damn face. I'm like a hobbit. I'll have my first breakfast in bed, then we'll head to the kitchen and I can whip us up some waffles for second breakfast." His nose wrinkled. "Unless you'd prefer pancakes."

His nerdy reference to being a hobbit only made her like him even more.

Rex was the walking definition of not judging a book by its cover. Because when she'd ogled him when he went for his runs or walked out to his truck for the last couple of months, never in a million years would she have guessed that he was a closet nerd with a penchant for puzzles and *Lord of The Rings.*

"You could not be further from a hobbit," she said, feeling her pussy pulse and tingle as he maintained eye contact with her and slowly wedged his free hand into the elastic of her panties.

His brows scrunched, and he made a mock dejected expression. "Are you saying I'm not courageous, brave and determined? Am I not a skilled listener? Do I not have good eyesight? I'd like to think that for my size, I'm still nimble and deft in my movements."

She sniffed a laugh. "Okay, maybe you have the *psychological* characteristics, along with the good listening and eyesight, but I'm more saying that you don't *look* like a hobbit. Aren't they generally short, fat and slow?"

He gripped her by the hips with both hands, making her yelp. "Maybe some, but not this hobbit. Now give me my breakfast." Then before she could complain—not that she would dream of it— he plopped her mound over his face, pulled her panties to the side and hit her clit with his tongue hard enough to make her leg spasm.

CHAPTER 9

HE'D DEBATED long and hard until he was long and hard about carrying the sleeping Lydia to his bed last night. But in the end, he just didn't think it would be right, and he'd left her where she'd zonked out on the couch. His couch was hella comfortable, so he knew she wouldn't be too bad off. But it was also hella comfortable for an average person to sleep on for several hours, not a behemoth like himself. He liked to lay on it to watch television, but it wasn't a place he could spread out and let his muscles relax, which was why he took his bed and left her on the couch.

But now she'd come to him of her own volition. Climbed into his bed in her underwear, swirled his precum around with her thumb and was currently sitting astride his face, drenching it with her juices as he licked her like a Popsicle.

His brother might be called "The Big Eater," but Rex loved eating pussy just like any sane, straight man.

The softness, the scent, the taste, the quivering and the way it made a woman moan, gyrate and lose her fucking head—that was his heaven.

And Lydia was doing just that.

She'd been reluctant at first, insecure about her overgrown shrubbery, but he had no idea what she was going on about. He'd been ears-deep in thicker bush than this and had never complained. And like fuck was he about to complain now. Not when she was gushing across his tongue and moaning every time he sucked hard on her clit and pressed his index finger against her G-spot.

Her hands were braced on the wall behind his headboard, and the few times she'd slapped it—which was right after he did some magic swirls of his tongue around her clit—he figured his neighbor Mrs. Herbert would be knocking on his door later to complain.

"Rex ..." Lydia whimpered, her thighs trembling on either side of his face. "I'm close." She tapped his head.

Did she think that meant he was going to stop?

Sure, a man did the head tap out of consideration and respect for the chick with her lips kindly wrapped around his dick, but this was different. He wanted all of her orgasms, and he intended to give her many. From his mouth, his fingers and if she was cool with it, his cock too.

He knew he was big, and he hadn't missed the flare of her eyes when she gripped him earlier. She was worried. But if they took their time, they could make it work.

He wasn't packing an eggplant in his trousers. More like a proportionately thick cucumber.

"Rex!" She tapped his bald head again. "I'm so close."

"Keep going, baby," he murmured, swiping his tongue up her folds and giving her clit a little flick, which made her legs tremble and her breath draw in.

She made a shaky cry, stilled, and then she came.

Warm, silky honey flowed from her center across her tongue, filling his mouth as she squeezed his face with her thighs, and everything that touched his lips swelled and pulsed. Her whimpers were muffled, so he guessed she'd pressed her mouth against her forearm, but the heavy panting and deep breaths in through her nose were unmistakable.

Next time she came, he wanted to hear her at full volume. Rattle the windows, shake the rafters, wake the neighbors. He'd deal with the cleanup and apologies.

Slowly, she started to come down from her climax, her body relaxing above his, thighs releasing their hold on his head. He knocked her clit with his tongue again, but she didn't flinch.

Good sign.

Some women needed a reprieve between orgasms and said they were too sensitive to go again right away. Lydia did not seem to be that kind of woman.

He liked that.

With his hands on her hips, he helped her down, but he didn't allow her to slide off him like she tried. He positioned her on his lap, his cock well aware of what had just transpired and eager to get in on the action. He hated being left out of the fun.

Her glazed-over, placid expression pulled hard at the strings of his heart, and he reached up and cupped her cheek. "Fuck, you're beautiful after you come."

Her smile was demure, and she tried to tuck her head, but he wouldn't allow it. Her cheeks were flushed but growing a deeper pink from his comment. A swath of her hair fell forward, shielding her face, and he used his other hand to tuck it behind her ear.

"Nothing to be embarrassed about."

The left corner of her bottom lip was tugged back by her top teeth, and she blinked at him. "You have a way with words. A way to use those words to make me blush."

"And I probably do it more than I should because I think you're fucking sexy when you blush."

That got her blushing even more.

"What do you want to do, baby?" If she wasn't ready for all of him, he wouldn't push her. She'd been doing a fine job with her hand. He'd also be just as happy to spend the day with his face between her thighs.

"Do you have a condom?" she asked, her gaze swiveling to his nightstand.

He nodded, released her face and opened the drawer. He pulled a sleeve out and tugged one off the strip. "Only if you're ready, though."

"I'm ready," she said, her throat bobbing on a swallow as she shimmied down his thighs a bit and pulled the sheet off his lap. Her eyes tripled in size when all of him was revealed. "Jesus."

"It looks bigger than it is," he joked, tearing open the condom packet, taking his cock and rolling the condom on.

"Objects in mirror are closer than they appear?" she murmured.

He chuckled. "Something like that. Objects on lap are bigger than they feel?"

Now it was her turn to laugh, but it came out breathy and through her nose.

"You set the pace, okay?" He gently took her hips and helped her lift up but quickly realized she was still in her panties, still in her bra.

That just wouldn't do.

With a quick, un-hobbit-like movement that made her squeal, he had her on her back. "Need you naked."

"Naked so we can get nasty?" Her grin seemed more confident than a moment ago, like she was mentally preparing herself and okay with his size.

"Exactly!" He hooked his fingers into the elastic of her panties on either side of her hips, and she lifted her butt off the bed so he could easily pull them off. "Now I want to see your tits," he said, eyeing the peaked nipples beneath the thin fabric of her bra. "But first ..." Leaning forward, he opened his mouth and latched onto one bud over the fabric. Her sharp inhale and the way her back bowed on the bed told him she liked it. She pressed her breast against his face, and he pulled her nipple deeper into her mouth.

She moaned and ran her fingers over his head, her touch gentle but purposeful. "I love that you're bald," she said. "Never been with a bald guy before. I like it."

"Hair is overrated," he said, switching to her other nipple and giving it the same attention as the first. A wet patch from where his mouth had been made the light pink of her bra darker. "Save money on the barber and shampoo."

Her chortle was deep and throaty. "Rex ..." She tugged on his ears until he opened his eyes and glanced up at her. "Inside me."

One final suck on her tit, and he was flipping back over to his back and hoisting her over his lap like she weighed nothing. Now there were two damp patches on her bra, but her nipples were still tight points, and he ached to take them in his mouth with no barrier.

"Bra off. I want to bury my face in your tits."

She complied instantly, wearing a wry smile as she reached behind her and unfastened her bra, tossing it onto his chest and sitting proudly astride his now painful erection. His eyes lasered in on her dusky areolas and the way the skin around her nipples puckered from the cool room.

She cupped them and ran the pads of her thumbs over the swollen peaks, biting her lips seductively. She knew what she was doing. She was playing.

He liked to play.

"Up on your knees," he said, grabbing his cock at the base.

She complied, just like she had with all of his directions, and her dripping slit hovered over his balls.

"Slow and steady wins the race, baby, okay?" he said, angling his cock so the head lined up with her. "We're not in any rush."

Though, by the way his balls were screaming and how hard his dick was, even with the condom, if she went *too* slow, he might blow his load too soon. Which wouldn't be great for him—or her. But he was also pretty capable of bouncing back in thirty to sixty minutes, so hopefully she wouldn't think of him as a one-trick pony and head home.

He really needed to get the fuck out of his head and deep into her pussy.

Too much thinking, not enough action.

His cockhead notched at her center and he watched as her pupils dilated and lips drooped to half-mast. She leaned forward and planted her hands on his chest, slowly sinking down, taking him inch by inch inside her slick, tight heat.

She paused, probably allowing herself to acclimatize to his girth and let her body stretch. He'd been told by past partners that the stretch was a pleasant feeling, and by the way Lydia had closed her eyes and her breathing had slowed, he would hedge to guess she was enjoying the stretch as well.

After another moment that felt like a fucking lifetime to his balls, she opened her eyes, pinned them on him and started to sink down again.

"That's it, baby. Almost there," he said, his voice hoarse as he dug down deep into his body and engaged in some biofeedback. He was the one who was supposed to be more in tune with his senses, with his surroundings and body. That should also mean he was more than capable of having a stern conversation with his genitalia and telling them to calm the fuck down.

Her mouth parted on a gasp, and her lips remained open, her bottom lip hanging open slack. She closed her eyes at the same time he finally hit the end of her.

Fuck, yes!

"Can we ..." She opened her eyes, her gaze unfocused. "Can we move up a bit, so you're sitting against the headboard?"

"We sure fucking can," he said, cupping her ass with one hand to hold her in place while using his other hand to scoot them upward until his back pressed against his headboard. Now her tits were right in his face, which was fucking perfect. "Excellent suggestion," he said, snagging a nipple between his teeth.

She drew in a breath and arched her back, her hair falling behind her, her long neck exposed. "I agree," she said on an exhale.

Her hands fell to his shoulders, and she slowly started to move up and down.

Fuck, yes!

With his mouth still laving at her tit, she pushed her chest against his face and made the lifts and drops of her hips much more deliberate, much more *tormenting*.

If she kept up this pace, he wouldn't be able to last long. Her tight fist of a slit was squeezing him the whole time she sank down until he was buried inside her, then she'd release for a moment, pause with him at the end of her, only to squeeze the whole way back up.

The woman was a fucking sadist.

A fucking sadist.

And he fucking loved it.

He couldn't be tied up, but he could be tortured and teased like this any damn day of the week. Especially when it was by a vixen with tits that fit perfectly in his palms, a pussy he was already craving to lick again and a mouth on her he couldn't wait to see wrapped around his cock. She could tease him any way she fucking pleased.

He still had one hand cupping her ass, and when he pressed his finger gingerly against her crease, she didn't tighten.

Didn't pucker.

Didn't slow her roll or swat his hand away.

He wasn't going to go there now, but he was intrigued to know she wasn't completely prepared to turn him down either.

He switched his mouth to the other breast, loving the way the nipple stiffened inside his mouth when he sucked it hard enough.

Lydia's pace was picking up. She was slamming down hard onto his thighs. Her breathing was growing more ragged too. Little breathy huffs and purrs tumbled from her parted lips. She left one hand on his shoulder but brought the other down between them to her clit.

Fuck, he loved it when a woman took control of her own pleasure. Next time they were in this position, he'd be sure to play with her clit himself, but watching her touch herself turned him on too. He'd love to just sit on the edge of the bed, or even better, go for a drive and have her stick her hands down her pants and get herself off. Then they could pull over, she could climb into his lap, sit on his dick and ride it until they both came.

"You close, baby?" he asked around her nipple, trailing his tongue up her chest, over the thin, delicate skin of her collarbone to her neck.

"Mhmm."

"Me too."

"Rex ... holy fuck. I'm gonna come." She picked up fervor, lifting and dropping on his lap until the slapping sound of skin on skin filled the room, competing with their moans and groans. The heavy scent of sex had already created a heady fog, and he'd probably have to open a window when they were done, but for now, it was just another element to enjoy. Another thing that turned him on. Their bodies mingling, her juices coating his lips and balls. He'd drunk down as much of her as he could, but he was already hungry for more.

After this, they'd have a shower and he'd go down on her again. He had to.

"Rex ..."

"Come, Lydia. Come for me, baby."

She squeezed her eyes shut, pressed her forehead against his, slammed down and detonated.

The squeezing of her walls around his shaft and the feeling of being balls-deep inside her were too much, and he exploded too. Grabbing the back of her neck, he pulled her in for a kiss, smashing their lips together and letting her taste her own flavor. She didn't seem to balk at it and drove in deeper with her tongue, breathing into him as the waves of the orgasm crashed into her. Tiny, feminine whimpers fled from her throat, but he caught them all, devoured each and every one.

The warm puffs of air from her nose with each ragged breath mixed with his, the heat in his belly intensifying as the pleasure careened through his body and his balls emptied.

By the time they were both done, their bodies were slick with sweat and their chests heaved. He'd kept them in a lip lock as he finished his orgasm, but she broke free when he sighed, and his body went lax.

"Well now." Her own heavy sigh hit his lips, and he smiled at the same time his phone on his nightstand beeped and vibrated with a text. "Just as you promised ... and then some," she murmured, pressing a kiss to his forehead.

"I never break a promise, baby." He kissed each of her breasts before reaching for his phone, their bodies still attached, though not for long. "It's a text from Chase."

Lydia's face lost its rosy, post-fuck glow, and she slipped off him and over to her back. "What's it say?"

He held his phone up and unlocked it. The message from his brother was simple and concise. *No prints besides your two.*

He held it out to her so she could read it too. Her eyes widened, then narrowed, then her expression turned sad. Without a word, she slid out of bed and went to the bathroom.

Shit.

He texted his brother. *Run them again.*

CHAPTER 10

In a fog of utter despair, Lydia returned from Rex's bathroom and tugged on her clothes. She needed to get back to her apartment. The apartment where nobody besides her and her cat—and Rex—had ever been.

Because clearly, she was losing her mind.

Nobody had tampered with her underwear drawer.

Nobody had pulled her shower curtain open.

Nobody had left her door unlocked.

Nobody but her.

"Hey, gorgeous, why're you getting dressed?" Rex was still naked on the bed, not the least bit concerned with that fact. He rolled over to his side and propped his head on his hand. "Come back to bed."

She shook her head. "I should get home. I should get Pia home. We've imposed on you and Diesel enough." She tugged her shirt over her head and put her arms through the holes.

She was losing her damn mind.

If she had a job, she'd look into what kind of benefits it had and book a consult with a therapist, but alas, she was still jobless. So any kind of mind analysis from a trained professional would have to wait.

Maybe she could just Google *Signs to look for that you're losing your marbles.*

Rex was off the bed and taking her pants from her. "What's going on?"

With a huff, she tore her hands back from him, but then he just tugged her to the bed and made her sit. He sat too—still naked.

"Can you put some pants or underwear on or something?" she asked, her eyes unable to avoid the snake between his legs. Even losing its *pep,* it was still a very impressive beast to look at.

Grinning but not getting up, he leaned over to his dresser in front of them, opened a drawer and tugged out a pair of plaid pajama pants.

The beast was shrouded in seconds, and Lydia let out a sigh of relief, which made Rex chuckle.

"Better?" he asked. "Can you think straight again?"

She rolled her eyes.

He wrapped an arm around her shoulder. "Come on. I'm trying to lighten the mood. What's going on?"

"I'm losing my damn mind, that's what." She shimmied into her pants. "Nobody was in my place. Your brother said so. Besides yours and my prints, there were no others."

"*Or* whoever was in your place wore gloves or wiped down the surfaces they touched. You'd be surprised the lengths weirdos will go to. And now that there are endless streams of crime and forensic dramas on television and YouTube videos for literally everything, it's more plausible than you think."

She gave him the side-eye. "You're just trying to make me feel better. Meanwhile, deep down you're wondering how you ended up with the crazy chick."

"I'm honestly not. I'm wondering how did I get so lucky to have such a hot chick for a neighbor and why won't she get naked and climb back into bed with me." He waggled his tongue. "Let me take your mind off your problems, baby."

He really was trying to make her laugh, and she appreciated his efforts. With a smile that felt forced, she bumped shoulders with him. "Thank you for trying, but I really should get back to my place."

"I asked Chase to run the prints again," he said, standing up and opening another drawer in his dresser. He tugged out a long-sleeved shirt and pulled it over his frame. "We'll get to the bottom of this. And if you *are* losing your mind—which I don't think you are—we'll get you the help you need."

"Why are you being so nice to me?"

She didn't get it.

She barely knew Rex. Sure, they'd just gotten to know a whole lot more about each other that morning, but truthfully, they hardly knew each other, and he was ready to help her no matter what the circumstances.

His big shoulder lifted, and he dug out some socks. "I like to help people. And I also like you, so it makes *wanting* to help you extra easy. Plus, it's the right thing to do. When someone is in trouble or having a hard time, you help them." He tugged gray and black socks over his enormous feet and then whistled. "D, let's go for a pee."

A snort, snuffle and then a throaty noise one usually makes when stretching filtered around the corner from the living room. The clickety-clack of Diesel's nails preceded him as he padded into Rex's room. Pia was behind him a moment later. She leapt up onto the bed and nuzzled Lydia's side.

"You two were awfully cozy on that big bed," Lydia said, scratching behind the cat's ears.

"D's a good judge of character. He likes you. He likes Pia. That's good enough for me." Rex scrubbed the dog's face, then kissed the top of his head. "We'll feed you, then go drain the pipes."

Diesel seemed to understand and followed Rex out into the living room.

Compelled by her upbringing to always make her bed for the morning, she straightened the sheets, pillows and duvet of Rex's bed, much to the irritation of Pia, who refused to get off the bed, before joining Rex in the living room.

Diesel was face-down in his food bowl and Rex was filling an electric kettle with water, a French press full of aromatic grounds perched on the counter. "You want coffee?" he asked, opening a cupboard that housed mugs.

Here she was mentally reeling inside, convinced she was losing her mind, and he wanted to know if she wanted coffee. She opened her mouth to respond when her phone on the coffee table started to ring.

She'd just bought a new phone—her first paycheck treat—and the battery life was awesome. Her old one would have died overnight if it wasn't plugged in. It was Jayne Wheatley, a friend from work. Her *former* work.

Lydia really didn't feel like rehashing the drama that encircled her embarrassing termination. But Jayne was a good friend, quite possibly her only friend. Jayne had been out of town for a funeral all week, so she was probably just hearing about Lydia's firing today now that she was back.

She answered her phone. "Hi, Jayne."

"Why in the bloody hell didn't you call and tell me that bitch fired you? Or the very least text me? I hate that I'm only finding out *today*. What the fuck?" Leave it to Jayne to ignore all pleasantries, rip the Band-Aid clean off and stick her finger on the scab. But because she was British, even her verbal flagellation came off as elegant.

"You were at a celebration of life for your aunt. I really didn't think my being fired was worth disrupting your mourning and family time." That earned her a lifted brow from Rex, who was now pouring the boiling water from the kettle into the French press. He mouthed the word *coffee?* But she shook her head.

"Tony's aunt was like ninety-three, and for the last two years, whenever she took ill, the family rallied and made peace thinking it was her time, then she'd bounce back and keep on going. We've all been ready for a while now. It was more of a party and family reunion than anything, and I certainly could have been interrupted for this. Come on. We're friends."

And that was one of Lydia's biggest flaws. She always thought she was imposing on people, interrupting or disturbing them, so she rarely asked for help or reached out. She just expected her call to be met with irritation, when in fact it never was.

She was trying to be better about asking for help and reaching out to people, but it wasn't easy when it wasn't a normal part of her makeup.

"How are you holding up?" Jayne asked, her earlier irritation replaced with concern.

"Not great," Lydia said. "I have a friend who's been helping me get through it, a neighbor, and he thinks he might have a nanny gig for me with some friends, but—"

"But you're a teacher. You need to be in a school with children."

"I know. Hopefully for September. But right now, I need to make some money."

"I'm not at work today," Jayne started. "Since it's Friday and I took the other four days of the week off to travel to back to the UK, I just figured I'd finish out the week and take today for myself. Plus, I'm bloody knackered from the jet lag. Let's grab lunch. My treat. We can brainstorm ways to get back at that bitch Odette and also find you a new job. Seriously, who the fuck does she think she is? Just because she used to manage an art gallery in butt-fuck nowhere doesn't mean she's qualified to run a day care. You were the best teacher we've ever had, and she made the stupidest mistake letting you go."

"You just said you were exhausted."

"Fuck that. I'm buying my friend lunch. If you say *no*, I'll hate you forever."

Lydia chuckled. Jayne just had this way about her that made the world seem a little less shitty. The *clink* and jingle of Rex attaching Diesel's harness alerted her to his imminent departure. "Lunch sounds great, Jayne. When and where?"

"McRae's at noon?"

She glanced at the clock on her phone. It was almost nine thirty. That gave her time to have a shower, clean her place and go grab some groceries for the week. "Sounds perfect."

"Great! I'll bring my voodoo doll that I used on all my old boyfriends. We'll make Odette have the worst case of diarrhea she's ever experienced in her life."

Laughing again and truly feeling less bogged down with plaguing thoughts of her possible madness, Lydia said goodbye to her friend and hung up.

Rex's hand was on the door handle of his front door. "You staying here or heading home?"

"Give me two secs, and I'll walk out with you so you can lock up."

No disappointment, just acceptance flashed in his eyes, and he nodded.

She quickly gathered Pia and her stuff and then joined Rex and Diesel in the hallway. He locked the door.

Diesel was getting impatient and pulling Rex toward the fire exit stairs. "That's good that you're meeting your friend for lunch. Hopefully, she can help you feel better. Is she a friend from work?"

Lydia adjusted a squirming Pia in her arms and nodded. "Yeah."

"Well, I'm not trying to be clingy or anything, but if you want to get together later or go for a walk or do another puzzle, just let me know. But I would like you to come to my mum's tomorrow for dinner. It'll give you a chance to meet the kids you'd be nannying. See if it's a good fit."

This man seemed too good to be true. Even before the accident, Dierks had never been so—accepting of things. He was kind and gentle, but there was something so relaxing, so disarming about Rex, it settled Lydia in a way she'd never felt settled before.

He was the calm during a turbulent storm.

She wanted more of it.

More of this feeling of ease and comfort.

She wanted more of Rex.

"Hmm?" he probed, snapping his fingers at Diesel to keep the pup from pulling. Diesel heeled immediately and sat down on his butt with a huff.

"Let's meet up later," she said. "Another walk or dinner or both."

Then the lightbulb went off in her head.

"I'll cook for you. As a thank-you. How does that sound?"

Oh, those dimples. Jesus Murphy. His smile seriously made the hallway seem like it was brighter than it had been a moment ago. "Sounds like one heck of a date. I'm in."

"Great! I'll make us dinner, then we can take Diesel for a walk after. Bring him over with you so he and Pia can do their snuggle thing."

Rex's brows bobbed. "And we can do ours?"

Yes, please!

"But of course."

His dimples were digging even deeper now. She had to get out of there before she tackled him in the hallway and dragged his body back to bed.

"All right. We'll see you tonight. Five?"

"Yep." She headed off to the elevator, a spring in her step, which was surprising, given how she was feeling just moments before—like she was on the brink of insanity. But that spring was because of Rex. He just made her happy.

Even when the chips were down and crushed to dust, he pulled a smile from her and made the good seem tangible.

"Hey, Lydia?"

She turned back around. He was halfway through the fire exit door. "Hmm?"

"Maybe you can show me your *blue ones?*"

"Only if you finish all your vegetables," she called back.

He tossed his head back with a laugh, waved and was gone through the door.

Nuzzling Pia, she hit the button for the elevator and stepped inside when it opened immediately.

Maybe things weren't as bad as they seemed? Maybe she'd just forgotten to lock her door. Forgotten to close the shower curtain and her underwear drawer. They were all easily forgettable things, particularly if she was distracted. And they didn't make a lick of sense as an act of torment by anybody that might be out to hurt her.

Didn't creeps and weirdos go a little more hardcore than that? Didn't they scrawl notes on bathroom walls in blood? Disembowel a beloved stuffed animal or poison your orange juice?

Of course, these were things she only thought weirdos would do, not things that she herself had ever thought of doing.

Oh God, maybe she was crazy.

Stop thinking like that. Rex doesn't think you're crazy. He believes you. He believes IN you. Doesn't that mean something?

Yes, it did mean something, and she needed to hold on to that something. Take solace in the new person in her life and how much he already cared for her and believed in her. It struck her hard and wonderful and warm in the chest just how much she already cared about Rex too. Sharing your darkest moments with another person will do that to you. Bring you close faster than normal. But it didn't scare her; it only excited her. Made her eager to keep traveling down this road with him and see where they ended up, where this journey would take them.

The elevator dinged and the doors opened. She and Pia headed down the hallway to her unit. She tried the door before putting the key in. It was still locked. That was a good sign.

She slid the key into the hole, unlocked it and stepped inside. Nothing weird stood out. There were no bizarre odors or feelings in the air. She set Pia down on the ground, along with her carrier and litter box.

She needed to shower, but first she needed to take inventory of her fridge and compile a grocery list.

She wanted to go super elegant and fancy for their dinner tonight. Like beef Wellington with pureed celeriac and green beans. She also wanted to make a dessert.

Her mother's famous pavlova with fresh raspberries and home-made whipped cream was always a crowd pleaser. It'd taken Lydia years to perfect, but she'd finally done it—after a lot of tearful phone calls with her mother complaining about stupid egg whites and a cursed whisk. Now whenever she was invited to a potluck, she brought that and received a lot of praise for it.

First things first, she needed to check to see how many eggs she had.

Humming, she opened her fridge and pulled out the carton of eggs. She was pretty sure she had a full dozen, but her mind was playing tricks on her with other things in her world, so maybe she didn't. She opened the carton and dropped it on the floor with a gasp, her hands shaking, heart rate going from zero to sixty in a second.

Every single egg inside was smashed.

And if they hadn't been, after she dropped the carton on the floor, they certainly would be.

But that didn't matter.

Because before she dropped it, the eggs were all cracked and open.

All twelve of them.

That didn't make any sense.

She always checked her eggs when she bought them at the store. Always.

Just like you always lock your front door and close your shower curtain?

Certainly, she would have noticed. Right?

Pia meowed and wandered into the kitchen, sniffing the egg shrapnel on the floor.

Lydia gently shooed the cat away so she didn't get yolk on her paws and reached for a roll of paper towels off the counter.

The fridge was still open but was rather empty—aside from four apples in her crisper and a block of cheddar cheese.

She opened the crisper, and her blood went icy. Every apple was bruised and dented. Like someone had deliberately, repeatedly dropped them on the ground.

What. The. Hell?

She pulled the opened but covered cheese from the dairy drawer. A giant bite mark was carved out of the side of the wedge.

Who?

With her hands trembling, breathing ragged, she set the cheese and apples on the counter, then closed the fridge and went about cleaning up the spilled eggs.

This wasn't her.

It couldn't have been her.

She didn't sleepwalk. And even if she did, she wouldn't crush all her eggs, take a giant bite out of her cheese or bruise all of her apples.

This was the work of a sick, disturbed person.

But who?

Panic started a hot, insidious trail through her limbs.

On her hands and knees, she wiped up the egg goo from the floor, her brain going at warp speed, heart rate doing its best to catch up.

She was going to hyperventilate or have a heart attack soon if she didn't calm down. Lifting her head to stand up and put the paper towel into the trash, she spied her three bananas on the counter.

She'd just picked those up on Tuesday night. She took one with her to work on Wednesday, like she always did, along with a little container of peanut butter. And the other three were to last her until grocery shopping day on Saturday afternoon.

But there was something weird about these bananas.

They were all brown.

She hated brown or even slightly brown bananas.

The greener the better.

She bought them as green as she possibly could and only four at a time.

Tossing the paper towel into the trash beneath the sink, she reached for the bananas but dropped them almost as quickly, like they were on fire.

A sick lotus blossom of dread unfurled inside her gut.

Someone—not her—had peeled back the skin on all three bananas, then carefully folded it back over to look like they were intact.

But they weren't intact.

All of them were oxidized and brown.

What the fuck was going on?

Without another thought, she scooped up a meowing Pia, who was circling her ankles for breakfast, grabbed her keys and phone off the counter and headed back out the door.

She was nearly at the elevator when she bumped into Rex's hard chest as she turned the corner. "Whoa!" He reached out and grabbed her shoulders. "You okay? You look like you've seen a ghost."

Her breath released shakily, and she crumpled against his chest, the tears coming on fast and furious.

"Hey, hey! What's wrong?" He rubbed her back. "What happened? I was just coming to bring you your sweater. You left it at my place."

But she couldn't get the words out.

Not only because she was crying too hard but because when she tried to say them in her head, they just came out sounding ridiculous and stupid.

Someone peeled all my bananas, bruised all my apples, took a bite of my cheese and broke all my eggs.

These were not the normal actions of a deranged psycho.

Would he think her crazy if she told him?

Because she was seriously starting to think that she might be.

CHAPTER 11

IT TOOK Rex a solid five minutes to get out of Lydia what had her so spooked. And when he finally did, he totally understood why she'd run out of her apartment as if a ghost was chasing her. Because one kind of was.

Not that he believed in *ghosts* per se. Maybe spirits of loved ones coming back to watch over you and celebrate with you, but not bad ghosts.

He liked to think his dad came back as a happy spirit and was there watching over him and his brothers with a smile on his face when they graduated from high school and the naval academy, and when his niece and nephew were born.

But the idea of a ghost breaking into Lydia's apartment, biting her cheese and peeling her bananas sounded seriously far-fetched and not something a ghost, let alone someone out to torment her, would even do. It was just plain bizarre.

He offered for her to come back to his place, but she shook her head and said she needed to shower, change and feed Pia, so he accompanied her back to her apartment and hung around until she did what she needed to do.

He also took pictures of the cheese, bananas and apples. The eggs were already cleaned up and in the trash, so there was no point taking pictures of them.

But now they had more surfaces where they could try to gather prints. He put in a call to Heath, who said he'd be by later with the print kit again.

By the time Lydia emerged from her bedroom wearing a pair of black skinny jeans that showed off all her curves, and a sexy red sweater that hung off one shoulder, she seemed to be a little calmer.

"You doing okay?" he asked, getting up from the couch and approaching her. Without hesitation, she went into his arms and rested her cheek against his chest. The shampoo she used—strawberries and summer sunshine—wafted up into his nostrils.

"I just feel so stupid," she said with a hitched breath. "Like none of this makes sense."

"You're not stupid. But you are right. None of this makes any sense."

She hiccuped a sob, her arms around him tightening.

"You want to have dinner at my place instead? I'll give you freedom in the kitchen to cook your fancy meal, and we can just chill there if you're more comfortable."

Lifting her head, she blinked up at him. He wiped away the one tear that had slid down her cheek. "You don't think I'm crazy, do you? Like you don't think I did all of this myself?"

If he was being honest, the unlocked door, opened shower curtain and open underwear drawer had him skeptical. Those were all easy things to forget. But the bananas, eggs, apples and cheese, that was just some fucked-up shit.

"I do not think you're crazy, and I don't think you did this yourself."

"I don't want to leave Pia here while I go out."

"Then leave her with me. She and Diesel can get their snuggle on again. No worries."

Big hazel eyes blinked at him. "Do you think whoever did this came *back*, or do you think we just missed it all yesterday?"

"Was your door locked when you opened it earlier?"

She nodded.

"Then I think we just missed these things and they haven't been back. They're easy things to miss. I know that when I'm on duty and either taking in a crime scene or surveying a house for bugs or tampering, the kitchen and fridge are not the first places I go looking."

She nodded again. "That makes sense." A laugh escaped her on a huff. "Which is refreshing, because not much right now *is* making sense."

"Finish what you need to do here. Leave your key with me. I'll go put Pia upstairs with D, and when Heath comes back, I'll let him into your place. You can stay at my place again tonight or as long as you need until you feel safe coming back here, okay?" He rubbed her back again and kissed the top of her head.

She did more nodding.

"Go have lunch with your friend. Clear your head and don't let this stress you out."

"Easier said than done."

"I know, but just try, okay?" He tucked his knuckle beneath her chin. "For me?"

A slow, calming breath released through her slightly parted lips, and she nodded again. "Okay. I'll try."

"And if you're not calm by tonight, then I can draw you a bath, give you a massage, and give you *plenty* of other things to think about ... like my tongue all ... over ... your ... body." He smiled at her, hoping that it pulled a smile from her as well.

It did, and it also made her blush.

"Rexwell, those dimples need to come with a warning label." The glitter of amusement was back in her eyes.

"You mean like: *WARNING: Dimples may cause panties to get very, very damp. Do not stare directly at them.*"

"Exactly that. They're like an eclipse."

"But instead of burning your retinas, they make your lady bits get all tingly." He waggled his eyebrows teasingly. "Are yours all tingly right now? Have I given you *the tingles?*"

She rolled her eyes. "Find the label. Put it on your forehead. Women need to be forewarned that they look at those things at their own risk."

"I did have a label. But I lost it. Might have gone through the laundry."

Another eye roll, which only made him grin harder. She swatted his chest.

"I can see about getting another label printed though. Would you like that?"

Her nod was playful. "Yes. Even a piece of green painter's tape on your forehead that issues a warning to any man or woman rendered weak and wanton by dimples. I think it's your duty to society."

"Fair enough, m'lady. I shall get on that posthaste."

Now he had her laughing, which was exactly what he wanted.

Her laugh was electric, along with her smile.

His smile might be lethal to dry panties, but hers was lethal to his heart.

She made to break away from their embrace, but he snagged her by the wrist and drew her back against his chest and took her mouth.

She didn't resist, not even for a second.

Lydia melted against him and wrapped her arms around his neck, pushing up onto her tiptoes to deepen the kiss.

They made out for a few minutes, but the painful scratch of cat claws on his leg had him breaking their lip lock. They both glanced down at the floor to where Pia was on her hindlegs and clawing at him.

"That means she likes you," Lydia said. "She only maims the ones she likes."

Rex snorted a laugh, bent down and petted the cat until she was satisfied in his attentions and wandered away. "You should head out. Go clear your head and run your errands. Have lunch with your friend."

Her head bobbed but almost absent-mindedly, and she glanced around her apartment as if trying to find something. "Now I'm thinking that we haven't checked the place out thoroughly enough. Like maybe whoever was in here has done more things, but they're so subtle that it'll be days or weeks before I find out."

He scrunched his brows. "What do you mean?"

Her shoulder lifted. "I read this joke online once about a husband and wife who divorced rather nastily. He got the house that they both wanted and was about to move in his mistress. The night before the wife moved out, she stowed a bunch of prawn shells into the hollow curtain rods. They ended up making the whole place stink so bad the husband and mistress had to sell. But nobody would buy it because of the smell, so the price kept dropping. The wife bought it for a steal, and when the husband and mistress moved out, they even took the curtain rods."

"That's a *very* specific story. And also genius and devious. Do you know somebody who has the brilliance to do that? To go to such lengths?" The level of thought put into the vengeance in her story almost made it seem made up, but then again, one could never be too sure about things they read online. Perhaps it had been made up or embellished. He couldn't fault her for reading it or remembering it though. It was a pretty ingenious story of revenge.

"I hardly know anyone here."

With a deep inhale, he snagged her keys off a small half-circle table against the wall between her bathroom and bedroom doors.

"Go. Clear your head. I'll take care of things here. I'll take Pia upstairs with me."

With another distracted nod, she pulled a light denim jacket off a row of hooks near her front door and shrugged into it. She grabbed gray suede ankle boots from the shoe rack and slipped into them. She looked hot as fuck, and he could tell she wasn't even trying.

With her purse now over her shoulder, she stood in her small foyer and looked back at him. "I'm really glad my drunk ass met you the other day."

Rex smiled. "I'm really glad my sober ass met your drunk ass."

Her smile was small, and even though it didn't trigger a twinkle in her eye, he could tell she meant it. "Thank you."

He flashed the dimples and winked. "Anytime. Now *git.*"

There we go. That was the smile he was aiming for.

She scrunched her nose, blew him a kiss and was gone.

Rex bent down and picked up a scrounging-for-affection Pia. "If only you could talk, eh? You could tell us exactly what's going on." He kissed her head, then went about gathering her travel stuff so he could get the hell out of there. It took a lot to scare a guy like him, and Lydia's apartment wasn't *scaring* him, but it also wasn't making him feel warm and fuzzy either.

With a shiver he had no control over, he gently ushered Pia into her carrier, grabbed her food dish, water bowl and bag of food, along with her travel litter box. Making sure he closed all of Lydia's dresser drawers and her shower curtain, he headed out into the building hallway and locked her door.

Something fishy was going on for sure.

But he highly doubted it was prawn shells stuffed into a curtain rod.

The question was: Who was doing this, and how far would they take it?

———

"WELL, that's just super fucking weird," Jayne said later at lunch, taking a sip of her mojito. "Like who does that to somebody's cheese? Or their bananas?"

Lydia had no stomach for rum after Wednesday night, so she'd opted for just a lovely pink lemonade. They were sitting outside on the restaurant's patio beneath big tower heaters, enjoying their SoCal quesadillas and homemade pico de gallo.

"I tell you, up until the bananas and cheese thing, I was starting to wonder if it was all just me and I was losing my damn mind. The eggs and the apples are a bit over the top too, but I could see how they *might* end up cracked and bruised in my grocery bags. It just seems unlikely." She dipped a wedge of her quesadilla into her pico de gallo and took a bite. "But Rex is looking into it."

"This Rex chap sounds dreamy," Jayne said, her bright blue eyes getting all sparkly. She and her husband, Anthony, had been together for nearly thirty years, but she still got all starry-eyed like a teenager when she spoke about their relationship, Lydia wanted that kind of love. "Do you have a picture?"

No, but she wished she did.

"He's hot, trust me. Big. Muscly. Dark blue eyes. Dimples as deep as the Mariana Trench, and did I mention he was bald?"

Jayne snickered over her straw. "Once or twice."

"So what's the news from the school? Has the new bitch on the block got her laser beam set on someone else to fire?"

Jayne's expression turned sad, and she tucked a strand of her blonde hair behind her ear. Even though she'd been away from the school for over a week, she was *the most* connected person there. Lydia was actually surprised it'd taken Jayne until Friday to call her. But then again, she was overseas and dealing with a family death, so ... "Everybody misses you and thinks Odette is a total cow for canning you. She had *zero* cause, and after all the extra things you did around there, she was just a giant fool. From what I heard, every single other staff member went to bat for you and challenged her. But she threatened their jobs, and they grew quiet."

"Fuck." Lydia shook her head. "And what about the big cheese? Reese, what did he have to say?"

Reese was the day care and preschool owner. He didn't give two shits about anything besides money, and in the month Lydia had worked there, she'd also learned the man didn't even like children.

Jayne made a noise in her throat. "Exactly what you would expect. He says he's paying Odette to make the tough decisions so that he doesn't have to, and she obviously deemed you not a good fit, so he supports her decision."

"Of course he does."

"The prick." Jayne reached her hand across the table and grabbed Lydia's, giving it a squeeze. "If I could get another job that paid like this one, gave me the vacation time and flexibility I get from this, I would leave Odette and Reese the heartless bastard in a heartbeat. But I've been there for almost ten years. I can't just walk away."

"I understand. I would never expect or ask you to quit your job —a job you *love*—just out of solidarity with me. The kids love you."

"But know I would if I could, love. I really would. If we had the money, we could start up our own preschool and then poach all the best families from Carrot Patch. Wouldn't that tell Odette and Reese to stuff it." Jayne was so feisty, Lydia loved it.

"Whichever one of us gets a fairy godmother first, we'll make it priority number one."

"Brilliant. Because I don't need to get all gussied up and ride in a pumpkin to a ball anyway. I have my Prince Charming." There she went getting all starry-eyed again. "And it sounds like you might have found yours too."

It was a little too early to make such a proclamation out loud, but Rex certainly seemed to be saving her like a prince or knight or whatever. And Diesel was most noble and valiant, even if he wasn't a steed.

"Not ready to say it to the heavens?" Jayne asked, her smile all-knowing.

"Something like that."

"But we *do* need to put it out there for our fairy godmothers to hear."

"You start."

Jayne nodded, clasped her hands in the prayer position atop the table, her brightly painted turquoise nails catching the sun's rays. She closed her eyes. "Oh fairy godmothers near and far, if you can hear us, please listen to our plea. Bestow upon us the money or opportunity to buy our own preschool, so we may be rid of the plague that is Odette Rockford and Reese Stone." She opened her eyes. "Now your turn."

Lydia wrinkled her nose. "I just don't know if they'll hear me."

Jayne made a motherly noise of dismissal and shrugged as she unclasped her hands. "You'll never know if you don't try."

Taking a deep, fortifying breath, Lydia mimicked what Jayne did with her hands laced together and her eyes closed. "Oh fairy godmothers near and far, if you can hear us, listen to our plea." She cracked one eye open, and Jayne was looking at her and nodding encouragingly. Lydia closed her eye again. "If you have the time, and maybe some extra cash lying around, do you think you could find it in your magical hearts to help us buy a preschool? Odette and Reese don't care about the kids. But children are the future, and if we don't nurture the future, then what will we have lived for at all? Even if you can't come up with the money, just a job offer or a nudge at an ad placement for a preschool teacher would be great. If you have the time." She opened her eyes but then immediately closed them again. "Thank you."

When she opened her eyes again, Jayne was tearing up. She

reached across the table and took both of Lydia's hands in hers and shook them slightly. "We'll find you your dream job, sweetheart. I promise."

Lydia pressed her lips together and attempted to lift the corners of her mouth into a smile, but only one lifted and just barely.

"In the meantime," Jayne said, perking up a bit and releasing Lydia's hands, "I brought some things for you." She started digging around in her enormous purse—the same shade as her nails, which was no coincidence, since Jayne always coordinated her accessories. "Here we go, darling." She plopped a little beanbag thing on the table. "I saw the print and knew it was for you."

As a side gig, Jayne—a very accomplished sewer—made little beanbag chairs for iPads and other electronic devices. She sold them on her Etsy shop. This particular one was big enough for Lydia's iPad and had cats dressed up like bananas all over it.

"This is fantastic," Lydia said, picking up the cushion and admiring it. "Thank you."

"Found that bolt at a little fabric shop in Doncaster, and I just knew I needed to make you something with it." She pulled something else out of her purse as well, which, the moment Lydia saw it, had her laughing until her cheeks and belly hurt. "Don't laugh. You should never laugh at voodoo."

"But don't we need a lock of Odette's hair or something? Wrap it around the doll before we stick a bunch of pins in it, so the doll knows which person to direct the misfortune to."

Jayne's brows bobbed deviously, and she pulled out a Ziploc bag from her purse with a single strand of hair inside of it. "Swung by the school when I knew she wouldn't be there. Was stuck to the chair in her office."

Holy crap.

Up until now, Lydia had only really been doing all of this fairy godmother beckoning and stuff to placate her eccentric friend. But now that Jayne had actually gone to the lengths of obtaining a strand of Odette's hair and had a voodoo doll in her hand, a doll that looked like it'd seen better days, Lydia was no longer sure she wanted to get sucked into these dark arts.

"I don't want to hurt her," she said, eyeing the doll and Ziploc bag like either might lunge across the table and bite her like a rattlesnake.

"And we won't." Jayne shrugged and pulled out a small black velvet bag with a drawstring from her purse. She loosened the opening, and four long pins with pearled heads spilled out.

"Shouldn't we be doing this at nighttime over a pentagram and with candles dripping a ton of wax?" Lydia asked with a forced chuckle. "Broad daylight at a restaurant doesn't seem right."

Jayne merely rolled her blue eyes and opened up the Ziploc bag. Carefully, she took out the single strand of hair and wrapped it around the doll's neck. She picked up one pin and held it out to Lydia. "It might work, it might not, but it's meant to be therapeutic. Do to the doll what you can't do to the person."

With her heart pounding like a gong in her chest, she took the pin from between her friend's long, decorated fingers.

Jayne placed the doll on the table between them. "Give her a headache, heartburn, diarrhea, a charley horse, whatever will make you feel better. Will make you turn the corner and forget that bitch and the job and move on. Because right now, darling, you're not."

Lydia sucked in a deep breath through her nose and stared at the doll. It didn't have any eyes, just a short, wide X where the mouth would be. It seemed to be sexually ambiguous and made out of straw and burlap. Truthfully, it was kind of creepy.

With a single finger, she flipped the doll over so it was face-down on the table, then, lifting the pin high in the air, she slowly dropped her arm until the point of the pin made contact with what would be the butt of the doll. She poked it a couple of times and then impaled it, pushing the pin in all the way. With her heart in her throat, she glanced up at Jayne. "Now what?" She felt like at any moment, lightning was going to strike her from the cloudless sky or the police would pull up in their squad car and arrest her for witchcraft or murder.

"Now, we wait. Sometimes it happens quick; sometimes it takes a few days. Just be patient." She sipped her mojito until it made a slurping sound in her glass.

"If I pull it out, will it stop it from happening?"

Jayne shook her head. "Doesn't really work that way, but you're welcome to try."

Releasing a long, slow breath from her nose, Lydia sat back in her seat. She still had half her quesadilla left, but she wasn't hungry. The thought that she'd just stuck a pin in a voodoo doll meant to represent her ex-boss was making her nauseous.

"Don't sweat it," Jayne said with a laugh. "It doesn't even always work, and I didn't bring the murder pins, just the pain, discomfort and gastrointestinal issues pins."

Lydia's eyes nearly fell out of her head. "Did you just say *murder* pins?"

CHAPTER 12

BY THE TIME Lydia got back to her apartment after lunch with Jayne, her fabric shopping bags and leftover quesadilla in her hands, she didn't feel the least bit better about the whole apartment intruder or the Odette Rockford situation. Not one bit.

Jayne, of course, insisted that Lydia keep the voodoo doll, since she was the one who needed it and who had put Odette's upcoming gastro problems into play.

But she didn't really want that doll in her house, let alone Rex's house, so she stuffed it into the glove compartment of her car before heading into the building.

She'd texted Rex just before leaving the restaurant, and he said he was home and that Heath had just left.

She went straight up to his apartment and was greeted with a kiss on the cheek, a wiggle-bum dog trying to sniff her grocery bags, and a cat who was hell-bent on tripping her before she even got her shoes off.

"How was lunch?" Rex asked, taking the grocery bags from her. "Feel better?"

Nodding, she plastered on a big smile and lied. "Much better."

He grinned back. "That's awesome. See, I knew an afternoon out and with a friend would be just the medicine you needed." Lydia just continued to nod. "While I was at your apartment with Heath, the mailwoman dropped off a package for you." He nodded at the shoebox-size box on his kitchen table.

Was it from her mother? A cookie care package perhaps? Or maybe some of her mother's delicious fudge? Even though her mother worked full-time as a receptionist for an insurance adjuster, her true passion was baking. Slowly, Lydia was inheriting that passion as well. But not without plenty of burnt cookies and soupy fudge along the way.

She left Rex to unload the groceries from the bags and went to inspect the box. There was no return address, which was not like her mother. And her name was not written in her mother's handwriting either.

A trickle of dread dribbled down her spine like a drop of water from a melting icicle.

"Gonna open it?" Rex asked, stowing the beef she'd bought for the Wellington in the fridge. He held out a pair of scissors from the cutlery drawer.

She accepted them and returned to the box. Slowly, precisely, she slid the scissors through the transparent tape that held the box closed. When the lid was free on three sides, she flipped it open.

Inside, nestled on a bed of panties—*her* panties—was a big, thick, veiny pink vibrator still in its original packaging.

"What the fuck?" She took a giant step back, her hand to her chest, heart beating wildly. Her back hit the wall, and she stared straight ahead at the box as if she'd been sent a severed head and not a sex toy.

"What is it?" Rex abandoned the grocery bags and moved toward her, peering into the box. His brows lifted, and he smiled. "Oh nice. Kinky."

But it wasn't nice at all.

It was fucked up.

Seriously fucked up.

"I—I didn't order that," she said, trying desperately not to stammer. "I didn't order it, and those are *my* underwear."

His smile instantly vanished, and his eyes darted between her face and the box. "What do you mean?"

Freaked the fuck out, she pointed at the box. "I *mean*, I didn't order that sex toy, and those are *my* underwear. I didn't think any were missing, but I guess I didn't look that hard, or ... but those are mine. I recognize them."

She'd gone to a bachelorette party last year, and at the party there had been this rep for a lingerie company. If you signed up then, you got a fifty-percent discount on their underwear of the month club. You paid thirty bucks for the year rather than sixty, and every month the company would mail you a fun new pair of panties. So far, she'd receive eight of the twelve pairs. They were cute and comfortable and made her feel sexy. And in that box, under the vibrator, were three of those pairs of panties.

Without hesitation, Rex retreated to the kitchen, dug around in a drawer for a moment, then came back over with a pair of metal barbecue tongs. First, he removed the toy, placing it on the table gingerly, then he went about pulling out each pair of panties. There were only three in total, but they were all hers.

"I thought you said nothing was missing," he said, his tone not quite accusatory but with enough of an edge, she felt her insides grow tight.

"I ... I didn't think there was. But I also didn't go through my entire underwear drawer and take inventory. I have like forty pairs."

"Jesus, why so many?"

That was neither here nor there, so she just lifted a shoulder and dismissed his question with a headshake.

"Need to get these checked for prints. Heath left me his kit, which makes way more sense than calling him over here every time."

Every time?

Did he think this kind of stuff was going to keep happening?

Was there something he knew but wasn't telling her?

"Chase says he'll run whatever we need him to, but he's tangled up with Stacey and the kids, so he's not doing a ton of field work right now."

Releasing the tongs, he stepped over to the living room, where the bag she recognized as the one Heath had brought over the day before sat on a side table. He grabbed it and brought it back to the kitchen table.

"Go put the groceries away or go do something else," he said gently. "I'll dust everything for prints. This is getting more and more fucked up as the days go by. What next? A voodoo doll with your face?"

Bile rose up in Lydia's throat at the mention of a voodoo doll. She gasped and choked to shove it down.

Rex dropped the equipment in his hands and went to her. "Are you okay? What's wrong now?" As if she were made out of porcelain, he guided her over to the couch. "Sit down for a sec. What happened?"

Pulling air deep into her lungs through her nose, she did her very best to settle her nerves and regain her composure. She wasn't going to tell Rex about the voodoo doll. Not after his comment. Then he'd for sure think she was crazy. "It's nothing," she finally said. "This whole thing —the unlocked door, bananas, cheese, and now this—it's all just *a lot.* You know?"

He nodded and rubbed her back. "I'll get you a glass of water."

He left her briefly but was back in moments, offering her a tumbler.

She took a few sips, allowing the last one to rest on her tongue for a moment before swallowing. She took her time looking up at him. "I'm getting scared, Rex."

He nodded, and his thick brows pinched tight. "I know, babe. But we'll get to the bottom of it, I promise." He pressed his lips together for a moment in thought. "Still don't think it's your ex?"

At first, she didn't think it could be Dierks. It just didn't fit the bill. He had not touched her or hurt her when they were together, and he had not gone super creepy when she broke up with him. He'd showed borderline stalker behavior but nothing like this. And even when he did show up at her house or work, it was always with the same plea: *Take me back. I can't do this without you.*

No threats though. Nothing aggressive.

But now ...

Now she had no idea what to believe.

Maybe it was Dierks. Maybe the head injury had gotten worse and he wasn't just angry and violent. Maybe he'd become obsessive and possessive too.

Rex rubbed her back again and kissed her temple. "I'm going to call my brothers, give them the skinny, then I'll dust it all for prints." He tugged his phone out of his pocket and stepped away from her into his bedroom.

As if they knew something was up, both Diesel and Pia leapt up onto the couch. Diesel snuggled in beside Lydia, his chin on her thigh, and Pia crawled into her lap, her butt in Diesel's face. He didn't seem to care.

She set her water glass down and petted them both, taking comfort in their warmth and calming presence. Pets really were the best companions, though Rex Hart was proving to be a close second.

Her eyes fluttered shut, and she leaned her head back against the couch, recalling the last three days and how everything had transpired.

In all of Victoria, she only knew a handful of people. And a handful was generous.

At work, even though she was friendly with all the other teachers and educational assistants, she'd only really bonded with Jayne. She chalked it up to her newness and that over time she'd get to know the rest just as well and build friendships.

Well, maybe not anymore.

But besides Odette, she didn't think she'd rubbed anybody the wrong way. Not even Reese Stone. Sure, the guy was an emotionless bastard, but the few interactions they'd had were pleasant.

Was Odette behind this?

She dismissed that thought from her brain before if really had a chance to take root.

No.

That made zero sense.

She hardly knew the woman. And Odette got the ultimate revenge for all the unpaid overtime Lydia put in—Lydia lost her job. Why would the woman spend any more of her energy tormenting a person she hardly knew?

No, it just didn't add up.

But Dierks ...

She didn't want to believe it.

Even though she'd ended it with him, she still held on to a few grains of hope that he would see the light and get the help he needed. She knew the man he once was, the man he could be again, if only he got the right help.

But he seemed resigned to the fact that he didn't need any help, which was why she left. Then he said he'd only get help if she took him back.

Maybe now he was angry about her leaving and was getting his revenge by slowly driving her crazy.

Whoever it was, their plan was working.

"We'll go back to your place and grab some clothes for you,"

Rex said, exiting his bedroom and stuffing his phone into his back pocket. "You can stay here until we get a handle on this."

As lovely as that sounded, it wasn't a permanent fix. She was also a grown-ass adult, and up until the vibrator mail, nothing had been scary ... just creepy.

Plus, she loved her apartment. It was southeast-facing, so it got all the sun, and she'd spent a great deal of time decorating it to her liking. It was her little haven of peace and joy—or at least it had been. But she needed to take it back from the intruder and reclaim the place as hers. It was her home.

"Thinking awfully hard there, gorgeous," Rex said, pulling a chair out from his kitchen table and picking up the fingerprint kit again.

"I need to be able to stay at my own place, Rex. I can't let whoever is doing this to me win."

He glanced at her but didn't turn his head. "Not tonight though. Tonight you'll stay here. Tomorrow we'll go to dinner at my mum's. You can meet the kids, and then we'll go from there. I can even stay with you at your place if you're hell-bent on sleeping there. Diesel can snooze anywhere."

Despite the circumstances, his authoritative tone and the way he was looking at her and taking control made tingles run rampant through her body, and her icy blood began to thaw.

With a gentle pat to the cat and the dog, she pried herself out from beneath them and headed back into the kitchen. As shaken up as she was right now, it would do nobody any good if she continued to just sit there and fret and stew.

She needed to be productive.

And what better way to be productive than by making a beautiful pavlova and mouthwatering beef Wellington?

It was what she always did when she was upset. Bake, cook or craft. It's how her single mother had raised her to cope with her frustrations. To channel her energy elsewhere, use a different part of her brain, and usually while she was collaging, scrapbooking or making brownies, the solution to what was bothering her revealed itself like a white chocolate chip in a triple chocolate cookie.

She was whisking her egg whites when Rex finally stood up from the chair, the vibrator back between the tongs. "I'm assuming you don't want to keep this."

She made the same kind of face she would if he'd just shown her a dead rat. She shuddered. "Get that thing away from me. The underwear too." She really hated to throw out her fancy panty of the month panties, but she'd never be able to look at them, or herself wearing them, the same way again. Not without getting the heebie-jeebies.

No. Panties were a dime a dozen, and once she landed a job, she could treat herself to either another subscription year or go to the lingerie store in the mall and hit their five for fifteen bin.

With a single nod, he used his free hand to point at the cupboard under the sink. "Grab me a plastic bag then, will you? I'm not going to toss them, but I'll put it all away and out of your sight. Take it all to Brock's or something."

She did as he asked, turning her back on him as he dealt with her *gifts*.

"Everybody is keen to meet you tomorrow," he said, sidling up beside her where she stood at the sink. She hadn't even noticed that he'd donned latex gloves. He ditched them into the trash bin beneath the sink before plopping a kiss to her cheek. "Particularly my mother. She was giddy on the phone when I told her I was bringing a date. Plans to make an extra special cake for dessert."

That reminded her. Her mother's words about showing up to a party blared inside her head. Still whisking, because she had strong-as-steel whisking muscles, she turned to face him. "What can we bring tomorrow? I can't show up empty-handed."

He gave her a weird look. "Why not? I always do. It's my

mum's house. Which used to be *my* house until I became a man and moved out."

"Because that's what you do," she said, whisking even harder. She needed to calm down. Otherwise, her stiff peaks would bypass perfection and then she'd have over-whisked meringue and have to start all over again.

Wouldn't be the first time.

But that was just a waste of eggs.

Particularly when she knew what she was doing now and didn't need five dozen eggs to make one perfect pavlova.

"No, Rex," she said with a calmer voice. "She might be *your* mother, but she's *my* hostess, and I need to offer to bring something. Can you call her, please?"

He was still giving her a weird face but nodded and pulled his phone back out. His big thumb slid across the screen, and in seconds he was putting it to his ear. "Hey, Mum. Lydia wants to know what she can bring tomorrow night. ... Yeah, I know. I told her that. ... I told her that too. ... She says that you're the hostess and she *needs* to offer to bring something. She made me call you, so I'm calling you. What can we bring tomorrow night?" He glanced at her. "She says just ourselves."

Lydia shook her head. "No. Tell her to come up with something. Otherwise I will show up with a giant bouquet of flowers."

She would still probably make Rex stop at a grocery store on their way to his mother's so she could grab flowers, regardless of whether or not they were bringing a dish as well. It was just what you did. Particularly when you were meeting your ... boyfriend? Neighbor? Neighbor with benefits? Savior? More than just a friend? Complicated sexual partner with feelings attached? All of the above's mother.

"She says if you don't tell her that she can bring something, she'll bring you a giant bouquet of flowers," he said dryly, giving Lydia a big, exaggerated eyeroll. She stuck out her tongue at him.

Glancing down into her bowl, she lifted her whisk.

Ah. Was there anything more satisfying than perfectly stiff peaks of egg whites?

Not to her, there wasn't.

"She says you could bring bread," he finally said.

"What kind?"

His irritation was palpable and came out in a huff. "What kind of bread, Mum?" He shrugged. "Like Italian, Turkish, naan, rye. I think that's what she means. I don't know." With a grumble, he pulled the phone from his ear and hit a button on the screen. "You talk to her."

"Hello, Lydia, dear?" a gentle voice said through the speaker.

Lydia's body began to tremble. "H-hi, Mrs. Hart."

"Call me Joy, honey. Listen, you really don't have to bring anything. I do dinners like this all the time for my kids, and I never expect them to bring anything. It's what a mother does."

"Yes, ma'am, but my mother taught me to never show up to a dinner party empty-handed. Please let me bring something. It'll make meeting the whole Hart crew a little easier if I know I contributed something to the meal."

"Your mother sounds like a very lovely woman. And you know what, my mother taught me the same thing. Stacey is bringing her artichoke dip, Krista is bringing a salad, so why don't you bring a side dish for dinner? I'm making a big beef tenderloin, so perhaps a nice roasted veggie dish or something."

As soon as Joy said it, Lydia immediately knew what she would make—her mother's famous (well, famous in *their* house) roasted Brussels sprouts. She grinned at the phone and then at Rex. "That's perfect, Mrs. Hart. Thank you."

"Call me Joy, honey. And I am very excited to meet you. Rex needs to start thinking about settling down."

Rex's face paled, and he quickly hit the speaker button on the screen to turn it off. He put the phone back to his ear. "We'll see you tomorrow, Mum."

Lydia could hear Joy chuckling on the other end of the call, even with the speaker option disconnected.

Rex stowed his phone back in his pocket and joined her in the kitchen. "Ignore her. She's got grandbabies and daughter-in-law fever. She's been outnumbered for so long, she's desperate to fill the house and family with more women." He came up behind her where she was washing dishes and wrapped his arms around her waist, resting his chin on her shoulder. "How about we take a break from this, hmm?"

She dried her hand on the tea towel and turned to face him, her lips twisted into a teasing smile. "Whatever did you have in mind?"

CHAPTER 13

"THAT'S NOT TOO TIGHT, is it?" Rex asked, making sure the Velcro on the last ankle strap wasn't cutting off Lydia's circulation or digging into her soft skin.

Sprawled out naked and with nipples pointing to the ceiling, she grinned down her body at him and shook her head. "Nope. Feels just right."

She'd been all too eager for them to get naked and do dirty things to each other. And he already knew from her excitement and revelation about her own restraints that she wouldn't take his mention of them as her cue to run screaming from his apartment.

For all his *kinks* and sexual proclivities, not that he had many besides swinging, orgies and a little slap and tickle, binding a woman to his bed spread-eagle was one of his all-time favorites.

And it wasn't because Rex liked all the power and to have a woman immobile, no way. It was because he liked a woman to just lie there and let him give her all the pleasure he could. It also got him off like crazy to hear her noises and watch her squirm and pull on the bindings the closer she got to climax, or when he did something extra wicked with his tongue or fingers.

He was hard as a fucking rock, and his dick was pitching a pretty impressive tent in his gray boxer briefs. But seriously, what man wouldn't have a massive stiffy with a woman like Lydia spread out on his bed like icing on a cupcake?

The icing always had been his favorite part.

He licked it clean off before he took one bite of the cake.

And he intended to lick Lydia until she *got* off.

"You know just how to distract a girl," she said. Her tongue slid across her bottom lip, and she made no attempt to hide where her eyes were laser-focused—on his junk.

"Ah, but you're not a *girl*," he said, trailing his fingers up her shins until gooseflesh broke out along her skin. "You're all woman, and that's how I like it."

Her smile warmed him, and he put one knee on the bed, then the other, his gaze still on her as he positioned himself on his belly. The scent of her arousal made his cock jerk, and he drew in a deeper inhale. He palmed her thighs wide, not that she could move, but the gesture was enough to make her gasp and wriggle on the bed.

Pressing his nose to her mound, he gently flicked out his tongue and smiled when she jerked and her body tightened.

But she had nowhere to go. Nowhere to hide. She couldn't squeeze her thighs or touch his head. She couldn't even pull on her own nipples if she wanted to. It was all on him.

It was his job—his *pleasure* to do all the work and bring her *all* the pleasure.

"Rex," she breathed out.

His tongue flicked out again, and she spasmed again.

"Rex ..."

Arching his brows, he kept his tongue where it was but opened his eyes and glanced up her body at her face. "Hmm?"

"I ..." Her head thrashed when he wiggled his tongue. She pulled on the restraints around her wrists, and her hips twisted.

"I ..." With one finger, he teased her center. It was already slick, and his digit slid inside easily. She clenched around him. "Oh God, don't stop."

Grinning, he closed his eyes again and got down to business.

Every woman was different. You couldn't come up with *The Master Technique* and expect every woman to react the same way. Nope. You needed to treat each woman just like she was—unique. Each new partner he had was a whole new adventure. He learned her tells, her likes and dislikes. He was a fast learner, though, and even though they'd only had sex once, and she'd sat on his face, which left little in the way for true experimenting and technique testing, he already knew where to start with Lydia.

Drawing her clit into his mouth, he sucked hard.

Her hips shot off the bed.

With his free hand, he reached up her body and cupped her breast, kneaded it, played with the nipple until it was diamond-hard. Only then did he tug on it.

Her hips leapt off the bed again, and her body twisted, a groan ripping from her throat, liquid gushing from her pussy.

Her hips churned, and he took that as a sign she wanted some circles.

He was nothing if not obliging and did as he figured she wanted. Counter clockwise circles around Lydia's clit had her moaning and crooning like a cat in heat. The words *Fuck* and *Oh God* spilled from her lips repeatedly and with increasing intensity the faster his tongue went.

He pushed a second finger into her tight slit, and a *Yes* escaped her thinly parted lips on a hiss. Her hips moved, slamming down on his fingers as best as she could, her legs twitching, knees bending, heels digging into the mattress.

He switched up his hand on her breast to the other one and tugged on that tight point, which caused another sweet gush of honey to flow across his fingers.

Well, now that just made him curious.

He tugged again. She gushed again.

He switched back to the first breast, then pulled the nipple. More honey dripped out.

"What are you doing?" she asked breathily.

"Every time I pull your nipple, you get wetter," he said, barely lifting his head up enough to answer her.

"Well, yeah, because I love it."

He lifted his head a bit more and smiled at her. "Should I order you a pair of nipple clamps?"

Her eyes flared with intrigue, and she nodded.

"One with a chain connected so I can tug it and they both pull at the same time."

"Why aren't you on your phone ordering it right now?"

Fuck, he loved her cheeky side.

"Got pressing matters, baby." He pressed the two fingers inside her up against her G-spot, and she sucked air in on a gasp. "First things first."

"Mhmm ... first things first." She melted deeper into the mattress. "Proceed."

Smiling like a kid who'd just been offered a *second* cupcake loaded with icing, he dove back between her legs and waggled his tongue over her clit until her breathing became erratic.

She was close.

The continued gushes, the clenching of her pussy muscles and the way her hips just could not decide which way to move were all the signs he needed to continue with what he was doing but just ramp it all up a couple of notches.

He sucked hard on her clit once, twice, and on the third time, he pressed up hard on her secret spot, and Lydia's limbs pulled at the restraints as her torso bowed on the bed and her pussy lips and clit swelled.

"Yes!" She stilled, her back still arched, limbs tugging hard at the bonds, toes clenched, fingers in tight fists. "God."

He continued to lick, suck and press, taking every lift of her hips, every press of her mound against his face as encouragement to keep going.

Her panting and squirming, whimpers and twitches fueled his need to pull all the orgasms from her he could. All of Lydia's climaxes would be his—unless, of course, she wanted to take care of herself; then she could totally go for it—but in the short time they'd known each other, he'd come to seriously care for the quirky, cat-loving day-drinker.

"Okay ... stop," she said breathlessly. "Too sensitive."

But he didn't let up.

Nope.

If he could pull another orgasm from her, he would. Hell, if he could pull twenty more from her, keep her distracted from all the shit bothering her, then he would. To hell with dinner and whatever the fuck she was making with all that whisking. He was getting a decadent feast right between her legs.

"Rex," she said, her voice just a breath above a whisper. "Stop. It's too much."

"Push through the sensitivity, baby. Think of my tongue on your clit and how good it feels." For good measure, he did a real thorough sweep of his tongue up through her juicy folds, finishing at her clit and doing a clockwise swirl a dozen times. So far, she'd preferred counter clockwise, but he wanted to mix things up.

She twisted her hips as best she could to try to pry his mouth from her, but he latched onto her clit like a limpet. "No, seriously. Please, stop."

With one more good lick to the center of her Tootsie Pop, he lifted his head, pulled his fingers from her, licked them clean, then wiped his hand over his mouth—which he was sure was shiny judging from the way she drenched the sheet below her ass.

Nothing wrong with a big wet spot on the bed.

It meant he was doing something right.

Still glassy-eyed and rosy-cheeked, she smiled shyly at him. "Get a condom on."

"Not finished eating," he said. "Want more than one helping. I'm a growing boy, don't you know?"

Since she was naked, he was able to witness the gorgeous bloom of color across her whole body, from her chest, up her neck and into her face. Her nipples peaked, the skin around them puckering.

Her bottom lip rolled inward, and she pinned her mouth shut.

"Don't tell me Little Miss 'I have those restraints in blue' is getting all bashful now. Not after you just creamed all over my face."

She rolled her eyes, but the smile that spread across lips he still wanted to feel around his cock one day made his body grow extra warm. Fuck, she was beautiful. And not just on the outside. Lydia had a good heart, too, he could already tell.

"You can have seconds after dinner. *After* dessert. I'm making pavlova." She jerked her chin toward the nightstand, since she was unable to move any other part of her body.

"I don't know what pavlova is, but I doubt it tastes as good as you do." Even though he was teasing her, his dick was getting irritated with the delay.

Standing up off the bed, a thick string of precum connecting the tip of his cock to the sheet snapping free and staying on the bed, he slid his finger along her thigh, hips and belly. "You can be bossy. You sure you're not a closet dominatrix?"

"Not in the slightest. I just know what I want, and that's *you* inside *me*."

He chuckled. His cock twitched, and she watched him eagerly, hungrily as he opened the nightstand drawer, pulled out a condom packet, opened it and slid it on.

He gave her a bit of a show, to be honest. Gave his length a couple of thorough tugs before slowly sliding the rubber on.

She'd snagged her bottom lip between her teeth and was gnawing on it, her eyes glued to his encased cock.

"You want me to untie you?"

She shook her head. "Nope. I want you to climb *on* and slide *in* so we can both get *off.*"

"Don't have to tell me twice." With a knee in the mattress, he climbed on and over her. Like a divining rod, his cock found her slick, hot center, but he didn't rush straight in. He wanted to take his time.

Tease her.

Watch her face contort to one of pure frustration as she lay beneath him, unable to do anything but wait for him to move, but wanting, craving him to sink deeper into her heat and fill her up.

With his hands on either side of her, his face just inches above hers, his cock notched right at her juicy center, he paused. "Fuck, you're beautiful." Leaning onto an elbow, he brushed a strand of unruly hair off her forehead before leaning down and pressing his lips to where the hair had been.

She blinked up at him, her chest moving up and down rapidly with each deep breath. She swallowed, but she didn't take her eyes off him.

They both felt it.

The connection.

The chemistry.

It was fucking electric, and it had been since the moment she rounded the corner in the lobby and rushed into his arms, her face full of tears, breath laden with rum.

And then how easily they fell into domestic bliss. It should scare him how perfectly she fit into his world, into his apartment ... but it didn't.

He'd known this woman two fucking days—not even—and she'd already burrowed so deep beneath his skin, she'd hit bone.

"This thing between us," she said softly, her breath hitting his lips in warm puffs. "It's kind of wild, isn't it? How fast it's all happening. I mean ... it's nuts, right?"

It was nuts.

But nuts wasn't necessarily a bad thing.

He happened to love nuts.

Macadamia, hazel, Brazil, almond, cashew, pecan.

He loved them all.

Well, not *all*.

He wasn't a big fan of *crazy* nuts, of course.

But this wasn't crazy nuts. This was awesome nuts.

He'd never felt a connection with someone this strong, this fast, and although a part of him remained cautious, hoping to God it all wasn't too good to be true, a bigger part of him was eager to jump in headfirst and see if he and Lydia were meant to go the distance.

Leaning on both elbows now, he cupped her face in his palms and kept them there, staring down into the beautiful mottled color of her eyes. When she was aroused, her eyes were more green than golden-brown. And right now, they reminded him of cedar boughs caught in a ray of sunshine.

"It might be a little nuts," he finally said. "But I don't think that's a bad thing. This all feels right to me. Does it feel that way for you?"

She nodded, still looking up at him with so much affection, so much ... *other* emotion, his body temperature instantly went up a couple of degrees. "It feels right to me, too."

"Then I think we just let what's meant to happen, happen. No need to analyze it all to death. We enjoy being together, so let's just do what we enjoy." He did a little hip swirl, which made her lips part slightly and her breath hitch. "And right now, I think *this* is what we enjoy, no?"

She nodded. "Very much."

He slid inside with the greatest of ease, her walls tight around him, hugging every inch of his cock as he seated himself deep within her. "I really like you, Lydia," he said, once he hit the end of her and paused. "And I *really* like fucking you." He followed that cheekiness up with a big grin.

"Seriously, Rexly, put those away before I lose all my inhibitions," she said, obviously meaning his dimples.

But her sass had him smiling more.

Her hips lifted up, and he smothered a groan that burbled up from his chest. "Seriously, put them away. They're lethal. You're going to be fucking nothing more than a puddle of goo in a minute if you don't stow those babies in a case and throw away the key."

"Yeah, but it'll be a sexy puddle of goo." He tried to hide the dimples, put her at ease, but the noise she made when he rocked his pubic bone against her clit made it really fucking hard not to grin like the cocky bugger he was.

"Kiss me," she demanded. "At least then I won't be able to see them."

"Don't have to tell me twice." He dove in and took her mouth, prying her lips apart with his tongue and setting a rhythm with his hips that moved in time with the way he was kissing her. Each dip of his cock was perfectly timed with a push of his tongue.

She moved with him as best she could, grinding up into his pelvis, trying to take more of him.

She had every last inch of him—he'd hit the hilt—but she hadn't balked in the slightest. If anything, she seemed to want more.

"Harder," she whispered, breaking their kiss for a moment, allowing them both to catch their breath. "Harder. Deeper."

Levering up onto his hands again, he picked up speed and drove into her with greater intent. Her tits jiggled with every pound, and he dropped his head and took a pebbled nipple into his mouth, sucking hard enough to make her gasp.

"Harder."

Fuck him.

He needed more leverage.

With one hand holding himself up, he used the other to reach for the straps around her wrists. She glanced up and watched him, her hips still moving in time with his.

He had to pause his thrusting for a moment, as it was becoming too difficult to do two technical things at once, but once he did that, her wrist was free in seconds.

He did the same to the other wrist.

Even though he was a filthy bastard, he was also all about taking care of people. He brought each of her wrists to his lips, and he kissed the insides, massaging the red marks with his thumbs to bring back any lost circulation or take away any kind of sting.

Once she seemed to be okay, he pulled out of her for a brief moment, tugged her body down the bed, lifted her hips up with his hands under her ass cheeks, then he slid back home, both of them sighing when he hit the end of her.

"Fuck yes," she said on a hiss.

Now that he had a better angle and more freedom to manipulate and contort her body, he could go balls to the wall and hammer her until she screamed.

On his knees, with his cock deep inside her warmth, he dug his fingers into the plump flesh of her perfect ass, and he started to move—slow, deep plunges at first, followed by torturously slow withdrawals where he left nothing but the tip inside. She would growl and give him the stink-eye if he did too many hip swirls with just the tip.

That only made him grin and do it more.

She was so easy to rile.

And yet, even though he knew he was frustrating her, the twinkle of amusement never left her eyes. She was loving every minute of it all, just as much as he was.

With her hands now free, she took advantage of the position they were in and wedged her hand between them, her fingers finding her clit.

He glanced down to where her hand was and watched in fascination as she rubbed quick circles around her nub with two fingers, her teeth crushing her bottom lip and eyes dropped to half-mast.

"Yes," she breathed out. "More."

He gave her more.

He gave her everything he had.

Harder.

Faster.

Deeper.

Whatever Lydia wanted, he gave her.

Her eyes were squeezed shut now, her lips practically chewed off and her pussy so slick, he wasn't going to last much longer.

He knew she was close, too.

Or at least he fucking hoped she was.

"I'm going to ..." Her fingers were a blur now, she was rubbing them so fast over her clit.

He kept going.

Easing up his speed just a bit but making his thrusts more deliberate.

Just when he didn't think he'd be able to hold on any longer at the sight of Lydia touching herself and her perfect tits bouncing around as he hammered into her, she broke with a sharp cry. Her hand stilled, body bowed and lips parted. The crown of her head pressed hard into the mattress, and her nipples pointed directly up at the ceiling.

It was fucking magnificent to see, like a goddamn masterpiece, and he gave himself a couple of seconds to just revel in the beauty that was Lydia coming.

The squeezing and contracting of her pussy walls sent him over the edge, and even though he'd paused his movements to just watch her, his cock and balls had had enough and were taking over. Warmth pooled in his lower belly, his nuts tightened, and tingles raced up and down his spine like he'd just stuck a fork in an outlet.

With one more pull out, followed by a hard, deep thrust that had him letting go of her ass and collapsing back over her body with his hands on either side of her, he found his release.

He stilled, grunted and closed his eyes. Dropping his forehead to hers, he let the feeling wash over him. The pleasure ricocheted through his body like a wave caught between two rocks. His cock twitched with each pulse as his balls emptied.

Hopefully soon they could have the birth control and STD test talk. He was clean, and chances are she was too. Maybe in time, they could go condom-free and he could experience her without any barriers.

With the last jerk of his dick, he let out a weighty sigh through his nose, his body now relaxed and his muscles sated.

Lips brushed the tip of his nose, and he opened his eyes.

"Hi," she said, blinking up at him. Everything about her was blurry since their faces were less than two inches apart. Even blurry Lydia was fucking gorgeous.

"Hi," he said with a grin.

She smiled and kissed the tip of his nose again. It was a sweet gesture that gave him more feels that he was prepared for. He tilted his head and dropped his mouth to hers, kissing her thoroughly, then easing off. Her chest heaved, and her breath hit his lips in ragged pants.

"That was fun," she said, her nails now doing a delicate dance over his shoulders and upper back. It felt really good, and he'd probably be asking her for more of that later. Even if it didn't lead to sex, her nails on his back were fucking near orgasmic.

"It was definitely a lot of fun." He adjusted himself onto his elbow and leaned over to one side, his cock naturally slipping out of her. "How are your ankles?"

"A little tender, but it was worth it." She glanced down her body and wiggled her toes. "Still have circulation, so we're all good."

He kissed her cheek and slid off the bed, removing the condom, tying it and stowing it in a piece of Kleenex from the box on his nightstand. Then he went about releasing her bonds.

Like he had her wrists, he kissed the red spots where the restraints had rubbed, massaging the marks with his thumbs. He planted a kiss to each of her insteps and the pads of each big toe, biting the last one just enough to make her pull her foot away, gasp, then smile.

"You're one dirty bugger," she said, affection tangible in her tone.

"I think the word you're looking for is *nasty*," he corrected, tossing the dimples her way again.

"Right, right. My bad. Naked and nasty, your specialty."

He lifted a shoulder, already halfway out the door to the bathroom. "Did I get the job done?"

She was still spread-eagle and completely naked on his bed. Her eyes were beginning to close, but she nodded. "And then some. I might need a power nap."

"Go for it, baby. Just tell me what a pavlova is and how to make it and I can take over for you in the kitchen." He was in the bathroom now and getting ready to shut the door when he heard a gentle *thud* on the floor in his room and her nakedness came careening around the corner.

She pushed her way into the bathroom and made to shove him out. "Don't you dare touch my pavlova. Get out so I can pee, wash my hands and get on with my day." She shoved his shoulder again, and if he wasn't so entertained by her energy and cheekiness, he could just stand his ground and she wouldn't be able to move him an inch.

But she was being playful, and he definitely enjoyed this side of her more than the worried side of her, so he acquiesced and allowed her to shove him out of his own bathroom. She shut the door.

"What happened to you having a power nap? Did I not fuck you thoroughly enough, woman?"

"You did. Yes, very thorough. Very thorough indeed. Mind blown and all of that. Never had a lover better than you. You've ruined me for all other men." Her tone was deliberately dry, but it made prickles of unease worm through him anyway.

"You're not very convincing, you know," he called through the door. "You *say* I'm the best, but your lack of enthusiasm right now isn't making that seem true."

The toilet flushed, and the sink ran.

She opened the door a moment later and patted his cheek gently. "I'm thoroughly fucked, truly. Gonna be walking bowlegged for days. But the thought of you touching my pavlova zapped any need for a power nap."

He scoffed and stepped into the bathroom, tossing the condom and Kleenex into the garbage. "You think I'm going to ruin your pavlova? I don't even know what it is."

"Which is precisely why you're not allowed anywhere near it."

He washed his hands. "You wound me. Not only with your lack of convincing words and enthusiasm about my sexual prowess, but also your lack of belief in my cooking abilities. A lesser man than me would be hurt right now."

"Don't care, bud. You touch my pavlova, ruin my perfectly stiff peaks, and we'll have a problem." She was already back in the bedroom.

He joined her back in the bedroom, where she was nearly dressed again. He located his boxers and tugged them on. "Fine, I won't touch your stiff peaks." She was just sliding into arms into her bra straps, so he took the opportunity, approached her and slid his hands beneath the cups before she could fasten it behind her back. "What about these *stiff peaks*? Can I touch them?" He tugged on her nipples between his thumbs and forefingers, causing them to grow even harder.

She squeaked in response.

"Hmm?" he probed, giving them each a gentle little tug and twist.

Her lashes fluttered. "Well, maybe you can touch these ones."

He dropped his head to the crook of her neck and kissed her while continuing to tug on her *stiff peaks.* "Yeah?"

"Mhmm." She tilted her head to the side. "And for the record ..."

"Hmmm ..."

"I wasn't kidding. You're the best I've ever had."

He lifted his head, grinning ear to ear. "Yeah?"

Her eyes rolled, and she swatted his chest. "But the list isn't very long."

"But the question is: Have I ruined you for all other men? That's the big one."

Rolling her eyes again, she finished fastening her bra. She pulled her T-shirt over her head, and he was forced to let go over her nipples. Still just in his boxers, he followed her to the kitchen. He was like a goddamn dog with a bone with this woman.

"You gonna answer me?"

She lifted a brow. "Hmm?"

"Have I ruined you for other men?"

She pulled the bowl with the whipped egg whites out of the sink and shrugged. "Did I say that?"

"Sure fucking did."

"Hmm ... well, what we did in there is getting a little blurry. I *might* need a refresher later tonight to confirm my statement."

He came up behind her like he had earlier, a move that had instigated their hour in his bedroom with her strapped to his bed. He was already sporting a semi in his shorts. He pressed it against her lower back and looped his arms around her waist, bending his face to the crook of her neck again. This time he nipped the soft, sensitive spot where the neck meets the shoulder. "I'll refresh all night long if I have to," he murmured. "As long as it takes for you to confirm that earlier statement."

"That you've ruined me for all other men?"

"Mhmm."

She turned her head, cupped his face and pressed her lips to his. "I look forward to your efforts, then."

CHAPTER 14

IT WAS LATE SATURDAY AFTERNOON, and to say that Lydia was nervous to be in Rex's mother's driveway and preparing to go inside and meet *all* of Rex's family was probably the understatement of the century.

But she was also excited.

She'd already met Heath, and although her phone call with Joy had been brief, it was still lovely.

She knew deep down that she shouldn't have anything to worry about. But tell that to the unruly butterflies currently going ape-shit in her belly.

She held the casserole dish of her mother's delicious roasted Brussels sprouts on her lap as Rex turned off the engine. They'd left Pia at home in Rex's place, as she was fairly self-sufficient, but Diesel was in the back seat of the truck, and the moment he spotted where they were, he started to whimper and act like a puppy on crack.

"Knock it off, bud," Rex said, glancing into the back seat at the dog. "I know you love Nana, but she really doesn't like it when you jump up on her. Remember that. You're almost as big as she is." He contorted himself in his seat more and cupped both sides of Diesel's face. "And watch that tail around all the kids. Zane's getting pretty tired of you always clotheslining him." He snorted a laugh and rubbed the dog's ears before focusing his attention on Lydia. "Ready?"

She nodded, sucked in a big breath through her nose and nodded again. "Yep. Let's do this."

They unbuckled their belts, and Rex opened his door, helping Diesel out of the back seat through the extended cab suicide doors. She climbed out of the truck carefully, her purse over her shoulder, casserole dish in hand. The sprouts were roasted. They would just require a mild reheat in the oven.

A soft creak near the front of the house drew her attention, and she spotted four little faces peering out at her curiously. One of those little people was being held by a beautiful strawberry-blonde woman.

"Uncle Rex brought Diesel!" a little boy probably around four called back into the house. "And a lady!"

Diesel was on his leash, but he resembled a deer trying to leap a fence more than he did a dog with the way he was jumping and bouncing all over the place. It was a good thing Rex had him on a torso harness and not a neck collar, otherwise the poor dog would be choking himself by the way he was pulling.

Rex turned back to her for a moment. "Diesel loves the kids. That's why he's so excited."

They approached the front door, and the two older children, the little boy who was about four and a little redheaded girl who was probably around three, held their hands out for Diesel to sniff. But the dog didn't bother with such formalities. He clearly knew them, and he went right in for a big, sloppy, dog French kiss.

Both kids giggled and turned their scrunched-up faces to deflect the brunt of the dog's affections.

Another little boy, this one probably about one year old or so, got right up into Diesel's face—most likely because his face was at the same level as the dog's—and he leaned forward, mouth open, tongue out. He licked the dog's face just like Diesel had licked the other two kids.

"Zane, buddy, we don't lick the dog," Rex said, ruffling the little boy's red locks. "Just because D licks your face doesn't mean you want to be licking his."

"Given the amount of weird crap this kid licks and tries to eat, he's going to have the best damn immune system out there," said a man roughly the same size as Rex but with brown, military-short hair, coming up behind the blonde woman. "Kid was sucking on a chain-link fence at the park last week. Just stood there for like three minutes. I thought he was staring at the ducks in the pond. Didn't think he was Frenching the gate." He picked Zane up under his arms and plunked the little boy on his hip before extending a hand to Lydia. "I'm Brock."

"Shit, sorry," the blonde woman with brown eyes and a face full of freckles said, doing a big face-palm. "I'm Stacey. Sorry. Nice to meet you."

They took turns shaking Lydia's hand, which forced her to balance the casserole dish on the other one.

"We'll let you get in the house," Stacey said. "Chase, come grab the dish from Lydia."

Before she had a chance to blink, a man alarmingly similar in appearance to Rex appeared and took the casserole dish from her. He was also bald, but his eyes were a luscious green instead of blue. He also had a darkness about him that Rex didn't have. It wasn't anything specific, not a face twist or brow pinch. The man just had an aura about him, a vibe, that seemed the exact opposite to Rex, like he'd been to hell and back and he was still dealing with the aftereffects of it all. Chase disappeared into the kitchen with her casserole dish, his broad back muscles moving beneath his tight black T-shirt.

The older boy and girl were still circling her and Rex like sharks at feeding time, their eyes wide and unblinking.

"Are you a new auntie?" the little boy asked.

"This is Lydia," Rex said, tossing her a big, deep-dimple smile.

Their eyes went even wider.

"Aunt Lydia," the little girl whispered. She glanced up at Brock, who was still holding Zane. "Daddy, I have another auntie."

Whoa! Aunt Lydia.

"Do you have any pets, Aunt Lydia?" the little boy asked.

"Connor, sweetheart, let her get her shoes off. Let her get into the house before you start hammering her with questions." Stacey adjusted the baby on her hip. The little girl was probably just shy of a year. She looked a lot like her mother.

"Are they here?" a voice she vaguely recognized asked. "Is *she* here?"

Lydia could hear Joy, but she couldn't see her.

"Move, you big buffoon," Joy said, which caused Brock to step out of the way with a grunt. "Like mountains, you boys are. Nice to look at but always in the way of where you need to go."

Lydia swallowed and took in the tiny, powerful package that was Joy Hart.

The woman would be pushing the lines of honesty if she claimed she was five feet tall. But she had a presence about her that made her seem so much bigger. Her eyes were a crystal blue, and her salt and pepper hair was tucked up into a no-nonsense bun on the top of her head.

She was a striking woman and had a sharpness about her gaze that said her boys had probably gotten away with very little when they were children. Eyes in the back of her head and all of that.

The older woman's eyes lit up when she saw Lydia, and her mouth split into a big grin. She wore a frilly white apron over dark jeans and a dark blue cotton blouse. "Well, aren't you a beauty," Joy said, not stopping and offering her hand to Lydia but rather going in for the full bear hug.

Lydia hugged her back and was surprised to feel how muscular the woman was.

They broke the embrace, and Joy turned to look at Rex. "Good job. It's about time you found a woman for more than one night." She glanced back at Lydia. "Did you meet on one of those apps?"

Lydia shook her head. "Uh ... no. We're neighbors, actually. We're in the same apartment building."

Joy tossed her hands into the air. "Oh, how perfect. Such a great story to tell your children."

Rex cleared his throat. He was still wrestling with a whining and eager-to-greet-everyone Diesel. "It's early, Mum. Less grand-children talk, please. You don't want to scare Lydia away and force me to go back on those apps, do you?"

Joy's expression turned fearful. "God, no."

Laughter echoed around the small, tight foyer.

Joy shook her head and made a perturbed face. "Come on, everyone, make some room." She started shoving Brock and the small children back so that Lydia and Rex had some room. Then she turned to Diesel. "And you, my big boy. Yes, hello. Nana missed you." She took the leash from Rex. "Let's go see what we have in the kitchen for my grand-dog, hmm? I may or may not have whipped up a batch of liver treats last night."

"Not too many," Rex called after his mother. "It gives him the farts."

Joy merely waved her hand in the air to dismiss Rex's instructions.

They toed off their shoes and followed the children, Brock and Stacey into the living room.

Rex motioned for her to take a seat on the love seat, so she did, and just as he was about to sit down next to her, Connor and the little redheaded girl ducked in under his butt and stole his seat.

"Why, you little monkeys," Rex said, taking a seat anyway, but gently. The kids were beneath him and giggling and squealing up a storm as Rex pretended to squish them. He turned to Lydia. "Does this couch feel bumpy to you? Is your cushion bumpy? Mine is *definitely* bumpy. And noisy too."

"Uncle Rex, it's us!" the little girl squealed. "Don't squish us with your big butt."

If he had a hairline, Rex's brows would have reached it. "Big butt? Zoe Hart, did you just say I had a big butt?" He turned around and started to tickle both kids, which only resulted in even more giggles and squeals.

The kids were out of breath quickly, and he seemed to know exactly when to call it quits. With a glance at Lydia, Rex stood up to his full height. "Can I get you a drink?"

"I plugged the kettle in for tea just before you guys arrived," Stacey said. "Should be boiled by now."

"Tea sounds perfect," Lydia said with a nod. Rex took off into the kitchen, leaving Lydia in the living room with Brock, Stacey and the children.

"So you're a preschool teacher?" Stacey asked, gently deflecting the probing fingers of her baby as they tried to make their way up Stacey's nose. She glanced down at the baby. "Thea, no. Stay out of Mummy's nose." The little girl tugged at her mother's shirt. Stacey rolled her eyes and went about getting her breast out for the baby. She was incredibly discreet about it, not that Lydia would have cared. She had two shirts on and lifted one just enough for the baby to spot the nipple and latch on. Then once Thea was nursing, you couldn't see anything but baby head and clothes.

Brock didn't seem fazed in the least either.

"Sorry," Stacey said. "She's such a feisty little monster sometimes."

Lydia held up a hand. "No need to apologize, and yes, I am a preschool teacher. I was working at a Montessori school for a few years in Vancouver and I loved it. But then I needed a change of scenery and a fresh start, so I moved over to Victoria. I didn't realize how difficult it would be to find a job here, though. I'd rather *not* work at a day care, seeing as I have a teaching degree, a preschool teaching degree and Montessori teaching certification as well as certification and training in teaching children with special needs. A lot of schools I applied to took one look at my resume and said they couldn't afford me."

"Overqualified," Brock murmured. "Not something you hear of often. I'd figure you'd be the holy grail of teachers and everyone would be after you."

Lydia shrugged. "You'd think so. But that's not the case. Not here anyway. It might be different in September, though. If I start applying for the new school year, I might have better luck. I came over at the wrong time. Spring is not when they hire new teachers."

"Why *did* you come over this time of year then?" Stacey asked, curiosity written all over her fair, freckled complexion. "You'd have to know it would be harder to find something. I'm surprised you moved here without a guaranteed job placement."

Wow, this woman was really giving her the third degree.

But Lydia couldn't really fault her for it either. If she had children, she'd want to know everything she could about the person caring for them. And if Lydia was going to look after Stacey's children, Stacey had a right to ask all the questions of Lydia she needed to.

"I was in a relationship, and it took a really dark turn," Lydia said softly, her eyes focused on the children. "He had a head injury, and it changed him ... aggressively. Breaking up with him and moving out of the apartment we shared proved not to be enough. I needed to get away. Move to another city. I figured the island was close enough to home and my mother in Hope but far enough he wouldn't bother taking the ferry to come look for me."

Brock made a noise in his throat. The look on his face wasn't one of surprise though. She figured Rex had probably filled in his brothers on the Dierks issue.

Stacey seemed somewhat satisfied with Lydia's answer, and her expression was now closer to compassion than concern.

"I loved my job in Vancouver, and I was devastated to leave. I moved here because I found a job covering a maternity leave that started in March, with the suggestion that it could turn into something more permanent when the maternity coverage was over. It was at a daycare and a preschool and it was great ... until it wasn't and I was ..." She glanced at Connor and Zoe before turning back to Stacey. "I was let go. And I don't know why."

The front door opened with the same soft creak as before, and a stunning redheaded woman with cornflower-blue eyes poked her head around the corner. Brock still had Zane in his arms, but upon seeing the new arrival, Zane shrieked "Mama!" with excitement and pried himself out of his father's arms. Zoe was ahead of her brother and already machine-gunning her mother with questions.

"Is it cute? What is it? How big is it? Did you hold it? Can I hold it next time? Did you take them my picture?"

"Zo-zo," Brock called, his tone one hundred percent *Dad*, "Let your mother get in the door before you talk her ear off."

"You can't talk ears off, Daddy. You need to rip them off," Zoe said, giving her father a *didn't you know that?* look.

The redheaded woman, now with Zane on her hip and Zoe at her side, entered the living room and smiled at Lydia. Her cheeks were rosy and her blue eyes bright and clear. "Hi, I'm Krista, Brock's wife. You must be Lydia."

Lydia offered her a wave. "Nice to meet you."

"Sorry I'm late. I was just visiting some friends. They just had their second baby, and after a couple of weeks in the NICU, they finally brought little Caden home. He's doing awesome."

Rex entered the living room again, a coffee tray with mugs, a teapot, and cookies on a plate balanced on his two hands. "I went in to make a cup of tea for my woman, and mother put me to work bringing out beverages for all y'all." He set the tray down on the coffee table and poured a mug for Lydia and handed it her.

"Did I just hear you say *my woman?*" Krista asked, giving Rex a coy smile.

Rex shot his sister-in-law a big grin. "Yep."

Lydia's insides warmed, and it wasn't because she was cradling her tea in both hands.

"So, Lydia," Krista started, settling down on the floor on her knees and reaching for a cookie from the tray, "let's hear about your teaching and childcare stuff. I have to say, when Rex called and told us he might have a nanny for us, I nearly peed my pants with excitement."

Brock made a face. "You pee your pants when you sneeze too hard."

"And you have your melon-headed son to thank for that," Krista snapped back.

Joy, with a much calmer Diesel off-leash and right on her heels, entered the living room, and Brock was quick to stand up and offer his mother a seat. Heath was right behind her, as was Chase.

Heath gave Lydia a brief nod and smile before settling down on the couch opposite the one Lydia and Rex were on. Chase sat next to Stacey and draped his arm around her.

"Well, this is wonderful," Joy said, petting Diesel's head. The dog was sitting right beside her, and he had his head on her lap and his eyes closed. "We're all here together. And it looks like we just keep growing." She pointed at Heath. "You're next."

Heath rolled his eyes and pulled what appeared to be a sandwich wrapped in wax paper out of the pocket of his hoodie.

"How long has that been in there?" Rex asked. "You just store food all over the place for a rainy day?"

Heath took a bite and grinned. "I just made it. But I put it in my pocket until I found a place to sit. Lay off."

"All of you, behave. We have company, and the last thing we want is to turn Lydia off at her first dinner." Joy turned to Lydia. "We're actually a very nice, normal family."

"If anyone asks, that's what we tell them anyway," Heath said with a snort, still chewing.

Joy shot her youngest son a look. "Quiet, buffoon."

Heath's grin fell.

"I want to hear about her teaching experience," Krista said.

"Me too." Stacey nodded. "I'm dying to get some time away from the kids. I'd also love to pick up some shifts if I can. I've been chatting with a local dermatologist here in town, and she's looking for a nurse two or three days a week, which would be perfect."

"And James and Emma are looking for something a few days a week, too," Krista said. "It could work out really well if we came up with a schedule. I mean, I get my schedule a month in advance, and between Brock, Joy and if Lydia wants the job, I'm sure we can work out childcare."

Before she asked Krista what she did, Lydia wracked her brain. She was sure Rex had already told her what Krista did for work.

She did a mental finger snap.

That's right!

She was a cop!

See, her memory wasn't going. She wasn't losing her mind. She would remember if she'd locked her door. She would remember if she'd closed her shower curtain or taken a giant bite out of her cheese. She would remember all these things.

Just like she remembered that Brock's wife, Krista, the beautiful woman with fiery red hair sitting on the floor beside her, was a police officer.

"You're the cop!" Lydia practically shouted. "I remember!"

The room went eerily quiet, and everyone just kind of stared at her.

Fuck.

"I am ... yes," Krista finally said.

Lydia's gazed bounced from person to person in the living room, lastly landing on Rex. He too was looking at her like she was a little bit crazy. "You okay?" he asked, rubbing her back.

Double fuck.

She set her tea down on the coffee table. "Sorry, everyone, I just ... some weird stuff has been happening recently. I know you *guys* know about it all, but ... it's really making me question if I'm losing my memory or, even worse, my mind. The fact that I remember Rex telling me that you're a police officer was just a big deal to me. It's been kind of scary thinking I'm not remembering things."

"I bet," Stacey said slowly.

Triple fuck. This was not how she'd wanted this afternoon and first meeting with Rex's family to go. They all probably thought she was straight-up Looney Tunes and wouldn't leave their children with her if their only other alternative was the devil himself.

"You're not losing your memory or your mind," Rex said, continuing to rub her back. "I keep telling you we'll get to the bottom of this."

But the looks on the faces in that room weren't nearly as convinced as Rex. In fact, his tone held a level of skepticism too.

Quadruple fuck.

Squeezing her eyes shut for a moment, she shook her head, blinked a few times and reached into her purse, which was on the floor between the love seat and Krista. She pulled out two manila envelopes and handed one to Krista and one to Stacey before standing up. "My resume. With references. I'm really sorry. I just ... there's a lot going on right now, and maybe today wasn't such a good idea." She glanced at Rex, the butterflies in her belly going ape-shit times ten. "I think I'll just call a cab and head home. Let you have your dinner with your family."

Rex shook his head, confusion filling the deep blue of his eyes. He reached for her. "What? No!"

She dodged Rex's hand, stepped around Krista and through the tangle of legs and little kid bodies until she stood next to the wall that divided the foyer and living room. "It was nice meeting you all." She ducked behind the wall to put on her shoes.

"Oh no, you don't, young lady. Get back here," Joy said, her voice drawing nearer until she stood in front of Lydia as she was pulling her ankle boots back on. "In the kitchen, now." She pointed in the direction she expected Lydia to go, and like the obedient, people-pleaser that she was, Lydia obeyed.

Everyone in the living room was quiet and statue-still.

Except for Heath. "Watch your back, Lydia. This one likes to throw her slippers at you if she's mad. I still have the scars to prove it."

CHAPTER 15

SHE COULDN'T BELIEVE the last time she'd been "told" to do something by a mother, even her own mother. Although Lydia and her mom were close and spoke weekly, since it had just been the two of them for most of Lydia's life, and Lydia's mom worked so much, Lydia and her mother's relationship became one more of friendship than mother-daughter.

She couldn't remember the last time her mother had scolded her or had to pull the Mom Card, as she called it. Lydia had always toed the line and done what was expected of her. She helped out at home, got good grades, showed respect to adults and her peers, had an after-school job to save up for school. She was a good kid.

To say that her body was currently the temperature of an icicle and her heart rate was beating at hamster speed would be a big ol' understatement.

She entered the kitchen ahead of Joy and stopped by the small breakfast nook. There was a bigger dining room table between the living room and kitchen where she figured they would all eat dinner tonight.

She turned around and watched Joy close the pocket door, then lock it.

From icicle to magma, her temperature spiked, and she resisted the urge to pull at her shirt to see if she had boob sweat forming under her bra.

"What was that?" Joy asked, her voice soft and gentle, like how one would normally speak to a child. She pointed to the bench seat in the nook. "Sit."

Lydia sat.

Joy sat across from her. "Now spill."

Lydia spilled.

All of it.

Dierks, Odette, being fired, the weird things going on in her house, the sex toy in the box with her underwear. She spared no detail, and by the end, she half expected Joy to stand up and tell her not to bring her drama into the Hart family based on the older woman's expression.

But Joy didn't say or do either of those things.

She did stand up, however, and came around to Lydia's side of the table, sat next to her and pulled Lydia in for another hug. "That's a lot. I'm sorry you're having to deal with all of that. It's not fair."

Joy's arms around her instigated a flow of tears she hadn't been prepared for. Sadness and pain, fatigue and hopelessness all bubbled to the forefront, spilling out as big fat tears and sobs that wracked her entire body. She clung to the older woman and sobbed, taking comfort in Joy's strong presence, her kind and gentle touch.

Joy did nothing but hold her, rub her back and make small, reassuring noises that actually helped ease the ache inside of Lydia.

When the sobs ebbed and she felt like was empty of tears, she pulled away from Joy and wiped the back of her wrist beneath her nose. Joy reached for a Kleenex off the window ledge and handed it to her.

Blotting her eyes, Lydia sniffled a few times before saying thank you.

"No thanks necessary, honey. You obviously needed a good cry. And from what you told me, it sounds like you've needed one for a while. That's a lot to take on all by yourself. Where are your parents?"

Her exhale rattled from her chest. "My dad passed away when I was eight. He was a high school chemistry teacher, and he had a brain aneurysm while teaching one day and just dropped dead to the floor. I was raised by my mum."

Joy's hand covered her mouth, and her head shook. "Oh, honey, I'm so sorry. My boys lost their father too. Not a day goes by I don't miss my Zane."

Not a day went by where Lydia's mother didn't miss Lydia's father either. She knew that. Even though her mother had tried dating—and picked some real asshole, creeper duds from time to time—she'd never had a serious boyfriend. Not that Lydia was aware of, anyway.

"My mum says I take after my dad a lot in my zest for knowledge and wanting to help people and work with children. He was always about shaping and encouraging the minds of tomorrow, building a better future, and I believe in that, too."

"And where does your mum live, sweetheart?"

"In Hope. She's a receptionist for an insurance adjuster. She's been doing it for over twenty years. She loves it. Has full benefits, a full pension, eight weeks of vacation a year. She has another five or six years to go before she says she'll retire, then she wants to move closer to me. Figures she'll have grandbabies to help babysit by then." She made a noise of disbelief in her throat. "But that won't be happening if I can't get a job to support those hypothetical babies. And it *definitely* won't be happening if someone is stalking me. And it definitely *definitely* won't be happening if I'm losing my damn mind.'"

"Which you're not, so just end that vein right here and now," Joy replied. "You say Rex is taking care of you. Well, I couldn't imagine a better man for the job. He and the rest of his brothers will get to the bottom of this. They'll find out who is tormenting you, and they will put a stop to it. In the meantime, I think you would be a wonderful person to help look after Zoe, Zane, Connor and Thea. And the Shaw twins—Grace and Claire—are lovely little darlings too."

"You don't think my behavior just now scared the crap out of everyone? That Krista and Stacey aren't thinking I'm some lunatic?"

Joy's brows furrowed. "I think you're building up your little outburst more than the rest of us. You exclaimed Krista was a cop. It's not like you outed her while she was undercover or something. Your enthusiasm was a little unexpected, but I think a lot of it is all in your head. You're worried you're going to appear crazy to everyone—which is exactly what whoever is tormenting you is trying to do. Don't let them win. I don't think you're crazy, and I'm a therapist, so I can legally and legitimately label you as crazy if I wanted to." Her smile was lopsided, but the twinkle in her eye had Lydia grinning.

"Thank you, Joy. I needed this. But now I have to go back in there and face all those people who saw me act like an idiot and then get scolded like a child."

Joy rolled her eyes. "And you don't think I've done the exact same thing to each and every one of them at some point? You're all still children who need a little dose of reality once in a while. Just last week, I had to throw my slipper at Rex and Heath because they started wrestling on the couch and nearly knocked their full beer mugs onto the floor. Bunch of big, burly buffoons with more muscles than brains sometimes, I swear it." She rubbed

Lydia's arm. "Don't sweat it, honey. Just go in there, apologize and move on. But I won't let you leave. You've been invited for dinner, and barring a case of explosive diarrhea—which you will never get from any of *my* food—or tea with the Queen, you're not leaving."

Snorting a laugh, Lydia took Joy's hand and squeezed it. "Thank you."

Joy squeezed her hand in return and smiled before scooting off the bench and pulling Lydia with her. "Now I see you've brought Brussels sprouts. Delicious. Do they just need to be reheated or ...?"

"Just fifteen minutes at three-fifty should do the trick," Lydia said, her breath still stuttering slightly on big inhales. But her shoulders seemed lighter and less bogged down, as did her heart. It felt good to let it all out, tell someone else her problems and let the tears purge her soul.

Joy was right. Sometimes you really did just need a good cry to feel better about things, and although nothing in her life was *solved* after crying, she did feel better about tackling it all.

"Ready to go back out there?" Joy asked, her fingers poised to unlock the door. "Or do you need a few more minutes?"

She blotted her eyes with the crumpled Kleenex one more time, drew in a big breath and nodded. "Let's do this."

"That's a girl," Joy said with a nod. She opened the door and waited for Lydia to step through first.

"I'm sorry I reacted that way, guys," she said, standing in front of a room of four bigger-than-life men, two beautiful women and four wild-eyed, confused children. "A lot going on right now."

Krista was the first to stand up. She went to Lydia and wrapped her arms around her. "Rex has filled us in. No need to apologize, and I honestly didn't think anything of your announcement about me being a cop. It's not exactly something I keep a secret." Her mouth fell next to Lydia's ear. "Let me know what I can do to help. This is some shady shit going down."

Lydia pulled away, her brows knitted. "But Rex said the cops wouldn't be able to do anything about it."

Krista rolled her eyes. "These four like to go rogue. It takes a lot of effort on my part to keep them following the law and even then ... but if you got a sex toy in the mail, that's some seriously freaky shit. You need to report it."

Lydia nodded. As much as she trusted Rex and his brothers, the idea of getting the police involved made her feel a lot better.

Rex's doppelganger cleared his throat. "Print analysis of everything came back."

Krista and Lydia both drew in a breath and stared at Chase, waiting.

Chase's expression grew uncomfortable, and it seemed like he was deliberately avoiding making eye contact with Lydia.

Uh-oh.

Quintuple fuck?

"Only prints that came up were yours and Lydia's, bro. I ran them all three times. And nothing came back on the *toy* or the box. Not one print besides Rex's. Not even the mail carrier's. Which is bizarre, but then a lot of them wear gloves."

A crater-sized pit opened up inside her stomach.

No prints.

None.

Skip the sextuple and septuple fucks. This went straight to a category octuple fuck, for sure.

"Not to worry," Rex said, his confidence in all of this visibly crumbling. "We'll figure it out. You can stay with me for as long as you need."

As lovely as that sentiment was, she had a place of her own— her home—and she wanted to stay there. Whoever was tormenting her couldn't win. He or she couldn't drive Lydia from her home. She wouldn't let them.

"Actually, bro," Brock said, his hesitation making the whole room seem to hold its collective breath. "Need you in Vancouver for a week or more starting Monday. Got a job."

"Can't Heath or Chase do it?" Rex asked, almost seeming angry. "Or you?"

Brock cleared his throat, and his face, hell, his whole demeanor, went stormy. "Not up to you. It's an order. Heath's headed down to Seattle for a job, and Chase isn't ready for field work yet. And I'm coming with you. It's a two-man job in Van."

His gaze swiveled to Lydia.

"I'll keep an eye on her," Krista said. "Can set up routine wellness checks and have cops cruising by the apartment building."

"Plus, I'll be around if things get dicey," Chase spoke up.

Stacey's face paled, as did Joy's.

What happened to Chase that he wasn't able to do field work? Was it something recent?

Stacey turned to Chase, gripped the front of his shirt and murmured something to him. He murmured something back, cupped her face with his hand and kissed her gently on the mouth before moving his head and kissing a sleeping Thea on the top of her head.

"Can Lydia maybe stay with you while I'm gone, Mum?" Rex asked, glancing at his mother. "It'll only be for a few days."

"At least a week," Brock corrected.

"And no," Lydia interjected. "I have a home, and I'm a big girl. I can't let whoever is doing this to me win. I need to be able to stay in my own apartment." She pinned her gaze on Rex. "I'm staying there tonight. Whether you're with me or not."

Brows shot up around the room.

"Another ball-breaker," Heath said, only half under his breath. "Guess it's up to me to find the mousy sister to bring into the family."

"Ha!" Joy laughed. "No, son, you need someone to put you in your place. But at this point, I'll take a mouse over a ghost or one of those soccer moms I hear mutterings about. Settle down already."

Heath's blue eyes went wide. "Who told you about the soccer moms?"

"I know everything. I keep telling you buffoons that." Joy's eyes rolled, and she glanced at Krista, Stacey and finally Lydia, appealing to them for understanding. "Right? Mothers know everything."

Heath managed to look a little chastised and pulled at the collar of his painted-on white T-shirt. "Awkward," he said, making an exaggerated frown.

"I'll be okay," Lydia said, ignoring the rest of the people in the room and focusing on Rex. "Leave Diesel with me for protection."

That seemed to mollify him a bit.

At the mention of his name, Diesel pried his muscular frame off the floor from where he'd been snoring on Rex's feet and came over to stand beside Lydia. "See, he's all ready to play guard dog. Aren't you, buddy?"

Diesel's tongue fell to the side of his mouth, and he panted, gazing up at her with big, soulful eyes and a smile.

Joy clapped her hands once. "Then it's settled. Now then, you boys can go and get to that list of yard work on the fridge."

All four men groaned.

"Do you want dinner?" Joy asked, her hands on her hips, watching her grown sons moan and complain about chores while standing up, joints cracking and popping.

Stacey stood up as well and quietly carried Thea down the hall. Krista scooped up a tired-looking Zane, who seemed ready to pass out where he sat quietly looking through a picture book. She followed Stacey down the hall but veered right rather than left.

Connor and Zoe were quietly playing blocks in the corner.

Rex came up to Lydia and took her hands. "I'm sorry. I really don't want to leave you."

She shook her head, dismissing his apology. "It's your job, plus, I can take care of myself. And if I can't, I have Diesel." She patted the dog's head. "Right, buddy?" Now she was damn sure the dog nodded.

Rex's face bunched into one of frustration and reluctance. "I know you can, but since that sicko sent you that sex toy, things are getting more serious."

"And Krista said I should report it, which is what I figured we needed to do in the first place."

Krista was walking back down the hallway toward them, child-less, a childless Stacey right behind her.

Krista stopped in front of them. "I agree with Rex's first statement, that the smaller things like an unlocked door and open underwear drawer wouldn't bring out an officer to your house, possibly not even the peeled bananas or bitten cheese—as weird and disturbing as it all is—but the mail is a whole other story. I'm not working tomorrow, and I'm also part of the WestShore precinct, so you may need to go to the Victoria PD or possibly Saanich PD depending where you live, but I can go with you either way if you'd like."

These people really were the salt of the earth and incredibly understanding. Even after her bizarre outburst and embarrassing attempt to flee, they still wanted to help her.

"Thank you," Lydia said. "I appreciate that."

"I took a look at your resume," Stacey added. "Sent snapshots of it to James and Emma, and they're really interested. I'm interested, too."

"Me too." Krista nodded.

"You mean, you're not scared off?"

She thought for sure Krista and Stacey would have figured out some kind and diplomatic way to say they no longer needed child-care but hoped Lydia got the help she needed. Or some other gentle canned response.

Both women shook their heads.

"No. And definitely not now that we know the whole story. Rex filled us in when you were talking to Joy. We hope you don't mind." Krista caught her husband's eye, lifted her brows and tilted her face. Brock stepped toward her and planted a kiss on her cheek. "You boys do right by your mama," she teased. "Clean those gutters and scrub that siding."

More groans drifted up from the foyer, where all four of them were currently getting their jackets and shoes on.

Stacey offered her a smile and squeezed her shoulder affectionately before heading into the kitchen where Joy was.

Krista lingered for a moment. "Just relax, okay? We'll get it all figured out. In the meantime, sit with the kids, have some tea and just chill."

"We're chilling," Zoe said. "You want to come chill with us, Aunt Lydia?"

Krista snorted a laugh. "That's a good girl inviting someone to come play with you, sweetheart. Very kind."

Zoe beamed.

"Yeah, we just chilling and making a block tower," Connor added. "You any good at towers?"

Krista smiled again, then retreated to the kitchen.

"Actually," Lydia started, grabbing her tea from the coffee table, then joining the kids on the floor, sitting cross-legged. "I've been told I'm *very* good at making towers."

Connor and Zoe both grinned, their eyes going wide.

Lydia let out a much-needed sigh and finally sipped her tea. It was lukewarm now, but she didn't care. She was in her happy place. With kids. With the future.

And judging by the two little humans in front of her, the future looked mighty bright.

The jury was still out on her own future though. It had dark, thick clouds looming over it no matter which direction she turned.

CHAPTER 16

LYDIA'S TOES CURLED, her pussy pulsed and her clit throbbed as the orgasm ricocheted through her. Rex's big palm that was kneading her breast loosened its grip, and he pinched her nipple.

Her gasp was fleeting, morphing into a moan that rumbled around in her chest as everything inside her hummed like a beehive.

His lips fell to her neck, replaced by teeth that scraped and nibbled, intensifying an already intense orgasm. His panting and grunting behind her said he was coming too. But now that they weren't using protection, she'd have known he was filling her up even if he'd been quiet.

She'd been asleep.

In her own bed, too, when a big, bare, muscular arm snaked around her torso, pulled her backward and against a boa constrictor made of pure steel.

They'd had the birth control chat on their way home from dinner at Joy's, and since Lydia had an IUD in and they were both clean, they practically raced upstairs from his truck to her apartment, engaging in serious restraint not peeling each other's clothes off in the building hallway.

Poor Diesel wasn't sure what to think, though, and kept trying to push his way into the action, jumping up at them and barking in excitement.

Eventually, he found Pia, and the two curled up on the couch and fell asleep, which gave Rex and Lydia an opportunity to sneak into her bedroom, close the door, undress each other completely and use her "blue" restraints.

After he'd sufficiently restrained her, he made her wait, naked and wanton on her bed, as he scoped out her apartment for anything nefarious.

Then he returned to her, still naked and still very hard. He slid between her thighs, condom-free, and made her forget anything and everything in her world besides the man inside her, on top of her and consuming her.

She took him in her mouth when he was able to get it up again, enjoying the heavy pants and manly groans that rumbled through him as she tugged hard on his balls and deep throated him as he came down her throat.

Then they lay in bed laughing and talking until well past midnight, cuddled up naked beneath the covers, touching and caressing until he rolled on top of her once more, brought her to climax and she fell asleep in his arms.

Her sleep had been blissful. Dreamless and deep.

No nightmares of weirdos in dark hoods creeping into her apartment or going through her cupboards and drawers.

An iron bar pressed into her back and a growling bear started to nip at her shoulder blades. She didn't even bother resisting, because that would have been a lie. Rather, she pressed her butt against him and let him slide inside from behind.

"Mmm," he hummed, tracing the shell of her ear with his tongue, "nothing like spoon sex in the morning."

"Agreed." She pointed her toes and stretched, enjoying the dull ache in her muscles from their marathon sexcapades last night.

He slipped out of her and rolled over to the other side of the bed, standing up and heading to the bathroom.

She stayed on her side, shut her eyes and waited for him to return, allowing her mind to drift back to just moments ago when Rex was inside her and the world made complete sense.

The toilet flushed, the sink ran and his naked gorgeousness appeared around the bedroom corner a second later.

They didn't say anything, just smiled like idiots at each other. She waddled to the bathroom and sat down to pee.

She forgot about the one real downside, besides getting pregnant when you don't want to, to going condom-free—the mess!

Ugh.

Oh well, whatever, it was totally worth it.

She did what she needed to do, washed her hands and rejoined him in the bedroom. He had jeans on but nothing else.

It was a *goooood* look for him.

"I'm going to make a motion that you're not allowed to wear a shirt ever again," she said, opening her dresser drawer and pulling out a sports bra.

"Motion denied. Maybe if we lived somewhere like Tahiti or Ecuador, but it's too cold here half the year." He rubbed his chest. "My man nips would fall off."

She snorted a laugh. "Your *man nips?*"

She went to reach for her underwear off the floor to toss them into the laundry hamper, but he was faster than her and snatched them first.

"Mine," he said.

She gave him a weird look. "Not my jam, there, Rexington. Seeing a dude in women's panties. If that's what you want to do on your own time, cool, but that's not what gets my engine revving, and I'd prefer if you bought your own."

His eyes rolled. "I don't want to wear them."

"Then why do you want them?"

"I'm going to be gone for a bit, and I want to keep a part of you … I want to be able to smell you whenever I feel like it."

"Eww. No!" She wrinkled her nose and went to take them back, but being well over six feet tall, he didn't even have to hold them very high over his head to keep her from getting at them.

"Mine now, baby. Anytime I want to get a whiff of that sweet pussy, all I have to do is …" He put her underwear to his nose and took a big inhale. "Ahhh."

"You're sick," she said, giving up the fight and grabbing a new pair from her dresser drawer and pulling them up her thighs. "A big ol' pervert."

Before she could blink, Lydia was bent over at the waist, her hands on the bed and her legs being forcibly shoved apart. "And you fucking love it!" he growled, dropping to his knees and ramming his tongue inside of her, where just moments ago he'd come.

She tried to wriggle away, but his hands kept her in place. "You just came inside me."

"So? Then you went pee, washed yourself and now you're clean. Besides, you *swallow* my cum …"

It's true. She had. And would again. He liked it when she gave him head last night, and she'd enjoyed giving it to him. His moans of pleasure were like primitive words of encouragement in her ears.

A painful but oh so wonderful little nip was delivered to her inner thigh, his way of telling her to shut up and enjoy. She heard him inhale through his nose while his tongue jammed in and out of her like a velvety cock.

"Mmmm," he hummed. "I'm going to miss this smell."

Dear God, the man was talented with his tongue.

He was talented with his cock and fingers too, and before she knew it, she was convulsing on the bed as his index finger waggled over her clit and his tongue fucked her center thoroughly. She was helpless to his ministrations. There wasn't a damn thing she could do but let him take her to Orgasm Town and enjoy the ride.

Not that she had any plans to open the car while moving and tuck and roll. Oh hell, no. The journey itself was beautiful.

Her toes curled on the carpet, and her fingers bunched in the unmade bed. Everything tingled, and the way he was twiddling her clit, she thought she was going to pass out from the intense pleasure.

The explosion was powerful, and for a moment, she thought she saw God—although he was far away and blurry, so maybe it wasn't him, or her—but either way, she had a brief out-of-body, spiritual experience when Rex's tongue, ramrod straight and so fucking slippery, pistoned in and out of her pussy.

By the time she regained her faculties and opened her eyes, she was ready for a damn nap. And here she'd been planning to go for a nice, long run.

He stood up from the floor and smacked her ass for good measure. "I'm keeping the panties."

With Jell-O for legs, she stood up straight, her thighs slick, pussy still throbbing.

Rex was all grins. And with a still shiny face and dimples that were filled up with her glossy arousal, he leaned in and planted a big wet kiss on her mouth. "Diesel and I will be right back. I'm just going to go grab my running clothes and feed the beast, then we'll meet you in the lobby."

She was still coming down from that orgasm, but she nodded. "O-okay."

He put her panties back to his nose, closed his eyes and inhaled deep. "Mmm, Eau de Lydia, the perfect scent."

Her eyes could not roll any harder if she tried. She picked up a pillow and tossed it at him. "Get out of here, you pervert."

His brows waggled on his forehead. "Shower sex after our run?"

Her clit and vagina made her mouth respond before her brain even had a chance to comprehend the question. "Need you even ask?"

————

IT WAS TUESDAY AFTERNOON, and Rex had been gone a little over twenty-four hours. He'd texted and called a few times to check up on her, then they did some super steamy phone sex as they went to bed Monday night. The man definitely knew how to talk dirty, and in no time, Lydia was coming, her fingers working hard between her legs as Rex made guttural noises and grunts on the other end.

He'd messaged her Tuesday morning to check in, nothing too clingy or smothering. Just a quick *Hope you have a good day. Stay out of trouble. Xoxo.*

Her body temperature would increase, her panties would get damp and her face would hurt from how hard she was smiling. Over the course of the day, she'd bring up his message again and re-read it.

Diesel and Pia were still getting along swimmingly, and she'd met with James and Emma Shaw and their twins Monday afternoon. They were excited to have her come over Wednesday and stay with the twins for a couple of hours to test things out. Emma was particularly excited, since she seemed frazzled and exhausted chasing after two precocious little girls all day.

Jayne had also texted and called a few times, along with Krista, Stacey and Chase. It seemed everyone was looking out for her but at the same time respecting her space.

Before he left Monday morning, Rex accompanied her down to the police station, where they filed the report about the weird mail and left the mail with the police for evidence. Once she gave her statement, including all the other weird occurrences, she was told that a cop would be in touch with her.

She wasn't overly hopeful that something could come of it, since there were no fingerprints, but at least now the authorities were aware of the situation.

She'd just finished lunch, and even though Diesel was contentedly sleeping on the couch wrapped around Pia, she knew the dog needed to get out for a long walk.

Just as she was getting on her lightweight, white puffy vest, her phone started to vibrate in the back pocket of her jeans.

It wasn't a number she recognized, and the ID came up *Private*.

Her blood turned frigid as she stared at the screen, contemplating whether to answer it or not.

Not a lot of people called nowadays. Most people texted.

So now, any unknown phone call made her instantly skeptical.

Should she let it go to voicemail?

It was probably just some scammer anyway, telling her she was in some kind of violation and if she didn't give her social insurance number over the phone right away, the cops would come pounding on her door and carry her away in chains.

But what if it was a cop? What if they'd miraculously found the person who was taunting her and had them in custody and were gearing up to throw the book at them? They just wanted to give Lydia a heads-up that she could now breathe easy.

She hit the green button on her phone and put it to her ear. "Hello?"

"Lydia, sweetheart? It's Joy."

She let out a sigh of relief, but there was also a mild touch of disappointment there too that it wasn't the police telling her they'd caught the weirdo cheese-biter.

"Hi, Joy."

"I hope you don't mind that I got your number from Rex. I

wanted to see if you'd like to go for a walk. It's such a beautiful day, we could go and walk up Mount Doug if you're interested."

She loved Mount Doug. The three-hundred-and-sixty-degree view of the city, peninsula and ocean, the criss-crossing trails around the whole mountain. What wasn't there to love? She'd just been planning to take Diesel for an extended walk around the block or to the off-leash park, but a rigorous hike up Mount Doug sounded far more enticing.

"I'd love to."

"Perfect. How about I come grab you and Diesel in fifteen minutes? I'm just finishing up at the dentist. I can meet you in the parking lot at twelve thirty."

"We'll be ready."

They said goodbye and disconnected the call.

It was incredible how easily—and quickly—she'd been welcomed into the Hart family fold. She hadn't even known Rex for a week and yet his mother was already calling her up to get together.

Was this normal?

Was this what a real adult relationship was like, and she'd just been goofing around in adolescent affairs until now?

Or was Joy keeping an eye on her for other reasons? Was she concerned for her son? Did she think Rex was hooking up with some crazy woman and she wanted to take Rex being on the mainland as an opportunity to better vet Lydia?

Was this walk such a good idea after all?

She stood in her kitchen staring at her phone, debating whether to call Joy back and cancel or just suck it up and deal with the walk, whatever might happen on it, when it started to ring and vibrate in her palm.

She jumped in surprise, nearly dropping her phone.

Blocked number this time.

Cops?

Rex from a burner phone?

A scammer wanting all her money?

She hit the green button on the screen and put the phone to her ear. "Hello?"

Silence.

"Hello?"

More silence.

"Who's there?"

Dead quiet.

She was about to hang up and chalk it up to some weird pocket dial or a wrong number when she heard a deep inhale on the other line, followed by the sound of distant traffic.

"All right, what the hell is this? Are you the person who has been trying to drive me crazy? Did you break into my house? Send me a fucking sex toy? What the hell is wrong with you, dude? Leave me the fuck alone! Get a life!"

Click.

The line went dead.

She hung up. Her hands shook so badly, she needed to put the phone down on her island. Her heart hammered in her chest, and her pulse filled her ears.

That had to be whoever was tormenting her. Only tormenters, only sickos did the call and deep breathing, right? That was their MO.

Her vision was blurry, and she swayed where she stood. Diesel was suddenly beside her, whimpering and hitting her thigh with one paw.

What the hell was going on?

Who was doing this to her?

Why were they doing this to her?

Who had she hurt? Who had she rebuffed or angered enough that they would break into her house, send her creepy mail and call her but not say anything?

Diesel's whimpering grew louder, and he nudged her wrist with his nose before licking the back of her hand.

That was enough to snap her out of her weird haze, and she blinked a few times, her senses refocusing, synapses reconnecting.

She rubbed the dog's head. "Thanks, buddy."

Slowly, leaving her phone on the island, she went to sit on the couch. Diesel followed her, keeping in step and gazing up at her with those soft brown eyes full of worry. "I'm okay," she said to him when he rested his chin on her thigh. "I'm okay."

He started to whimper again and sat down at her feet, his head still resting in her lap, tail swishing softly on the carpet.

Who was doing this to her?

Was it Dierks?

She couldn't think of another soul who would want to cause her any kind of torment. She wasn't the type of person to make enemies. And she didn't think she knew enough people in Victoria to earn a stalker.

Pia stretched from her spot on the couch and gracefully stepped into Lydia's lap. Both animals seemed to know she needed the comfort right now.

Animals really were the best companions and form of therapy out there.

She closed her eyes for a moment and petted her cat, allowing Pia's purrs and warmth to soothe her. To absorb the tremors of worry that raced through her and ease her wildly beating heart.

By the time she opened her eyes, things were better.

Not great.

Not fixed.

But better.

She could breathe without the feeling of a hippo on her chest. The twisted sensation in her gut was still there but not as tight.

The ornate wrought-iron clock she had on her mantel said it was almost twelve thirty. Joy would be waiting for her.

They needed to get a move on.

Careful not to jostle Pia too much, she pried herself off the couch, grabbed her phone from the island and strapped Diesel into his harness. Then, just like Rex had advised her, she videotaped herself locking her front door.

Though if the perp really wanted to get to her, they wouldn't let a flimsy deadbolt stop them.

The question was: What was their end game? Was their goal just to harass her? Drive her crazy? Or should she start looking over her shoulder and wear a Kevlar vest while out buying groceries? Was her life in danger? Did someone want her dead?

Okay, that was more than one question, but the fact that she had so many and didn't have an answer for any of them only made her worry all the more.

What if someone *did* want her dead?

Should she move?

Would they just follow her?

More questions.

So many questions.

Should she call Dierks and ask if it was him who'd been harassing her? Sic the cops on him?

But if it wasn't, then he might just start worrying about her and try to find her anyway. He hadn't been a bad boyfriend or a bad person, but after his brain injury, he definitely needed help.

She didn't think he would be the type to come after her and start stalking her, but then again, you really don't know people as well as you think you do. And even when you do ... they often surprise you, and not necessarily in the jumping out of a cake or proposing on top of the Eiffel Tower kind of surprise.

Now she was wondering how well she knew Rex.

All of this started happening after she met him.

Was there a connection?

Did he have an ex who wanted her out of the way?

Was Rex who he claimed to be? Who his family knew him to be?

Did he have a darker side to him? One where he got off secretly taunting and harassing a woman while simultaneously playing her hero?

Seemed like a far-fetched possibility but not a completely impossible one.

She'd been duped by nice guys before. So had her mother, and that duping could have ended very differently, very badly if her neighbor hadn't come knocking at just the right time.

There wasn't a breath of a breeze in the freshly blooming leaves on the trees as she stepped out of her apartment building, and yet the hair on the back of her neck stood straight up, and she hugged her arms around her body like an icy northeaster had just swept across her skin.

That was the first time she'd thought about Lyle in years. She'd effectively blocked out the memory of him, but now that weird shit was happening ... the man *was* a locksmith, after all. It would explain how someone got into her apartment so easily.

But he was also back in Hope, right? How on earth would he know she was in Victoria? Especially since she'd been living in Vancouver for the past eight years up until two months ago. And why, eighteen years later, would he start bothering her now? After Mr. O'Flanagan put the fear of God in Lyle, she and her mother hadn't seen or heard from him again.

Good riddance, of course.

But still ...

A white Toyota Corolla pulled into the apartment complex parking lot, and the lights flashed. It had to be Joy.

The fact that all four of her sons had big, black, beefy Chevy pickups and little Joy had a small, white compact sedan was a hilarity not lost on Lydia, even given her mental anguish. She wouldn't put it past the sprightly woman to have bought the car on the premise of it being the antithesis to her son's vehicles. Possibly just to spite them or needle them in some way.

Joy was barely visible behind the steering wheel, but she managed to stop right in front of Lydia and Diesel. When Diesel saw his nana, he started to bark in greeting.

Joy rolled her window down. "I laid the dog cover in the back seat. He knows what to do."

Still shaken by the sudden thoughts of Lyle Whigby, particularly after all these years of repressed memories and blissful ignorance, she opened up the rear door and Diesel hopped right in. He instantly lay down on the back seat, his tongue lolling out of his mouth as he smiled wide.

Shutting the back door, Lydia moved around to the front passenger door and opened it, sliding into the seat and buckling up. She barely gave Joy a smile and hello.

Joy put the car in gear and backed out of the lot. "I'll give you a minute to collect whatever thoughts are currently causing you to have the Grand Canyon between your brows, but then you're going to spill."

Diesel barked.

Joy hooked her thumb over her slender shoulder, but her blue eyes twinkled and were laser-focused on Lydia. "See, even he agrees."

CHAPTER 17

REX HATED that he'd been away from her for so long, particularly after that weird phone call she'd received on Tuesday, but Brock needed him in Vancouver, so he had to finish the job.

It was now the following fucking Tuesday, and finally, at long last, the job was done. They were in charge of transporting and guarding an FBI informant. He and his family were being moved to Canada temporarily until some of the heat surrounding them died down, then they'd be moved up to Alaska and put into witness protection.

It was his and Brock's job to fly down to LA, pick up the informant and fly back with him, all the while making sure he didn't die.

Another team was in charge of bringing his family to Vancouver.

All in all, it had been a pretty uneventful job. The informant was a nice guy and complied with everything Brock and Rex told him to do.

So once they got to the safe house in Maple Ridge, it was just a sit and wait game until his family was brought to him.

Rex had talked with Lydia every night and sometimes during the day, too.

Nothing else had happened to her since the phone call, and although she was still shaken about it, she seemed to be in better spirits, particularly since she'd started working for James and Emma watching their twins, and she'd also looked after Zoe and Zane while Krista was on some day shifts.

Either way, he was eager to get back to her. Their relationship had started unconventionally and been whirlwind ever since.

He liked her.

Actually, he *really* liked her, and just because things between them were new didn't mean they weren't intense.

She'd also proven just how dirty she could be during their late-night call last night. The sound of her coming over the phone, knowing her fingers were inside her slick, warm pussy, had made him so fucking hard. He'd needed half a dozen Kleenex to clean up his load once he was done.

After they ended their call and he had a shower to get the sticky cum off his belly, he started to do a bit of hunting.

They had a lot of downtime on this job, so he'd already done the majority of his searching, but he hadn't gotten an address yet.

By the time he went to sleep, he had an address, a phone number and half a dozen pictures of the person he was looking for, and before he and Brock left home for Victoria tomorrow, he intended to go and pay someone a much-needed visit.

"There's a two o'clock sailing," Brock said, lifting his head from where he'd been scanning his phone. It was Tuesday morning, and they were packing up their gear to leave. The informant's family was now in Canada and at a different safe house near Whistler. The police had come and picked up Rex and Brock's charge to take him to his family. "We can make it if we leave in the next fifteen minutes."

Rex, too, was staring at his phone, but he wasn't looking at the ferry schedule.

"Bro?" Brock grunted. "Two o'clock sailing work for you?"

Rex pinned his gaze on his brother. "Got a few things to take care of here. You head home. I'll catch a later ferry or see if I can grab a flight with Harbor Air."

Brock's bushy brows bunched, and a darkness fell across his features. "No vigilante stuff. I'm having a hard enough time keeping tabs on Heath. I can't be dealing with you going off the grid, too."

"Heath's hunting pedophiles. It's not like he's off chasing a poltergeist."

Brock grunted again. "Might as well be chasing a ghost with how little he's finding."

"Dakota Creed is still out there, and with Chase doing the legwork on the computer but not ready to return to the field, it's up to Heath and I. And Heath seems to be keen on heading down to Seattle as often as possible." A grin tugged at his lips. "It's not *all* business when he's down there. He's finding time for pleasure."

Brock grunted for a third time. "And you? What are you planning then?"

"Gotta go check out a lead, that's all. Ask some questions. Not going rogue, I swear. Won't even touch 'em if I don't have to."

Brock grabbed his duffle bag from the corner of the bedroom and started filling it with his belongings. "This have to do with Lydia?"

"I told you she got a weird call last week, right?"

Brock grunted.

His eldest brother did a lot of grunting but not much talking. Chase was the same way.

"Not liking not having any answers. Not even a fucking fingerprint."

"Anything else happen since the call?"

Rex shook his head. "At least nothing that Lydia relayed to me. She could be keeping other incidents a secret not to make me worry, but she doesn't seem like the type. She's putting on a brave face through all of this, but she's really scared."

Brock tossed his black hoodie into his bag after giving it a quick sniff test. "And you still think it's someone else doing this shit to her?"

Rex gave his brother a look that he hoped conveyed just how pissed off he was at his suggestion that she might be faking it. It was tough to tell if it did convey anything, though, since Brock's expression remained blank.

"You suggesting she's doing this all herself? Why?"

"Attention? Maybe she's got some mental health issues? You've known this chick less than two weeks, and eight of those days, you've been over here. She doesn't know anybody in Victoria, she's lonely, and she just got fired. All I'm saying is, look at this from *every* angle, including the ones you don't want to think about." Brock shrugged into his signature black leather jacket. He even wore it in the summer, which was just plain insane.

"You're letting her look after your children and you're suggesting she might be mentally unstable?" Rex countered, his hackles rising along with his blood pressure.

Another grunt.

Fuck, he was getting tired of the grunts.

"I'm sure she's totally fine and not mentally unstable, but I'm trained—as are you—to approach a situation with an open mind and a willingness to examine all sides. Have you done that?"

No. He hadn't.

He'd been so caught up in their whirlwind romance and saving her, he hadn't stopped to really think that maybe there was more to this than he was seeing. After all, it all only started happening *after* she met him, didn't it? She hadn't mentioned any other incidents before they met.

Was this her cry for help?

Brock zipped up his bag. "Do what you gotta do, bro. I'm not going to stop you. Trust your instincts and shit. But just give what I said some thought, and stop by the house when you get back, if it's not too late. Just had an inquiry for a new client pop up. I'm meeting her at five." He lifted his chin, looped his hand through the duffle bag handles and hit Rex with a big-brother look. "Stay safe."

Rex nodded, his mind now reeling with all that Brock had said.

Was Lydia behind all of this? Was that why they could only find her fingerprints on things? Because it was her doing all along?

He reached for his own bag off the floor and haphazardly shoved his belongings into it. The person he needed to see lived in East Vancouver, so he needed to figure out the fastest way there from where he was in Maple Ridge. Luckily, Vancouver public transit was impressive, and by the time he got downstairs to the foyer of the empty safe house, he'd planned his route.

He would be there within the hour, and then hopefully, by the time he left, he'd have more answers and fewer questions, because right now, his brain was overflowing with questions, and a lot of them were about Lydia.

———

FATIGUE AND UNCERTAINTY slowed his movements as Rex parked his truck in his brother's driveway and shut off the engine.

Brock's truck was in the driveway, as was Krista's SUV.

With a weary sigh, he grabbed his phone from the passenger seat and opened his door. Although his efforts in Vancouver hadn't been fruitless, they hadn't provided him with the answers he needed. And as he sat on the ferry for ninety minutes, stewing in his own thoughts, only more questions popped up, their answers invisible, even to his extra powerful senses. Brock's words stuck to him like an uncomfortable humid breeze. *Was Lydia doing this all as a cry for attention?*

He was about to knock on the door when it opened and Brock stood in front of him, stone-faced, a crease so deep between his brows, it was probably pressing on his brain.

"We need to talk," Brock said gruffly, jerking his chin toward the basement.

Shit.

Had *he* uncovered something about Lydia?

And if so, what?

With a stomach full of knots, he followed his brother down the half flight of stairs to the basement and into his office. "What's wrong?"

Brock jerked his chin at the door, and Rex closed it.

"New client."

"Need to give me more than that." But Brock didn't really have to. His brother wouldn't be looking at him like that if it didn't have something to do with Lydia.

"New client is Odette Rockford."

As if liquid nitrogen had been poured in his veins, Rex's body turned ice cold. His hand tightened around his phone and keys, and his jaw locked.

Brock's brows lifted, reading Rex's reaction for what it was. "She is claiming that Lydia is harassing and stalking her. Says it's been happening since just after Lydia was fired from the day care for being unprofessional, erratic and showing signs of mental instability."

"She's fucking lying," he finally said, but even he could pick up the subtle inflection of question and hesitation in his voice. Brock definitely could. "First, she fires Lydia and now this? How do we know it's not the other way around?"

"You haven't found any prints, have you?" Brock asked gently. "I mean, it makes more sense for Lydia to be taunting the woman that fired her than the reverse, right? She has motive. What motive would Odette have?"

Rex scoffed. "We know fucking well you don't always need a motive to be a psycho. We've seen enough sick fuckers in the world whose only motive is the fact that they derive joy from hurting others. Odette could be the same. How much have you looked into her? How do we know she's not just a huge sadist and Lydia is just her most recent victim?"

Brock's shoulder lifted. His leather jacket was hung up on a hook behind him. "Not a ton ... *yet*. But we will. I've already sent everything to Chase, and he's going to start digging."

"Don't you wonder why, of all the security companies out there, she came to *us*?"

"Of course I do. But if she *is* a threat, now we can keep an even closer eye on her. Maybe she'll inadvertently reveal her hand and we can put it all to rest. But we have to look into her accusations."

"Which are?" Rex spat out.

"Harassing phone calls, weird packages in the mail, following her. She even mentioned voodoo. Said before Lydia left, she put a curse on Odette."

Oh, for fuck's sake. Rex rolled his eyes so hard his brain hurt.

"Voodoo? Really? Come on. This bitch is whacked. I'll go ask Lydia right now—"

"This is a case, and we are bound by confidentiality. You cannot talk to Lydia about this. Don't even mention Odette. Just do what you do best and feel her out in other ways. Do some snooping."

The thought of rooting through Lydia's personal belongings in search of evidence *against* her made the knot in his stomach pull extra tight. His knuckles were starting to ache from how firmly he was holding on to his phone and keys. He shoved them into his pocket, pulled his hands free and wiggled them to get the circulation flowing again.

"How the fuck am I supposed to look Lydia in the face and not feel like a lying asshole?"

"Because it's your job." His big brother crossed his arms over his chest and leaned back in his office chair, causing it to creak in response to his bulk.

Fuck. Sometimes he really fucking hated his job. He'd thought more than once about giving his big brother his notice and going to work for Rick and his plumbing company full-time. Plumbers made good coin and could work nine to five. No more weeks on end away. He could sleep in his own bed every night, walk Diesel every day and have a normal fucking life. He also wouldn't be forced to lie to the woman he was seeing because he'd just taken a job that could possibly result in her going to prison.

Son of a bitch.

"Check out her car. Glove compartment, trunk. Hidden storage compartments. When she's in the shower, take a peek in her dresser drawers. Look for buried boxes and things put in unexpected places," Brock suggested. "Be subtle about it."

"I know how to do my fucking job."

"Yeah, but you've never been sleeping with a suspect before."

"Should I talk to Heath, get some pointers from him?" He regretted those words the moment they came out of his piehole. And the look on Brock's face was as fatherly and scolding as they come. Last year, Heath had fallen hard for a woman, only she ended up not being who they thought she was, and he got hurt in the process. Not only his heart but physically. She'd ended up being one of the baddies, and it was a twist none of them—especially Heath—saw coming.

"Be the good boyfriend but also do your job. Are you capable of both? Or do I need to be the one to make up an excuse to come by her apartment and root through her closet and medicine cabinet?"

Rex glared at his brother. Brock was deliberately taunting him now. "You know I can do it."

Brock's eyes closed slowly, and he nodded once. "Good. Let me know what you find out."

Rex's nostrils flared, and he spun on his heel to leave, shoving his hands into his coat pockets so he didn't suddenly get the urge to punch one of his brother's office walls.

"With any luck, Lydia's not guilty and it's Odette stalking her, but either way, you know we need to take this shit seriously before it escalates," Brock called after him.

He didn't respond.

"Did you get done what you needed to do in Vancouver?"

Rex only grunted, taking a page out of his brother's playbook.

"Answer some questions or just breed more?"

He paused in the doorway. "Both."

Brock inhaled and clucked his tongue. "That's usually the way. Sorry."

Rex knew his brother's *sorry* was intended for more than just the fact that Rex hadn't gotten the answers he sought out in Vancouver, but he was too pissed off at the world to acknowledge it. He climbed the stairs to the front door, the sounds of children happily having a bath in the tub on the main floor echoing through the house.

He should go say *hi* to his sister-in-law, niece and nephew, but right now he was just not in the mood. He was expected back at the apartment. He'd texted Lydia earlier to say that he was just stopping at Brock's and would be home shortly.

She hadn't responded, but he figured she was probably out for a run with Diesel or something. At least he hoped that was the reason.

Worry spiraled through him.

What if she was in trouble and that's why she didn't answer?

Or what if she was *up to* trouble and that's why she didn't answer?

Fuck.

Brock had planted even more seeds of doubt in his mind. More seeds than he'd had earlier that day—also planted by Brock—but the lack of answers he got from the person he found in East Van had only caused those seeds to sprout.

Opening the front door, he stepped out into the cool spring evening. The heavy scent of blooming flowers hung in the air, and the sun was still visible in the sky to the west. Summer would be here before they knew it.

Longer days. Warmer nights.

He couldn't wait.

And yet, his normal excitement for the solstice wasn't there. It was too bogged down with worry and confusion and the reluctance that came with knowing what he would have to do once he got home.

It'd only been a couple of weeks, but he'd come to really care for Lydia, and now he had this big secret he had to keep from her and he had to betray her trust and start snooping.

He hit the fob for his truck, drank in a big gulp of fresh air and stared up into the clouds for answers.

They didn't have any for him. Instead, it felt like they were mocking him.

He climbed into his truck, started the engine and backed out of his brother's driveway, hoping to God that his gut instinct about Lydia wasn't wrong and that this was all just one big clusterfuck that she was not at the center of.

But if family history proved anything, the men in his family were notorious for finding their way to the nucleus of clusterfucks and catastrophe.

Their dad, Brock, Chase, even Heath.

Now, it seemed like it might just be his turn to face the rapture.

He just hoped to fuck he wasn't wrong about Lydia. Otherwise, he'd take it as a sign he was better off becoming a celibate monk.

He already had the hair for it.

CHAPTER 18

AFTER A GREAT FIRST day with Chase and Stacey's kids, Connor and Thea, Lydia arrived home feeling good. She'd looked after James and Emma's twins, Grace and Claire, three times so far, and the little girls were hilarious, wonderful and cheeky. Krista and Brock's kids were also great, and little Zoe was her sidekick, helping her with Zane.

Even though she didn't want to be a babysitter or a nanny, the fact that she woke up every day and had a job to go to and a sense of purpose was doing wonders for her mood and psyche.

She barely thought about the weirdness that had happened to her last week. Particularly since nothing had happened to her since the creepy phone call.

Had the person given up tormenting her? Was she not a willing and terrified participant in this charade, shrieking like a scream queen on the big screen every time something sinister took place in her home?

Well, whoever was bothering her would be sorely disappointed, because she wasn't easily scared off. She refused to give them what they wanted—which was obviously Lydia scared out of her skin.

She was scared, but she wouldn't let them see it. She wouldn't let them see her fear, because fear was their fuel.

She was a big girl, raised by a strong single mother, and she wouldn't let anybody push her around or scare her off. She would stand and fight if she had too.

Though she really hoped it wouldn't come to that and all this weirdness was finally behind them once and for all.

So to keep the good vibes going, she harnessed up Diesel, and the two of them took advantage of the nice weather and went for a beautiful run through their neighborhood to work up an appetite for dinner.

She didn't realize until she pulled her earbuds from her ears and fished her key out of her sock that she had a missed text from Rex. He was on his way home.

She couldn't wait.

It surprised her, but in a really good way, how much she'd missed him.

Hopefully, he didn't have any more away jobs for a while.

She was also feeling lonely without him, despite having Diesel and Pia to keep her company. She'd come to enjoy their instant but comfortable dive into domestic simplicity. Not to mention the soul-consuming sex, both in person and on the phone.

The man *definitely* knew how to talk dirty. So much so that even though she had her cellphone on speaker when they were getting digitally dirty, she gave it a good wipe-down with a Lysol wipe after they disconnected the call.

Rex was a filthy fucker.

With a heaving chest and warm face, she opened the front door to the lobby and let Diesel lead the way. She had just enough energy left in her to take the stairs instead of the elevator, though by the way he pulled on his leash, Diesel had enough energy for another five-kilometer run.

Crazy puppy.

They were at her door in no time. She used her other key to unlock her door, letting out the sigh of relief she'd kept locked in her lungs when the door revealed itself to still be locked.

Not that that meant much. But it was still a small boon of comfort.

She turned the latch, and Diesel pulled them inside. It was like he had a bunch of stuff to tell Pia about the outside world, the way he ran up to her, his tail wagging, nose sniffing and snuffling like crazy.

"You're a nut," she said, rolling her eyes at the dog and unhooking his harness. He and Pia were now nose to nose.

She set his harness down on the side table next to the sofa and was about to toe out of her shoes when a smell unfamiliar to her home hit her in the nose like a fart on the wind.

Only it wasn't pungent.

It was sweet.

Floral.

But nonetheless unfamiliar.

It hung in the air of the apartment as if someone had run through the room with a can of air freshener.

She didn't own any air fresheners. She preferred her essential oil diffuser, and she hadn't turned that on in several days.

She also hadn't burned any candles, and the smell wasn't like her bodywash, dish soap or shampoo.

It smelled strongly of artificial lavender, and she *hated* artificial lavender.

Real lavender extract was fine, as was real dried lavender, but the kind of lavender scent that was usually found in bubble bath or hand soap damn near made her gag.

She was having a hard time breathing now, the terror was so consuming. It had gripped her lungs, and her breaths came in shallow pants as she raced to her sundeck sliding glass door to see if it was open, then her bedroom window. Both were closed and locked.

She opened them to let the breeze sweep through and cleanse the air, purge her home of the foreign, putrid stench.

Someone had been in her apartment again.

There was no other explanation for such a strong, unfamiliar, unpleasant smell, particularly because the hallway hadn't smelled like this, and no scents from her neighbors on either side, or above or below her, had ever permeated her unit this strongly.

Not sure what else to do, she started opening cupboards and drawers in her kitchen to see if anything else had been touched or tampered with.

Nothing seemed out of place ... except for the phone.

An antiquated black flip phone she'd never seen before was tucked into the corner of her cutlery drawer. She tried to turn it on, but it was dead.

What the hell?

She was pretty sure she'd never seen that phone before in her life.

However, it *did* vaguely resemble one of her first cell phones back when she was a teenager. But she wasn't a hoarder and didn't hold on to unnecessary things simply out of nostalgia. She'd watched the Marie Kondo special on Netflix. She knew how to purge things that didn't bring her joy.

She put the phone on her island and continued on her hunt for weirdness.

Whoever was tormenting her seemed to have a penchant for the undramatic. The bananas, the cheese, the apples, the shower curtain, her dresser drawer. All seemingly harmless things and almost inconsequential if they'd happened individually, but they were all happening together and at the same time.

She opened the cupboard above her fridge and found the

brand-new tub of Americone Dream that she'd bought yesterday but hadn't opened sitting in a warm puddle.

What the hell?

She knew she hadn't put it there. Knew for a fucking fact. She remembered distinctly unpacking her groceries, opening her freezer and having to play Tetris with the contents inside to accommodate the tiny tub of ice cream. She'd been mighty proud of herself too, only having to sacrifice one ice cube tray to get it all back in.

She'd then promptly made herself a vodka soda. No sense letting good ice cubes go to waste, right?

Grabbing the ruined ice cream from the cupboard, she set it next to the phone on her island.

This was not how she saw the first several minutes of her reunion with Rex going. Her telling him all the new creepy things she'd found when she came home.

She thought they'd spend those first minutes tearing each other's clothes off while he walked her backward to the bedroom, fell on top of her and reminded her just how talented his tongue was.

Now she had to tell him about this the moment he walked through the door.

She knew she should be scared, and she was, but in a lot of ways, it just felt surreal, too. Like who tormented someone this way?

Wasn't she supposed to find a severed foot in her bed or a bloody note scrawled on her bathroom mirror? Wasn't that what tormenters and weirdos did?

Who took bites out of someone else's cheese?

Who defrosted their victim's ice cream and peeled all of their bananas?

This was so fucking fucked up, the only thing she could think of to do as she stared at her ruined ice cream was laugh.

That too was fucked up, but it was all her brain would allow.

She'd lived in the city for all of two months, had retained, then lost a job, found a dreamy new boyfriend and apparently also a weird, passive-aggressive, fruit-hating stalker.

What would be next? Would they sneak out onto her deck and overwater her plants? Steal her leftovers? Vacuum her house? Give her cat a new toy?

This person was unpredictable and warped.

Still giggling, even though she knew it was totally wrong, because truthfully, she was scared out of her skin, she went back to her foyer and toed off her shoes.

She needed a shower.

Rex had left her with the key to his place in case she didn't feel comfortable to stay in her own for whatever reason, but since he'd left last week, she hadn't gone in there besides to get the dog treats for Diesel. Otherwise, she was determined to be a big girl and stay in her own apartment. The apartment she paid for. The apartment she loved.

She peeled her sweaty tank top off, then her workout tights, finally followed by her socks, throwing everything into the hamper in her room.

Diesel and Pia were snuggled on his big dog bed in the corner of her living room, paying her nakedness no mind.

She stepped into her bathroom and was about to turn on the shower when there was a knock at her door.

Diesel huffed a bark and stood up.

"Lydia, it's me, Rex."

She blinked and drew in the deep breath that she'd been denying herself since smelling that horrible fake-ass lavender.

"Just a sec," she called out, ducking back into her room and tossing on her robe. She was still sweaty and hated putting her robe on her body while sweaty, but whatever, she'd do laundry.

Barefoot, she wrinkled her nose as she approached the door.

Even though he'd already announced himself, she peeked through the peephole just in case. He was standing all beefy, bald and bodacious on the other side.

Her pussy pulsed and insides quivered in response to his sexiness.

Rein that shit in, girl. You're supposed to be terrified here.

And she was.

She seriously was.

Someone kept coming into her house and doing shit to drive her crazy, for no reason she could think of, and yet her body reacted in opposition to her brain when Rex was in sight.

She opened the door and had to keep a tight grip on the handle to keep herself from launching forward and into his arms.

His midnight gaze swept her from head to toe. "Did I wake you?"

"Diesel and I just got back from a run. I was about to hop into the shower."

He nodded, but she could tell his thoughts were elsewhere. He was distracted, and the way his eyes darted around her apartment and his nose wrinkled said he knew someone had been in here too. "What's that smell?"

Even though she knew she shouldn't because it would inevitably turn her stomach, she took a deep breath anyway. Gag! "It's lavender."

"It's terrible."

"I didn't do it."

His bushy brows narrowed, and he pivoted to face her. "What?"

"When Diesel and I got back, I noticed the smell. I hate artificial lavender and would never use anything like this. I like the essential oil, or real lavender, like in a sachet for my underwear drawer, but not like this. This is like cheap bodywash or something." She took his hand and led him over to her kitchen island. "And I found these, too."

A crease formed between his brows and another emerged on his forehead as he picked up the ice cream. "What do you mean?"

"It was in my cupboard. I remember specifically putting it in my freezer yesterday after I bought it, and yet when I opened my cupboard a minute ago, I found it in there all melted. I didn't do that. I *know* I didn't."

The flick of a look he gave her was fleeting before he focused back on the black flip phone. This time though, he didn't touch it and rather reached for the dish towel hanging from the handle of her oven. He picked it up and flipped it open. "And this?"

"Never seen it before in my life before today. Found it in my cutlery drawer. Its battery is dead, though."

"Easily remedied," he murmured more to himself than to her. He set it back down on the island. Something about the man was off.

Since the moment she opened her door, he'd been guarded, suspicious and withdrawn. Their calls and texts while he'd been gone had been flirty, sexy and fun. Even their phone call last night had turned steamy, with him describing a plethora of dirty things he wanted to do to her when he got back.

Between then and now, what had changed?

Why was he looking at her like he didn't believe someone had once again snuck into her apartment and taken her ice cream out of her freezer and left an ancient flip phone in her cutlery drawer?

Did he think *she* was doing all of this?

Why the sudden change of heart? What—or *who*—had suddenly prompted this lack of belief?

She didn't even have to ask him if he believed her to know that he was on the fence. It was written all over his damn face.

She took a step back and pulled her robe tighter around her body. "What's going on, Rex?"

His large Adam's apple bobbed thick in his throat. "I went to see Dierks."

Everything in her went tight, cold and painful. She held her breath and didn't blink. "And?" was all she managed to squeak out.

"It's not him."

"How can you be sure?"

"Because I'm sure. He's in therapy. He's in a support group. He's getting the help he needs. He knows he can't use his health as a bargaining chip for your relationship, and he only wants you to have the very best life. He wanted me to apologize to you for all the stress, grief and heartache he caused."

Her pulse in her ears was like a goddamn church bell. She reached out to the counter for support. "What did you say to him?"

Rex shrugged. "Not much. Asked him where he'd been these last two months. And his story checks out. He's been in Kelowna at an intense anger management and counseling facility. Says he's getting the help he needs. He only just got back to Vancouver two days ago, and he hasn't left his apartment. His neighbor can attest to that, and she did."

"It has to be Dierks, though. Who else ..."

She'd told Joy everything about Lyle Whigby and the two of them had ruled him out as a suspect. He just didn't fit the bill. He was a pedophile, and since Lydia was now an adult, she would no longer be his target. He wasn't even worth mentioning.

Rex's gaze was serious, and it was starting to scare her. "I want to believe you, Lydia, I do, but you have to admit, all of this is really unusual."

What did he mean by he *wanted to believe her*? Did that mean that he *didn't* believe her?

Her hackles rose up, and she took a step back from him, tightening her robe again. "You think *I'm* doing this?" Her nostrils flared. "You think *I'm* torturing myself—for what? For attention? Oh, the lonely little jobless neighbor is so bored out of her tree she's going to pretend to stalk herself so the sexy bald man with nail-gun dimples comes to her rescue. Is that what you think, Rex?"

Diesel whimpered and stood between them, his head swiveling back and forth. He was just as confused as she was. Where had Rex's sudden disbelief in her come from? Why now?

"I'm trained to get *all* the facts, Lydia, that's all." His words were spoken slowly, softly and carefully. Like she was some rabid raccoon in the corner of the garage and he was trying to coax her into the live cage so they could take her away and dispose of her.

She shook her head. "Yeah? And what about listening to your gut? Because I could be making the same accusations against you, you know."

His eyes narrowed, and his head cocked ever so slightly.

"None of this stuff started happening to me until I met you. What's to say it's not *you* who is doing all of this creepy stuff to me? Hmm? Just so you can swoop in and save the day. Got a hero complex that's not being satisfied, Rex? Get your sick jollies scaring women, then acting like their knight with a shiny bald head? You *did* take my underwear, after all. Hmm?" At this point she was just trying to get some kind of a reaction out of him. He was so calm and stoic compared with her, standing there, taking all of her ire and frustrations. She wanted to break that composure and make him feel just as hurt as she was for his horrible accusations.

And when she accused him of the hero complex, she finally noticed a slight fissure in his stony exterior.

The intense scrutiny in his eyes changed too. She could see the doubt forming. A muscle ticked in his jaw, and she watched the pulse in his neck pick up tempo.

Squeezing her hands into tight fists, she took a deep breath, closed her eyes for a moment and tried to regroup. When she opened her eyes again, her pulse had slowed down, and her body wasn't nearly as warm. Choosing her words carefully, just like he had, she spoke slowly and calmly. "I'm not doing this, Rex. I swear to God. Someone is fucking with me—with *us*. Do you have any scorned and angry exes who might try to take revenge on someone you're seeing? Any jobs gone bad, where someone might be out for justice? We need to think *outside* the box and not just start throwing accusations at each other. That's not going to solve this. That's not going to get to the bottom of who is doing this."

She could practically see the cogs turning in his big brain. He was scrolling through the Rolodex of past relationships and people he'd put away in his head, searching for an unstable nut in the bag of trail mix.

God willing, that bag would be mostly full of dried fruit and raisins and maybe a handful of M&Ms.

After a moment of the two of them just standing there staring at each other, his shoulders slumped, his tight mask fell, and he dropped his head. "I'm sorry."

"Me too."

He stepped toward her, his gaze still wary but far less so. He reached for her hands, and she let him take them. "After I ruled out Dierks, my mind started to go in a bunch of crazy directions," he said, running his thumb over the top of her left hand. "It's all so fucked up."

"Seriously fucked up." She nodded.

"I believe you when you say that it isn't you."

Oh, how she wanted to believe him when he said that right now, but there was still something he was holding back, something that he wasn't telling her. She could see it in his eyes, in the way he was looking at her. He was at war inside. Torn by something he couldn't tell her or *wouldn't* tell her.

She knew that his job with his brothers would come with a lot of secrets. Classified information only those in the business could be privy to. There would be cases he wouldn't be able to talk about. That just came with the territory. It was probably very similar for Krista and her job as a cop.

But if what he couldn't tell her involved her in some way, didn't she have a right to know?

"I believe you when you say that it isn't you." She repeated his own words back to him, even though she knew hers were far more truthful than his.

He still held some doubt.

She knew it.

She could see it.

She could feel it.

He didn't entirely trust her.

And yet she didn't doubt him at all. She knew her thoughts about him being the stalker were far-fetched and the machinations of her tortured mind. It couldn't be Rex. It just couldn't. She trusted him. Believed him.

His hands squeezed hers, and his smile, although small, eased the ache she felt in her chest. The ache placed there by his doubt in her. By the unsure way he was looking at her, like he didn't know her as well as he thought he did. "It's good to see you."

Yeah, this was not at all how she saw their reunion going.

Stupid fucking stalker messing with her happy, sexy-time reunion.

If she ever met them—which she hoped was never—she'd be sure to give them a serious piece of her mind. If, of course, they weren't in the process of peeling off her face to make a mask of her skin. Then she'd have bigger fish to fry.

CHAPTER 19

THINGS WERE MORE awkward than when they'd discussed her propositioning him while drunk once she'd sobered up. She would gladly go back to that moment rather than be forced to live another second in the uncomfortable place they were now. Not to mention that nauseating lavender smell that seemed to be worming its way into her pores.

He released her hands but maintained eye contact, the pain flitting behind his gaze so strong, she could feel it in the air. Feel his sad energy and the weight of it.

She swallowed hard. "It's hard for you to trust, isn't it?"

Something dark passed behind his eyes and the muscle in his jaw seemed to double in size he was squeezing it so tight. At that moment she felt so much smaller than him. And in reality, she was small than him. By nearly a foot at least, but at that moment she felt even smaller. Puny. He was like this giant, foreboding mountain, blocking out the sun and casting her into a dark, cold shadow.

A shiver raced up her spine and out into her arms from his icy stare.

But she knew the warm Rex that resided inside and she wasn't ready to stop trying to bring him back out. This Rex, the cold Rex didn't scare her. But he did worry her.

"You don't have to tell me what happened, but ... I'm here if you ever want to talk about it. Or anything. I'm a good listener."

Rex rolled his lips inward and pinned them together, his mouth forming a slash. He looked at her with an intensity that made her squirm inside. What was he thinking right now? What was going on in that big bald head? Who had betrayed him so badly he struggled to let anyone else in?

"Go have a shower," he said softly. "I'm going to go unpack upstairs, then we can grab dinner."

Dammit.

He wasn't ready to melt and let the warm Rex come back out.

After her shower, she'd have to try harder.

With a disappointed nod, she turned away, taking one step toward the bathroom, but was halted in her efforts when a big, warm, strong hand gripped her roughly by the waist and she was hauled up gruffly against hot steel. His lips took hers like they owned them, and even though her body had gone stiff at first, she dissolved into his embrace within seconds, opening her mouth for him and letting him claim her.

He took the lead, controlling the kiss, molding her lips to do as he pleased.

She had no problem with his demands, not when she knew where they would lead. He controlled her mouth like he controlled everything. With calm, measured precision. He made the kiss—he made her—his own. All she had to do was keep up with his intensity, keep up with his moves and the way his tongue plundered her mouth and his lips sucked at her lips.

A thrill skittered the length of her spine, and she trembled. Her breasts felt heavy, and her nipples were diamond-hard.

A delicious heat pooled between her legs, and she knew if she moved an inch, a droplet would either slip down her inner thigh or land on the floor at her feet.

The man made her so wet, so fast.

Slowly, he backed her up, one of his hands shoved into her damp, sweaty hair, the other unfastening her robe. She stumbled backward into the bathroom, and her heels hit the tub.

He only broke their lip lock for a moment to pull back the curtain and start the water. Then he returned to her, taking her mouth again and thrusting his tongue inside to taste. He pushed her robe over her shoulders, and it fell in a heap at her feet that she promptly kicked out of the way.

She was naked now.

He was still fully dressed.

She was sweaty.

He didn't seem to care.

"Not exactly fair," she murmured when he dropped his head, took a puckered nipple in his mouth and sucked hard enough to cause a hickey. She'd have a mark there for sure. A reminder for days to come of his need for her. Of just how much he burned for her.

He bit down just hard enough to make her gasp, but the gasp quickly turned into a groan, which he swallowed when he released her breast and lunged up to take her mouth again briefly. "What's not fair?" His voice was gravelly and hoarse and made a trickle of arousal escape her pulsing and wanton center and run down her inner thigh.

"You're still dressed."

He latched on to the other nipple and sucked just as hard as he had the first. Pleasure mixed with pain shot through her, landing where it had before—right in her clit—and her hips shot outward, the V of her legs making contact with the top of his thigh. She ground down, desperate for friction.

Her hands left his neck and went to work shedding him of his coat and long-sleeved thermal. He didn't stop her, didn't stop sucking on her nipples, besides to clear the shirt off his head. His fingers trailed a path of fire down her sides, over her hip and between her legs.

His teeth scissored over her nipple before clamping down and tugging, not enough to break the skin but enough to cause a shock-wave to sprint through her and land firmly on her clit, causing that sensitive nub to swell and pulse like it had a heart of its very own.

Two digits pressed firmly against her clit, which she was still rubbing on his thigh, and she spasmed in his arms.

"Pants off," she demanded, her legs going to jelly when he pushed those two fingers between her slick folds and into her pussy. She squeezed around them and slid up and down.

From where he was still latched on to her breast, his tongue twiddling the nipple like it was the tip of her clit, he tipped his gaze up to her. Blue flames of lust flickered back at her in those midnight orbs.

"Pants." Her breath hitched when his thumbnail scraped across her clit. "Now."

He stood up, releasing her breast and pulling his fingers from her. She watched his shiny fingers that had just been inside her unbuckle his belt and release the button on his cargo pants.

A very obvious tent was pitched in his gray boxer briefs, but it was the heart-shaped damp patch right over where the tip of his cock would be that had her licking her lips.

He ran his palm over it. "You want this?"

She nodded slowly, crushing her bottom lip between her teeth to keep herself from licking her lips again like a lioness staring at a herd of gazelle.

Only he was no gazelle.

Not even close.

Rex was a hunter.

A proud, virile male lion. King of the fucking jungle. Emperor of the savanna, almighty ruler of the pride.

Her knees threatened to buckle when he pushed his boxers down and his cock sprang free, bobbing slightly before whacking his thigh.

She swallowed and stepped over the tub and into the spray, the heat of the water instantly soothing her muscles and washing away the sticky sweat from her run.

Her adrenaline was still pumping though. But it was no longer from the run.

Rex got her engine revving. Her chest lifted and fell erratically, and her blood ran hot as she stared at the bobbing head of his cock, dark purple and shiny with a perfect dewdrop of salty precum glistening on the tip.

Rex ditched his socks and stepped in after her, crowding her.

Normally, when it was just her, the shower and tub felt plenty big enough. But with this giant hunk of man meat in there with her, she barely had enough room to turn around.

His hands cupped her breasts from behind, tugging on the nipples, kneading the heavy mounds that were now tender from his earlier affections.

He was rough, but she liked rough.

Still plucking one nipple, he moved the fingers of his other hand down her belly and between her legs. Her breath stuttered as his middle finger double-tapped her clit.

Teeth scraped across her neck and shoulder, and the warm water hammered her head and back. She'd pushed herself on the run, not only because Diesel seemed to only have two speeds, walk and turbo, but also because she wanted to be able to keep up with Rex better. She knew when they'd gone for a run last week that he'd slowed down his pace for her.

But she'd feel that extra hill and increased speed in her legs and back tomorrow. So right now, the water felt divine. As did the finger the man behind her had slipped back into her pussy.

Her head fell against his chest, and he held her up with his arm under his breasts. Her eyes closed as the pleasure he was giving her built like a perfect storm inside her. Her limbs tingled, belly warmed, pussy pulsed and clit swelled. The heel of his palm rubbed against her clit, and she rocked into it. He only had the one finger inside her, but it was all she needed.

A ribbon of heat swirled through her, tangling around her most sensitive body parts, the parts Rex was so expertly touching.

His other finger and thumb tugged at her nipple, and she exploded.

Like a barge full of fireworks being hit by a grenade, everything detonated at once. Her toes curled on the wet tub floor, and she would have lost her footing if he hadn't been holding her up. Like she'd just been shot with a Taser, her chest shook and convulsed. Her eyes squeezed closed tight, and bright starbursts flittered behind her lids. Her pussy throbbed and squeezed around his one finger. His thumb on her clit refused to cease, and the orgasm just kept going, unfurling like a never-ending roll of ticker tape or one of those trick handkerchiefs that magicians use.

His thumb waggled over her clit again, and just when she was about to tell him to stop, that she couldn't take anymore, that it was all too sensitive, another climax crashed into her like an out-of-control train.

Helpless to the euphoria and boneless, she slumped in his arms, her eyes still closed, head still back against his shoulder as the second orgasm careened through her, navigating its way to each erogenous zone and spreading its warmth.

Her pussy spasmed, her clit pulsed and her nipples ached for his mouth.

With the last remaining fragments of energy, she spun in his arms the second the orgasm ebbed enough for her to move. Gripping his head with both hands, she brought his mouth down to her breast.

He knew what to do, and without hesitation, Rex latched on to her tender bud and sucked.

"Harder," she murmured. "More teeth."

Growling, he lifted his head, hoisted her up onto his hips and plowed into her, wasting no time hitting the end of her.

Her impalement drew out her emergency reserves of adrenaline, and she grappled at him, her fingernails raking down his back as he powered into her, pressed her back to the wall and started hammering into her good.

Arching his back, he dropped his head and took a nipple into his mouth again, sucking before biting the areola and nipple hard.

Rex continued to pump up into her, his pelvic bone scraping across her ultrasensitive clit in a way that had her already jelly legs struggling to keep purchase on his hips.

She was enjoying this immensely, but she wasn't sure she'd be able to get off again. At least not without a bit of reprieve.

Rex switched his attentions to the other nipple and scissored his teeth over it until she sucked in a sharp breath. She released that breath in a soft hiss and squeezed her eyes closed tighter while digging her nails harder into his back.

He grunted but didn't tell her to stop.

His pace quickened.

Opening her eyes and blinking through the spray, she leaned over and glanced down, taking the opportunity to look behind him and watch his oh-so-fine ass muscles clench and release with each hard, measured thrust.

Goddamn, the man was perfect. Chiseled from marble and brought to life to be a pleasure god she had the fortune of being seduced by.

He lifted his head, and his teeth found her neck. They scraped across her collarbone and to her trachea, where he ran his tongue, swirling it around the hollow of her throat.

His grunts and moans fueled her, and she felt another orgasm beginning to brew deep in her belly. Heat swirled, and tendrils of ecstasy grew.

But just when she thought she might be able to come again, he lifted his head, stepped back and plopped her onto her feet.

"Wh-what?"

Without saying a word, his fingers wrapped around her long, wet hair at the nape of her neck and he guided her to the ground on her knees. The spray hit her back, keeping her warm but not getting in her eyes. His cock bobbed in front of her face, heavy, thick and hard as granite.

She took him in her palm and eased his length into her mouth, but he didn't give her a chance to adjust and with a firm tug, seated himself in her mouth as deep as he could go.

She gagged slightly, and he pulled back, but once she relaxed her jaw and tongue, he started to move her head, using her hair for leverage. He fucked her face and swatted her hand away when she tried to use it to help her mouth get him there faster.

"Just your mouth." He grunted and kept going.

Even though this rougher side of him was more than welcome, she couldn't mistake the tenderness he still possessed. The look of need and craving in his eyes as he watched her take him to the back of her throat, the way his other hand gently cupped her jaw and his thumb tugged at her bottom lip. He would never push her too far, but he would push her to the edge.

She liked the edge.

And even though they'd only been together for a short time and doubt still clearly niggled at the back of his mind, the connection they had, the deep care she felt for him already and knew he felt for her came through in every one of their interactions.

She'd fallen hard for this man. And not because he'd *saved* her.

Not because she was no longer lonely. Because Rex was her friend, her lover, and he was a good, loyal man through and through.

He would never hurt her. Not the way she'd started to fear Dierks might.

His hips bucked, and his cadence picked up fervor. Another grunt rumbled from his well-defined chest, and he tightened his grip on her hair. She had one hand on his thigh and the other one snaked between his legs until she found his soft, hairless balls.

Cupping them, she squeezed them gently, then tugged.

His groan prompted her to do it again.

He fucked her face harder.

Tears sprang to her eyes from how deep he was hitting her, knocking her tonsils.

She tugged harder on his sac.

He grunted.

Salty precum coated her tongue. But it wasn't foul-tasting, and she swallowed it down with ease.

His rhythm was beginning to wane. She knew how to get him to the point of no return. The question was, would he let her?

Only one way to find out.

Dipping her index finger between her own legs to gather her slick arousal, she wrapped that hand around Rex's thigh and waited for his ass cheeks to relax as he pulled out of her mouth slightly. She took her opening and pressed her finger against his tight hole, at the same time tipping her gaze up to his.

He was staring down at her now, fire in his eyes.

She pushed a little more and waited for him to shake his head, grunt and pull away. He didn't.

She pushed more. He pushed out with his muscles, and she breached him.

Past the tight ring of muscles her slippery finger went.

He continued to pump into her mouth, his eyes open, chin

tucked into his chest as he watched her take all of him. Every last inch.

When her finger was about two inches inside, she felt around until she pressed on the spot that made his knees wobble.

Found it!

She pressed harder.

His knees wobbled more.

A rush of salty, warm liquid vaguely tasting of chlorine seeped from the tip of his cock. She swept the tip with her tongue and swallowed it down, pressing harder on his prostate, then tugging his balls.

With a deep breath, she pushed him to the back of her throat and held him there.

His body went stiff.

A harsh grunt rumbled so deep and echoey, it was as if it had come from his toes. His grip on her wet hair tightened, his balls cinched up in her palm, and his anus contracted.

Hot cum shot across her tongue in thick spurts as she continued to stroke his prostate and pull on his testicles. She swallowed as best she could each time he shot more of his load, her throat muscles contracting around the head of his cock.

The veins of his length were bulged against her tongue, and his cock jerked as he finished coming.

A sigh and the loosening of his grasp on her hair were the first signs that he was done, followed by his cock slowly pulling from her mouth. She released him with a wet *pop* and gently pulled her finger from his anus. He helped her up with his hands under her arms, and before she could blink, his mouth was on hers again, swallowing her squeak of surprise as his wet, warm body plastered her against the shower wall.

His kisses were frantic. Not like before, where every move seemed calculated and precise. His control had crumbled as he came down her throat, and he seemed almost needy for more of her.

Gathering her wrists in one of his hands, he pinned her arms above her head and dropped his head to her breast, sucking a nipple back into his hot mouth. But he didn't stay there. His lips roamed farther down her torso, across her mound. Then, releasing her wrists and lifting one of her feet, he put it on his shoulder and dove in face-first to her center.

Her head tilted back against the shower wall and she shut her eyes just as he slid two fingers into her soaked center. Giving Rex head had made her so fucking wet, she was like a damn slip and slide.

Taking his cue from her earlier, he used her arousal on another finger and dipped his finger behind her, probing at her anus. She let him in willingly.

Every time they had sex or made love or whatever you wanted to call it, Rex was like a marathoner or the Energizer Bunny. The man just kept going and going and going. If he wasn't fucking her, he was eating her out or fingering her. He kept demanding more orgasms from her, more than she ever thought she could have in one sexy session. But he kept proving her wrong and pulling another one from her, almost always unexpectedly.

Maybe he was a magician.

Instead of coins from her ears, he pulled orgasms from her body she didn't know were there.

Only today seemed different.

Today, now, the man currently ears-deep between her legs had an intensity about him, a determination she hadn't felt before. Up until now, all the sex they'd had had been playful. But at that moment, there was nothing playful about Rex.

He was all passion. All business.

It was like he was caught up in some swirling vortex of doubt and self-flagellation and the only way he could exorcise himself of the feeling was to pour every last ounce of his energy into making her come. Into fucking her senseless.

He was still upset about earlier.

When he'd accused her of doing all that tormenting shit to herself?

Was he saying sorry for not believing her? Even though she could tell deep down, he still harbored seeds of doubt. He still didn't trust her completely.

Was this how Rex Hart apologized?

His tongue on her clit was working magic circles, and his finger in her ass and fingers in her pussy pumped in sync. She wasn't going to last long. Possibly not even long enough to finish this train of thought—

And she detonated.

That extra erogenous zone being played with was what tossed her clear over the edge. She had no way to reach for a tether or scramble for purchase on the overhang. When Rex's fingers pressed and rubbed against each other inside her, she was shot off the cliff by a cannon.

But rather than fall with the ground growing closer by the second, she fluttered her wings and soared. Higher and higher up into the atmosphere until she saw stars.

The attention Rex's tongue paid her clit never stopped, never slowed, and his fingers just kept going. It wasn't until she was tapping him on the head and begging him to stop that he finally relented.

With a shiny face and a smug smirk, he pulled his head up from between her legs.

She blinked through the spray and swallowed just as he reached for her bath pouf from the suction-cup hook, squirted some of her bodywash on it, handed it to her, then turned around. "Scrub my back. I'll scrub yours."

CHAPTER 20

FUCKING LYDIA SEEMED like the best way to clear his mind and make sense of every doubt and whisper of confusion he had swirling around inside his big, bald head.

Plus, he'd missed her body and her mouth, and up until his brother had delivered that horrible fucking news an hour ago, he'd been gung-ho to take her to pound town for the entire night.

But when she threw the accusation back in his face, that's when shit got real.

Here he was, torn between believing and doubting her; meanwhile, she was dealing with the exact same shit.

He'd been so caught up with his own trust issues, he forgot that she might very well have some of her own. Particularly after the Dierks fiasco.

He did feel a bit better now that he'd put a face to the name and met Dierks in person. The guy seemed troubled, but Rex had used his ultra-keen senses and his lie detector skills and determined that Dierks was being truthful. He wasn't a threat to Lydia and seemed to finally be ready to turn his life around for himself.

As far as Dierks was concerned, Lydia didn't need to worry

about him any longer.

But the fact that she was suspicious of him was like a slap to the face with a cold, wet washcloth. He'd always been one of the good guys. One of the heroes. Which made having his uncertainties about Lydia turned around on him, all the more shocking.

Because honestly, it made sense. If everything nefarious had started when they began seeing each other, of course she would have suspicions about him. Who wouldn't?

There were plenty of stories out there about stalkers, molesters and psychopaths who got their rocks off by being "the hero." Only the reason they were the hero in the first place was because *they* were the one tormenting their victim.

It was seriously fucked up and gave Rex the willies if he thought too hard about such a thing, but he couldn't blame Lydia for thinking it.

He'd thought she was doing it all to herself for attention, so why wouldn't she suspect him of doing it to her for attention, too?

Now that he'd ruled out Dierks as a possible suspect, his focus was on Odette. Although he hadn't met the woman, it was all too convenient for her to suddenly pop up on their radar claiming that Lydia was stalking *her*. And to go to Rex's family business, of all places.

Something smelled particularly fishy, and it wasn't the tuna sandwich he'd had for lunch.

After their shower sexathon, they seemed to be in a better place. She got dressed, and he rooted around in his duffle bag for a fresh set of clothes. They ate dinner, and although they were quiet while they ate and sat on the couch watching a movie, when he tugged her into his side and wrapped his arm around her, she didn't balk and she wasn't stiff. She melted against him with a sigh of contentment, drawing one out of him as well.

He could start digging tomorrow. But today—tonight—he just wanted to do what he wanted, which was hold the woman he was falling for until she fell asleep and convince himself she wasn't crazy.

Easier said than done when you were a man like him though.

Trained to think the worst. Trained to be prepared for the worst.

It didn't help that he'd been betrayed in the past by someone he trusted. Strung up and tortured because he'd put faith in the wrong person, and his gut had failed him.

It made trust all the more difficult to come by now.

The only people in his life he truly trusted, without question, were his brothers, their wives and his mother.

Everyone else was viewed as a possible turncoat.

It was just safer to live life that way.

Sad.

But safer.

But when Lydia finally did fall asleep on him as they watched television, he gently carried her to her bed, pulled the covers over, kissed her and then went back to the living room.

He hooked up Diesel's harness. "Come on, buddy, let's go for a pee." But he didn't just grab his own keys from the side table next to the couch. He grabbed Lydia's too.

Even though he'd promised himself one night, he just couldn't wait.

Outside in the parking lot, he waited for Diesel to finish lifting his leg on a fire hydrant before he went to Lydia's car.

It was dark outside, and the parking lot was quiet. There were two big streetlamps providing the lot with light, but where Lydia was parked lent him the perfect amount of shadowed coverage.

However, he was using her key, so it wasn't like anyone would think he was breaking into her vehicle. Even so, he kept his body low and hushed Diesel when he barked at a bunny sprinting across the lot.

Double-checking that she wasn't standing in the lobby

watching him, he opened her car door. She had a box of Kleenex on the floor behind the passenger seat, and he grabbed one, then used it to open the center console.

Nothing weird or stalkerish stood out.

Just a phone charger, pens, lip gloss, sunglasses, baby wipes, a granola bar. Typical stuff.

He closed it.

She kept her car pretty clean, but most sedans had hidden compartments for storage, so he'd be sure to check those, too.

Diesel let out another huff of impatience.

Rex dug into his hoodie pocket and handed D a treat. The dog chewed it, swallowed and groaned a thanks. Then he twisted his body and started licking himself, resigned to the fact that they would be there a while.

As gross as it was, Rex had to admit that if his body could bend that way, he'd probably try at least once to take himself in his mouth. Humans were naturally curious creatures.

Using the Kleenex again, he opened up the glove compartment, and what tumbled out had him lunging backward in the seat.

Diesel snuffled and barked once in surprise, lifting his head from his crotch and sniffing the object that had fallen to hit one of Rex's sneaker-covered feet.

A motherfucking voodoo doll.

Holy fucking shit.

His body was ice. Hard, cold and unmoving.

Was Odette right?

Was Lydia the one doing all of this?

Was she tormenting Odette? Did she believe in voodoo?

His gut told him Lydia was innocent, but fucking hell, the evidence against her just kept piling up.

Dragging his phone out of his hoodie pocket, he snapped a picture of it on the floor mat, then carefully, so as to not touch the pin poked in the belly or disturb any other part of the creepy-ass doll, he picked it up with the Kleenex, stuffed it back in the glove compartment and shut the compartment door.

With a shudder to his spine he just couldn't shake, he finished snooping in her car. Nothing else weird or sinister could be found. But the fact that there was a fucking voodoo doll in her glove compartment gave him the serious willies.

He let Diesel mark a bush one more time before taking the dog back into the building.

She'd be suspicious if he didn't return to her place.

In her mind, things between them had settled. She believed he believed her. They'd had sex multiple times in the shower, ate dinner and watched television like a normal couple.

To Lydia, they'd merely had a lovers' spat, but things were A-OK now.

Not to Rex, they weren't.

Using the key, he opened up her apartment door, stowed both of their keys back on the table where they'd been before and unhooked Diesel.

Diesel waited for another treat, and once he got it, he nudged Rex's crotch for a second, sniffed, snorted, sneezed, then went to go curl up with Pia on the dog bed again.

If Rex knew any better, he'd think Diesel was trying to tell him he needed to go get an STD test. But Diesel just liked to sniff crotches. Dog crotches, people crotches, tree crotches. And if he couldn't find a crotch to sniff, he turned to his own.

He removed his sneakers, turned off all the lights in the apartment and headed back to the bedroom. Lydia was still asleep, hugging her pillow but facing the side of the bed he would take.

He shucked his sweatpants and pulled his hoodie and T-shirt off before sliding beneath the cool covers next to her in just his boxers.

His eyes had adjusted enough to the dark that he could make out most of the features on her face.

Her features were delicate. Her nose adorable. She had an angular chin and high cheekbones, but they weren't sharp. There was a softness to them that lent her a sweetness that he'd been drawn to immediately. Her round, heart-shaped face with the long, feathered lashes and perfectly shaped lips that looked just right wrapped around his cock. She was beautiful. Inside and out. And it had been that beauty, that gentleness, and the fact that he just couldn't get her out from under his skin, combined with her inherent and deep-seated strength, that he'd been initially drawn to.

Even though she'd been drowning her sorrows in a mickey of cheap booze when they first met, she was still incredibly fierce and determined to not let getting fired ruin her life. She'd worked too damn hard, gone to school for far too long to let one lost job get her down.

And yet, she still smiled.

She smiled through it all.

Laughed even.

The show they'd been watching on television earlier had been a comedy, and her chuckles had warmed his chest, made him tighten his hold on her and press more than one kiss to the top of her head.

When he'd kiss her like that, she'd glance up at him, her smile reaching her eyes and causing them to sparkle. Then she'd make some silly comment about his dimples, poke them and tell him to put them away before she straddled him on the couch.

Careful not to wake her, he brushed a strand of hair off her face with one finger.

She sighed deeply, snuggled deeper beneath the covers but didn't wake.

Slowly, he pulled the covers free from her shoulders and upper back. She wore a tank top and pajama pants, but enough of her soft skin was exposed that his finger, as if drawn by magnets, swept across her shoulder closest to him.

She sighed and moaned, but her eyes remained closed.

Leaning over, he pressed his lips to her shoulder where his finger had been.

She sighed again and squirmed, rolling over to her side more, giving him a better view of her face.

Her lips were puffy, and faint circles marred the delicate skin beneath her eyes. Even if she was getting enough sleep, all this shit happening to her had to be exhausting. Had to be weighing on her.

It was fucking weighing on him.

That same, stubborn lock of hair as before had fallen back over her face, so this time, he tucked it behind her ear.

Her lips parted, and warms puffs of air from her even breaths hit the back of his hand that rested on the bed, propping him up.

He leaned over again and kissed her shoulder.

He wasn't sure if he wanted her to wake.

He wasn't sure of a lot of things right now.

He just knew the woman lying in the bed next to him wasn't a bad person. She might be troubled, possibly lonely and lost. Possibly hungry for attention and affection. But she wasn't a bad person.

"What's the plan here, handsome?" she asked groggily, her eyes still closed, but her lashes now fluttering against her cheeks. A small, placid smile curled her lips. Lips that had sucked his cock like a Hoover vacuum earlier in the shower. Fuck, she gave great head. And that added finger in his ass—he'd only had it done to him a few times—but he'd never say no if a chick offered. Never fucking ever.

"No plan," he said, twirling his tongue over her shoulder cap again before moving it along her upper back, dragging the covers off her body as he did.

She hummed softly. "Not like you at all. You're a man with a plan."

He smiled against her skin and nipped her other shoulder.

"You've got me there." With one hand, he pushed the hem of her tank top up along her back while the other dragged the sheet down past her perfect ass cheeks, which were encased in booty-short PJ bottoms. But really, they were just loose underwear based on how much they covered. They reminded him of the silkies they wore while training in the Navy. He tugged those down to reveal her crease and dragged his tongue along the length of her spine.

She trembled slightly when he reached those sexy little twin indents at the small of her back and swirled his tongue around each other them. Gooseflesh seemed to chase him the farther south he traveled.

He flicked the top of her crease with his tongue, but she didn't let him get any farther before she was rolling over and pulling the shorts off. "Come here." She reached for him, her smile sleepy and placid.

He shucked his boxers and settled over top of her. She spread her legs wide for him, planting her feet on the mattress.

Her hands were warm and soft and her fingers gentle as she lifted one hand and traced the outline of his brow, allowing her finger to drift along his cheek and jaw. "You okay?"

He nodded.

But he couldn't be further from fucking okay. Not after what he just found in the glove compartment of her car.

Even in the dark, he could see the concern building on her face. Her eyes were dark shadows, but the tension in her jaw, the pinch of her brow was unmistakable.

He swallowed. "I'm really falling for you, Lydia. Like *hard*."

Her eyes began to sparkle. "I'm really falling for you, too. It's been fast, but it feels really right." Her fingers tickled an itch down his back, and he grinned through the turmoil inside him when she playfully dug her nails into his ass cheeks.

"You know you can tell me anything, right?" he said, his cock confused about whether it should be getting hard, so staying soft.

The mood wasn't sexy, but he'd started the seduction routine and was currently naked between her warm, soft thighs, so the moment would suggest something sexy this way cometh.

She nodded. "Yes. I trust you." She kissed his shoulder. "And that goes double for me. I know there are things that you *can't* tell me because of work, but you *can* tell me anything."

Oh, how he wished he fucking could.

How he wished he could just tell her all about Odette coming to Brock for help and claiming that Lydia was stalking her. In a lot of ways, it would be a hell of a lot easier if it all just did come out into the open. If he told her what he knew and they could work together to get to the bottom of it all. His gut told him that Lydia was innocent, but when he found that voodoo doll in her glove compartment, his gut no longer felt confident in its initial reaction.

"There's something you're not telling me, isn't there?"

With a heavy sigh, he rolled off her and propped his head in his hand, facing her on his side. She mirrored him, but it was still dark in the room, so her expressions were distorted.

"Is there anything *you* would like to tell me?" he countered.

Her brows scrunched.

Fuck, he needed to be able to see her face.

They didn't call him The Lie Detector back in the day for nothing. But in order to be The Lie Detector, he needed to be able to see who he was trying to squeeze the truth from. He pivoted in the bed and turned on the bedside lamp.

When he turned back to face her, her pupils were rapidly shrinking to accommodate the light, and the hazel of irises seemed to almost swirl with intensity. It unnerved him as much as it turned him on, and the way her breasts moved beneath her tank top on deep, long breaths made it feel like spiders were dancing down his spine.

She was troubled. He could see the conflict on her face as clear as the freckle beneath her left eye.

"Lydia?"

"What are you getting at, Rex? What do you think I know that I'm not telling you?" Ire had her nostrils flaring, and she sat up in the bed and glared down at him. The sheets pooled at her hips, and anger flashed in her eyes, causing the gold to overtake the green. Her mouth became a harsh slash as she plopped her hands on her hips and waited for him to respond. "Hmm?" she probed when he didn't say anything.

Rex squeezed his eyes shut for a moment and rolled onto his back with a sigh that felt shallow in his chest. The weight of all of this was making it difficult for him to breathe.

Why oh why did he bring this up now?

Why couldn't they just have had more sex and then tackle this disaster in the light of day?

Because you found a motherfucking voodoo doll in her glove compartment and won't be able to get a stiffy until you get to the bottom of why she has that freaky thing in her possession.

Right.

That.

With as deep of a breath as he could muster, he opened his eyes and turned his gaze to her. "I just want to make sure we haven't left any stone unturned. Is there anyone, anyone at all that you think might be out to get you? Who has a score to settle or something? No detail, no person is too small or insignificant."

Her gaze narrowed.

She didn't believe him.

Fuck, he didn't believe himself. He'd pulled that out of his ass, and it fucking stunk.

But when her eyes shifted down to the duvet and she began to pick at a loose thread, he realized maybe his question didn't stink as much as he thought it did.

"I don't see how any of this is relevant, but ..."

He sat up in bed abruptly, adjusting the pillows behind his

head and back and leaning against the headboard.

He didn't want to appear *too* eager, but if she came to him about the voodoo doll, then he wouldn't have to feel so fucking guilty about his snooping. He could pretend it never happened. It would be even better if she just came clean about harassing Odette and that everything that was happening to her was a cry for attention.

His mother was a therapist. If she couldn't help Lydia, he was sure she could recommend someone who could.

She cleared her throat. "My dad died when I was eight. And when I was ten, my mother started dating again. She works as a secretary for an insurance adjuster and has since shortly before my dad passed. She didn't introduce me to any of the men she dated until this one guy—Lyle Whigby. They were together for about five months, and he seemed nice. He was a locksmith."

Every single hair on Rex's body immediately stood up, and the ghostly fingers that tap-danced the length of his spine had him fighting off the squirm he so desperately wanted to do.

A locksmith!

A motherfucking locksmith.

"Lyle was nice to me. Friendly. I didn't think anything of it, really. We mostly saw him on the weekends, or a few nights a week, he would bring takeout over after my mom got home from work. Since I only lived a few blocks from the school, and my mom worked until five, I usually walked home and stayed there by myself until she got home. I did my homework, my chores and sometimes started dinner. It was just the two of us, so I wanted to help out where I could."

"That's kind of young to be staying home alone."

She nodded and shrugged. "Yeah, but after-school care wasn't cheap, and the wait list to get into some of those were so long, I would have been in high school before they called my name. Hope is also a really small commuter town, so options were limited. Our neighbors next door—the O'Flanagans—were a married couple, and both were retired police officers. Every day, I had to go to their house after school first, call my mom to tell her I was home safe, then I'd walk across the lawns and do my homework. I was really only home alone for two hours, and I was—*am*—a responsible person."

This wasn't the direction he thought their conversation was going to go, but the mention of a locksmith had him on high alert. As soon as she finished her confession, he would text Chase the name Lyle Whigby and have him dig up every last speck of dirt on the man that he could.

"I was home one day by myself—with all the doors locked—and I had my headphones in and my Discman playing while I dusted and swept the floors. I didn't hear him come in."

Nausea filled him, and he had to push down the taste of bile that covered his tongue.

"He shocked the crap out of me, to say the least. But I knew Lyle, I liked him, so I figured maybe my mum gave him a key—she hadn't, of course. He seemed different. Said he brought me a present. I didn't know what they were at the time. I wasn't quite eleven. But I know now that they were sex toys. A vibrator and a ball gag."

Holy fuck.

His breathing was shallow and quick now, all coming out his nose like a bull gearing up to charge the matador.

He could also tell that she was suffering, telling him this. It was taking its toll on her, emotionally, mentally and even physically. Her complexion was ghostly, her eyes laser-focused on the duvet. She hadn't looked at him once since she started. Her fingers also trembled as she plucked at the loose strand.

"He asked me if I'd ever seen a penis before. I said *no*. Then he asked me if I would like to see one. He told me that a man's penis changes when he finds a woman pretty, that it grows and gets hard and that a woman should be happy when a man gets hard. Take it as a compliment, because it means he likes her. I said that was weird and seemed like a huge inconvenience for men, since pretty girls were everywhere." The corner of her mouth lifted slightly, and she huffed out a sardonic laugh.

He wasn't laughing though.

Not in the fucking slightest.

"He told me that he thought I was pretty and asked me if I'd like to see his hard penis as proof. I told him that I didn't want to see it. I even told him that he was making me uncomfortable, and I asked him to leave, that I didn't like him at the house without my mum there."

"Good for you." He knew his praise was unnecessary and that it was decades too late, but at this point in her story, he had no idea what else to say. His bloodlust for this motherfucking pedophile was making the pulse in his ears thunder to the point where he was struggling to even hear the rest of her story.

As he expected, she didn't react to his comment. She just kept picking at the duvet thread. "He started to walk toward me, coaxing me, complimenting me. All I had was the broom and a can of Lemon Pledge. Then he asked me if I'd gotten my period yet. I hadn't, but I didn't tell him that. He said that girls who hadn't gotten their periods yet could have sex but not have to worry about having a baby. He then asked me if I would like to be better and more mature than my other friends and have sex before they did."

Rex pinched his eyes closed, pressed the back of his head hard against the headboard and ran his hand over his scalp. "Jesus fucking Christ. Please tell me ..."

"Mr. and Mrs. O'Flanagan to the rescue. They saw his truck parked out front, knew he didn't have a key, and they also knew I was home by myself. They knocked on the door, and when I didn't answer, they used *their* key to come in."

"Thank fuck," he breathed, opening his eyes and tilting his

head forward again.

She was finally looking at him. "It could have gone a lot differently if they hadn't shown up when they did."

"And thank fuck they did." He reached for her hands. They were cold and trembled slightly in his. "What happened to Lyle?"

"Mr. O'Flanagan put the run on him, and neither my mum nor I ever saw him again. Apparently, my mum was getting ready to dump him later that day anyway. She said he was overly curious about me, and for a person with no children, he certainly had a lot of opinions on how to raise them. It made her uncomfortable and also frustrated her. She said that I am her number one priority and that no one would ever come between us or allow her to question how she was raising me."

"But did he go to fucking jail for breaking and entering?" Rex practically yelled.

She shook her head. "He had a key. He'd cut one."

"Fuck almighty."

"What about getting him on a sex offenders watchlist or ... or ..."

"He didn't touch me."

"But you reported him, right?"

She nodded. "We did. But nothing came of it because he didn't touch me and he had a key. Yes, he propositioned a minor, but there was no evidence. It was my word against his at the end, and even though we tried, eventually my mum just wanted to put it all behind us."

"And you think this Lyle motherfucker might be the one coming into your apartment now? Where is he now?" If she didn't know, Chase would find out as fast as his fingers could move. They'd find Lyle, and if the motherfucker was still breathing *and* he was the one tormenting Lydia, Rex would make sure the man wished he'd never been fucking born.

She lifted a shoulder. "I don't know. I haven't thought about

Lyle in a long time. I've done a pretty good job of blocking the man from my mind and memory. But when I recorded myself locking my door like you told me to, the memory of him being a locksmith and cutting himself a key came back to me, and I started to wonder."

"Who else knows about him?"

She swallowed. "Your mum."

His eyes went wide. "My mother?"

"I'd started thinking about Lyle at the same time we were meeting for a walk. She's got some serious Spidey-sense, that woman." Yes, she certainly fucking did. "And she pulled it out of me."

He nodded slowly. "And what did she say?"

"Not much. Just that she was glad he didn't touch me. She said he was grooming me and that he exhibited classic signs of a child molester with his behavior. We figured that he's probably a pedophile, so since I'm an adult now, I'm not on his radar as a target. Your mum is a really good listener."

She could be. But Joy Hart also knew how to lecture until he and his brothers thought their ears were going to fall off. He was glad his mother had taken the listening and therapist approach with Lydia, though, and not the all-knowing mother approach like she did with him so often.

"This all happened back in Hope?"

She nodded again. "Yeah. I honestly never saw the man again after that day. I thought that I might. So did my mum and the O'Flanagans. So for a long time after he let himself into our house, I stayed at the O'Flanagans' after school until my mum came home. But he never tried anything."

"And the sex toys ... you think because he gave you some that day and then you were sent another one—on your own underwear —that it might be him again?"

Another shoulder lift. "Maybe. I don't know. I mean, why after eighteen years is he doing this to me? I'm adult. How did he find me?"

"Social media," he said blandly. "You can find anyone. It's how I found Dierks, and he's not even as bad as some people with what he posts."

"I guess ... I mean, I don't post much either. Is Lyle in Victoria?"

He grabbed his phone off her nightstand. "I'm going to text Chase and get him to figure that out. He should have an answer for us by the morning if I know my tech-savvy brother."

She glanced at her own phone. "It's late, though. Isn't he probably asleep?"

"Then he'll have it by noon. Either way, it won't take long for us to figure out where Lyle Whigby is and perhaps pay him a visit."

"Are we okay, Rex?"

Her question sobered him, and he quickly finished his text to Chase, set his phone down and turned off the lamp before scooping her into his arms and sliding them both down beneath the covers. "We are. We just need to get to the bottom of things."

"It's just ... the way you were looking at me, it's like you think I have some big secret that I'm not telling you." She glanced up at him from where her head rested against his chest, her eyes holding almost a pleading look to them. "I'm not. I swear."

He kissed her head and pulled her tighter to him. "I know, baby, I know. First things first. We need to find Lyle Whigby and see what the fuck is going on."

Then he'd deal with the voodoo doll and Odette's accusations.

One thing at a time.

Slow and steady won the race.

He just hoped that when the finish line came into view, he and Lydia were holding hands as they crossed it and she wasn't sweeping a leg out in front of him so he ran face-first into the dirt.

Wouldn't be the first time someone had done that to him.

CHAPTER 21

EVEN THOUGH SHE was warm and toasty with Rex's big body wrapped around hers in bed, Lydia hardly slept at all after telling Rex all about Lyle. She rarely slept well after reliving that memory.

He didn't have to touch her or show him his penis for the knowledge of what *could* have happened to be burned in her brain for eternity. She knew very well what *could* have happened if the O'Flanagans hadn't shown up when they did. She and her mother had had a long discussion about it, and then she'd been sent to speak with a child counselor.

She was well aware of what Lyle could have done to her if she hadn't had guardian angel neighbors with licenses to carry.

But it wasn't just the Lyle stuff that kept her sleep at bay. It was the way Rex had looked at her even before she started talking about Lyle. Like he was waiting for her to come clean about something. Like she harbored this deep, dark secret and if he stared at her long enough, she'd break and spill all the beans.

The problem was, she had no beans to spill.

Nothing.

She was a victim in all of this. Just like she had been with Lyle.

And yet, Rex wasn't looking at her like she was innocent—not anymore, anyway.

What changed? Between when they spoke on the phone when he was in Vancouver to when he arrived at her house later that day, what changed her Hart's heart? Even more so, after their little head-butt in her foyer followed by white-hot sex in the shower, he seemed to be more himself. Then he took Diesel out before coming to bed and he was back looking at her like she was guilty of peeling her own bananas and biting her own cheese for attention.

Just because she'd been lonely in a new town with no friends didn't mean she was desperate enough to start stalking herself for attention. If push came to shove, she'd just move back to Hope where her mother was and find a job there.

But a few summer vacations to the island as a child had ingrained her love for the coast and Vancouver Island in particular. The salty air and gentle sound of the lapping waves, or even the crashing waves during a storm, were soul-cleansing.

Before she knew it, it was six thirty in the morning and Rex was letting go of her and rolling out of bed. "Need to get Diesel out and head to work." He checked his phone. "Nothing from Chase yet."

She shifted to her side and watched him dress.

They'd both slept bottomless, since they'd shucked their drawers when he'd started kissing her awake, but it hadn't gone to sexy time.

Even in turmoil, she allowed herself a moment to just appreciate the perfect specimen of a man before her—the breadth of his back and shoulders, each well-defined muscle bunching and flexing as he pulled on his boxers, followed by his pants.

She was chewing fiercely on her bottom lip and contemplated moving her fingers between her legs under the sheets, but the no-nonsense scowl on his face crushed that thought before it'd fully formed.

Now what was going on in that shiny, bald head of his?

"Gonna go up to my place after. Grab some fresh clothes and head to Brock's. You gonna be okay?"

Yes, of course she was going to be okay. She had to head to James and Emma's to watch the twins for the day while their parents went to work. She had a purpose, and she was going to be spending time with children, so she would most definitely be *okay*.

That didn't mean she wasn't going to keep whatever was plaguing Rex from eating way at her.

She nodded. "Watching the twins today."

He tugged his shirt over his head and shoved his phone into the pocket of his sweatpants. "'Kay, then I'll see you later."

Was he going to kiss her goodbye?

Should she ask for a kiss?

It was weird to say that this felt like the beginning of the end, because it was still just the beginning of everything—their relationship, her new job—but the inescapable crushing feeling in her chest and her heart was all too real.

He was distant, and he hadn't busted out the dimples since they'd been snuggled up on the couch watching television.

Rolling her lips inward to keep herself from asking for a goodbye kiss, she pulled the covers up and tucked them beneath her arms.

He placed one hand on the bed and leaned in toward her, his lips brushing across her cheek. "Have a good day."

She forced a smile, but it felt like weights were hanging off the corners of her mouth. "You too."

Then he was gone.

The sound of Diesel's nails on the parquet floor, followed by the open and close of her front door, echoed through her small apartment.

Moments later, as she sat there staring straight ahead and wondering who she'd wronged in her life for them to wreak such havoc in hers, Pia pounced up onto the bed and ran her tail beneath

Lydia's nose. That was the cat's way of saying she was hungry and if she didn't get fed soon, she would poop in Lydia's favorite shoes.

With a throat full of razor blades and a lump the size of a peach, she swallowed, swung her legs over the side of the bed and started to get dressed.

At least she had a job—for now.

But that job had been because of Rex's connections. Hell, two thirds of the children she was looking after were related to Rex. If he ended it between them, would that mean her nanny gig ended, too?

Once dressed, she fed Pia, fed herself, tidied her hair and slathered on just enough makeup to hide the worry lines and circles under eyes, then she was out the door. She'd stop on her way to work and grab a sandwich at the grocery store. Her fridge was pretty bare, and she also just didn't have it in her to stay in her place any longer. The lavender smell had pretty much disappeared, but now her place—particularly her bed and room—smelled like Rex, and that was just another kind of pain, to smell him but not be near him.

Even though he'd kissed her goodbye, things between them weren't normal.

Things in her life weren't normal.

And what sucked more than anything was that she had no idea where to start to try to fix it. Not a clue, and the one man who'd promised to help her harbored doubts about her and her claims. So now she really was on her own.

Maybe that was how it was supposed to be.

She'd need to get more cats to fit the bill of the crazy cat-lady.

Pia wouldn't be too happy about that though.

———

IT WAS ONLY ten o'clock when he heard from Chase.

"Last known address of one Lyle Whigby was 1456 Tremaine Terrace in Hope, British Columbia. But I checked further, and he doesn't live there anymore," Chase said over the phone as Rex sat in Brock's office on one side of the desk, Brock on the other. "Thinkin' he changed his name, but why?"

"'Cause Lydia wasn't the only child he tried to groom and molest. He probably changed his name before he could be on a registered sex-offender list. Might have gone off the grid." Brock leaned back in his chair until it creaked and brought his coffee mug up to his lips.

Rex had an identical mug steaming in front of him as well.

"Think he changed both his names?" Rex asked. "I mean, the guy's a locksmith. Can't you cross-reference locksmiths with the first name Lyle in B.C.? Fuck, across Canada?"

Chase made a noise in his throat. "Already did. Nothing popped up. But I'm going to keep digging."

"In the meantime," Brock said, setting his mug back down on the desk, "I'm going to send Heath to Odette's to try to pull some prints and hair, see if her accusations against Lydia hold any truth. How are we coming on the burner phone?"

"That burner is old as fuck," Chase replied. "I need to go buy a different cable to charge it."

Brock grunted.

Chase grunted.

Rex flared his nostrils and welcomed the too-hot coffee and its burn across his tongue.

He hadn't told his brothers about the voodoo doll yet. But that fucking creepy-ass thing and Lydia's story about Lyle had kept him awake all goddamn night. He knew she was awake all night too. But they remained silent, both of them pretending to sleep, his body wrapped so perfectly around hers.

"How long is Lydia working at James's?" Brock asked.

Rex lifted a shoulder. They'd barely spoken that morning, and he fucking hated it. But he knew that if he talked too much, he'd come clean about the voodoo doll and his snooping, as well as the fact that Odette was accusing Lydia of stalking her. He was good at keeping secrets but not from the people he cared about.

It felt wrong.

And keeping that shit from Lydia felt really fucking wrong.

Brock's big sausage fingers punched a bunch of shit into his phone. He was probably messaging James or Emma. The phone vibrated in his palm, and he glanced at it. "She's there nine to four." He lifted his gaze to Rex. "Which gives you more than enough time to go back to her place and do a thorough sweep."

"Of what, exactly?" He already knew the answer. He just needed his brother to tell him so his brain could compartmentalize all this shit. This was HIS JOB.

Brock lifted a brow.

Chase snorted.

"Anything that could provide us with evidence corroborating *our client's* story."

"Gonna run to the store and find a cord for the burner," Chase said. "Call you back when it's charged." He disconnected the call without saying goodbye.

Rex and Brock sat across from each other, their eyes locked.

"Don't like this any more than you do," Brock finally said. "I like Lydia. My wife likes Lydia. My kids like Lydia. But if she's a nutter, we gotta find out before anybody gets hurt."

Rex nodded. "Odette at work?"

Brock's caterpillar eyebrows kissed. "She's on stress leave for two weeks because of what this is doing to her ... apparently. Why?" His green eyes widened, pulling the caterpillars apart. "You're not going over to her place with Heath. I forbid it."

He rolled his eyes. "Just wanna fucking meet this chick. Give me a break. I can follow orders."

Brock shook his big, square head. "Not a good idea."

"But I'm the fucking Lie Detector. Give me ten minutes with her and I can tell you whether she's making all of this shit up or not."

The chair beneath Brock squealed as he hinged forward and planted his hands on the desk, his expression fierce, his voice just above a roar. "You're also *fucking* the suspect, *and* you've spent more than ten minutes with her, and can you tell me whether she's making it all up?"

Rex growled and stood up. "That's fucking different."

No, it wasn't.

Brock's expression relaxed. "No, it's not, and you know it. Now, go do the job your boss *assigned* you to do and stop pouting like a toddler." He bent his head, picked up a pen and started writing something.

Rex glared at the top of his brother's head.

"Go!" Brock shouted, not bothering to look up.

Rex headed for the door, the pit in his belly expanding the more footsteps he took. He paused in the doorway and glanced back at his brother.

"I hope to fuck we're all wrong and Lydia is innocent. But we've been hired by a client, and we have to take this shit seriously. Now let's all do our jobs, get to the bottom of it, and hopefully, with any luck, your girlfriend will be in the clear." He finally lifted his gaze to Rex's, the green in Brock's eyes extra dark and stormy. "I want her to be in the clear just as much as you. She's watching my kids, for Christ's sake."

Rex nodded, pinned his lips together and left.

He took the long way back to his apartment building, delaying the job he had to do because he sure as fuck didn't want to do it.

What good, decent human being would?

Snoop around the apartment of the woman he was falling for to *hopefully* find something to incriminate her in the stalking and harassment of the woman that fired her.

Could this get any more fucked up?

He knew better than to even think such a thing, because when he finally pulled into his apartment parking lot and glanced at his phone, there was a text from an anonymous number with a link.

Normally, he would have deleted the number, blocked it and reported it as spam, but the message that accompanied the link had him pausing.

You're going to want to see this. Did you agree to this?

What the fuck did that mean?

He clicked the link to a fairly well-known shaming website. People posted everything from videos of neighbors stealing packages at the front door, to sexual images and videos. It was often used by a partner trying to shame their cheating partner after catching them on film, but that wasn't always the case. Sometimes people just posted videos there for attention, or to be an asshole.

Why the fuck was someone sending him a link to this site? He had no account at this site and never visited it, but that didn't mean he wasn't aware of it.

His question was answered a second later when the sounds of two people having sex echoed through the cab of his truck before the video appeared on the small screen.

But even with the small screen of his phone, it was easy enough to see just *who* those two people getting it on were—and where they were.

Dread coiled through him like a suffocating vine.

He recognized that room.

He'd spent the night in that room.

It was he and Lydia last week. The first time they'd had sex in her bed and he'd tied her up. She was spread-eagle, restrained, and he was going balls-out, hammering into her as she encouraged him to give it to her harder.

They were both completely naked.

You could see everything.

Her tits, her pussy, his ass, his cock.

There was absolutely nothing left to the imagination.

What in the ever-loving fuck was going on?

He texted back the number. *Who are you? How did you get this?*

The person responded almost immediately. *Just a concerned citizen. The link was sent to me. It has over two hundred views, and it's only been posted for thirty minutes. Your girl a camera babe?*

The way the person was talking made him think it was a guy. But then, anybody could *pretend* to be the opposite sex, particularly in texting or emails.

Who are you? He texted back. *How do I know you? Who sent you this link?*

But whoever it was didn't return his questions with answers, and Rex was left sitting in his truck, watching himself on his phone bite Lydia's nipples and then come inside her.

Sick to his fucking stomach, he forwarded the link to Chase, along with the message. *Track down the IP address for this video. We need to know who the fuck posted it.* Then he sent his brother the phone number that had texted him the link. *And find out who the fuck this number belongs to. Send a cease-and-desist letter and pull the video the fuck down.*

He waited until his brother texted him back.

Chase's message was as expected. *What in the fuck? On it.*

Rex was regretting dropping Diesel off at his mother's right about now, as he climbed out of his truck and hit the fob to lock it. He could use some puppy snuggles and love, because the sick feeling in his stomach only grew worse the closer to the door he got.

He didn't want to think it, certainly wouldn't say it out loud, but ...

How on earth could things possibly get any worse?

CHAPTER 22

SHE'D JUST GOTTEN the twins down for a nap and was closing their bedroom door when her phone began to vibrate and warble in the back of her jeans pocket.

Lydia made sure the door was closed and the baby monitor on before she answered Jayne's call and put the phone to her ear. "Hey."

"Hey, how are you holding up?"

"I'm a nanny for now, so at least I can keep the roof over my head and food in my belly. How are you?" Lydia trudged downstairs with sandbags in her feet, grabbed her sandwich out of James and Emma's fridge, then sat at the kitchen bar to have her lunch.

"Odette's on two weeks' stress leave, effective immediately."

Lydia paused, her sandwich not fully out of its package. "What the fuck does that bitch have to be stressed about? She's not even a teacher. She's a preschool administrator. Parents breathing down her neck about why their three-year-old isn't doing his times tables yet?"

Jayne made a noise of agreement. "That's what we're all wondering. Except ..."

Lydia finished opening up her turkey and Swiss sandwich and took a bite. "Except what?"

"Except Reese made some offhand comment about you being the cause of her stress. None of us knew what he was talking about, and when we probed further, he shook his head, dismissed it all, jumped in his Jag and took off like he was late for his hair-plug appointment." She snorted. "I wish the man would just embrace the bald."

Lydia could attest that bald wasn't bad—at least on some men. She wasn't sure if her former big boss Reese Stone could pull off no hair like Rex could.

Thoughts of Rex made her melancholy, and she pushed her sandwich away. "Do you have any idea what Reese meant by that? How am I stressing Odette out? I don't even work there anymore." Her eyes went wide. "You don't think the voodoo doll did more than give her diarrhea, do you?"

Jayne clucked. "No. I don't even know if it did. I more just did that to help you feel better and get over being fired."

She knew that, but there was still a thin thread of skepticism coursing through her that perhaps the doll had worked and perhaps a little too well.

"How's the nanny job working out, darling?" She could hear Jayne chewing. She was probably on her fifteen-minute lunch break.

"It's good. Kids are all great. The parents are great, too. But ..."

"But it's not what you want to be doing. It's not what you're highly educated to do."

"Exactly."

"We seriously need some rich guy to just say, 'Hey, I'll fund your preschool if you run it. Here, have all this money and teach the future.'"

"From your mouth to the universe's ears." She picked at a piece of turkey breast hanging from the corner of her sandwich and popped it into her mouth. "I think Rex and I are over."

"What? Why?" Jayne's voice had turned slightly shrill, and Lydia had to pull her ear away from the phone.

"He's beginning to think that all the weird shit happening to me is of my own doing."

"Like you pissed someone off, so they're rightfully tormenting you?"

"No, like I'm doing it all to myself for attention because I'm lonely and lost."

"Did he say that?" Jayne's pitch was even higher, and Lydia pulled the phone away even farther with a grimace.

"No. Not in so many words. But he did say that he went and saw Dierks and that it can't be him. Then he kept probing for information, like I have some deep, dark secret I'm keeping from him. He said he *wants* to believe me, but this is all very unusual and he's trained to listen to his gut."

"Fucking twat."

"Well, no. I mean, I get it, but it still hurts."

"Did you throw those accusations right back in his face?"

"I did. I said that none of the shit that's been going on started happening until I met him, so what was to stop me from thinking it was him doing it all and getting his rocks off being the hero to save me? He didn't like that very much, but it seemed to knock a little bit of sense into him. Do I think he's the one doing it? Of course not. But when he accused me of doing it, I couldn't just keep my mouth shut."

"And I'm fucking glad you didn't. Men need to be put in their place."

Lydia snorted. "Yeah, well, his place probably won't be the same as my place for much longer. I can already see the writing on the wall. He thinks I'm crazy, and what man willingly invites crazy into his life?"

"More men than you think, darling. And you are *not* crazy. He's the crazy one if he lets a catch like you get away."

Lydia exhaled a big breath through her mouth and stepped down off the barstool. "Thanks, friend."

"Coffee and a walk soon?"

"Yes, please. I could use the distraction and friendship."

"Always, love. You know I'm here if you need me."

They said goodbye and hung up.

The twins usually napped for a solid two hours, so Lydia had an hour and forty-five minutes to tidy up. James and Emma said she didn't have to clean, that they had a cleaner, but in all her years as a babysitter, she'd never left the home she was working in not tidy. She did dishes and swept, put toys away and whatever else. Plus, she needed the distraction.

Her head was spinning, thoughts colliding with each other. This didn't make any sense. None of it did.

The person stalking her and tormenting her, Odette claiming that Lydia was the reason for her stress leave, and Rex accusing her of doing all the crazy shit to herself.

She reached for the broom from the kitchen pantry and started sweeping. Maybe if she just kept her head down and focused on work, all the bad shit in her life would just disappear. Like a fart on a breeze, her father used to say.

That thought brought a tear to her eye, and she wiped the back of her wrist beneath her nose. He'd been gone twenty years, but she still missed him. Still remembered him. Remembered his smell, his voice, his laugh.

Hank Sullivan had been an incredible father, and they had been a happy family. Until suddenly they weren't.

He'd been taken from them far too soon, and even though they were okay now, she wasn't sure she or her mother had ever fully recovered from his death. How do you *recover* when a piece of your heart is ripped out? The heart doesn't regenerate that piece. It just heals over it with scar tissue.

Her father would know exactly what to do in this situation. He was a man who always had the right answer. Whether it was which chemicals when mixed together would cause an explosion or which unicorn was the most friendly in her Unicorn Party books, he always knew just what to say.

And she knew beyond a shadow of a doubt that he'd know what to do now.

Thoughts of her dad had her grabbing her phone off the counter and punching in her mother's cellphone. Her mother always took her lunch between twelve and one. Most likely, she'd be sitting in the small lunch room at her office with her earbuds in and some feminist podcast playing in her ears while she ate her green salad with chicken breast, nuts and cranberries. Her mother was a very predictable creature. It was one of the things Lydia loved most about her.

The phone rang three times before her mother's gentle voice broke through. "Hello, sweetheart, what a nice surprise."

"Hi, Mum."

And as predictable as Kim Sullivan was, she was also just as astute about her daughter's moods. There rarely went a time when Lydia called and her mother didn't pick up on something with just the tone of Lydia's voice.

Now was no exception.

"What's wrong, honey?"

Tears welled up in Lydia's eyes. The broom dropped to the ground, followed by her, and the entire story tumbled from her nearly as fast as the tears fell.

By the time she was through, regaling her mother with her woes, Lydia's heart felt lighter and her eyes burned from all the tears.

Her mother was very quiet, as she usually was. An exceptional listener.

Lydia used to tell her mother that she should go back to school and become a counselor, that she just had that calming way about her. But her mother would do no more than just smile and say she liked her job and that she didn't want to make a living listening to other people's problems. But she would listen to Lydia's because Lydia was her daughter and she loved her.

"Lyle doesn't live in Hope anymore, honey," was the first thing her mother said.

Ice slithered down Lydia's spine. "What?"

Was she still in contact with him? And if so, why? Had her mother been keeping tabs on Lyle, even now that Lydia was an adult?

"After what he tried to do to you, I kept tabs on him. Mr. and Mrs. O'Flanagan did too. He was quiet for a couple of years. Then, when you were about twenty, he just vanished. No body, no trace of him. We don't know if he's dead or alive, but we know he's not in Hope anymore." Her mother's voice held a tremor to it that Lydia didn't like. Her mother was worried.

"Do you think he'd come after me now? After all this time?"

"I don't know, honey. I can't answer that. I hope not. God, I hope not, but ..."

"But ..."

"But I didn't think he was capable of what he tried to do to you, so who's to say *what* he's capable of?"

Lydia stood up from her pile of mental agony on the floor and reached for a Kleenex from the side table next to the couch in the living room. She blotted at her eyes and her nose. "Did you ever hear of Lyle taking up with any more women? Any more mothers with daughters?"

Her mother's next words came out with such heavy regret, Lydia felt it all in her chest. "No. As much as I kept a bead on him, I didn't pay attention to who he was seeing. I just wanted to know where he was. And the fact that I was a single working mother didn't allow me the opportunity to be in the know at your school like some parents. I wasn't there for school pickup, keeping up on all the gossip."

Yeah, Lydia kind of figured that question would result in a dead end.

"All I want to do is hug you right now, honey. Wrap my arms around you and take away all this pain and confusion. I wish you'd called me sooner and told me all of this. I have vacation time saved up. I could have come and stayed with you. I still can if you want me to. I can be there by Monday. I just need to call the temp agency."

Lydia blotted at her eyes and nose more before walking into the kitchen to toss the Kleenex in the garbage. "No, Mum. It's okay. You save up those vacation days for your cruise with Aunt Molly. I know how much you're looking forward to it."

"That's only two weeks, sweetheart. I have eight weeks. I can come if you need me to."

As much as she wanted to see her mother, she also knew that there wasn't much her mum could do. Plus, the last thing Lydia wanted was to put her mother in any kind of danger. Who knew what this freak was capable of and whether they would up their game to a dangerous—possibly lethal—level?

"I'll let you know, okay, Mum?"

"Call me tomorrow? Let me know how you're doing."

Lydia inhaled on a stutter, and she swallowed the still very large lump in her throat. "I will. I promise."

They ended their call with their usual declarations of love. Lydia glanced at her phone after she hung up. The twins would be up shortly. She needed to finish sweeping and get a handle on her emotions.

The girls were expecting their nanny to be happy and smiling, not crying her eyes out.

She finished sweeping and putting away the toys just as one of the twins started to make noise on the baby monitor. Ascending the stairs, she pulled her phone out of her pocket when it chirped and vibrated.

It was a text from Rex along with a link. *Did you post this video of us?*

CHAPTER 23

Thank God James was able to come home and relieve Lydia sooner than four o'clock, because after seeing that video and being accused by Rex of posting it, Lydia was barely able to function, let alone take care of two little girls.

She didn't even remember getting into her car or driving, but somehow she wound up in her apartment complex parking lot unscathed and without a police siren wailing in the background as a squad car pulled up behind her. Even completely out of it, she was a decent, law-abiding driver.

At least she had one thing going for her.

With concrete in her feet and a pounding heart, she entered the building. Rex said he would meet her in her apartment and that they *had to talk*.

That could only mean one thing.

Especially now that he thought she'd posted that video online of them having sex.

How utterly mortifying. The video had over five hundred views, too. And loads of comments. The only saving grace in all of it seemed to be that neither of their names were attached to the video. But it wouldn't take much for someone in the comments to out either her or Rex or both of them. Nobody was safe or anonymous these days, not with hackers, tech gurus and keyboard warriors with nothing better to do than hide behind their screen and hurt others.

She didn't want to step foot back into her apartment now, not ever, knowing that someone had videotaped her having sex.

What else had they recorded? Her masturbating? Her and Rex having phone sex? Her changing? Was all of it just stored in some cloud waiting to be unleashed on the world? Was whoever did it preparing to blackmail her?

Where else did they install cameras? In her shower? Did they watch her use the toilet?

It seemed there was no limit to the lengths evil people would go to or the kind of fetishes out there people got off watching.

To say she felt violated would be a gross understatement.

She felt icky. As if it wasn't just a video of her having sex that had been released online, but it was as if she was actually having sex in person in front of hundreds of people. Like they were all gawking at her naked body, whispering and commenting, watching an intimate, private act between two people and turning it into nothing more than a roadside spectacle or one of those Ping-Pong shows she'd heard about in Thailand.

The door to the building felt extra heavy, and she had to use two hands to heave it open. She took the stairs. Delaying the inevitable.

Her apartment was unlocked, as she expected it to be, since Rex said he would meet her there and she'd given him a key before he left for Vancouver. That way, he could get Diesel if he returned early and she was at work.

She turned the knob slowly, gritted her teeth, straightened her back and stepped inside.

What waited for her was a man barely able to contain his rage.

He was a bottle of Coke and Mentos that some idiot had decided to shake.

Only she wasn't the idiot, even though at this point, she was sure he was one hundred percent convinced that she was.

"What the fuck?" was the first thing out of his mouth.

She stood in front of him, arms at her side, lips pinned together to keep from trembling. "I know, right? I don't know how ..."

His head snapped back and he gave her an incredulous look. "What do you mean you don't know how? Chase tracked the video to your IP address, and I found a small camera hidden on your vanity. The text message came from a burner phone, so that's a dead end."

Her head shook frantically. No. This was not happening. "I ... I didn't do it. You think I posted it? I would never. I told you that in my text message back to you. I feel just as violated as you do. My body, intimate moments between the two of us are on display for the world to see and I hate it." Every word seared her tongue like a hot poker, while the lump that felt more like a small orange at the back of her throat caused her jaw to throb.

But Rex didn't seem to be buying any of her horror or devastation. He stood there with a brow raised and his arms crossed over his chest. "Are you actually going to stand here and deny that you secretly videotaped us and then loaded it to the internet?" Anger as white-hot as the surface as the sun blazed back at her. "Chase has pulled down the video, but I want all the copies. I want every fucking video you have. Now."

Her feeling of relief from the video being pulled was fleeting, and her resolve to not turn into a puddle of tears was quickly crumbling, too. Her breath rattled from her chest like she was fighting a chill, and she shook her head emphatically. "I don't have anything. I didn't do this. I didn't record us, I swear. I am as devastated and as violated as you are. I am a victim! We are *both* victims!"

Rex's lip curled up into a sneer, and he walked over to her

kitchen counter and picked up a box. "Yeah, then what are these for?"

It hurt to swallow.

It hurt to think.

It hurt to breathe.

She blinked through the tears and focused on the box. "Wh-what is it?"

With a scoff, he tossed the box at her, and it landed in a *clunk* at her feet. It was a box of purple disposable latex gloves. She'd never seen that box before in her life.

"Where did you ... what ... those aren't mine."

"I found them under your bathroom sink."

She squinted. "Okay ... what are you implying? That I used the gloves to orchestrate all of this in order to not leave *my own* prints in *my own* house? How does that make any sense?"

If this was the extent of his detective skills and what he based his accusations on, then he could go and fully fuck himself.

He blinked a few times, like what she was saying about not leaving prints in her own house actually made sense. But that uncertainty didn't last and he shook his head stiffly. "Chase charged that old flip phone. Thirty-two calls to Odette Rockford's phone from *that* phone. All within the last two weeks."

"What?"

Now she needed to sit down, otherwise she was going to faint or puke or have an aneurysm. Was she in the Twilight Zone? What was going on? Why did a flip phone that she'd never seen before in her life in her cutlery drawer show thirty-two outgoing messages to Odette Rockford?

"We found hair that resembles yours at Odette's house as well."

"My hair?" Now she really was going to puke. Her jaw went slack, her vision cloudy. She reached out for the wall and leaned into it. "My *hair?*"

"We'll need a DNA test to confirm, but it looks like yours, not hers. Why do you have a voodoo doll in your glove compartment?"

This all had to be a dream. One big, colossal fucking nightmare. She could wake up any time now. It wasn't funny anymore. Sure, the sex with Rex was great and she'd be sad to see that go, but nothing else that was happening to her made any sense. She'd obviously been in a dreadful car accident and was in a coma in some hospital and the last several months of her life were all just a ruse, fabricated by her brain as it tried desperately to heal.

It had to be.

Otherwise, there was no logical, practical, realistic explanation for anything that was happening. None. Nada. Zip. Zilch.

Just like before, it was all so utterly unbelievable that her body's fucked-up reaction was a giggle.

She fucking giggled.

Rex's eyes widened in horror. "You think this is *funny?*"

Lydia squeezed her eyes shut for a moment and shook her head. She opened them again, still leaning against the wall. "No. This isn't funny at all. In fact, Rex, it's a fucking nightmare, and I'd really appreciate it if I could fucking wake up now, because I'm done." She glanced up at the ceiling. "You hear that, I'm fucking done. Wake up from whatever coma or dream you're in, because this isn't fun anymore. Wake up!"

"You do realize that what you've done, stalking and harassing Odette, breaking into her house, are criminal offenses, right? Like, we have to call the police." He was looking at her like she was crazy now. Like at any moment she might just whip out a gun—or a rubber chicken—and start either shooting or making *bok bok* sounds.

"Stalking? She's accusing *me* of stalking *her?* Since when?"

His expression was stony. "She hired Brock after we got back from Vancouver. Claims you're harassing her because she fired you."

"This is rich. Honestly." She huffed a laugh and lifted a shoulder. "So you're done believing me, huh? You're done going with your gut. You snooped through my stuff, my car and God only knows what else, and the few things you've found—that have been *planted*, besides the voodoo doll—have led you to believe that I am not only doing all of this shit to myself, but that I'm also stalking the bitch that fired me? Is that correct?"

A muscle ticked in his jaw, his nostrils flared again, and the strong, sexy cords in his neck popped. "Why do you have a voodoo doll?"

She rolled her eyes. "Because Jayne gave it to me when we had lunch. She was trying to cheer me up after Odette fired me. We stuck one pin in her belly with the hopes of giving her diarrhea. It was harmless, cathartic fun. You don't actually believe in that shit, do you?"

One of his brows rose. "Do you?"

"No! I just told you, it was harmless fun. And even if it *did* work, it was only for diarrhea. I didn't want the woman to die or anything. I'm not some sadist. She fired me, and she's a bitch, but I don't want her dead. Forced to sit on the toilet for a day or two? Sure, but nothing more nefarious than that."

"And the gloves?"

She shrugged again. "Never seen that box before in my life. The same for the phone. And the camera in my bedroom. And as far as my hair at Odette's goes, well, that's just fucked up and I have no explanation for that, besides the fact that maybe she took home something from the school that I had touched and it had some of my hair on it. I cannot even tell you where the woman lives."

Now it seemed his resolve was crumbling and he wasn't sure what to believe once again. The turmoil on his face was palpable, but she had to stop herself from running to comfort him. His accusations to her burned against her skin like hot coals. He'd launched them with such force, she'd be feeling them for days if not weeks later.

He didn't trust her.

He didn't believe her.

Instead, he ignored his gut instinct and let others turn him against her.

She could tell he was clenching his molars and watched as he squeezed them extra tight and the muscles on either side of his jaw popped. "Brock's building a case against you to take to the police."

She shrugged, determined to remain calm on the outside, even though inside she was freaking out and an absolute mess. "I'm innocent, and the police will see that. The police *will do their jobs* and prove that the right person is innocent."

"I hope they do," he said quietly. "And I hope it's you."

"Are you done with the accusation assault, or did you find a chainsaw covered in blood under my bed, too?"

Anguish swirled in the midnight blue of his eyes, and his lips formed a thin, flat line. "I'm done here."

"Then *we're* done here." She released the wall and moved out of the way so his big body could lumber to the door.

She made sure not to inhale his sexy scent as he walked past. But she also knew that she wasn't in the wrong here and refused to not meet his eyes. "I'm going to assume that I'm fired from my jobs, too, at least with Chase and Brock, but I'm sure you'll be calling James and Emma after this and letting them know I'm a crazy stalker bitch who they shouldn't let anywhere near their children, right?" Her upper lip curled into a sneer.

He paused, and she watched the muscles in his back tighten beneath his black T-shirt before he turned around to face her. His expression said it all.

She was one hundred percent correct in her assumptions.

She nodded once and snorted through her nose. "Figured."

"I don't want to be right, Lydia."

"But the evidence is pretty damning, hmm? To hell with listening to your gut. With listening to *me*. To trusting *me*."

His gaze was searing.

"Gotcha. Well, *neighbor*, it was nice knowing you for the brief time that I did. Give Diesel a kiss goodbye for Pia and I."

His face turned grim, and he spun back around to face the door and opened it.

"Don't come crawling back expecting me to just forgive and forget when the cops prove that I'm innocent. Definitely shows you who your true friends are when the chips are down," she called after him as he stepped out into the hallway and before he closed the door.

But then he closed it.

And she stared at it.

For a really, really long time.

It wasn't until Pia came wandering toward her from the living room, meowing, that she peeled her gaze from the door. One glance at her cat, and all the pretend strength she'd been using to keep her knees from buckling, her voice from hitching and the tears from flowing vanished with a flick of a cat's tail, and she vomited, barely missing the cat.

When her stomach was empty—not that she'd eaten much that day to fill it—she picked up a confused-looking Pia, pressed her back to the wall and slumped to the floor.

She clutched Pia to her chest, and thankfully, the cat allowed her to. She cried for longer than she thought she ever could. Longer than she thought she had tears for. When she finally stopped and wiped her eyes, it was dark outside.

Pia scurried from her arms, skirting the vomit, but didn't go far. It was dinnertime, and she wanted Lydia to know that.

With what little energy she had left, she pried her sobbing ass off the floor and went into the kitchen to get the cat food.

Then she cleaned up her mess and filled her essential oil

diffuser with calendula and ylang ylang to mask the stench of her puke.

Her fridge was practically empty, since she wasn't too keen on buying groceries and having them get ruined by a phantasm. But her pantry had a couple of packs of ramen and a can of peaches. She wouldn't go hungry.

She put Pia's food out for her, boiled the kettle for her ramen and sat down at the island on a barstool, her face in her hands.

How did her life come to this?

And what the fuck was Odette's angle? Why was her ex-boss claiming that Lydia was stalking her? What on earth did she have to gain from that?

She'd already made Lydia's life miserable by firing her for no reason, and now she was messing with her by claiming Lydia was stalking her?

Was this all Odette?

Was she behind everything that had happened to Lydia, but was claiming Lydia was stalking *her*, to throw Rex and his brothers off the scent of the truth?

Did Odette had some fucked-up ax to grind and was getting her rocks off by tormenting Lydia.

The problem was, Jayne said Odette was on stress leave—caused by Lydia—and Lydia had no idea where Odette lived. She'd reached a dead end without even lifting a butt cheek off the stool.

She could call Odette and ask her what the hell was going on, since she still had all the contact information for all the staff at the preschool. But that might just perpetuate Odette's ludicrous accusations toward her, and the cops would be pounding on Lydia's door before she went to bed.

No. She couldn't make contact with the woman.

But she was also burning to understand the *why* behind it all.

Why come after someone you've already terminated? Why make their life even more miserable? Why waste that energy?

The kettle finished boiling, and she poured the steaming water over her noodles, watching as they softened.

Maybe tomorrow she could ask Jayne to call Odette and ask her why she was doing what she was doing to Lydia. Why she was accusing Lydia of stalking her. Maybe Jayne could just ask Odette to stop and everything could be put to rest and they could all go on with their lives.

With food in her belly, it all seemed so easily fixed.

Ask Odette to stop. She stops. Life goes back to normal.

Lydia was a realist though.

She'd always been, but it'd become a lot more a part of her everyday life after her dad died.

"Bad things happened to good people and good things happened to bad people. There is rarely a rhyme or a reason why. It just is what it is and what it is, is fucking stupid." Her Aunt Molly had said that to her after her father's funeral, and it'd stuck with her ever since.

Aunt Molly could not be more right, especially right now. Because as hard as she tried to think of a reason *why*, she just couldn't.

And that was fucking stupid.

CHAPTER 24

"And you actually think she did all of that?" Rex's mother asked him the following morning as he sat at her kitchen table and ate waffles and drank coffee.

Even though he was thirty-six years old, when shit hit the fan, his mother was the best sounding board there was. Joy Hart held no judgment, no preconceived ideas or notions, and when he asked her to just listen and not lecture, she did. He could tell when she was itchy to give advice though. Everyone had a tell, and his mother's was a little nose wrinkle like a bunny.

Her nose had been twitching like crazy all morning. He almost wanted to get up, go to the fridge and get her a carrot.

"I don't know," he finally said after taking a sip of his coffee and setting the mug down on the table. "My gut is rarely wrong, and yet, right now, I don't know if I can trust it. The evidence against her is really damning."

His mother cocked her head to the side and delicately sipped her tea. "And yet your gut keeps telling you to trust *her*, not the evidence?"

He nodded. He hadn't been able to sleep after heading to his apartment from Lydia's, so at five in the morning, he packed up Diesel and headed to his mother's. He knew she'd be up, since she'd always been an early riser. And she was, running on her treadmill in her office like she did every morning.

He hadn't expected her to cancel her morning client for him though, but she also wouldn't take *no* for an answer when she invited him to stay for breakfast and called her client to reschedule. "My babies come first, always and forever," she said, as she pulled the waffle iron out of the kitchen cupboard. "Now do you want blueberry or cranberry orange?"

He'd obviously gone with blueberry.

"You've talked with her, Mum. What do you think?" He swirled a chunk of waffle in his maple syrup before shoveling it into his mouth.

His mother was quiet for a while, her fingers steepled in front of her and the tips pressing sideways against her mouth as she thought. She closed her eyes for a moment and sat back in her seat. "I think Lydia is a lovely young woman who is very lonely. But I think she is a *good* person, and if I'm going to listen to *my* gut, which I usually do because it's rarely wrong, I am going to say that she is the victim of a meticulously plotted conspiracy against her. But she is not doing this. I also don't think she is the type to be a stalker."

"But the voodoo doll ..."

His mother rolled her blue eyes. "Oh, for Christ's sake, you buffoon, have you seen my office and all the weird sexual and otherwise paraphernalia I have in there? I have like six voodoo dolls."

A warmth of embarrassment burned his cheeks. He and his brothers had always made sure to lock their mother's office door before they ever had friends come over when they were kids. Their mother's "collection" of sexually accurate and liberal carvings, painting and paraphernalia were a bit much to try to explain to friends whose parents weren't sexuality and relationship therapists.

Big wooden phalluses, vagina diagrams, paintings of couples in various sexual positions, and a big hairy pillow with flaps and folds meant to resemble a vagina adorned her office. Not to mention all the dolls. Most of them overly anatomically correct. And now that she'd mentioned it, he had seen a few voodoo dolls on the shelves too.

"Do you use them?" he asked.

She rolled her eyes again, reached for a strawberry half from her plate and popped it into her mouth. "No. A couple were gifts from a client, another was a gift from a colleague, and then I bought a few when I went on that sex education mission to Haiti, remember?"

Right. She and a bunch of other women—doctors, counselors, therapists and the like—had gone down to Haiti for six weeks to bring free birth control and women's sanitary supplies and educate the younger generation on safe sex and their bodies. She'd brought him and his brothers back some weird fertility necklaces and said that they should wear them when they found the right women and wanted to give her grandchildren. Apparently, a voodoo priestess had blessed them and said they would make the wearers extra virile. Then his mother had tossed her head back and laughed until tears formed in her eyes at Rex and his brothers' expressions of fear.

His mother was a firecracker. All four feet eleven inches of her.

He pushed his finished plate away and reaching for his coffee. Diesel was snoring under the table like the diesel truck he was named after. When Rex first found the pup, he'd snuggled right into Rex's jacket and fell asleep. His snoring—for his size at the time—had been crazy loud and rivaled the rumble of the diesel truck parked at the gas station that served as their raid team's muster point. The dog had been called Diesel ever since.

"We need to follow the evidence and abide by the law," he said on a long sigh. "I just hate which direction the evidence is pointing us."

"You do," his mother said, sipping her tea again. "That's true. Follow the evidence. Follow the law. But listen to your gut. Even good cops know to follow their instincts." Her lips twisted into a lopsided smile. "That's one of the things that sets you apart from your brothers. You trust your gut far more than they do. You are in tune with your body and your senses and you let them guide you in the right direction. You always have. It's why you were the earliest to walk out of all of you. Brock is too blinded by responsibility, and the safety of this family weighs like a thousand cinder blocks on his shoulders. Chase is battling too many demons to listen to his body, and Heath ..."

She shook her head and glanced upward for a moment.

"My big baby boy ... he's got a lot going on in that fluffy head of his. He's always been such a happy guy, but ever since ..." His mother choked on her next words, and her throat rolled on a swallow. "What she did to him changed him. He's harder now. Darker. I still see flashes of who he used to be, but it's not the same." Anger infused the last few of her words, and her cheeks turned ruddy.

Of course, his mother was referring to what happened to Heath last year when he'd been kidnapped by the woman he fell for.

In addition to having his knee dislocated by some thugs, his heart had also taken a beating. And from what Rex's mother was saying just now, Heath's heart still hadn't recovered.

She perked up a bit and forced a smile. "But you, my darling empath, have always listened to your gut and your body. And I think you need to ignore the evidence and get back to what you're good at. *Be* the lie detector."

"I don't think she'll talk to me again. She's pretty mad."

Her brows pinched. "And any normal person would be. Not only does she feel violated by whoever is doing this to her, and now this video being posted, but she feels violated by *you*. You went through her things to find incriminating evidence against her. She trusted you, and you broke that trust." She lifted a shoulder. "I'm pissed at you for doing it, too."

He scoffed, ran his hand over his bald head and scratched the back of his neck. "Fuck, Mum, I was just doing *my job*. Brock told me to."

"*Brock told me to*," she mimicked. "Brock told me to jump off the roof so I did and that's why I have a broken leg. Same song and dance for the last thirty plus years, it would seem."

"It's different and you know it. This is my job. Odette Rockford hired us."

"And did you obtain a warrant to search Lydia's place?"

"No. She gave me a key."

"As her *boyfriend*. Not as the bald behemoth that makes up twenty-five percent of the Harty Boys."

He ground his back teeth.

"You're angry at yourself, not me," his mother said plainly. "And you definitely shouldn't be mad at Lydia, because we both know she hasn't done anything wrong. You have a hard time trusting people. I get it. All four of you do, given your line of work and the shit you've seen. But has she given you any reason *not* to trust her?"

He lifted both brows and gawked at his mother in shock.

"All the evidence and crap aside. Has she?"

No. Lydia hadn't. She'd been honest and genuine—or so he thought—right from the very beginning. It was why he was so drawn to her. When she'd run into him in the hallway, broken up over losing he job, she'd worn her heart right out there on her sleeve, and it was endearing.

But, trusting a woman he thought was on his side was what got him caught and tortured. Up until all this evidence against her, he'd been ready to let her in. To tell her more about himself, about why he didn't trust people the way he used to. About those white scars on his back. He hadn't let anyone in in a long time. And he really wanted to.

But now ...

"You're torn," his mother said. "You want to believe her. Want to trust her. You heart is telling you to listen to her. But the evidence is holding you back."

Fuck yes, he was torn.

He was torn between listening to his instincts, like he'd done for his whole fucking life, and following the blatant clear-as-day breadcrumbs that seemed to lead him right to the suspect, who just happened to be Lydia.

"You need to talk to her. Help her. Right now, I bet she's feeling more alone and helpless than she's ever felt before. She's in a town where she hardly knows anyone, and nobody believes her. She feels like the world is out to get her, and the one person she did trust —*you*—has turned against her, too. How would you feel in her shoes right now?" His mother's eyes held a sadness that he felt right to his toes. She reached across the table and took his hand. "Out of all my boys, you're the one most like me—you feel deeply and care intensely. Brock is like your father. Chase is a lot like him, too, and Heath ..." She huffed a laugh and shook her head. "If Heath wasn't the spitting image of your father, I'd say he was the mailman's baby based on how he acts." Her gaze turned whimsical. "Of course, our mailman was an ugly, cranky bastard and your father was wonderful and gorgeous—so no way would I stray—but you know what I mean."

Yes, he knew what she meant. He squeezed her hand back.

"Go to her," she encouraged. "Help her. Make it right. Help her fight for her innocence, because you and I both know that she is."

He squeezed his mother's hand again and forced a smile.

Just as he was about to stand up and head home to find Lydia and make things right, his phone lit up and Chase's face and number came up on the screen.

"Hey," he answered.

"Been digging, bro," Chase said, the tone of his voice making all the hairs on Rex's body stand straight up. "Got lost down a scary-ass rabbit hole."

Fuck.

He put the phone on speaker but held it. He and his mother exchanged worried glances. "What did you find?"

Chase cleared his throat. "I've been digging around on Lyle Whigby. Thought it was weird as fuck that the guy just vanished. Turns out he changed his name, and you'll never guess to what ..."

The suspense was fucking agony.

"Lyle Whigby took up with a Rita Cottam about twelve years ago. Rita Cottam had a daughter—Odette Cottam. Ten years ago, Rita Cottam committed suicide, and although the case was closed, the cops I talked to about it said they never felt right about the decision to rule it a suicide, that something just felt off," Chase went on.

Rex's mother's eyes were as wide as saucers, and Rex had to set his phone down before he crushed it in his hand. He was also really worried he was going to lose his waffles.

"A Mr. Lyle Rockford and a Mrs. Odette Rockford have moved around a fair bit these last eight years—after she graduated high school, that is—since he was still with her mother when she died and it would seem stuck around to *take care* of Odette afterward."

"He didn't *take care* of her, he groomed her," his mother spat out.

"And now where do they both live but right in little ol' Victoria," Chase said.

"Holy shit!" Rex picked up his phone again and pushed his chair back so quickly, it toppled behind him. But he didn't have time to stop and pick it up. He needed to get to Lydia.

"Brock and Heath are already on their way to Lyle's work,"

Chase said. "But you need to get to Lydia. These two are connected, and although we don't know *why* they're doing this to Lydia, we know now that she's not doing it to herself. She can't be." Chase's voice was the calm in the storm Rex needed. "I'm leaving now, too. I can meet you at her apartment."

He stumbled as he put his shoes on. He could feel his mother behind him, feel her fear and worry.

Opening the front door, he turned to his mother pleadingly. "Call Lydia, Mum. She might answer your number before she does mine. Tell her to get out of her apartment. Tell her to get in her car and drive here."

His mother nodded. She already had her phone in her hand.

Rex debated waiting around to see if Lydia picked up or if he should just get on the road.

His mother put the speaker option on and held the phone out.

It started to ring.

And ring.

And ring.

"Hello, you've reached Lydia Sullivan. I can't take your call right now, but please leave me a message and I will get back to you shortly. Thank you. Goodbye."

Beep.

Son of a bitch.

"Lydia, honey, it's Joy. If you get this, please call me. Or better yet, don't even waste time calling me. Just come over. Chase has new evidence, and the boys believe you could be in danger."

Rex nodded at his mum. "Keep trying."

His mother's head bobbed, her expression of concern only causing the cables of dread inside him to tighten to the point of excruciating pain.

If something happened to Lydia, he'd never forgive himself.

This was the last fucking time he ever ignored his gut.

Ever.

CHAPTER 25

Lᴙᴅɪᴀ ʙʟɪɴᴋᴇᴅ ᴀɴᴅ ɢʀᴏᴀɴᴇᴅ. A dull ache in the back of her head throbbed in time with her heartbeat, and she winced. She needed to get herself an Advil.

She tried to rub her eyes, tried to lift her hand, but her arms wouldn't move. She tugged. They still wouldn't move.

She kicked her legs, but they were bound too.

What the hell?

Her eyes flashed open, and her head swiveled from side to side as the fear of where she was and what was happening seeped into her consciousness.

She was in her bedroom, on her bed, clothed but bound by her restraints.

This was not making any sense.

"Hello?" she cried out. "Someone help me, please."

She winced again when the pain in the back of her head intensified.

A figure appeared in the doorway, but the way the morning light in her bedroom was filtering in, she couldn't quite make out who it was. She could tell they were female though.

"Who are you? What do you want with me? Are you the one who has been doing all of this to me?"

The figure stepped forward, and Lydia's mouth opened and her eyes went wide.

"He calls you *the one that got away*," Odette said, a glass of water and a bottle of pills in her purple-latex-gloved hands.

"Who did?" Lydia eyed the bottle of pills. She couldn't tell what they were.

"Lyle," Odette said. "My husband."

Her husband?

"Odette, what are you talking about?" Lydia pulled at her restraints, but she knew better than to think they'd budge. They weren't meant to, so they wouldn't.

Then she remembered walking into her apartment after going for a soul-cleansing morning walk—not that it'd worked—and being hit over the head with something.

"Lyle Whigby? Or should I say, Lyle Rockford. You remember him, right?" She pulled up the seat next to Lydia's vanity, where she normally kept the clothes she was too lazy to put away after folding laundry, and sat down in it beside the bed.

"Of course, I remember Lyle. He cut himself a key to my house when he was dating my mother, then he showed up one day when I was home alone, gave me sex toys and asked me if I'd like to see a hard penis. I was *ten*." She made sure she watched every single thing Odette did, where she placed her hands, the water glass, the pills. If she got out of this alive, she needed to be able to remember every minute detail.

"Yes, well ... when your mother ended things with him, he eventually started dating *my* mother."

"And then he started grooming you?"

Odette's brown eyes turned nearly black, and her top lip curled up enough to reveal her top front teeth. "He didn't *groom* me. He loves me. He's always loved me. I am the one he loves. Not you. Not my mother. Me. It's only ever been me."

Holy shit. This woman was fucking crazy. It was like she had some kind of weird version of Stockholm Syndrome or something. Only Lyle hadn't kidnapped her. He'd dated her mother and slowly groomed Odette to become his child sex pet, to the point where she fell in love with him.

Oh dear God. Had that been his plan with Lydia?

"Do you remember *me?*" she asked.

Lydia shook her head. "I don't. Should I?"

"We went to the same primary school. You were a couple of grades ahead of me."

Lydia's bottom lip dropped open. "Odette Cottam?"

Odette nodded. "I had a feeling you wouldn't recognize me."

"It's been like fifteen years."

Odette shrugged.

"You were a mean girl back then, I remember that. Pushing kids down into the mud, teasing, stealing things out of students' backpacks. I even heard a rumor that you snuck into the fifth-grade class, took the class hamster out of his cage and set it free into the bushes behind the school."

Odette merely shrugged again. But her expression wasn't one of denial. It was one of pride.

"Whispers said you were acting that way because your parents were separating and you were lashing out, but ..."

"But people gossip. I wasn't *mean.* I was assertive."

"You were *mean.* There's a difference. I don't remember *you,* but I remember talk *of* you. And the talk of the school—and it wasn't a *big* school—was that Odette Cottam was a mean little girl."

Odette's eyes rolled and her lips twisted. "The years have blurred your memories. Which isn't surprising since you've clearly gone crazy. Poor little Lydia."

This bitch was the crazy one.

Lydia scanned her bedroom, checked to see if the window was open at all. If it was, maybe someone outside could hear her scream.

It was closed up tight.

Her breath stuttered out of her nose in shallow pants, and her fingers tingled from how hard Odette had fastened the restraints. It wouldn't be long before she lost all feeling in her hands.

Odette's dark gaze narrowed, and she leaned back casually in the chair. "I'm not sure how *your* first sexual experience went, but Lyle made me feel so comfortable, so loved, so ... special. He started out by introducing me to self-pleasure. Helping me learn how to bring myself to orgasm. He bought me toys, watched me touch myself, then he showed me how to make it better by guiding my hand with his."

Lydia was going to be sick.

"Then, one day, we finally made love, and it was wonderful. No pain. Just pleasure. I was the first girl in my class to become a woman. To feel the touch of a man. Even before I got my period, I had become a woman."

Oh dear God.

"We kept our love a secret for a few years behind my mother's back, but eventually I just got tired of watching him with *her*. She was in the way."

In the way?

What the hell did that mean?

Shit. She knew *exactly* what that meant.

"Odette, did you kill your own mother?"

Odette's nostrils flared, and she carefully tucked a strand of her thick black hair behind her ear. It was in a ponytail at the nape of her neck, and she appeared to be wearing a lunch-lady hairnet, but a few tendrils had escaped. "The police report says she killed herself. Just like the police report—and the suicide note on your kitchen counter—will say for you."

Her what?

Her *suicide note?*

She glanced at the bottle of pills again, but the label wasn't facing her.

"Do you have *any* idea how easy it is to overdose on fentanyl? It's like crazy easy. Particularly in its pure form." She pouted. "But I had to go with what I could find. So a bottle of pain meds containing fentanyl will have to do. Amazing the things you can buy on the streets, huh?"

Her smile made Lydia shudder and an acrid taste coated her mouth.

"Then I found a tutorial online about how to make your own pharmacy labels. And bing bang boom." All proud of herself, she picked up the bottle and held it in front of Lydia's face to show her the label.

She'd printed a prescription for Lydia Sullivan from a pharmacy Lydia hadn't heard of before, and the drugs prescribed were for something Lydia hadn't heard of before. But the warning label was very clear. TAKE WITH FOOD. MAY CAUSE DROWSINESS. ONLY TAKE ONE—OVERDOSE COULD BE FATAL.

Plain as freaking day.

"Why are you doing this, Odette?" Her words shook from her throat, and hot tears stung her eyes. "I don't want Lyle. You can have him. Please, just stop."

Odette's top lip curled again, and she glared down at Lydia. "Do you know how it made me feel when I came home after my first day of work at the preschool and told him who my coworkers were and his eyes lit up like fireworks at the mention of your name? I felt like I didn't exist. To my own husband!" She screamed that last bit. "His eyes got all wistful, and he said *the one that got away,* like you were the golden chalice and I was just some fucking sippy-cup consolation prize. I knew then that I'd never be able to work with you, as hard as I tried."

"So then why not just fire me and be done? Why torment me?

Why sneak into my apartment and make me think I'm going crazy? Did Lyle come with you? Is that how you got in here? Did the locksmith pick the lock?"

Odette rolled her eyes as if bored. "We've been together for years. He's taught me how to pick a lock. Plus, you can find out how to do anything online if you search long enough."

"But why post a video of me and my boyfriend having sex? Why ruin my life? Wasn't firing me from a job I loved enough?"

"Because you were still out there. In the same town. Breathing the same air. I can't have all of his love if you're still around." She placed the pill bottle back on the nightstand. "But I also needed to set up your suicide. Make it look believable that you have in fact gone crazy. And it all started with getting fired, which was why you started stalking me, right?"

Lydia's head thrashed side to side on the bed. "You know I didn't."

Odette's expression turned innocent. "But of course you have. You were let go from work because of your erratic behavior and your mental instability. You're also desperate for attention, so you made it look like someone was harassing *you* so your hunky boy toy would come to your rescue. Sad, lonely, stupid girl. It was so easy to break you?" She laughed, but to Lydia it sounded more like a cackle. "Just enough to plant seeds of doubt in everyone around you. And it worked brilliantly."

"Why go to such lengths? I don't want Lyle. I don't ..."

Odette ignored her and kept talking, her pride in her scheme evident in her tone and the way she tossed her shoulders back and smiled. "But if those cries for attention weren't enough, then you started stalking and harassing the boss that let you go. You broke into my home, killed my cat, left notes on my mirrors. And all the phone calls. I mean, come on, Lydia, in the middle of the night, really? That's pathetic. It really is."

"Your cat ..."

Pia! Oh God.

"Where is my cat? Please, don't hurt my cat. Pia? Pia! *Psst. Psst.*" Tears ran down her cheeks and onto her pillow unchecked.

If Odette had hurt her cat ...

Clearly, the woman wasn't above killing animals if she killed her own pet and framed Lydia for it.

Poor Pia. She was a good kitty. Only two years old. Lydia had had her since she was a kitten. She didn't deserve this. Neither of them did.

Odette flicked her hand behind her shoulder dismissively. "Put some sedative in a bit of cat food. She'll wake up just as you're falling into an endless sleep, and with any luck, now that Lover Boy is gone, nobody will find you until sweet little Pia gets so hungry she has to start nibbling away at her mommy."

Lydia's head shook, and her heart rate picked up until her pulse beat like a gong in her ears. "P-please, don't do this. I'll move, I swear. I'll leave Victoria. I'll leave the island. I'll leave the country. You'll never have to see me again. I won't breathe the same air as Lyle or anything. I know he loves you. He doesn't love me. He just sees me as a failure, because in the end, I wasn't the woman for him. You were. You *are*. You are the one he loves. Please, Odette. Please."

Odette's sigh of frustration had Lydia's body turning to ice. The woman stood up and reached for the pill bottle.

She opened it and pulled out three pills.

"Now, I have no idea how many it will take to do the job. So I figure, we'll just down the whole bottle and then cross our fingers, hmm?"

Lydia pressed her lips together and shook her head.

Odette rolled her eyes for the umpteenth time. "You might as well just resign yourself to your fate, Lydia. I've won. Now open up." Holding the pills in her palm, she used the fingers from both gloved hands to wedge their way between Lydia's lips.

Lydia kept her jaw locked tight and twisted her head back and forth across the pillow, causing the hair from her ponytail to break free from the elastic and fall across her face. No way was she going down without a fight. The longer she could delay the inevitable, the better. Maybe Odette would just get weary of the game and suffocate her with her pillow. Harder to rule that as suicide these days.

"You little bitch, fucking open your mouth." She got one finger into Lydia's mouth and tried to maneuver the pills past her lips, but Lydia bit down hard on the finger until she heard a crunch. "Fuck!" Odette screamed, pulling her finger free.

The hard smack to the side of Lydia's face wasn't entirely unexpected given the fact that she'd just nearly bitten off a woman's finger, but it was still really painful and had Lydia seeing stars.

It also had her gasping out in pain, which gave Odette her opening to swoop in and shove the pills into Lydia's mouth.

But Lydia wasn't going to swallow them. She spat them back out, causing them to land on her chest.

"HELP!" Lydia screamed. "SOMEONE HELP ME! She's trying to kill me."

Rage ignited in Odette's eyes, and she smacked Lydia again before scooping up the pills and trying once again to force Lydia's mouth open as Lydia's head spun and she fought through the pain in her cheek and jaw to regain her senses.

She wasn't fast enough.

Odette got two of the three pills into Lydia's mouth, and before Lydia could spit them out, Odette was holding her mouth open and pouring the water from the glass down her throat.

She gargled and spat as best she could, causing water to spill down her chin, cheeks and neck. Some even ended up in her ears. But even still, she felt one pill slip down her throat.

She needed to keep the other one from sliding down too.

She had no idea what was in that bottle and whether two pills was too many. The warning label did say, ONLY TAKE ONE. OVERDOSE COULD BE FATAL.

She didn't want to die.

She wanted to live.

She wanted to teach children and help mold the minds of the future.

She wanted to get married one day and have babies of her own. Grow old with her husband and take her grandchildren camping, go on big, noisy, chaotic family vacations.

This could not be how her story ended.

Not at the hands of some Stockholm Syndrome psychopath mother-killer.

Her head thrashed, and she broke free of Odette's hold for a long enough moment that she was able to spit out the other pill.

Odette growled, climbed onto the bed, straddled Lydia's stomach, reached for the pill bottle with one hand and pinched her nostrils with other.

"You're going to have to breathe sometime, sweetie," she said, her mouth curling up into an evil smile.

Lydia held her mouth shut.

Odette set the pill bottle back on the nightstand but picked up the pill Lydia spat out onto her chest. She also appeared to have the third pill from earlier still in her palm.

Lydia's lungs were beginning to burn. She needed to breathe.

But if she opened her mouth, even the slightest, that could give Odette the opening she needed. The woman's fingers pinched her nose even tighter, but the pain there was no match for the pain in Lydia's lungs, the fire that was slowly spreading through her chest. Spots started to cloud her vision and alarm bells began to go off in her brain as it begged for oxygen, pleaded with her for one tiny inhale of delicious air.

But she couldn't.

She wouldn't.

Odette fished her gloved fingers into the top of Lydia's shirt and beneath her bra. She pinched and twisted Lydia's nipple so hard that she was unable to stop herself from opening her mouth on a harsh gasp that morphed into a cry of anguish.

NO!

With quick reflexes, Odette took her opening and shoved the two pills into Lydia's open mouth. She was still pinching Lydia's nose, so either Lydia opened her mouth to breathe, which would give Odette another opportunity to pour water down her throat, or she risked passing out from lack of oxygen.

Either way, she was coming to the realization that this was how she was going to die.

"Bad things happened to good people and good things happened to bad people. There is rarely a rhyme or a reason why. It just is what it is and what it is, is fucking stupid."

Her aunt's words rang through her head as her lungs began to burn again and her vision started to get blurry. A heavy pounding started in her frontal lobe.

Maybe she should just swallow the pills and get it over with.

She was helpless, and everyone who had been helping her had walked away, believing her to be the bad guy.

But she wasn't the bad guy in this story.

She wasn't.

She was the good guy.

She was the victim.

They say drowning is a nice, peaceful death. Maybe holding her breath long enough or taking the pills until she fell asleep would be similar.

She could just slip away and forget all of this.

Would anyone besides her mother miss her anyway?

She closed her eyes and pictured her last wonderful moment with her mum and dad. It had been right before he died.

They'd celebrated his birthday and gone on a weekend family trip to Harrison Hot Springs.

She treasured that time with her parents. With her father.

For a long time, she'd begged her parents for a sibling, envious of her friends at school with their live-in playmates and co-conspirators. But her birth had nearly killed her mother, so the doctors advised against any more children.

But that trip for her dad's birthday just made her appreciate the bond that the three of them had. How much she loved her parents and they loved her. She was their miracle baby, and as much as she wanted a brother or a sister, she realized on that trip just how lucky she was to have two incredible parents, and in the end, they were enough.

They weren't a rich family, but they had love, and that made them as wealthy as kings.

With her eyes squeezed shut and the image of her father smiling and laughing on the back of her eyelids, she swallowed the two pills that had already started to dissolve on her tongue.

She had very little control anymore.

Odette had stripped her of that.

But if there was one thing she could control, it would be the last thing she saw before she died, and it sure as hell wasn't going to be Odette Rockford's face.

She opened her mouth and took a big gulp of air.

Odette poured the water in, but that didn't matter.

She'd already swallowed the pills.

She accepted her fate now.

This was her time to go.

She heard the pill bottle rattle and more pills get shaken out.

"Open up."

Lydia complied, no sense fighting it.

She'd already swallowed three when the bottle said ONLY TAKE ONE.

Her fate was sealed now.

She prepared herself for more pills to land on her tongue, but it didn't happen.

Should she open her eyes?

She'd have time to close them again and conjure another image of her parents, surely. She was about to pry one eye open when Odette screamed and her weight disappeared from Lydia's body.

CHAPTER 26

LYDIA'S EYES FLEW OPEN. Rex stood over her, his face full of horror as he took in her predicament.

Chase was with him, and he had Odette in a hold. The woman's body slumped to the ground a moment later, and he dragged her out into the living room.

"Police are on their way. Chase just knocked her out. She's not dead." With trembling fingers, he started to release her bonds.

Her eyes darted across the harsh, angular plains of his face as he loosened the straps at her wrist.

She was shaking.

Was this the drugs?

Were they fast-activating?

How much time did she have?

He moved on to her ankles. She waited until the circulation had returned to her hands and fingers enough before she helped him by releasing one as he released the other. Then he glanced at the pill bottle on the floor, empty and surrounded by the remaining pills. "How many have you taken?" he demanded.

"Th-three," she stammered.

He grabbed the bottle off the floor and read what it was. "Fuck. You need to puke now."

He didn't wait for her to climb off the bed herself. He had her scooped up and was carrying her to the bathroom and lifting the toilet seat up before she could register what was happening.

Rex set her down on her knees, sat on the edge of the tub, grabbed her chin in one hand and ordered her to open her mouth. Then he stuck two big fingers down her throat until her gag reflex engaged and she peeled away from him with urgency and leaned over the toilet.

"We need to get them all out, Lydia. You have to keep going," he said, rubbing her back as she gripped the cool porcelain and emptied the contents of her stomach. His other hand pulled her hair off her face. "Can you see the pills?"

Saliva and vomit hung from her lips. She wiped at it with the back of her hand and glanced down into the bowl. Three little yellow pills floated among her breakfast of instant oatmeal and coffee.

Thank God.

She nodded.

"Thank fuck," Rex breathed.

Noise in her apartment filtered in through the open bathroom door.

"She okay?" an unfamiliar female voice asked from the doorway leading from the living room to the bathroom.

"Yeah, only took three and they're all out," Rex said.

"Good. Police are on their way to pick up Lyle Rockford as well. Your brothers have him detained."

Rex stiffened beside her. "I'd like to talk to him."

The woman—who was probably a cop—laughed humorlessly. "Not likely. We'd like our suspect to be able to talk, and something tells me you'd render him speechless one way or another."

Rex merely grunted.

"Paramedics are on their way for her, too," the officer said.

Rex grunted again.

"She okay?" Chase's voice replaced the female officer.

Rex handed Lydia a towel, and she wiped at her mouth before sitting back on her heels. "Yeah, I think so."

The female police officer had disappeared into the living room, and Chase leaned against the doorjamb in her place. His expression was grim as he asked, "Just a little shaken up?"

Lydia huffed a laugh through her nose. "Just a little."

"Heath and Brock found a fuck-ton of kiddie porn on Lyle's work computer. Along with half a dozen ongoing social media conversations with underage girls. He was grooming them, making plans to meet them and posing as either a teenage boy or a modeling scout."

Rex ran his hand over his bald head. "Jesus Christ. Makes you wonder why he was with Odette if he was in to kids."

"She was probably just a cover," Chase said with a shrug. "Once she turned legal, she lost her appeal, but he kept her around to keep up appearances."

"Fucking disgusting," Rex growl.

"Guy's going straight to jail. No passing GO, nothing. Same with his psycho wife." Chase glanced into the living room, where the voices of probably four cops echoed. "Glad you're okay," he said, turning back to Lydia. "Sorry for not believing you and how things turned out."

She swallowed and nodded. "Me too."

Chase disappeared into the living room, leaving Rex and Lydia.

He helped her to her feet and stood as well, his eyes sad, mouth turned down into a deep frown.

With hesitation, he took her hands.

She allowed it.

"I'm so sorry," he started. "Sorry that I didn't believe in you. I should have listened to my gut, which was telling me that you were innocent. I ..." He hung his head. "I will never forgive myself for what she's done to you, for not putting a stop to it sooner."

After what she'd just been through, Lydia was in no mood for forgiveness or reconciliation. Maybe in a day or two, she and Rex could talk, but right now, as grateful as she was for him coming to her rescue when he did, she was still incredibly hurt.

He didn't trust her. He didn't believe in her.

Even though their relationship had been fresh and new, they both felt the connection and the chemistry. It had gone from zero to sixty faster than either of them had anticipated, but with that intensity should have come trust, too. And with Rex, it hadn't. And she needed some time away from him to think things through, to figure out what she really wanted and whether Victoria was even a good fit for her.

She let go of his hands, opened her bathroom medicine cabinet and grabbed a bottle of Scope. She quickly rinsed the taste of vomit from her mouth.

Two paramedics with medical bags entered her apartment and turned to see them in the bathroom.

The male paramedic with red hair spoke first. "You Lydia?"

She nodded.

He jerked his head toward the living room. "Let's get you checked out, eh?"

Nodding again, she stepped away from Rex and through the bathroom doorway into her living room.

"Lydia," he called after her, his tone so full of confusion and remorse, she felt it like a sledgehammer to her chest.

But she needed to be strong. If there was one thing she'd learned through all of this, it was that when the chips were down and crushed to dust, the only person she could truly lean on was herself, and she needed to have a mighty strong backbone for that. She couldn't let Rex's feelings of guilt stomp all over her own feelings of hurt and frustration. His feelings were not more important than hers.

She glanced at him over her shoulder. "Thank you, Rex."

Understanding and despair swirled in the midnight blue of his eyes.

Odette was now awake. She was in handcuffs and being spoken to by the police. Lydia didn't bother looking her in the eye. She'd stared into those soulless orbs enough to last a lifetime.

Chase held a sleeping Pia, and he approached her. "I'm going to run her to the vet, okay?"

She nodded and thanked him, pet her limp but still breathing cat, kissed her head and finally sat down on her couch so the paramedics could do their thing.

Rex slowly approached in the living room, his steps calculated, his face unsure.

"You can go," she said to him, refusing to look him in the eye, instead focusing on what the paramedics were doing.

"I'm not leaving you," he said gently.

She lifted her gaze to his, pinning him with the most determined and serious look she could muster at the moment. "Yes, you are. This is my apartment, and I'm kindly asking you to leave. I am safe now. See, they're carting Odette away, and the paramedics are here. Please go."

He worked his jaw back and forth.

The two paramedics were trying their damnedest to do their jobs, but they had working ears and were clearly interested in the intricacies of this exchange.

She turned away from Rex and addressed the female paramedic. "Do you think I'll need to go to the hospital?"

The woman, with blonde hair tucked up into a bun nodded. "I think so. They'll want to run a tox screen to make sure she didn't inject you with anything while you were unconscious. We also want to make sure all those pills were thrown up. We can take you in the ambulance."

Lydia nodded and waited for the male paramedic to remove the blood pressure cuff before standing up. "Okay, let's go."

Rex was still standing there as she stepped past him and grabbed her purse and keys from the hook and table next to her couch.

The paramedics packed up their stuff and stood to join her.

A few cops were still milling around, taking pictures of the crime scene.

"I'll come to the hospital with you," Rex offered.

She released a breath and closed her eyes for a moment before facing him. "No, you won't." Then she turned to go, one paramedic in front of her, one behind, and a cop in their wake, undoubtedly to take her statement.

Rex followed them to the elevator.

She stepped inside, hit the *M* for the main floor and was joined by the cop and paramedics.

Rex was about to step in too, but she shook her head and said a firm, "No."

His breath caught, then his throat rolled, and she watched as his fingers twitched at his sides, like he was trying his hardest not to reach out for her or to stop the doors from shutting.

"I'm sorry," he said, his gaze beseeching.

The elevator doors began to slide closed, and just before they did, she looked him square in the eyes and whispered, "Goodbye, Rex."

———

He gave her a week.

And it was the longest week of his fucking life.

She hadn't returned to her apartment, he knew that much, but he had no idea where she was staying.

Chase had offered to do some digging to see if they could find out where Lydia was living, but he told his brother to stand down.

She didn't deserve to have any more of her freedoms or privacies tampered with. Not after what she'd just been put through.

She was staying hidden for a reason, and as much as it killed him, he knew that if he found out where she was staying and showed up, it would not go well for him—or them.

And he desperately wanted there to be a *them*.

After a week, though, he finally spotted her.

He'd been working as a plumber for the last five days, having told Brock he needed a break from the cloak and dagger shit for at least a month, so his hours were more consistent with a banker's. He spotted her just as he was getting home from a long day of installing gas stoves in a new apartment complex. She was loading boxes into her car.

Was she moving?

Shit.

Slowly, he approached her, made sure she saw him long before he got to her so she wasn't caught off guard. She'd had enough of that bullshit to last a lifetime.

She didn't cast him a warning glance or tell him to go away, so he took that as a good sign and stopped just six feet in front of her.

"Hi," he said, swallowing hard and resisting the urge to drop his gaze to his feet.

"Hello."

"How are you?"

She shrugged and glanced away from him for a moment. "Been better." A breath shook from her lips like it would a horse's. "Also been worse."

"Are you moving?"

Her head bobbed. "Yeah. Going to move home to live with my mum for a bit. Need to clear my head and get some things sorted."

Fuck. No.

"How's Pia?"

"She's good. Was a little groggy for a day or so, but she's back to her old self."

He needed to keep her talking, needed to break this icy wall between them and encourage her to see that what they had, even if it had been brief, was real and intense and worth fighting for.

He glanced inside her car. It was pretty full. "Where have you been staying?"

"With Jayne. She let Pia and I crash in her guest room. But I need to give her and her hubby their space. Guests are like dead fish. They start to stink after three days."

Even though it was April now and the sun had lent them a beautiful day of warmth, the breeze was still cool, and she was in no more than a T-shirt. He watched her shiver and rub her hands over her arms, the goosebumps following in the wake of her fingertips.

He didn't think twice and was unzipping his hoodie and handing it to her. "Here."

She shook her head and pressed her palm forward to resist. "It's fine. I can go grab one upstairs. Now that they've taken down the crime-scene tape, I can go back into my apartment."

"I don't want you to go," he blurted out, still holding the hoodie out for her. "We're not over."

Her brows lifted on her forehead. "We very much are, Rex."

He shook his head, opened his hoodie, circled around behind her and draped it over her shoulders.

She rolled her eyes but didn't shrug it off. Rather, she tugged it tighter around herself, put her arms through the sleeves and gave him a look of irritation mixed with amusement. "Thank you. I'll drop it off in front of your door once I grab my own from inside."

"Keep it," he said with a headshake.

She released a breath through her nose, and her shoulders slouched slightly. "Rex ..."

He faced her again and made sure they were standing less than six feet apart. "Please, Lydia. I know I fucked up."

"You didn't trust me, Rex. And what kind of relationship or future could we possibly have without trust?"

"I know."

"You kept telling me to trust *you*, but refused to trust *me*. How does that make sense? Trust is a two-way street."

"I know." He swallowed down the spike in his throat and took a deep breath.

"I can't be with someone who is going to constantly think I'm going to betray them. Someone who refuses to believe me when I tell them the truth. I don't deserve that."

"I know you don't. Nobody does. I just ..." He blew out a long breath, rubbed his hand over his head and glanced away for a moment, searching for strength from the clouds. He turned back to face her, knowing he owed her an explanation, a glimpse into his world. Into his head.

She was watching him with a patient expression, but he could tell that patience wouldn't last much longer.

With a fortifying inhale, he started. "A few years ago, my brothers and I were working a job in Montana. There was this weird religious cult made up of a bunch of families. They lived off the grid a bit, up some mountain. Kids didn't go to school, they kept to themselves mostly besides getting groceries and necessities in town. They had a leader who called himself Reverend Bliss.

"The men were revered and treated like gods, while the women and children were considered property and for lack of a better term, slaves. There was incest and rape like you wouldn't believe. If a man wanted to have sex with a woman—or a child—all he had to do was ask her husband or the father for permission. If it was granted, then the wife or child had no say. Most of the women had no idea who the father or fathers of their children were, since birth control is forbidden, and anyone could have sex with anyone as long as the men permitted it. The youngest pregnant women there was eleven, and she said the baby was her brother's—but she wasn't sure *which* brother."

Even now, years later, the memories of it all made his stomach do a big flip. Saying it out loud wasn't helping either.

The look of horror on Lydia's face was nothing compared to what he'd felt when he witnessed it first hand. He'd seen a lot of shit over the years in his line of work, but that cult compound was by far some of the most fucked up shit he'd ever seen. The image of that eleven-year-old girl's protruding belly and hearing that the baby belonged to one of her older brothers was enough to make Rex and his brothers all return to their motel rooms and puke.

"One of the wives had been brave enough to reach out for help. And that led to us being called and offered the job of extraction. A lot of the women and children wanted help escaping out of the lifestyle. Several were brought into the cult without consent. Kidnapped or runaways who were lied to and then not allowed to leave. Very few were there willingly. Our point of contact was another woman, one of Reverend Bliss's many wives. She was close to him and fed us the information we needed to get in, get the women and children out and to safety without the men—who were all heavily armed—knowing. Only, she had a last-minute change of heart and even though my brothers were able to get the women and children out, I had been working with Ruth and was with her when she sounded the alarm."

Lydia's eyes flared.

"Reverend Bliss and his 'deciples' tied me naked to a metal pole and whipped me with a switch, demanding I tell them where their women and children were taken. Luckily, none of the women or children had been given that information prior, out of fear they might be coerced into spilling the plan. So Ruth had no idea where they were."

"Thank God," Lydia breathed.

"They held me for almost two days. Beat me every few hours. Kept me bound to the pole. My arms were tethered above my head, while my feet remained on the ground. I wasn't able to lay down or kneel. I had to stay standing for the entire time. They also wouldn't let me sleep. If I tried to sleep, they'd throw ice water on me to wake me up. Or blast some weird fucking religious music. They wanted to know where we'd taken their 'property'. They said we 'stole' it."

"Oh my God."

He nodded and scratched the back of his neck. "My brothers eventually got me out, with the help of the cops. The organization was shut down, and to the best of my knowledge it still is. The men were charged with rape, child molestation, incest, kidnapping and probably a dozen other offences. But this is why—"

"You find it hard to trust."

He closed his eyes for a moment and nodded again. "And why I can't be restrained. I trusted Ruth. We all trusted Ruth. My gut told me she wanted out just like the rest of them. I asked her all the questions I knew to ask to try to trip her up, to get her to reveal that she wasn't an ally like she claimed to be, but she passed. Answered everything perfectly. And yet, she still turned on us. I'd been wrong. My gut had been wrong. Yes, she was brainwashed, was a master manipulator, and 'in love' with Reverend Bliss, but even when the cops came with my brothers to free me and arrest anyone left in the compound, she was screaming for Reverend Bliss and telling everyone that he was innocent and the one true messenger of God. The more I think about it, the more I believe she never had a change of heart but had been secretly plotting to ruin the plan the entire time."

"I'm so, *so* sorry that happened to you," she whispered. "I can't even imagine." A tear slid down her cheek and her bottom lip wobbled.

"I know I accused you of some pretty horrible stuff, and didn't listen to you, didn't listen to my gut when it was telling me that you were innocent, but it was a mistake ... and I ... I don't want this to be over. I really like you, and when I listen to my gut now, it's telling me that you're the one. That we're supposed to end up together. Get married. Have babies. And go on big, family vacations. That's what my gut is telling me." He bunched his fists at his sides to keep himself from reaching for her, but his gut gave him a swift kick in the pants, and he extended one hand and took hers.

She didn't pull away.

He took that as a good sign.

"We can take it slow if you want. As slow as you need to. But please, give me a chance to make this up to you. To show you that I *do* trust you. That I *do* believe in you." His thumb grazed the back of her hand over the silky-soft skin of her knuckles. With hope, he squeezed gently. "If you want to tie me up," he swallowed, the thought of being restrained making the back of his neck itchy, "you can. If that's what it will take to show you that I trust you, then I'm willing. I owe you at least that. I broke your trust, didn't trust you and because of that, I almost lost you." His shoulders slumped. "I *did* lose you."

Light flared in the hazel of her eyes, and one corner of her lip turned up into a cute, crooked little smile. "You'd let me tie you up?"

"I would, yes."

The sheer thought of being restrained had him feeling nauseous. But he pushed down the sensation and focused on the woman in front of him. On hope, and the fact that she hadn't dismissed him yet. She hadn't walked away and told him to go to hell.

That had to mean something, right?

"Wow." She blew out a breath. "That's a big deal."

"It is," he nodded. "But I trust you."

Her words were quiet. "Thank you."

"If you want to take a few steps back, and go back to being just friends, we can do that, too. I'm willing to do whatever it takes to prove to you that I trust you, and that I believe what we have is real. But please, don't give up on me. Don't give up on us. And don't give up on Victoria. There are a lot of people here who like you, who care about you and want you to stick around."

"Rex ..."

"Haven't you ever made a mistake?"

She snorted.

"Okay, well, maybe not one as big as mine, but still. We all make mistakes, right?"

That earned him a small nod.

"But then we learn from them. We grow. But I'd rather *grow* with someone—with you—than by myself. I want to *grow* old with you."

The other side of her mouth lifted too, completing the small smile. "But you're already old."

Her cheekiness had him grinning.

She pressed the back of her free hand to her forehead and tilted her head back like she was swooning. "What have I said about those dimples?"

"That they should come with a warning." His heart felt lighter than it had in a really long time. He took her other hand when she dropped it back to her side. "Can we try again?" He squeezed both her hands. "You want me to grovel even more?" Still holding on to her hands, he made to get down on to his knees. "Because I will. I will grovel right here in the parking lot, in front of any neighbor watching. I'll do it, I swear."

Her brows scrunched and she tugged on his hands. "Get up. You're groveling quite well while standing. Let's not make a scene."

Chuckling, he stood back up, grateful that she let him keep hold of her hands, and also seemed to have regained her sense of humor.

She was serious again though, suddenly and an uneasy feeling spiraled through him. Her head was tilted down, her gaze focused on their hands, but she lifted her eyes to him, looking at him from beneath her lashes. "We grew pumpkins in our garden when I was a kid, and one year the cutest little one didn't turn orange, but I loved it so much I wouldn't let my mum carve it. I put it under my bed. I don't know what I planned to do with it, but I didn't want it to get butchered. But I forgot about it until the smell of rotting squash had my room nearly uninhabitable. My mother was *not* happy."

He lifted up one brow. "Okay ..."

"I make mistakes, too."

Ah. Now he got it.

That pulled a big smile from him, but when her breath hitched, he dropped his lips into a frown and said, "Warning, dimples about to come out." Then he smiled again.

Her laugh was like the sweetest birdsong, and he tugged her hands until she was wrapped up in his arms, her chest smashed against his.

Her hands fell to the middle of his back, and she gazed up at him, still laughing. Still smiling.

"I'm really, really sorry for what happened to you." The way her fingers flitted across his back it was like she was searching for the scars beneath his shirt. They were barely visible, thank God, and she wouldn't be able to feel them. But when his shirt was off, if she stared long enough, eventually, she'd see them. "If you ever want to talk about it, or—"

"Thank you. But I'm mostly okay. I have some tried and true distraction techniques that do the trick at blocking out the memories. Working out helps. Puzzles help. Sex helps." He grinned.

She squinted and smiled coyly. "Is that so."

He nodded. "I won't fuck up again, Lydia. I promise."

It was her turn to lift one brow.

"Okay, I probably will. You're right. But I won't fuck up *this* badly next time. I swear. It'll probably be something more like I forgot to take the recycling out, or I'm *too* amazing of a husband and your friends are getting mad at you because your husband is making all of their husbands look bad." He hit her with the dimples again.

She snorted a laugh and rolled her eyes, but the smile never wavered from her lips. Lips he'd really missed kissing. "Already talking about being my husband, eh? Pretty confident there, Rexworth."

"Not confident. I'm just listening to my gut."

"And what is your gut telling you?"

"That this is worth fighting for. What's your gut telling you?"

She smiled up at him and tightened her hold, gripping the back of his shirt in her little fists. "That people make mistakes, but it's those who learn from them that are the ones worth giving a second chance to."

"And I'm worth a second chance?"

Slowly, she nodded. "I think you're worth fighting for."

"Is it telling you *we're* worth fighting for?"

She nodded again.

Thank fuck. "My gut's telling me something else, too."

"Hmm? And what's that?"

"That if I don't kiss you right now, I'm really going to fucking regret it."

Goddamn it, her smile had the whole day suddenly appearing brighter. "My gut is telling me the exact same thing."

"Better listen to them then, hmm?"

Then he dipped his head low, took her mouth and held on to her for dear life, because his gut told him she was his happily ever after, and no way was he ever not going to listen to his gut again. No fucking way.

EPILOGUE

18 months later ...

"AND YOU MADE sure that the justice of the peace knows it's *husband and wife* and not *man and wife*, right?" Lydia asked Rex for probably the twentieth time in the last two weeks.

He nodded. "Yes, dear."

"I won't have any of this patriarchy, I'm your property, you stay a *man* but I become a *wife* bullshit at my wedding."

"Yes, dear."

"And you double-checked that the word *obey* is not in the vows at all, right?"

"Yes, dear."

"And you—"

He grabbed her from behind, where she was busily chopping vegetables for dinner, spun her around and promptly took her mouth with his.

That shut her up.

But she was still holding a knife, so he needed to tread carefully.

Their baby in Lydia's belly kicked him, and they both grinned through their kiss.

Not removing her lips from his, she blindly set the knife down on the counter and wrapped her arms around his neck, deepening their kiss.

Their kid kicked even harder.

He or she was going to be just like their mother. Fierce, strong and with their daddy wrapped around their pinky finger the moment they were born.

And he was A-fucking-OK with that.

After a few moments, Lydia broke the kiss, her eyes glassy and her smile gentle. "That's not going to shut me up, but thank you."

He busted out the dimples.

"Put those away." She turned back to the counter and went to pick up her knife, but he wasn't letting her get away that easily. He scooped her up, and she squealed as he carried her over to their couch.

With the baby on the way, they'd decided a few months ago to get a bigger place. And it perfectly coincided with Chase and Stacey's move to the new home they built on Prospect Lake. Rex and Lydia just moved into the townhouse his brother vacated. The townhouse was owned by James and Emma, so it was the easiest move Rex had ever done.

Eventually, he and Lydia would like to own their own place, but for now, the townhouse was perfect and more than enough space for their growing family.

He fell onto the couch first, bringing her into his lap.

She was all sexy grins, and her arms looped around his neck, but then her smile drooped and she gently traced a finger over his head. "Need to put some more aloe on that burn. We don't want it to peel and have you looking like a leper in the wedding photos."

He shrugged casually. "I'll just wear a beret if it starts to peel."

That earned him exactly the reaction he'd been hoping for.

Her hazel eyes went dinner-plate wide, and her bottom lip dropped open. "No berets in my wedding."

"*Our* wedding, dear. Remember?"

She nodded. "Right. Sorry. *Our* wedding."

The baby kicked him again, and their gazes fell down to Lydia's belly. She was six months along now, and although the pregnancy had come as a surprise to both of them, he could not be happier to be having a baby with the woman he loved.

"Did you have a coffee today? Little Bug is a wild thing."

She shook her head, eyes sparkling as she rubbed her belly affectionately. "The baby gets like this when they hear your voice. They love their daddy."

That made his heart soar.

"You ready to find out what we're having?" she asked excitedly.

Lydia had known for a full day now, and was champing at the bit to tell him. But Rex remained on the fence. Boy or girl, he'd love the baby no matter what. Did it really matter knowing ahead of time? Wasn't that part of the surprise?

She reached into her apron pocket and pulled out a black sash. He eyed it curiously. "What's that for?"

She nibbled on her lip. "I'm going to blindfold you."

Unease wormed through his belly. He still didn't like being tied up or blindfolded—not that they did it on the regular—but for her, he'd do anything. She had his complete trust now and forever. If there was anyone he would to let tie him up or cut off one of his senses even temporarily and in good fun, it was Lydia.

He allowed her to fasten the sash around his eyes, blocking out the light and everything else, while he inhaled deep to calm his nerves.

She shifted slightly in his lap, her wiggling against his crotch not at all unpleasant.

"What are you doing, woman?"

"Just give me a minute. I'm big."

"You're sexy."

She plopped an unexpected kiss to his mouth, then resumed her wiggling, which was accompanied by a few grunts as well.

"Ready?" she asked, the giddiness in her tone so real he could probably reach out and touch it.

He made a "Mhmm" noise.

She reached for his blindfold, pulled it free from his eyes and he blinked a couple of times to allow his pupils to readjust.

She sat there grinning at him while wearing a hot pink bra that showed off her luscious, full, pregnant lady tits.

Pink.

A pink bra.

Pink for ...

"A girl?" he asked, his voice hoarse. "We're having a girl?"

She blinked through tears and nodded, still smiling brighter than the sun. "We are. We're having a little girl."

Boy or girl, he would have been ecstatic for either one, but if he was being entirely honest, he was secretly hoping for a little girl maybe five percent more. He saw the way his brothers were with their daughters and how strong and fierce Zoe and Thea were growing up to be, and he wanted to be part of that. He wanted to help the next generation of women grow up to be powerful and rule the world.

As Stacey often pointed out, if women ran the world, there would be fewer wars and people would be more taken care of. Women were nurturers, but they got shit done.

And he fucking believed it.

He'd been raised by such a woman.

He was getting ready to marry such a woman.

"Are you happy?" she asked, her gaze wary but hopeful.

Emotion clung heavy in his throat like a sticky wad of peanut butter. "So happy. We're having a baby girl." He was going to raise a warrior princess. A warrior princess who would befriend the dragon rather than slay it and rule the world with her iron fist of compassion and strength.

He kissed the mother of his child hard, feeling her smile against his lips.

She chuckled and broke their kiss when the baby kicked again.

He placed his hand next to Lydia's, and they watched her belly move, their foreheads instinctively migrating until they leaned against each other and watched their daughter stretch and move like a healthy baby should.

"Can you believe we're getting married in two days?" she asked. "And that in three months we're going to be parents. This is all so surreal. I'd hoped for all of this to happen in my life, but the fact that it's actually coming true is ... like a dream." The last three words were said on a sigh, and she closed her eyes for a moment.

"I'm over the fucking moon, babe. Life is on the upswing, and we're going to ride it all the way to the stars."

She opened her eyes and looked at him sideways, one brow lifting on her forehead. "Waxing poetic now, are you?"

He shrugged. "Hard not to when life is this good. You have your dream job, thanks to James." James the millionaire, decided to make Lydia's dream come true and provided her with the start-up funds for her own preschool.

"Thanks to James for the money, but you for believing in me," she replied.

"I'll always believe in you," he said. "Forever and always."

Her smiled made him feel like he was floating.

"We're getting married. We're having a baby. Life is perfect." She smiled and pulled her head away from his, removing her hand from her belly and cupping his cheek instead. "Thank you. Thank you for fighting for us. For demanding a second chance and for our amazing life and the amazingness yet to come."

He shook his head. "I'm the one that should be thanking you. You gave me a second chance when I didn't deserve it, and now you're giving me a baby girl to love and a perfect life with a woman I'm crazy about."

She blinked back at him with fresh tears forming in her eyes. "You're going to make the hormonal pregnant lady cry, Rexthalomew. Not cool."

But her smile was illuminating, and even though when she pressed her lips against his and her salty tears dripped down, mingling with their kisses, he knew she was happy.

She pulled away and used the hem of his T-shirt to wipe her eyes. "I suggest you take your wife upstairs to our bedroom, get naked and limber up that tongue, because when you say such wonderful things, all she wants to do is ride you bareback like the virile stallion you are."

She had him tossing the dimples at her again with full force.

"Now you're throwing those things at me? You know I can barely contain my orgasms at this stage in the pregnancy as it is. I sneeze and I either pee or come. Put them away or get naked."

He scooped her up again, making her squeal, and he made his way toward the stairs. "I choose option B."

She held on tight to his neck and kissed his cheek. "Good choice."

"I'm listening to my gut." He started to ascend the stairs. "Won't make that mistake again."

Then he laid his wife-to-be down on their bed and made love to her, because any other choice would have been going against his gut and frankly, just plain stupid. If the last two years had taught them anything, it was to trust your instincts and not let go of the good.

And Lydia was all good.

And he was never letting her go.

———

FOR A DELETED SCENE FROM *TORN HART*
CLICK HERE: whitleycox.com/bonus-material

SNEAK PEEK - DARK HART

Read on for a sneak peek of Chapter 1 from
Dark Hart
Book 4 in The Harty Boys series

CHAPTER 1 - DARK HART

"Spread those legs baby, I'm starving!" Heath Hart called out into Pasha's house as he closed the door behind him and dropped his bag in the foyer. He peeled his shirt over his head and started to unbuckle his belt and unfasten his jeans as he wandered through her house to the kitchen which was where the only noise in the whole place was coming from. "Baby? Where you at? You already naked? Don't tell me you started without me."

He glanced into her dark bedroom, but no figure laid on the bed with her hand between her legs.

Stroking the heel of his palm over his jeans and his erection, he continued talking. "Been hard for the last thirty minutes, Pash. Two weeks is too fucking long." He stepped into the kitchen, his jeans unbuttoned, zipper almost all the way down only to find a woman who looked a fuck-ton a lot like Pasha, only half her damn age, staring at him with wide eyes and a gaping mouth.

"Shit!" Pasha's voice behind him had him spinning around and zipping up his pants. She was standing in the jamb of sliding glass door that led out to her patio and he could smell barbecue. His belly rumbled.

He grabbed an oven mitt from the counter and held it in front of his crotch.

"Didn't you get my text?" she asked, her brown eyes with flecks of gold were in full-on panic mode. He also didn't miss that her eye color was exactly the same as her younger doppelganger.

He shook his head, causing his blond hair to swish across his shoulders, his gaze bouncing between the two women.

The younger one now appeared amused and had her phone out. She snapped a few pictures of Heath. "Are you and my sister boning?" she asked. "Pash, he's fucking hot."

Sister?

He grabbed his phone out of the back pocket of his jeans, careful to keep the oven mitt in front of his slowly deflating junk, and checked his messages. Nothing from Pasha since last night—which has been a pic of her tits and oh what perfect tits they were.

She had her own phone out now. "Fuck. I didn't hit send." Her head rolled on her shoulders. "Rayma's been getting into trouble back home in Baltimore, so my parents thought it would be a good idea to ship her out to me for a week or two so I could knock some sense into her. They didn't, however, consult with me first, and Little Miss Trouble here just arrived on my doorstep two hours ago."

Rayma grinned. "Like a baby at a fire station."

Shit.

His cock seemed to have softened enough that he was able to pull the oven mitt away from his crotch and refasten his pants. He also tugged his shirt back on. Thanking God he hadn't tossed it aside into the entrance way.

"Oh, don't do that," Rayma protested. "I quite liked the view. What is that, an eight pack?" Her smile was sassy and she bobbed her brows. "Never seen arms that big either. Bet you could bench press a Civic."

Pasha flicked her sister in the back of the head as she wandered toward Heath, setting barbecue tongs down on the counter before she came to stand in front of them. "I'm sorry."

He bent his head and kissed the tip of her nose. "No need to apologize, babe. A bit awkward on my part, but family comes first, so I get it. I can head out and leave you two to your sisterly bonding if you want me—"

"No!" Pasha nearly shouted.

That had him grinning.

She loved his cock and wasn't shy about expressing it. He knew she'd be pissed right the fuck off if she had to wait another two weeks for it because of her bratty sister and her incommunicative parents.

"We'll just *adjust* our weekend plans."

"Yeah, less boning on every surface of the house, and more humping behind closed doors," Rayma teased.

Pash shot her sister a glare over her shoulder. "Rayma!"

Rayma adopted the perfect look of innocence, but it was plain as day that this cat devoured all the canaries. "What? He's the one who came in here telling you he was starving and to spread your legs."

Heath's cheeks grew warm, he snorted and a smirk tugged at his lips.

He wasn't a man who embarrassed easily. He preferred to just roll with the punches, but hearing it from Pasha's little sister's mouth has him blushing none-the-less

Pasha's head swiveled back around and her gaze landed on him. She elbowed him. "Not funny."

"It is a little bit funny," he admitted, wrapping his arms around her from behind and nipping her neck. "And she is right," he whispered. "I was looking forward to eating you on the kitchen table like a buffet."

"I heard that," Rayma said with another big smile.

Fuck, it was scary how much the sisters looked alike. Right

down to the cute button nose. The freckles, the eyes, the heart-shaped face, even the caramel-colored hair with thick blonde streaks. The only difference—besides their ages—seemed to be that Rayma had thinner lips, while Pasha's were plump and full and looked so fucking good wrapped around his cock like it was a Popsicle.

"We need more wine if we're going to do this weekend the three of us," Pasha said, glancing at him over her shoulder. "I only grabbed one bottle from the store on my way home."

He knocked his heels together and did a salute. "I shall go and get us some wine then. Any preferences?"

She turned her body, escaping his hold on her, and took up post at the counter to begin chopping vegetables. "It's hot out, so I usually go with white when it's warm out, but I could do a rosé if you can find a good one."

He nodded. "A rosé it is."

"I'm partial to vodka sodas myself," Rayma added.

"You're partial to ginger ale, *child*," Pasha lectured. She glanced at Heath. "And a big bottle of ginger ale for the whipper snapper, please."

Rayma growled. "You're just as bad as Mom and Dad."

"What? Determined to see you *not* end up passed out in some ditch with no pants on? Yeah, I'm okay saying our goals are aligned."

Rayma's eyes rolled and she lifted her chin at Heath. "Grab some ice cream, too, Surfer man."

"Surfer man?" he asked with a chuckle.

Rayma lifted a shoulder, reached for a grape from the fruit bowl in front of her and popped it into her mouth. "Well, we've never even been properly introduced. So it's either Surfer man, since you look like you just rolled in with the tide, or Man-who-wants-to-eat-out-my-sister, take your pick."

Fuck.

Rayma was trouble.

"How about you call me Heath," he said. "And what kind of ice cream?"

She popped another grape into her mouth and smiled through the chewing. "Anything fruity. I like mango ice cream. Or strawberry. Thanks, *Heath*."

He nodded. "Wine, ginger ale and ice cream it is." Walking up behind Pasha, he ran his hand over her ass. "Anything else?"

"Earplugs," Rayma added. "Something tells me you two are going to be fucking loud and I'd like to get some sleep."

It was Pasha's turn to growl, but she didn't look up at him, and it was a good thing, too, since he was struggling to keep from smiling.

Pasha was fucking loud when they had sex—and he loved it.

"All right then. Wine, ice cream, ginger ale and earplugs. Coming up. I'll be back shortly." He squeezed Pasha's butt, kissed her on the side of the head and left, gathering his phone and keys where he'd dropped them on his way in.

He slid behind the steering wheel of his black Chevy Silverado HD, turned on the ignition and let it purr for a moment.

This was definitely not how he saw the July 4th long weekend going with Pasha, but then again, nothing about their relationship— if you could call it that—was conventional, so why would he expect their long weekend to be?

Pulling out of her driveway, he headed to the grocery store closest to her house. Pasha lived in downtown Seattle, and worked at the hospital as a pediatrician. Their meeting had been unconventional, since she was brought in to help with a group of trafficked children Heath and his brothers rescued earlier that year. Then, when his brother got hurt, Pasha was the first doctor on site. Their relationship—albeit only sexual—had blossomed from there and for the last five months they'd been bouncing back and forth between his place in Victoria and her place in Seattle, humping like bunnies.

Was she his girlfriend?

Fuck no.

He was done with relationships of that kind.

Been there, done that, had the scars to prove it wasn't worth it.

But they were exclusively sleeping with each other.

She's even suggested no condoms since they weren't sleeping with other people.

Not that he had any real problems with condoms, but obviously sex with anyone, let alone someone as hot as Dr. Pasha Young, was a million times better when you rawdogged it.

Neither of them wanted anything serious, they just wanted someone to fuck and not have to worry about STDs or condoms. She had an IUD and the sex was fucking fantastic.

~~Win. Win. Win.~~

He pulled into the grocery store parking lot and turned off the ignition. His phone vibrated in the back pocket of his jeans and he tugged it out just as he climbed down out of his lifted truck with the duallies on the back.

It was another message from Pasha. *Kill me now. Teenagers are the worst. Buy ALL the wine.*

***

"So, is it serious?" Rayma asked, half paying attention to Pasha as Pasha finished making the salad for dinner, and half gawking at her phone. In the two hours Pasha's baby sister had been at her house, Rayma had spent at least ninety minutes of that on her phone.

Ugh.

Sure, Pasha was on social media and liked playing Candy Crush as much as the next person, but there was more to life than Instagram or whatever the latest social media platform was occupying the minds of Generation Z.

But try telling that to a seventeen-year-old.

They were sixteen years apart, so Pasha and Rayma hadn't

even grown up in together. That didn't mean she didn't love her sister, it did however, make her feel like she barely knew Rayma and was completely out of touch with her world.

Maybe this was their opportunity to change that.

There were five of them in the Young family

Five girls.

Pasha was the oldest at thirty-three, then Triss was thirty. She was a speech pathologist in Connecticut. Mieka was twenty-seven and loving her life as a dancer with Royal Caribbean Cruises, and Oona was twenty-three and doing her masters in psychology at McGill University in Montreal.

So, yeah, Pasha understood the pressure Rayma was under, following in the footsteps of a doctor, a speech pathologist, a dancer and a soon-to-be psychologist, but that didn't mean she had to act like a delinquent to make her own mark on the world.

"Hmm, sister dear?" Rayma probed again. "Are you and the blond hunk of burning love with the German sausage in his jeans just making the beast with two backs for fun, or are there strings attached?"

Ugh!

Pasha finished tossing the cucumber pieces into her Greek salad before hitting her sister with a look she hoped conveyed everything she was thinking but would rather not say.

Rayma rolled her golden-brown eyes. "Don't look at me like that. I just asked a question."

"We're casual," Pasha said on a huff. "We're both too busy for anything more. He lives in Victoria—"

"Which is where?"

"In B.C. Just across the strait on Vancouver Island."

Rayma was still looking at her like she was speaking another language.

"In Canada!"

"Oh! A foreigner. Sexy."

Oh dear God.

"Sure. His accent isn't as sexy as an Aussie's," Pasha said sarcastically, "but I have to work with what I got. Anyway, he's super busy with his job, and I'm busy at the hospital, so we do what works—"

"Which is crazy-hot monkey sex for forty-eight hour stretches, right?"

Yes.

But she wasn't going to admit that to her seventeen-year-old sister.

"We're doing what works for us." Even though the more time she spent with him, the harder it was to keep her heart out of the equation. "We're not serious, but we're also not seeing other people. We're content with the way it is." *At least that's what I keep telling myself.* "We've only been seeing each other since March, so it's still new."

"And hot. I bet he's dynamite in the sack. The way he came in here, demanding you spread your legs." Rayma's eyes sparkled. "Fuck, I'd love for a man to talk to me like that."

"You're seventeen!"

"But I'm not a nun. You do know that like nearly all of my friends are having sex, right?"

But are you?

Not that it was the end of the world if Rayma was, but Pasha worried about her baby sister. STDs were no joke, not to mention rumors and reputations that haunted you for years later.

She'd kept her nose down and stuck to her studies during her high school years, determined to graduate a virgin, so she didn't run the risk of adding a kid to her high school's daycare. Then once she was in college, she dated a bit, had a few boyfriends, but nothing really lasted until med school.

There, she'd met Frank and they were inseparable for three years. Only, he got a killer offer at Johns Hopkins and she received an offer from her first choice at the Mayo Clinic. From Mayo she moved to Seattle after her residency was up, and she was enjoying her fellowship in Seattle immensely.

Frank was rocking his fellowship in diagnostics at Johns Hopkins, and they texted on the regular. He also had a new girl-friend and she was lovely. Pasha wished them nothing but the best. Then there was her whirlwind five-month romance with Ivan—a neurologist—at the Mayo Clinic.

He proposed, she said yes, it was magical.

Emphasis on the *was.*

He claimed he loved her, wanted to marry her and start a family with her. Only to pull the plug a month after proposing, and right before Christmas, saying he just couldn't picture himself growing old with her.

That harsh slap in the face was what prompted her to accept the fellowship in Seattle. She moved to the west coast New Year's Day and could not be happier about the change of scenery, or the distance between her and Ivan.

"Were you always this big of a space cadet?" Rayma asked, causing Pasha to jerk her head up, but move her knife down, slicing off the pad of her finger.

"Fuck!"

"Shit."

Even though she was a doctor, human nature—animal instinct more like it—had her shoving her finger into her mouth to stop the bleeding.

"Blondie got you that zoned out, huh? Thinking about all the orgasms?" Rayma teased, sliding off her stool to come around into the kitchen. She grabbed a piece of paper towel off the roll and handed it to Pasha. "Band-Aids in the bathroom?"

Pasha nodded, wincing in pain as she pulled her finger from her mouth to survey the damage. She wouldn't lose the finger, but it also wasn't great. She should stitch it up. She moistened the paper towel under the faucet with ice-cold water, before pressing it to her finger. The cold would slow down the bleeding, and the damp cloth would keep the paper from sticking to her injury.

"Grab the suture kit, too," she called after her sister, making her way into the dining area and pulling out a chair to sit down. "It's in my medical bag which is on the bench at the end of my bed. Thank you."

Dammit. She was not normally this lost in her own thoughts.

Rayma showing up on her doorstep like a runaway, and then Heath appearing ready for the ultimate erotic takedown had thrown her for a serious loop.

She loved her parents dearly, but they were a bit out of touch with reality sometimes, particularly the demanding life of a pediatric fellow. She didn't have two weeks to just *knock some sense* into her little sister. She had work. A lot of work.

She also had a life—sort of.

And a no-strings friend with benefits, whose body she'd been very much looking forward to enjoying this weekend. She'd gone so far as to take the entire long weekend off, so that she and Heath could spend the majority of it naked. Then, she'd gone and gotten waxed yesterday, had her eyebrows threaded and shaved her legs this morning, all in preparation for their weekend.

So much for that plan. So much for all the effort.

He's a no-strings fling, you shouldn't be going all out on the preening anyway.

She rolled her eyes at herself.

That was true. Heath was a non-strings fling, but that didn't mean she couldn't do a little self-care in preparation for their weekend.

She deserved to feel human. To feel beautiful and sexy. Desirable.

Especially after the way Ivan made her feel when he broke off their engagement.

Like she wasn't settling down material. Wasn't mother or wife material.

She wasn't looking to settle down and have a family right now anyway. She was focused on her career. She was only thirty-two, she had time to have it all.

Rayma returned carrying a box of Band-Aids and Pasha's suture kit, she set them down on the table in front of Pasha and took the seat across from her. "Thinking so much about his head between your legs that you nearly cut off your own finger?"

Pasha rolled her eyes, refusing to give her sister an answer. With one hand and a few fingers from the other, she began preparing a suture needle and thread. Her finger throbbed.

"Are you going to do it without freezing?" Rayma's voice was high-pitched. "Like some ... army guy in the field. God, let me at least get you an ice cube." She stood back up and went to Pasha's freezer.

As annoying as her teenage sister could be, Pasha was actually grateful to have her there at this moment. Not that Pasha wouldn't be able to get the Band-Aids or suture kit herself, but because more often than not she *was* alone and would have had to do it all herself. Though to have someone with her, sort of taking her care of her was nice.

The sound of Heath coming through the front door drew her attention away from the throbbing pain in her left index finger.

Rayma returned and set a paper towel with an ice cube in it beside Pasha's hand. "Need any help?"

"Help doing what?" Heath's voice slid through her like warm honey. Damn, he had a nice voice. Everything about him was *nice*. More than nice. Everything about him made her tingle and grow increasingly hot.

He set the shopping bag on the counter, his blond brows pinching in concern as he approached them. "What happened?"

"I tried to kill her," Rayma said with a wide grin. "Didn't work. Just cut her finger."

Pasha rolled her eyes. "I cut my finger. I just sharpened my knives yesterday."

"She was daydreaming about your head between her legs and nearly made herself an amputee," Rayma added.

Heath was trying hard not to smile, but it wasn't working. He nudged Rayma out of the way and took up post in the chair across from where Pasha sat. "Let me see."

Gently, she peeled the paper towel away.

Heath clenched his teeth and sucked in a breath. "You really were daydreaming about my tongue, weren't you?"

Rayma snorted.

Pasha rolled her eyes and swatted his shoulder. "Shut up."

His deep chuckle had tendrils of desire spinning through her belly. "It's deep."

"That's what she said," he murmured.

She swatted his shoulder again.

"You got the suture ready?"

She handed it to him.

"Hold the ice to it for bit."

She did as he instructed.

"You can go and finish the salad for your sister," he said, turning to Rayma. "I can take care of whatever is on the barbecue."

"Shit!" Pasha stood up and grabbed the paper towel, putting it back on her cut. "The chicken! I completely forgot about the chicken."

The calm in the storm, Heath put his hand on her shoulder. "Sit. I'll take care of it."

"But it's probably burnt, by now," she whined.

"Then I'll order us pizza. Sit."

With a pout she sat and watched his fine ass head out the sliding glass doorway that lead to the patio of her townhouse.

He closed the door behind him.

"Damn, he's hot," Rayma purred from her spot at the counter, the sound of chopping filling the quiet kitchen. "And bossy. I like it."

"Down, girl," Pasha said, shaking her head at her horny sister, but also smiling because her sister wasn't wrong. Heath was hot and bossy and she liked both qualities a lot.

"He's not my type though," Rayma went on. "I like brunettes."

Not Pasha.

She liked them blond. Tanned. Built.

Like a surfer emerging from the sea, his body glistening with water as the sun rays hit him just right.

Like Heath.

IF YOU'VE ENJOYED THIS BOOK

If you've enjoyed this book, please consider leaving a review. It really does make a difference.
Thank you again.
Xoxo
Whitley Cox

ACKNOWLEDGMENTS

There are so many people to thank who help along the way. Publishing a book is definitely not a solo mission, that's for sure. First and foremost, my friend and editor Chris Kridler, you are a blessing, a gem and an all-around terrific person. Thank you for your honesty and hard work. You really helped me with this one, and your feedback was spot-on (as always). You helped me give Rex that edge he was missing and I think it made him such a better character because of it.

Thank you, to my critique groups gals, Danielle, Jillian and our newest addition, Felicia. I love our meetups where we give honest feedback. You three are my bitch-sisters and I wouldn't give you up for anything.

Author Kathleen Lawless, for just being you and wonderful and always there for me.

Author Jeanne St. James, my alpha reader and sister from another mister, what would I do without you? You get an extra special thank you as well for your very brutal, but necessary feedback on this one. Your help was so needed. Thank you.

Tara from Fantasia Frog Designs, your covers are awesome. Thank you.

My street team, Whitley Cox's Fabulously Filthy Reviewers, you are all awesome and I feel so blessed to have found such wonderful fans.

The ladies and gent of Vancouver Island Romance Authors, your support and insight have been incredibly helpful, and I'm so honored to be a part of a group of such talented writers.

Author Cora Seton, I love our walks, talks and heart-to-hearts, they mean so much to me.

Author Ember Leigh, my newest author bestie, I love our bitch fests—they keep me sane. You helped me SO much with this book, and I am so very grateful for that. Sometimes it just takes talking it through with someone to have the lightbulb come on. Thank you for helping me find the light switch.

Ana Clemente, the only fan I've met in person, and now a dear friend. Thank you for proofreading this one and always supporting me and checking in.

My parents, in-laws, brother and sister-in-law, thank you for your unwavering support.

The Small Human and the Tiny Human, you are the beats and beasts of my heart, the reason I breathe and the reason I drink. I love you both to infinity and beyond.

And lastly, of course, the husband. You are my forever, my other half, the one who keeps me grounded and the only person I have honestly never grown sick of even when we did that six-month backpacking trip and spent every single day together. I never tired of you. Never needed a break. You are my person. I love you.

ALSO BY WHITLEY COX

Love, Passion and Power: Part 1

mybook.to/LPPPart1

The Dark and Damaged Hearts Series Book 1

Kendra and Justin

Love, Passion and Power: Part 2

mybook.to/LPPPart2

The Dark and Damaged Hearts Series Book 2

Kendra and Justin

Sex, Heat and Hunger: Part 1

mybook.to/SHHPart1

The Dark and Damaged Hearts Book 3

Emma and James

Sex, Heat and Hunger: Part 2

mybook.to/SHHPart2

The Dark and Damaged Hearts Book 4

Emma and James

Hot and Filthy: The Honeymoon

mybook.to/HotandFilthy

The Dark and Damaged Hearts Book 4.5

Emma and James

True, Deep and Forever: Part 1

mybook.to/TDFPart1

The Dark and Damaged Hearts Book 5

Amy and Garrett

True, Deep and Forever: Part 2

mybook.to/TDFPart2

The Dark and Damaged Hearts Book 6

Amy and Garrett

Hard, Fast and Madly: Part 1

mybook.to/HFMPart1

The Dark and Damaged Hearts Series Book 7

Freya and Jacob

Hard, Fast and Madly: Part 2

mybook.to/HFMPart2

The Dark and Damaged Hearts Series Book 8

Freya and Jacob

Quick & Dirty

mybook.to/quickandirty

Book 1, A Quick Billionaires Novel

Parker and Tate

Quick & Easy

mybook.to/quickeasy

Book 2, A Quick Billionaires Novella

Heather and Gavin

Quick & Reckless

mybook.to/quickandreckless

Book 3, A Quick Billionaires Novel

Silver and Warren

Quick & Dangerous

mybook.to/quickanddangerous

Book 4, A Quick Billionaires Novel

Skyler and Roberto

Hot Dad

mybook.to/hotdad

Harper and Sam

Lust Abroad

mybook.to/lustabroad

Piper and Derrick

Snowed In & Set Up

mybook.to/snowedinandsetup

Amber, Will, Juniper, Hunter, Rowen, Austin

Hired by the Single Dad

mybook.to/hiredbythesingledad

The Single Dads of Seattle, Book 1

Tori and Mark

Dancing with the Single Dad

mybook.to/dancingsingledad

The Single Dads of Seattle, Book 2

Violet and Adam

Saved by the Single Dad

mybook.to/savedsingledad

The Single Dads of Seattle, Book 3

Paige and Mitch

Living with the Single Dad

mybook.to/livingsingledad

The Single Dads of Seattle, Book 4

Isobel and Aaron

Christmas with the Single Dad

mybook.to/christmassingledad

The Single Dads of Seattle, Book 5

Aurora and Zak

New Years with the Single Dad

mybook.to/newyearssingledad

The Single Dads of Seattle, Book 6

Zara and Emmett

Valentine's with the Single Dad

mybook.to/VWTSD

The Single Dads of Seattle, Book 7

Lowenna and Mason

Neighbours with the Single Dad

Doctor Smug

mybook.to/doctorsmug

Daisy and Riley

Hard Hart

mybook.to/hard_hart

The Harty Boys, Book 1

Krista and Brock

Lost Hart

The Harty Boys, Book 2

mybook.to/lost_hart

Stacey and Chase

Torn Hart

The Harty Boys, Book 3

mybook.to/torn_hart

Lydia and Rex

Upcoming

Dark Hart

The Harty Boys, Book 4

mybook.to/dark_hart

Pasha and Heath

Quick & Snowy

The Quick Billionaires, Book 5

Brier and Barnes

ABOUT THE AUTHOR

A Canadian West Coast baby born and raised, Whitley is married to her high school sweetheart, and together they have two beautiful daughters and a fluffy dog. She spends her days making food that gets thrown on the floor, vacuuming Cheerios out from under the couch and making sure that the dog food doesn't end up in the air conditioner. But when nap time comes, and it's not quite wine o'clock, Whitley sits down, avoids the pile of laundry on the couch, and writes.

A lover of all things decadent; wine, cheese, chocolate and spicy erotic romance, Whitley brings the humorous side of sex, the ridiculous side of relationships and the suspense of everyday life into her stories. With single dads, firefighters, Navy SEALs, mommy wars, body issues, threesomes, bondage and role-playing, Whitley's books have all the funny and fabulously filthy words you could hope for.

DON'T FORGET TO SUBSCRIBE TO MY NEWSLETTER

Be the first to hear about pre-orders, new releases, giveaways, 99 cent deals, and freebies!

Click here to Subscribe
http://eepurl.com/ckh5yT

YOU CAN ALSO FIND ME HERE

Website: WhitleyCox.com
Twitter: @WhitleyCoxBooks
Instagram: @CoxWhitley
Facebook Page: https://www.facebook.com/CoxWhitley/
Blog: https://whitleycox.blogspot.ca/
Multi-Author Blog: https://romancewritersbehavingbadly.
blogspot.com
Exclusive Facebook Reader Group: https://www.facebook.
com/groups/234716323653592/
Booksprout: https://booksprout.co/author/994/whitley-cox
Bookbub: https://www.bookbub.com/authors/whitley-cox

Subscribe to my newsletter here
http://eepurl.com/ckh5yT

JOIN MY STREET TEAM

WHITLEY COX'S CURIOUSLY KINKY REVIEWERS

Hear about giveaways, games, ARC opportunities, new releases, teasers, author news, character and plot development and more!

Facebook Street Team
Join NOW!